A Life Without Fear

Sins of The Father: Book Two

By Leo King

grey gecko press

Grey Gecko Press
565 S. Mason Road, Suite 154
Katy, TX 77450
www.greygeckopress.com

Printed in the United States of America

Also available as an eBook

Library of Congress Cataloging-in-Publication Data
King, Leo
Sins of the father: a life without fear / Leo King
Library of Congress Control Number: 2013935826
ISBN   978-1-9388216-1-5
First Edition

To Janna and Carol,

the two women in my life
who told me to just "write it down."

A Life Without Fear is the second volume in the
Sins of the Father trilogy. Sam's story begins
in *The Bourbon Street Ripper* and concludes in
the final volume, *Face Behind the Mask*.

Acknowledgements

When I started working on *A Life Without Fear*, I really thought it was a one-man show, seeing as how writing is such a solitary thing. Boy, was I mistaken. Unsurprisingly, there are a lot of people to thank for this book:

First off, a massive thank you to Jason Aydelotte, the owner of Grey Gecko Press, for making a reality out of my dream of being an author. As much as I, and pretty much all of the GGP crew, tease him, none of this would be possible without him.

Then I have to thank Hilary Comfort, my editor. Not just for being the best editor I have ever known, but for putting up with me. Artists and writers are notoriously prickly little pears, and I'm no different. So a huge thanks to Hilary for working with me, over email and Skype, to make sure this book got done properly and on time.

Also, a big hug and thanks to Staci Reed, who made the beautiful cover for both this book and *The Bourbon Street Ripper*. Her art skills are surpassed only by her ability to take a design idea over email and turn it into reality.

Next I have to thank my critique group, affectionately called Team Armageddon, for tearing this story apart page by page and putting it back together.This wouldn't be possible without you guys. And an extra shout out to Dominick D'Aunno for lending the team his bungalow every month.

A very special thanks to Andrea Reagor, Erik Hailey, Hal Werner, Robert Pevehouse, George W. Padgett, and Jeremy Hochhalter.

Without you all, this book would not be around right now. Thank you for believing in my work!

Now for the long list. A thanks to Kristina Hanck for all those long nights of chatting about totally unrelated writing projects whenever the burn on this book would start to sink in. Thank you to Shannon Winton for those just-as-long nights drinking coffee at Denny's and bouncing ideas around. A special thanks to Lee Lackey for some of the best *Sins of the Father*-related brainstorming I've ever done.

Thanks also to Keri Bas for running the Houston Science Fiction and Fantasy Writers Meetup, for without her, I wouldn't have met most of these people. A thank you to Cherie Campbell for standing around and giving me a page-by-page critique one night—and for letting me pose with Boudreaux. And a special thanks to Vijay Kale and Gini Koch for supporting me as I move forward and to all the fellow writers and readers I've met who have made this journey possible.

And of course, a thanks to my family. Thanks to Carol and Gerry, my parents, for always believing in me. A thanks to Sarah and Ryan, my siblings, for telling everyone how cool their big brother is (their words, not mine!). A thanks to Grandma Kay, Aunt Judy, Uncle Ronnie, Aunt Suzie, Uncle Marvin, Aunt Holly, Uncle Mark, Aunt Jolie, Uncle Andrew, Aunt Mary, and my cousins Allison, Jonathon, Jessica, and David. And . . . wow . . . I have a lot of family . . . so thank you to everyone in my family for the support and showing how much you care!

Finally, thanks to Janna, the best wife a guy could have. It's been a great journey, hun, and it's just beginning. We'll make it to Munich yet!

If you want to solve the mystery . . .

keep an open mind . . .

question everything . . .

and pay attention to what Sam writes.

— Leo King

Contents

Contents

Prologue

Date: **Saturday, August 9, 1992**
Time: **12:00 a.m.**
Location: **Office of Kent Bourgeois**
               Central Business District

"I don't care how high the property tax in that area is, just buy the damn place." Kent spoke into the receiver, a barbed edge to his tone. He was silent for a few moments as someone spoke to him from the other end.

"I already told you, it's for a charity that Madame Castille is investing in this autumn." His voice was starting to sound strained. Taking out a white cotton kerchief with an embroidered "G.C." on it, he wiped some sweat off his brow. "No, don't use the usual account, she'll never sign the check in time. Poor thing has been in a knot lately over the new Bourbon Street Ripper murders."

After a moment, he said, "Yes. Use that account. It's better for everyone that way, I think."

After another pause, he nodded. "Yes, that's it exactly. Very good. Corner of Bourbon and Canal. Call me—no, email me—when the transaction is complete. I'll be busy all day today with the Castille accounts. Huge mess to clean up there."

With that said, he hung up the phone and mopped some sweat from his brow. "Christ, the weather is muggy. Are we due for a storm soon?" He absentmindedly played with his gold wedding band, which shone with a newly polished luster. He hoped not. It was the middle of hurricane season, and a bad storm could spell big trouble for the Big Easy.

Kent's phone rang again, jarring him from his thoughts. He nearly jumped out of his seat from the sudden noise. Grabbing the phone, he said, "Eddie, didn't I tell you to—oh, hello, son." His voice went from irritated to cool. "Yes, everything is fine. Please stop worrying. No, there's no need to do anything like that. If you need more money, I'll transfer some into your account tomorrow."

He loosened his necktie and finished mopping the sweat off his brow as he listened. Finally, he said, "It's not rocket science, son. You just have to follow the instructions I gave you. They were exceedingly explicit. God, if your mother saw what a disappointment you turned out to be . . ."

He pulled the receiver away from his ear as incoherent yelling ripped through the other end of the line.

After the noise died down, he put the phone back to his ear and said, "And you prove my point, son. Instead of using the education that I paid for to do something useful, you work for that low-class newspaper. Instead of becoming something admirable, like a police officer, you choose to just screw one. And instead of helping your father out when he needs you the most, you call him while drunk and complain about how broke you are. What a model son you are."

Again, he lifted the receiver away from his ear as the shouting crackled out like fireworks on New Year's Eve. When Kent finally spoke back into the phone, his tone was considerably colder. "We had a deal, son. You help get me out of this jam I'm in and I make sure you have all the money you need to booze up, shoot up, or get messed up with that little cop friend of yours. Are you trying to back out?"

After a measure of silence, the voice on the other end of the line responded. Kent smiled wryly. "Good boy. Then I'll contact you tomorrow. For now, try to sleep off whatever you're on. You sound like a damn moron. Good night."

He hung up the phone.

For a few moments, he ran his fingers over a neatly folded letter on his desk. Then he placed it in his desk drawer and pulled out a bottle of Scotch. He poured himself a third of a glass, removed his necktie completely, and then took a long draft.

He sighed. "I swear, if my marriage doesn't get me killed, my stupid son will." He sat back, closed his eyes, and continued to sip his drink. "This new Bourbon Street Ripper couldn't have come at a worse time."

Chapter 1
Old Friends and New Leads

Date: **Sunday, August 9, 1992**
Time: **6:00 a.m.**
Location: **Esplanade Apartments**
                 New Orleans City Park

Water. Cool, clean, comforting water. Water that washed away the dirt, the grime, and the sins of the previous day.

Junior Detective Dixie Olivier's eyes were closed as she felt that water cascade down her back, over her buttocks, and down her legs to the shower floor below. Leaning back, she reached up and massaged her scalp, rubbing in the shampoo. Her motions were slow and deliberate. They eased her troubled mind—and she had a lot troubling her.

The copycat serial killer dubbed "the new Bourbon Street Ripper" had the city in a panic and had caused some sort of harm to almost everyone she cared about. Her best friend, Junior Detective Michael LeBlanc, was still unconscious in the hospital, having been shot in the line of duty. Her partner, Senior Detective Kyle Aucoin, was being torn in three different directions—the case, his failing marriage, and his missing daughter. And her superior, Commander Louis Ouellette, was being pressured by City Hall to do whatever it took to find and arrest the killer.

Needless to say, quiet moments like these were getting rarer for her.

Rinsing off her hair, Dixie renewed her resolve to keep the investigation on track. Once Aucoin arrived, she'd bring up her list of notes on the case and suggest their next move. As a detective, she was organized and well-practiced at sorting facts, not to mention she had a reputation for being damn good at interviewing. However, she felt that her true strength lay in analyzing situations and discovering patterns. She only hoped she'd get a chance to let that side of herself shine.

Hair rinsed, she turned off the shower and dried off before throwing on her robe, slipping on her slippers, and heading out of the bathroom.

The bedroom was mostly dark, the sun still down and the drapes drawn closed. In the shadows of the room, she made out the sleeping outline of Gino, her long-term boyfriend. His muscular form lay still beneath the sheets, his chest slowly rising and falling. She felt a flush come to her cheeks and an increase in her pulse. She dearly loved him.

Dixie hurriedly got dressed in a fresh pair of slacks and a blouse. Once her socks and shoes were on, she softly and quietly kissed Gino on the cheek. "Love you, honey. Be here when I get back." It was something they always said to each other.

Without another word, she went to the front of their apartment.

The Esplanade at City Park was way out of the price range for someone living on a detective's salary, but fortunately for her, the apartment was in Gino's name. Besides being independently wealthy, he made a comfortable income writing scripts for a nationally syndicated soap opera, as well as the occasional Harlequin romance novel. He preferred a life of seclusion. To most of the other residents, he was simply "that nice, quiet Greek fellow."

As she entered the front room, the cordless phone in the kitchenette rang. She hurried over and picked it up. Her voice was low and scolding. "Whoever you are, don't you realize it's six in the morning? Are you out of your—"

"It's Ouellette," came the voice of her commander.

Immediately, Dixie straightened up and cleared her throat. "Apologies, sir. What's going on?"

"I'm taking Aucoin off the case for a few days," Ouellette said. "He's obsessed over Cheryl's disappearance and has convinced himself that she's going to turn up as the third victim."

She didn't flinch. She was used to her commander being less than sensitive about others' problems. "Can you blame him, though? Cheryl may not fit the profile Michael and Rodger have been working on, but his daughter did just go missing."

"Teenage girls go missing all the time," he said, irritation in his voice. "That doesn't mean every one of them is the victim of a serial killer."

Asshole. She waited to hear what he had to say next.

He sighed, the irritation in his voice replaced by a noticeable strain. "But I'm giving him a few days to get his shit straight, find her, and get back with the program with the rest of us. Whoever this killer is, he's moving much faster than Vincent—one victim every other day instead of one a week. So we need to step up our game as well. For now, you're paired up with Bergeron. He's on his way to get you. Report to me before heading out." Ouellette hung up.

For a few moments, Dixie stood there holding the phone and then slowly hung it up. She had thought the pressure would be getting to her commander, and she was right.

She picked up on others' emotions very easily, a trait that helped her considerably as a detective. While she didn't consider herself to have Michael's level of brilliance—something she admired—she was able to combine her analytical skill with an understanding of people's emotions. This also gave her an edge in interrogation.

Except in some cases, such as when she and Aucoin had interviewed Richard Fastellos, the bumbling goof who was Sam's boyfriend. She hadn't been able to get a good read on him, and he had snatched the interview from them with a smirk on his lips.

Dixie felt her mouth tighten and her skin heat up as he remembered how Richie had played her. She hated him for that. She hated it anytime an arrogant, domineering man got the best of a situation, and she had good reason to. *I'll get that son of a bitch back for showing me up.*

She pushed away those angry thoughts and turned on the lights to the front room.

The dinner table in the dining area was covered in hers and Gino's paperwork, as well as his word processor and her overcoat, pager, and holstered pistol. She finished getting ready by strapping on her holster, throwing on her overcoat, and making sure that her badge was secured.

Not sure how long Rodger would take to arrive, she sat on the leather couch in the living area and turned on the television. It was the usual morning broadcast. The weather was hot and muggy, the traffic was terrible, and the top story of the hour was, of course, the new Bourbon Street Ripper.

Dixie shook her head in disgust. The media sensationalism was amazing. It seemed like the news stations and the *Times-Picayune* alike were more interested in the ratings than the real story. Talking heads gave theories ranging from the sound to the ludicrous, and everyone had an opinion.

Of course, the prime suspect was the unknown writer called Sam of Spades, who had published the first chapter in a serial story that had detailed the second murder before it had even happened.

She was grateful that the district attorney had placed a gag order on the *Times-Picayune*. If the public discovered that Sam of Spades was none other than Samantha Castille, granddaughter of the original Bourbon Street Ripper, she'd be lynched by a mob of frightened, angry citizens before anyone could blink.

"In other news," said the anchorman, "Saint Tammany Parish deputies arrested a man late last night for domestic violence. Mr. Gregory Descheneaux was arrested in his home after neighbors called in complaining they could hear his eight-year-old daughter crying out for help. The girl, Noella, was taken to the hospital with severe injuries."

Dixie sat, transfixed in horror. She never liked watching the news alone, for fear that a domestic violence story like this one would trigger memories of when she was a little girl.

She did not like remembering her childhood.

She had been born Dixie Electra Gateaux and had grown up in Slidell, a city northeast of New Orleans, just across Lake Pontchartrain. Like most families in Slidell, Dixie's was poor. She grew up in a trailer park with her parents and older sister. Throughout her childhood, poverty and instability tore her family apart.

As long as she could remember, her father had been unemployed and almost constantly intoxicated. Emotionally and verbally abusive, he would take his drunken frustrations out on every single member of the family on a daily basis. Her mother was an enabler who just kept making excuses and claiming he'd get better once he found a job.

Her older sister had reacted by staying out late, taking to smoking and extreme promiscuity by age twelve. By her fifteenth year, she had become pregnant with the child of a twenty-six-year-old man.

When her father had found out, he had snapped, and his verbal abuse had turned physical. Dixie had been only ten years old when she had watched her drunken father beat her older sister into a miscarriage. When her mother had finally tried to intervene, he had broken her jaw. The police were only called after Dixie, who had been hiding underneath her bed, ran to a neighbor and begged for help.

Immediately, her and her older sister became wards of the state, placed into separate foster homes.

Dixie was jarred out of the emotional trip down memory lane by the doorbell ringing. She realized she had been crying, and she took a moment to wipe the tears away before answering the front door.

"Morning, Dixie," said Rodger. The bags under his eyes were apparent, but she must have looked even worse, since he looked at her with concern. "I can wait down in the car if you need a few minutes to, um, finish getting ready."

"Thank you," she said, giving him an appreciative smile. It was obvious that he knew she was crying but was too much of a gentleman to say anything. After he left, she washed off her face. She appreciated his not asking what was wrong.

A few minutes later, she went downstairs and found him parked at the roundabout in front of the apartments, leaning against his squad car and smoking a cigarette. Nearby, a doorman was motioning to a public ashtray.

Seeing Rodger like that made Dixie smile. Despite his looking more and more like he was at the end of his career, he had a reputation for being a good cop who wanted to do the right thing. Everything about him reminded her of a detective from a gritty noir film—a hard-boiled cop with a heart of gold.

"You ready to go?" Rodger asked, tossing his cigarette into the public ashtray. The doorman mouthed a "thank you."

She nodded, and the two got into the car. "Do we have an agenda today, Rodger?" she asked as she latched her seatbelt shut.

"One moment," he said, fighting to get his seatbelt to catch. Once it did, he fished out a series of Post-It notes and flipped through them. "Let me see what we're doing today."

Dixie watched him and tried not to laugh. The way he flipped through his Post-It notes with a look of concentration was the same way her foster father would concentrate when sorting through bills. That made her very comfortable.

"Here we go," Rodger said at last. He was holding out a single note. "What we've got is a lead for the Nite Priory."

She recalled that the Nite Priory, currently believed to be a cult of some sort, was the group who had left instructions for three out of the four accomplices of the original Bourbon Street Ripper. Topper Jack, as well as Mad Monty and Fat Willie, who were both now deceased, had all been contacted by this group to assist them with the new murders. The only accomplice not accounted for was Blind Moses, the supposed courier who had carried Vincent's orders to the others.

"Good to know," she said, reading the note. "Jonathon Russell, eh? Never heard of him."

"You can thank Richie for this lead. One of the few things he's done right," Rodger said as he pulled out of the apartment's roundabout. "Jonathon's a rich guy. You know, old money. Lives on Lake Pontchartrain in a mansion, like the Castilles. A bit of a recluse, actually. Took Ouellette himself calling in a favor to get us the interview."

Dixie's lips tightened again at the mention of Richie's name, but she fought back any snarky comments. Instead, she focused on the task at hand. "Old money like the Castilles, eh? We're headed there right now, yes?"

Rodger shook his head. "Nope. Need to head into the precinct first. Ouellette wants to talk to us. Probably to give us some instructions we have to follow . . . or else." He accented the words "or else."

Despite herself, she giggled at his display. That helped them both relax. She found herself sliding into the same kind of groove as she had with Aucoin. She thought they'd get along just fine. She was looking forward to working with him.

It was two hours later when they finally finished meeting with Ouellette. On their way to Lake Pontchartrain, they stopped at a convenience store to get some coffee. While Rodger had gotten the usual, a dark roast with very little added to it, Dixie had bought one of those premade coffee drinks. It was more her style. As Rodger made a call to Tulane hospital to let Michael know the results of meeting with Ouellette, Dixie sipped the sweet vanilla drink and reflected on the meeting with Ouellette.

It hadn't been a pleasant meeting. With one officer in the hospital, two victims in the morgue, and the city getting the same paranoia as twenty years ago, City Hall was tightening its grip on Ouellette. Already his competency was being called into question, and with the recent mass murder of Giorgio "Blue-Eyed" Marcello and his men, the mayor was one more murder away from putting the city under martial law.

Ouellette, who was in a substantially foul mood, had even informed Dixie and Rodger that the mayor was considering calling in Sergeant Arsenault and his team from reserve duty. Arsenault headed up a special SWAT team affectionately called Arsenault's Arsenal. They were known for their ability to bring in a perpetrator no matter the danger. They were normally kept in reserve because of their reputation for using extreme tactics, and Arsenault himself had as many reprimands as commendations.

Everyone knew that when the Arsenal was called, shit had gotten real.

"All right, I've updated Michael on everything," said Rodger. While he still looked tired, the coffee had him looking less haggard. Rodger loved coffee—a lot.

"You know, Rodger," said Dixie, finishing up her coffee drink and tossing the bottle away, "you don't have to call Michael every time we learn something. Ouellette will update him, like he said he would. You need to let him rest and heal." She was unable to hide the concern in her voice. Michael was someone she cared for very deeply. A part of her secretly wished that things had been different between the two of them, even though she knew that would never have worked out. But the friendship she had with him was one of the few absolutes she felt she had in her life.

"Yeah, forget that," said Rodger, starting up the car and heading toward the lake. "Just the night before he got shot, Michael was furious with me for hiding some stuff from him. For the first time since I was paired up with the kid, I felt like I was losing a partner and a friend. And then when he needed me the most, when some crazy-ass John Woo Ninja bitch started pulling stunts from a Bruce Lee film, I could barely keep up."

"But you saved his life," she interjected.

Like everyone else, she didn't know what to make of the superhuman stunts that Michael and the indigo-clad assassin, who had just killed a Jefferson Parish deputy, were rumored to have performed. Ouellette had said it was more important to find the copycat killer than to investigate "this comic book bullshit."

Although she was on the fence about that part of it, Dixie knew that if Rodger hadn't been there, Michael would likely have died. "At the last moment, your bullets got the assassin away from him, Rodger. It's plain and simple. When he truly needed you, you were there for him."

When Rodger didn't reply, she reached over and rested her hand on his. "You're a good partner, Rodger Bergeron, and Michael knows that."

That seemed to scare away the dark cloud gathering on his face. "Thanks, Dixie."

When they pulled up to the Russell mansion, the mechanical front gate was closed. Rodger pressed a small button underneath a speaker. A moment later, an older man's voice rang out in a distinctive Creole accent. "Yes? Who is it?"

"This is Detective Rodger Bergeron with the New Orleans police," he said. "Our boss, Commander Ouellette, called to let you know my partner and I would be showing up to speak to Mr. Russell?"

"Detective Bergeron? Well, I'll be damned. I'll ring you right in."

As the front gate opened up on its own, Rodger leaned back with a confused expression.

Dixie looked over at him, cocking her head. "So this person knows you, Rodger?"

He sat there for a few moments before shaking his head and driving onto the property. "Not that I know of. I guess we'll find out. At this point, there isn't much left that could surprise me."

He drove alongside a pretty, well-tended garden with assorted trees and shrubs, as well as a few water fountains. Parking in front of the main entrance to the mansion, he shrugged. "So long as he doesn't try to feed me into a grinding machine, I'll be fine."

Dixie groaned as she got out of the car.

As they headed up the front steps, an elderly African-American male with curly gray hair and a gaunt face, dressed as a butler, came down the steps. "Detective Bergeron! I haven't seen you in so many years. How are you? How is Miss Samantha? You two still talking, right?" He shook a very surprised-looking Rodger's hand.

Dixie took a step back and rubbed her chin while regarding the man. He seemed to be well into his seventies and too frail to be an effective manservant.

Meanwhile, Rodger seemed to be faltering. "This is embarrassing, but I don't remember—"

"Oh, Lordy, forgive me," the butler interrupted. "You knew me back when I worked for"—his voice hushed, as if he were saying a bad word—"Master Castille."

Rodger's eyes widened with recognition. "Wait, Reggie?" he asked. "Reginald Washington? The chauffeur?"

Reggie smiled brightly and, clapping him on the back, led both of them into the mansion. "That's right, Detective Bergeron. After Miss Marguerite passed, Miss Gladys done canned all of us. Fortunately, Miss Samantha arranged it so that we'd be taken care of for the rest of our lives."

Dixie listened intently to Reggie's story as he led them through a foyer and up some stairs to the second floor. The interior of the house was beautiful, with dark oak beams interspersed regularly along the walls from the floor to the ceiling, several expensive-looking pieces of artwork adorning the walls, and hardwood floors covered in exqui-sitely detailed rugs. She noted that the architecture had a distinctive rustic look to it that made the mansion feel homey despite its size.

She also noticed that the interior of the house was clean and ev-erything here was as well-kept as the grounds, though she hadn't seen any maids or other servants as they passed through.

"So you received a quarter million in severance," Rodger was say-ing as the three of them stopped in front of a large oak door, "and yet you still came to work for Jonathan Russell?"

"Oh, yes, Detective Bergeron, that I did," replied Reggie. "I don't feel right not working. And Master Russell was always kind to me when he'd come by the Castille house. So after Miss Gladys done let me go, I asked Master Russell if I could be his chauffeur."

"And what happened?" asked Dixie, inserting herself into the conversation.

Reggie turned to her. "Well, Master Russell said he didn't need anyone to drive him, on account of him staying inside all the time, but he'd be happy to hire me on as a manservant."

"Been with him ever since, eh, Reggie?" asked Rodger.

Reggie bowed his head. "Yes, sir. But that's my story and no rea-son to bore you with it. Let me announce you two." He knocked on the door. After a few moments, the door opened by itself.

Dixie blinked as this happened. "You don't see that every day."

"Oh, almost everything here is like that," he said, motioning the two detectives into a study. "I do feel bad for the burglar who tries to break in here, though. The security system Master Russell has is not very friendly."

She was about to ask him what he meant when a gruff old voice from the far side of the room said, "That'll be enough of that, Reggie."

They turned to see an elderly gentleman sitting behind a desk. He had white wispy hair and was as thin as a skeleton, his skin hanging from the bones of his face and hands as if it were moss on a tree. He wore what looked like a dark bathrobe and was breathing into an oxy-gen mask attached to a large tank. The mask was painted to look like the mouth and jaw of a skull.

Dixie felt that was a bit too freaky for her tastes.

Removing the oxygen mask, the old man said, "Good afternoon, Detectives Bergeron and Olivier. I'm Jonathon Russell." He motioned toward two chairs before his desk with a bony hand. "Please take a seat."

She looked at him with a mixture of curiosity and concern. She had met more than her share of elderly people, and more than her share of sick elderly people, but Jonathan surpassed them all. He looked like he could pass any day now.

She noted that the most prominent thing on his desk was a sizable red button. She also noted that behind him was a small altar with an assortment of miniature statues, skeletons in tuxedoes, beautiful half-naked women, and a portrait of the Virgin Mary.

With a congenial smile, she took a seat. "It's a pleasure to meet you, Mr. Russell." Rodger also took a seat.

Reggie approached the desk. "Is there anything else I can gets you, Master Russell?"

Jonathon waved him off. "No, Reggie. Thank you. That will be all. Please leave me with the detectives."

Reggie bowed politely before heading out, leaving the three of them alone.

"You'll have to forgive me if I don't shake hands. The cancer that is eating me alive makes simple movements very painful. If not for Reggie, I don't know what I'd do," said Jonathon, taking a few moments to breathe from his mask, which made him look even more dead.

"I'm sorry to hear that," said Rodger, shifting some in his seat. "Reggie seems to enjoy working for you."

Dixie recognized the tactic of getting personable with someone they were about to interview, as it was a tactic she had used successfully many times before.

"Reggie is a good man. I felt bad when Gladys Castille fired him. He's not a very useful servant, but he's loyal and he looks after me. And at my age, I really appreciate loyalty, Detectives."

She looked him over, noting an ornate ring with a crest on it—a red cross with a golden crown. Sorting that design away for later, she said, "If you don't mind me asking, Mr. Russell, where is the rest of your staff? I only saw Reggie here, and there's no way just one elderly man can care for this entire estate."

He chortled. "My dear Detective, I don't have anyone else on staff. I contract out a maid service and a gardening service to care for my home. I have my meals catered to me every day." He took a deep breath from his mask and then he coughed a few times. "I don't generally like people. Not anymore."

"And I'm sure it's more cost effective," Dixie said politely, trying to keep the conversation going. "Much more so than having a full-time staff."

Giving a short, loud snort, Jonathan said, "I don't have any heirs or any family left, Detective. When I die, whatever I have left goes to Reggie. Why should I care how much of the Russell estate I squander?"

Dixie shook her head. *Wow. What a jaded old grouch.* But she figured she probably would be, too, if she were dying a slow, painful death.

"But enough talk of my short remaining lifespan," he said, leaning forward in his chair. "Your commander told me that you have something very important to talk to me about. And Louis wouldn't bother me if it wasn't important. So then, what is it, Detectives?"

Dixie blinked, surprised that he was on a first-name basis with her commander.

Rodger pulled a folded-up piece of paper out of his overcoat. "I made this at the library last night. It's a copy of a newspaper clipping of you, Vincent and Gladys Castille, and someone named Gerald Robichaux. It mentions a 'Modern Priory.' Do you remember that?" He passed the paper over to Jonathon.

Jonathon slid his bony fingers over the image. He smiled in a way that looked more bitter than reminiscent. "Ah, yes. Our donation to Southern Baptist Hospital. I remember that. Vincent was so happy the Priory was supporting modernized medicine." Pushing the paper back toward Rodger, he said, "But this isn't about a trip down memory lane, is it, Detective?"

Rodger shook his head. "No. I'll be honest with you, Mr. Russell, we're at a dead end with an important lead in our investigation of the new Bourbon Street Ripper."

"Oh? What lead is that, Detective?"

Rodger leaned forward on one elbow. "We keep coming across something called the Nite Priory. What is it?"

To their surprise, Jonathon laughed, so hard in fact that he started wheezing and hacking, his eyes bulging in considerable pain and his face turning red.

Quickly, Dixie got up and helped Jonathon get his oxygen mask back on.

As he breathed deeply and calmed down, she noticed dozens upon dozens of buttons behind the desk. *What the—? What are those for?* She wondered if they controlled parts of the house, like the door that had just opened. She anxiously eyed the large red button, remembering Reggie's statement about feeling bad for a burglar. She had a feeling it was not a nice button.

Once she was sure he was breathing normally again, she went back to her chair. He and this house were starting to creep her out. She just wanted the interview to be over.

"Are you all right, Mr. Russell?" asked Rodger, concerned.

"Yes, yes. I apologize for that," said Jonathon. "But this is my own penance for my own sins. The good Lord saw fit to strike me down with an aggressive form of cancer that will, to be blunt, end my life in excruciating pain."

Dixie was about to offer more condolences when he said, "But you want to know about the Priory. Instead of telling you about it, I'll show you." With a trembling hand, he pressed a button under his desk.

There was a click, then a motorized sound, and then the wall panel beside Rodger slid open. Both detectives watched as a small bookcase, framed in black velvet, rolled forward. In it were what looked like old, leather-bound tomes and dozens of rolled-up parchments. It looked like something from a monastery.

"The dark red book on the top, Detective," said Jonathon, pointing with a skeletal finger. "Can you read Creole?"

"A little," said Rodger, taking the book. It was as dark as blood. The cover had an embossing of the same design as Jonathon's ring— a cross with a crown.

Dixie took note of this. Perhaps that was their emblem, a family crest.

Jonathon gestured toward the book with a shaky hand. "The page you want is where the black ribbon rests, Detective."

Dixie traded glances with Rodger, the anxiousness on his face matching her own. The interview had officially become creepy.

When Rodger opened the book to where the black ribbon was marked, Dixie saw an intricate drawing of what looked like a group of men in black hooded robes. They were all holding chalices up toward a heart pierced by a sword and wrapped in thorns.

Rodger read slowly. "The Knight Priory of Saint Madonna." He looked over at her. "Knight spelled like, um, a knight. You know, armor and swords. Not the way we've seen it spelled."

She looked at the picture more closely. Something wasn't right, but she couldn't put her finger on it.

"The Knight Priory of Saint Madonna," said Jonathon, leaning back in his chair. "Formation dates back to the founding of New Orleans.

"Originally, the Knight Priory was a group of French nobles who believed in the purity of blood as a right to rule. They believed that as some of the first founders of the Port of New Orleans, that rule was their right. Over the course of this city's history, the Knight Priory gained complete control over the trade routes, businesses, and even its construction."

She suddenly realized what was off-putting about the image of the hooded men. "Mr. Russell," she said, pointing at the image, "the eyes of each of these men are hollow, lifeless. Like they're all dead."

Jonathon nodded. "Yes. Indeed, Detective. Very observant. You see, the Knight Priory, for all its roots in Christianity and pledges to the Virgin Mary, put considerable stock in Haitian voodoo. While homage was always given to the mother of Christ, the real deities worshipped were Papa Ghede, Madame Brigitte, and Baron Samedi, the three chief loa."

"Loa?" asked Dixie.

"Spirits," said Rodger, his lips tightening. "Sam called it correctly. There is a voodoo cult involved here."

Jonathan snorted sarcastically. "Well, if this 'Sam' you are referring to is Samantha Castille, I'm not surprised that she would think that. You see . . ." He leaned forward and stared at them. "Samantha is the reason the Knight Priory of Saint Madonna isn't the same organization it used to be."

Dixie blinked, feeling quite lost.

"Please, tell me what happened with Sam," Rodger said, finally sitting down again.

Jonathon again leaned back and took a long series of inhales from his mask. Then he started speaking.

"The Knight Priory was always run by the Castille family. Vincent, his father, his father's father, and so on. While their public face changed over the centuries to include groups such as the Mardi Gras Krewe of Comus, behind closed doors, the Knight Priory basically remained a secret order that ran New Orleans. And they—we, I should say—routinely practiced voodoo rituals."

"Voodoo rituals? Like what?" asked Dixie. In the back of her mind, she was trying to understand how this Knight Priory related to the Nite Priory referenced by the copycat killer. She wasn't completely sure it was the same thing.

"Oh, the usual," he said casually, as if he were teaching a class. "Blood sacrifices of barnyard animals, maddened dancing as if possessed, and sexual rituals. What you'd expect from a Haitian religion."

She felt yet another degree more disturbed.

Rodger seemed unfazed by that. Instead, he asked, "So what happened with Sam? You said 'we' practiced voodoo, so, obviously, you were a member." The concern and urgency in his voice was apparent.

Dixie flashed Rodger a look and shook her head. *Don't get too worked up about Sam, Rodger.* Sam was a suspect and Rodger was already on the edge with Ouellette. One more screw-up like he'd had with Dr. Klein and he would get suspended.

Jonathon pursed his lips in obvious pain and continued. "Indeed, I was. What happed with Sam was truly a mistake. Vincent was concerned over her health when she was younger. I don't remember the details, but she had medical problems. Vincent had been searching for a way to help her when he learned about an African compound called the *tkeeus.*" The foreign word had an African-style *click* at the beginning.

Taking another breath from his oxygen mask, he added, "Vincent was convinced that doing a ritual with the *tkeeus* would help Samantha's condition."

Dixie furrowed her brow. He was talking about a voodoo ritual with Sam when she was only a child, in a group that practiced blood and sex rituals. *What in God's name did they do to her?*

She found her mind going dark places, postulating the horrible things that could have happened. Quickly pulling herself back before she could succumb to those thoughts, she said, "Well, it sounds like Vincent was doing some crazy stuff with his granddaughter. What happened?"

"Well, if you had asked Vincent, he would have told you that the ritual worked. If you had asked anyone else, they would have told you it was a disastrous failure." He chortled morbidly.

"The ritual started just fine. But halfway through, Samantha went into a convulsion. According to Vincent, she suffered a massive seizure. Now, I'm no doctor, but I've never seen a seizure that would make a five-year-old girl strong enough to knock back grown men. Samantha, for a few moments, had strength no human being could possess."

Dixie stared, completely transfixed by Jonathon's story.

"After that night, the Knight Priory only met two more times. They met once to try the ritual with a different girl, and then they met so that the older members, such as myself, could announce retirement. After that, the younger generation took over, turning the Knight Priory into more of an underground political group and less of an occult secret brotherhood." He coughed a few loud, hacking coughs.

"Everything I know about voodoo says that rituals are only as malevolent as the will of the people performing them, but something evil happened that night with young Samantha. Ever since then, most of the old guard like myself have been dying off from some disease or another. It's like we're cursed." He took a few deep breaths from the mask. "Or maybe that's exactly what happened. Maybe we all cursed ourselves that night."

A light went off in Dixie's head. An exotic incense had been mentioned in Michael's report. He had said that soon after inhaling it, he had started doing things that would be considered superhuman. One look at Rodger, and she knew he was wondering the same thing—could Michael have inhaled the *tkeeus*?

She didn't believe in voodoo or demons, either, but a drug that enhanced people's strength wasn't completely impossible.

"So where did Vincent find this tah-keese?" she asked, stumbling over the word.

Jonathon rubbed his chin for a long time, a contemplative look on his face. "You know, I actually don't remember. I know he learned about the *tkeeus* from someone. But that was so many years ago. I'm going to have to think on that one, Detectives."

She nodded. "We'll follow up with you on that, Mr. Russell. I'm sure it's important."

"So two more questions, Mr. Russell, and then we'll get going," said Rodger. "First off, who was the other person this ritual was performed on? Second, the copycat killer is spelling 'Knight Priory' as 'N-I-T-E' Priory. Any idea what that means?"

Jonathon took a long breath from his oxygen mask. "The other person was one of the daughters of the housekeeper, Josephine Patterson. Don't ask me which one, because I don't remember."

Dixie looked over at Rodger. She had no idea who the Pattersons were. However, when he nodded thoughtfully, she was sure he had to know.

She could grill him for what he knew about the *tkeeus*, the Pattersons, and everything else on the ride back.

Leaning forward, she asked, "And the other question, Mr. Russell? About someone spelling 'Knight Priory' incorrectly?"

To her surprise, Jonathon laughed again. "My dear Detective Olivier," he finally said after more than a few hacking coughs, "I do believe the killer is playing the police for fools."

Chapter 2

A Condition of the Heart

Date: **Sunday, August 9, 1992**
Time: **11:00 a.m.**
Location: **Sam Castille's townhome**
                Uptown New Orleans

Sam's eyes were closed as the water from the shower poured over her. She braced herself as she leaned forward. The rhythmic pounding of the water was in perfect sync with Richie as he moved in and out of her, his hands tightly gripping her hips. The water added beautifully to the sinful carnality of their love-making.

She tensed as another wave of pleasure seized her, making her entire body shake, and he grasped her tightly as he cried out. She wanted him to stay inside of her as long as he could. The feeling of being that close to another human being, someone she loved, was the absolute zenith of fulfillment.

Only when she felt him soften did she slide forward and dislodge herself. She turned, embraced him, and kissed him passionately, holding him close. They stayed that way for a long time, and when she pulled back, she rested her head on his chest and closed her eyes.

Today was the first time in years that she'd felt that genuinely happy. As soon as they had woken up, they had started making love again and had kept it up until well past morning. Even once they were in the shower, it had only been a matter of time before the cleaning had stopped and the playing around had commenced.

Despite all those feelings of mirth and desire, a part of Sam felt genuinely disgusted with herself. It was like that part of her felt that she was not only wasting time with Richie but was also doing something gross. She kept pushing those thoughts out of her mind, figuring it was just her laundry list of psychological problems. She was sure that Dr. Klein, her psychiatrist, would say that she wasn't ready for a relationship, but she didn't care. For the first time in her life, Sam felt safe and comfortable.

She had never believed in true love until now.

She looked at Richie's face for a long time. His eyes were still closed. At rest, he looked less like the goofball he normally was and more like someone with an amazing inner strength. She was certain that if it came down to it, he could show a force of will far beyond the human norm. Also, the sense of familiarity was overwhelming. She felt like she had known him her entire life.

"I love you," she finally whispered.

He opened his eyes and grinned cheekily. "I love you, too. But staring up at me, Sam? Kinda creepy." He winked and kissed the tip of her nose.

Sam said nothing at his silly behavior. She just smiled, leaned up, kissed his lips softly, and then proceeded to wash him off. In a matter of minutes, they were both out of the shower and drying off.

"When do you have to go back to Philadelphia?" she asked, combing through her long, blond, wet hair to get out the tangles.

Richie was perched on the toilet lid, wrapped in a towel. "Two days," he said, sounding less than pleased. "Then I'm booked solid for almost two weeks, possibly more if Gordon feels vindictive about missing his flight here."

She smirked and put down her comb, remembering him saying that his publicist was extremely sore about losing his ticket to New Orleans.

"Why don't you come with me, Sam?" he asked, touching her arm gently.

Sam frowned and covered his hand with her own. "I can't, and you know that, Richie. I'm a suspect. If I go out of town, I'm sure that

Ouellette and everyone else will see it as an admission of guilt." She couldn't hide the bitterness in her voice.

She also failed to hide her contempt as she said Ouellette's name. She really hated that man. He had threatened her father, Edward, when he was implicated in being complicit with a serial rapist, Giorgio "Blue-Eyed" Marcello. Something about Ouellette set her teeth on edge, and she was convinced he'd frame her for the serial murders if given the chance. She just didn't trust him.

"Ow! Ow! Sam, your nails!" Richie tried to pull his hand away.

She suddenly realized that as she had allowed those dark thoughts to enter her mind, she had dug her fingernails into his hand. With a gasp, she let go.

He pulled his hand back and gritted his teeth. The nail marks were an angry-looking red.

"Oh, crap, Richie, I'm so sorry," said Sam, hurriedly opening the medicine cabinet. A few moments later, she was applying peroxide to the wound. He look-ed away the entire time, like a little kid with a skinned knee. "I don't know what came over me. I really—"

"It's OK," he interrupted. "I shouldn't have brought any of that up. I know you can't stand Ouellette. I should be the one apologizing."

"That's no excuse," she said, wrapping the hand in gauze. "I let my mind into dark places, and I ended up hurting someone I love. I need to take control of that if I want to get through this situation with my sanity and relationships intact."

Richie snickered with amusement. "So long as you don't go thinking that negative thoughts invite problems into your life."

She rolled her eyes. "Yeah, right. Can you imagine how messed up the world would be if people really believed that?" Leaning down, she gently kissed his hand. "There, all better."

As she started to get up, he pulled her back onto his lap. With only the towel between them, he looked into her eyes and said, "We may not be able to investigate the murders without Ouellette following through on his threat and throwing us in jail, but we can still find a way to prove your innocence."

Sam blinked and looked at him. "How's that?"

Richie waggled his eyebrows. "We keep you busy and in front of other people besides me. Ya know, witnesses. It's called an alibi, Miss Mystery Writer. We keep you busy and in public, and when the next victim shows up, you'll have an airtight alibi. You can't be killing someone if you're drinking daiquiris on Bourbon Street."

She smiled again. Touching his face, she said, "Clever boy. I like that. There's just one problem. Neither of us is very sociable. And there's only one person I know who is, and that's my best friend, Jacob. Even though he's been pretty worried about me, I'm not completely sure if he'll do this, considering that he's an editor at the *Times-Picayune* and could lose his job if he helps me."

Her hands drifted down Richie's body toward the crescent-shaped scar on his chest. She wanted to ask him about it, but no time seemed appropriate.

"Let's give Jacob a visit, then," he said. "If he's your best friend, he'll find a way to help us. Besides, I want to meet him, and I'm sure he wants to meet me. How does that sound?"

Sam didn't answer him verbally. Instead, she leaned down and deeply kissed him. As he returned the kiss, she felt him swell underneath the towel. She felt a rush of desire. It felt almost unnatural. Every time they started to make love, she'd feel this intense internal craving, like a part of her wanted the sexual contact the same way one wants food.

As soon as they finished, she'd feel disgust.

But for now, she didn't care. With a sultry look, she removed the towel from between them and said, "One more time before we get dressed."

Two hours later, they arrived at the apartment of Jacob Hueber.

Richie had driven them. On the way there, Sam had worked on the notes to her story. Using her notebook and the silver pen she had found after Rodger and Michael had first visited her, she had come up with some pretty gritty storylines. Despite the published story being similar to the actual copycat killings, she was having fun. Working on the story felt as therapeutic as it did compulsory.

They parked at Jacob's apartment. She was dressed in a short-sleeve button-down blouse with blue jeans, and he was in his freshly laundered clothes from the day before, blue jeans and a polo shirt.

In one hand, she held a red plastic shoe charm. It was a keepsake of her mother, Mary Castille, whom she had been told had died shortly after her birth. Just holding it and squeezing it gave her a sense of security. Her other hand held Richie's, which was just as nice.

He whistled as they headed into the apartment building. "I'm impressed. Jacob lives well for a guy in the newspaper business."

Sam hadn't thought much of it before, but she agreed with Richie. Jacob lived in the St. Phillips Apartments on St. Phillips Street in the French Quarter. Being from a wealthy family herself, she hadn't given much thought to the cost of living in such a place.

"I guess," she said as they passed through the lobby and into the elevator. "His parents died and left him a trust fund. I think he just invested it and is living off the interest."

"Must be nice. If I had that kind of money, I'd really live it up," he remarked.

She giggled as the elevator stopped and the two made their way toward Jacob's apartment. "Oh, yeah. Normally, he's pretty relaxed and reserved. But when you get him partying, he's a real nut. It's like he leads a second life when he's not working. Did you see that black and purple motorcycle out front?"

"You mean the one that looks like it belongs in an action film?" asked Richie.

As Sam rang the doorbell, she said, "Yeah, that's his. He also para-sails, bungee jumps, and sky-dives. Not to mention rock climbing and the occasional ski trip. Like I said, though, you wouldn't know it from looking at him."

"A real thrill-seeker, then, eh?" he asked.

"You could say that, but only when I need to blow off stress," came a voice from behind them both.

They both turned. For a moment, Richie tensed up like he was ready to punch someone, one of his hands curling into a fist.

Jacob was standing there in riding leathers, holding a paper grocery bag and stepping back. "Whoa, whoa there, guy. Calm down. Didn't mean to make you jump like that."

Sam quickly squeezed Richie's hand reassuringly. His ears turned red and he unclenched his fist, muttering, "Sorry. Old habits. Don't like getting snuck up on."

Jacob looked over at Sam. "Let me guess. This is Richie Fastellos, right?"

She nodded.

He looked Richie over and shrugged. "Well, other than being a bit jumpy, he looks like a pretty decent guy." He unlocked the door to his apartment and headed inside, leaving it open. "Well, pleasure to meet you, Mr. Fastellos. Why don't the two of you come inside? Just don't punch me, OK?"

Sam followed with Richie behind her.

"Crap, Sam, I'm already messing things up. Sorry." He squeezed her hand.

"Don't worry about it," she said. "Jacob is not one to beat around the bush. He's a straight shooter. If he didn't like you, he'd say so."

He mumbled another apology and followed along.

A few minutes later, they were all sitting in Jacob's front room, drinking iced tea. Jacob reclined on a big comfy chair, while Sam and Richie sat on a couch. The first few minutes of conversation had been spent bringing Jacob up to speed. They had made certain to detail the recent acts of harassment she had suffered—people leaving threatening messages, phone calls, and notes at her townhome— some even inside the townhome.

Not surprisingly, Jacob was angry over the entire situation, and he and Richie went back and forth over how much ass they'd kick if they ever caught anyone threatening Sam. Before the testosterone in the room could rise to choking levels, however, Sam steered the conversation elsewhere. "I love the new furniture and artwork you've gotten, Jacob," she said. "Is this a new couch?"

Both men took the cue and settled down.

"Agreed. Quite a place you've got," said Richie, looking around the apartment and apparently noting the leather couches, giant projection TV, and full bar.

For the first time, Sam noticed that his fingers weren't covered in bandages anymore. Last time she had seen him, they had been covered in gauze so rough it had actually scratched her when he had rubbed her hand.

"Your fingers," she said. "Your burns are already healed?"

He looked down and wiggled his fingers, chuckling. "Yeah. Ended up only being first degree. Still, stove burns are not the kind of thrill I go for." He then got a look of recollection. "Oh, while I'm thinking about it—Caroline called me this morning and told me about you and Richie visiting her yesterday. She was furious that the both of you stood up to her like you did."

Sam had forgotten about Caroline Saucier, the editor-in-chief of the *Times-Picayune*. Shrugging, she said, "I don't care if that rich bitch and every member of her rich, old family hates my guts, Jacob. I just want her to treat me fairly." She squeezed her plastic charm a few times to keep the anxiety at bay.

Jacob smirked and leaned forward. "Yeah, but here's the thing. You actually impressed her with how you stood up for yourself. That's how those elite types think, ya know? She'll never admit it, but she thinks you've got moxy, and she likes that." He then jerked his head at Richie. "She hates your boyfriend's guts, though."

"The feeling is mutual," replied Richie, his voice a bit darkened. He looked tense again.

"That reminds me, Jacob, I need to ask you something," said Sam, patting Richie on the thigh. She wasn't offended by him bowing up every time someone opposed her. She figured that was just how guys acted toward their girlfriends. "Caroline mentioned you were taking a vacation to help me prove my innocence or something. Is that so?" she asked.

Jacob furrowed his brow, looking deep in thought. "Well, yes and no. I've been having some problems of my own to deal with. Plus, I'm not a detective, and I feel pretty helpless. But I do want to help prove your innocence. I just don't know how."

Sam smiled to herself. Richie's idea seemed that much more golden now. "I know what you can do, Jacob," she said, resting her arms on her knees. "Richie suggested that I stay busy with other people, in public, every single night. You know some of the party spots in town, right? Why not take us around, go out with us, ya know?"

Jacob sat up and clapped. "Sam, that's a great idea. I know of a lot of places we can go. Restaurants, shows, dance clubs, anything you want. Lots of people. Lots of alibis. Brilliant!"

She patted Richie fondly on the back. "It was his idea." She was so proud of him.

Jacob looked over at him and gave him an appraising gaze, nodding. "Not bad, Richie. Not bad at all."

"Thanks," he said. Sam could feel his tension lowering. Maybe he'd been tense because of what had happened at the front door. Without his meds, he'd surely had to work through it on his own. *We should probably get that prescription refilled.*

Richie leaned back. As Sam leaned against him, she asked, "So, Jacob, what places do you recommend we—"

"Hey, Jake, honey," came a female voice with a thick Creole accent. "Who are these people? Friends of yours? Not the regular crew."

Sam sat up and looked. The woman in the nearby doorway was in her mid-twenties, a bit on the short side, and dressed in a pair of boxers and a tank top. She was toned like an athlete and had tanned skin, black hair, and brown eyes. The bags around her eyes were red and puffy, and she smelled so strongly of marijuana, Sam feared she'd get a contact high.

The woman slid into Jacob's lap, who looked notably uncomfortable at the woman's public display of affection. He put an arm around her and said, "Emilie, honey, this is my best friend, Sam, and her boyfriend, Richie. Sam, Richie, this is Emilie Guidry, my . . . girlfriend."

Sam grinned awkwardly. She knew him very well, and she couldn't imagine him dating a drug user. It seemed completely out of character. "So, Emilie," she finally said, "good to meet you. I'm Sam Castille."

Jacob, who had started making throat slashing motions as Sam introduced herself, looked exasperated.

Already, Guidry's expression had stiffened. Her eyes were a bit narrowed as she said, "Yes. My name is Emilie Guidry. But you may call me Officer Guidry, Miss Castille."

Sam felt the color drain from her face. Next to her, Richie tensed up.

Jacob chortled nervously. "Whoa, whoa. Calm down, ladies. Emilie, we talked about this already. You don't think Sam is the killer, right? Sam is my best friend. Let's not make this awkward." He sounded like a man who had already lost control.

"It's already awkward," Sam said between her teeth, looking away. She felt Richie's hand over hers, but it hardly helped. She wanted to leave. She began to squeeze her charm rapidly.

"Right, sorry," said Guidry, her tone still on the cool side. She slid off Jacob's lap. "It's hard to stop being a cop, even when I'm with Jake. It's just that you've been—"

Her comment was stopped by a sudden slapping sound.

Sam quickly looked over to see Guidry rubbing her butt. Jacob was glaring up at her, a dark look in his eyes. Sam blinked. It was like he had become someone else for a moment. She couldn't believe that the same gentle soul who had been her best friend for years would slap a woman's rear end in such a derogatory manner.

Guidry's cheeks flushed. "Right. I won't talk about it anymore." Rubbing her eyes, she said, "Honey, I need to get ready for work. I'm going to go take a shower. A real long one."

And with that, she headed to the back of the apartment.

Sam shook her head. "Seriously, Jacob, you're dating a police officer? And one with a drug problem?" She wanted an answer from her friend.

Next to her, Richie felt tenser than ever. It was like he was ready to pounce.

Jacob nervously bit his bottom lip. Any vestige of darkness from when he had slapped Guidry's butt was gone. In its place was a look of pity. "Man, Sam, I wasn't going to trouble you with this. I didn't want to hide stuff from you, but this has gotten really messed up. I mean, *really* messed up."

"What has gotten messed up, Jacob? Spit it out," said Sam, starting to get angry. Richie was looking at Jacob with narrowed eyes, as if sizing him up.

Jacob leaned back and rubbed his eyes. "So, I've been dating Emilie for a short while. Not long enough to build some kind of relationship, but long enough that she trusts me. So a few nights ago, she comes here in hysterics. Why? Sam, she's the one who discovered the body of the new Bourbon Street Ripper's first victim. She's only been active on the force for about a year. Then, would you believe it, the poor thing discovers the second body as well."

Sam was shocked. Most of her anger immediately washed away. She could see the look of concern and disquiet on his face.

"And so I do the best I can to help her, because that's just what I do, right? So last night, she shows up strung off her ass on pot. I can't even imagine how much she smoked. She's never done it before, either. She won't tell me where she's gotten the stuff from. All it takes is one random drug test and Emilie's career and life are pretty much screwed."

Sam felt bad for starting to doubt her best friend. Beside her, however, Richie was still tensing up, his fists tight. *What's his problem?* Richie was starting to grate on Sam's nerves. "So, Jacob, this is the personal issue you were talking about?"

He nodded. "I can't say I'm in love with her or anything. I mean, she's a lot of fun and she's really cute. But, hell, I don't need this kind of problem. But what am I going to do, throw her out on her butt? I mean, who can understand the horrors that she saw?"

"I can," Sam said softly. "I saw what Grandfather did to people. I know how it looks. She's not handling it well. No one can."

"No, she's not," Jacob said, leaning forward. "Sam, I never talked about Vincent Castille because I knew it would upset you. However, I gotta say that I've always admired how you've been able to go on with life after living through all that. Emilie just doesn't have your strength. She's falling apart and there's nothing I can do."

Without a word, Sam got up and hugged him. That was the Jacob Hueber she knew—someone who was always concerned with others.

Someone who made it their mission to save poor girls in danger of falling out of life—girls like Sam when she was in college and in dire need of a friend.

She kissed his cheek and said, "I understand. You do what you have to do, just don't beat yourself up if she screws up her own life, OK?"

He nodded once more as Sam sat back. She noticed that Richie was looking away, totally disengaged from the conversation. She glowered a bit. *He and I are going to have a little chat when we get to the car.*

"Anyway," said Jacob, clearing his throat, "Emilie is working tonight, and I've got to make sure she doesn't look strung out or smell like weed. I'll be free around seven, so why don't the three of us grab dinner and hit the town?"

Sam nodded. "Yeah, that'll work. Someplace public and fun. What do you think, Richie?"

Richie quickly looked over and smiled, but it looked insincere to Sam. "Sounds great. Dinner and fun. Love it. Let's do it."

She scowled at him.

Jacob must have sensed the tension, as he hastily stood up and said, "Right, well. Let me go tend to Emilie. You two lovebirds go do your thing. I'll stop by your townhome this evening. Don't worry, Sam, we'll make sure you have a strong alibi. I won't let you down."

"You never do, Jacob," she said, heading out of the apartment. She felt good having her best friend at her side.

"It was a pleasure meeting you, Jacob," said Richie. The two men shook hands for what felt like a few seconds too long. It was like they were sizing each other up.

"Take care of Sam, Richie," said Jacob, and then showed them out.

Soon, Sam was driving back home with Richie. He was staring out the window. She was holding her charm so tightly her knuckles were white. She was not pleased with her boyfriend and felt like arguing.

"Okay," she said with annoyance. "What gives? You've been acting weird. What was all that about at Jacob's?"

"I don't like him. I dislike druggies. And I really despise guys who hit girls," he said very matter-of-factly.

"What the frick, Richie?" she said, glaring at him. "This from the guy who pops anxiety pills like they're Pez. And he didn't hit her. He smacked her butt. Yes, it's degrading as shit, and if you ever smack my ass to get me to shut up, I'll beat the taste out of your mouth, but that doesn't mean Jacob's an abusive type."

He looked at her. His eyes were uncharacteristically cold.

For a moment, Sam felt like she didn't know who he was.

Then Richie sighed. "You're probably right. He's probably a good guy who's trapped between a rock and a hard place. Sorry. Just. Bad memories. Really, really bad memories."

In that instant, she felt her annoyance and anger start to melt away. Something about the pained look on his face, something about the way his eyes watered, made her heart ache. Reaching over, she placed her hand on his. "What happened, Richie? Share with me. Please."

"It's a shitty story," he said. "You sure?"

She nodded.

With a grim expression, he closed his eyes and started talking. "It's hazy because I blocked out most of the details, but I pretty much grew up without a father. It's like he didn't want me or my mother around, like we were an embarrassment, so he ignored us and just did his drugs. Heroine, mostly. The bastard was always high on the stuff."

Sam squeezed Richie's hand.

"So one day when I was around ten years old, Mother borrowed a spade from a neighbor, took all of his drug crap, and buried it in the backyard. Just buried it. His needles. His pills. Everything. When he found out . . . Sam, he went ape-shit on us. He slammed that spade into me until my ribs cracked. And he beat my mother so badly that . . ."

His voice choked. Tears ran down his cheeks.

She felt a sudden wave of nausea start to build up inside her. Like when they were at the Patterson shop on the dark ride, she was getting severe motion sickness. It felt like something in her guts was wiggling around.

"If a neighbor hadn't heard me screaming, Sam, he woulda killed her. He woulda killed us both. Sam, I . . . Sam! *Sam!*"

Sam's head lolled, her eyes rolling back, as she felt Richie grab the wheel and swerve. A few seconds later, there was a tremendous jerk and a squealing sound—the sound of brakes. Then all those sensations were replaced by a tranquil coolness, the sounds replaced by someone else calling her name.

"Sam! Sam!"

It was her grandfather.

It was over twenty-five years ago when little Samantha awoke in Southern Baptist Hospital. Barely five years old, she was too weak to move. Through blurry vision, she saw people standing around her. One was a doctor wearing a white coat. Another was a doctor wearing green scrubs. Standing at the doorway was a middle-aged man she didn't know. Seated next to her was her grandfather, his hands covering his mouth. He looked terrified.

"Sam!" Vincent rubbed his face. "Dammit, she's still not responsive."

"So she just passed out?" asked the doctor in the white coat.

"Yes," replied Vincent. He had never looked so upset before. "She was just playing in the nursery when she said she was tired. Then she just fell over."

The haze was parting. Samantha could see people more clearly. Her chest hurt. Her arms and legs felt numb.

"We did an EKG. Her heartbeat is very labored, Dr. Castille," said the doctor in the scrubs.

Vincent didn't say anything. He just rubbed his face anxiously.

She wanted him to hold her. She was getting frightened.

"Does the mother have any health conditions?" asked the doctor in the scrubs.

The man at the doorway stepped inside. "Yes. Mary Castille suffers from a weak heart. She's been on medication since childhood. Her nighttime job is very strenuous. When not working as a nurse, she—"

"That's enough, Jonathon," said Vincent, gritting his teeth. His sudden anger made Samantha even more frightened.

"They need to know everything, Vincent," replied Jonathon. He wasn't backing down.

Vincent glared at him, motioning his head toward Sam.

Jonathan sighed. "Fine, all right. If you come this way, Dr. Hofmann, I can fill you in on the details about Samantha's mother. We need to be discreet."

After they were gone, the doctor in the white coat placed a hand on Vincent's shoulder. "It's genetics, Vincent. There isn't much we can do about it right now. Give us a few more decades, and we'll—"

Vincent's outburst made him recoil. "She doesn't have a few more decades!"

Samantha whimpered on the inside. Everything was so confusing. She wanted to cry. What had happened to her?

Vincent paced around the room as the doctor tried to calm him down. "There has to be something we can do. The thought of losing my princess . . . No, it's inconceivable. There must be a way to strengthen her heart."

The other doctor folded his arms. "It's not that there's nothing we can do, Vincent. There's nothing we can safely do. You know that we're limited by science and technology."

Samantha tried to call out. She wanted her papa. She wanted her grandpa. She wanted to be held, to be safe.

Vincent was still pacing. "I know that, Lazarus. But if modern science and technology fail, there must be other options. Chinese healers have been cheating death for thousands of years. Men have purged sickness from their bodies through sheer will. There must be a way, even if it defies convention."

Dr. Lazarus shook his head. "Vincent, my dear friend, you are treading dangerous ground. Need I remind you what happened to your fa—"

"Papa!"

Samantha's voice was suddenly free. While Edward was not there, her little cry made Vincent stop in his tracks. In a moment, he was at her side, holding her hands. "Sam! Sam!"

He turned to Dr. Lazarus. "She's coming around. Please, my friend, go get Dr. Hofmann."

Dr. Lazarus nodded and headed out. He stopped at the doorway and regarded them both for just a second. His expression was troubled.

"Grandpa," Samantha said, crying, "I'm scared!"

"I know, Sam," Vincent said, kissing her tiny hands. "I know, my princess. I'm here. Grandpa's here."

"I can't move, Grandpa," she cried. She felt so weak. Even breathing was hard.

"Try to move for me, Sam," he said, squeezing her hands. "Show me that you have the will to live. Show me that you have the will to cheat death. Move for me, Sam! Move for me!"

"Move, Sam! Move!"

Sam's eyes fluttered open as Richie shook her shoulders. He looked both out of breath and terrified. Glancing around, she realized she was lying on the sidewalk and was surrounded by quite a number of onlookers. Nearby, EMTs were getting out of an ambulance.

Groaning, she sat up. The people around her gasped and scooted back.

"She ain't had no heart attack," someone yelled derisively.

"Yeah, she just passed the hell out," someone else said.

Richie snarled at them. "Back off, the lot of you." He then motioned for the EMTs.

Letting them examine her, Sam looked wearily at her boyfriend. "Richie, what happened? How long was I out?"

He held tightly onto her hands. "You passed out. About ten minutes, I think. You scared the shit out of me, Sam. I thought you'd had a heart attack."

She blinked and peered up at him. "Heart attack?"

He leaned in and kissed her forehead. "You were grabbing your chest and gasping for breath. Then you fainted. Guess I overreacted, though, huh?"

"Come on, miss," said an EMT, helping her stand. "Let's get you checked out at the ambulance. Then we'll see if you need to take a ride."

"Is my car OK?" Sam asked, uneasy on her feet.

Another EMT chuckled. "I think she's fine if she's asking about her car."

"Your car is fine, Sam," said Richie, following along.

At the ambulance, they gave Sam a more thorough exam, including listening to her heart. Someone asked, "Do you have any medical conditions?"

"No. Not to my knowledge," she said, wondering if that was true. She was certain she had just had a dream, a distant memory, where someone had said she had a condition of the heart. But why wouldn't anyone have ever told her?

"Well, you seem OK. It was likely a fainting spell," said an EMT. "However, I recommend you go to the hospital anyway and get checked out. Tulane is just up the road. We can bring you, or your boyfriend can drive you."

"I can drive her," Richie offered, again squeezing her hand.

Sam smiled at him and squeezed his hand back. "Yeah, I'll let him drive me. Thanks."

The EMTs took her information for billing and then left.

Once in the car, she pointed down the road and said, "You see that big building with the word 'Tulane' on it?"

He started up the car. "I do."

"Take me there," she said, leaning back in her seat. She still felt tired. She wondered what the heck was going on with her. That was twice in a row she'd passed out while under stress. Maybe she needed different medication. Maybe she needed to see Dr. Klein after all.

A few minutes later, they pulled into the parking lot for Tulane University Hospital.

The conversation they had been having before Sam passed out started coming back to her. She said, "So, Richie, that scar on your chest. Is that from when your father . . . ?"

Richie parked the car, flexing his jaw. "Yeah. That's where it's from."

She didn't know what to say, other than to show that she cared. "I love you."

He helped her out. "I love you, too," he said. "Although there is something you should know."

She slung her arm around his neck and they started walking through the parking lot. Her feet felt heavy and it was hard to focus. "Oh? What's that?"

"Um, you got a moving violation for nearly causing an accident. The traffic cop, um, took your driver's license."

Sam blew a raspberry. "Richie, I'm a suspect for serial murder. Losing my right to drive is a bit trivial right now."

The two shared a laugh as they entered the hospital.

Chapter 3
Theories and Postulates

Date: **Sunday, August 9, 1992**
Time: **2:00 p.m.**
Location: **Tulane University Hospital**
              Downtown New Orleans

Junior Detective Michael LeBlanc was still getting used to the sound of beeping monitors and the feeling of pads taped to his body. He had been awake for a couple of hours, having regained consciousness just after lunchtime. Lying there dressed in nothing but a hospital gown, his left shoulder and lower abdomen taped up, he stared up at the ceiling. All around him were gifts from just about everyone in the homicide division, a bouquet of flowers from Dixie, and a card from Rodger. And even though both gestures from the people he was closest to had touched him deeply, he was no longer focused on them.

For the moment, he was focused on the case. Without any distractions or interruptions, he felt he was in a better position now than ever to solve the case.

We're being led around in circles by someone who wants us to believe anything but the truth. It's like we're being delayed, he thought, holding onto his notebook, which Rodger had left with his get-well card.

Clicking the lever on the side of his bed, Michael tilted it forward until he was sitting up. He winced as he moved, the pain from the stab wound in his gut twisting through him. He gritted his teeth and endured it.

When the bed stopped moving, the pain subsided to an ache. "Ironic that the stab wound hurts worse than the gunshot wound," he said to the empty room. Complaints aside, he counted his blessings that the bullet had gone clean through his shoulder.

He sat up and opened his notebook. His eyes fell on the words "Bourbon Street Ripper? Jack the Ripper?" on the middle of a page.

The media had called Vincent Castille the Bourbon Street Ripper because of the brutality of the original murders, harkening back to Jack the Ripper. However, what if he had been more like Jack the Ripper than just that? A common theory was that Jack the Ripper had killed all his victims to hide only one killing. What if both Vincent and the copycat were doing just that?

Michael closed his eyes. In his mind, he visualized the information about the original victims. They were just names on paper to him, but he had read their statistics so many times during the past week that he had become intimately familiar with them. However, only two names stood out as relevant to the present case.

Maple Christofer, Vincent's last female victim, and Edward Castille, Vincent's final victim—his son and Sam's father.

Maple had been murdered a day or so before Edward. Vincent had been captured by Rodger soon after murdering Edward. It was like Vincent had wanted to get caught, but not until he had killed a certain person. *Let's start with Maple.*

Opening his eyes, Michael flipped through his notebook, stopping on the page he had dedicated to Maple.

"Maple Christofer and her son, Dallas. Vincent killed Maple in front of Dallas."

Michael blinked at that and quickly flipped to his notes on Edward's death.

"Edward Castille and his daughter, Samantha. Vincent killed Edward in front of Samantha."

The similarities were so obvious, he wondered why no one had ever picked up on it.

"So, both parents were murdered in front of their respective children. Both children were paralyzed with a low-level sedative. Dallas was buried alive with Maple and left for dead. Samantha was not. Why? Why do the exact same thing twice? Unless . . ."

Everything seemed so rehearsed, down to the last detail. It was like a ritual or a play or a—

Michael's eyes widened.

"Could it be that Maple's murder with Dallas was practice for killing Edward in front of Sam?"

Despite his goal of always trying to remain dispassionate when investigating a case, he felt sick to his stomach over that idea. Even for Vincent Castille, that was too cruel. *And all the evidence I've seen shows he really cared for Sam. He loved her.*

"Detective LeBlanc," said a sultry voice from the doorway. Looking up, he saw a woman with dark red hair, her eyes a deep blue and her lips a red so dark they were almost the color of blood. She wore a nurse's outfit, which strained to keep back her sizable chest and hips. He name tag bore only the Tulane logo and her first name, "Camellia." She was holding a tablet and approaching him.

Michael cocked an eyebrow at her. "Yeah, that's me." She looked unfamiliar, but he had already seen two other nurses, even if they hadn't been quite so memorable.

Camellia smiled at him and tapped the tablet in her hand, which she held against her chest. "My name is Camellia, Detective, and I'm assigned to your case."

"All right, Camellia. Have at it."

Without a word, she put down her tablet and started checking his bandages. Her touch was cool, like a refreshing breeze, and he felt himself relaxing.

"You'll need to have your bandages changed out later tonight. Doctor's orders," she finally said, jotting down notes on her tablet. He just sat there and waited for her to finish.

"Okay, now I just need to ask you a few questions," she said.

"Go for it," Michael said.

Camellia checked his pupils with a small pen light. "Do you feel tired and drained right now? If so, by how much?"

He thought about it for a moment. "I feel a bit drained. Not tired like I'm sleepy, just drained like I've run a marathon." He hadn't thought anything of it, figuring it was because he had been shot and gone through surgery.

Taking his wrist with her cool touch, she timed his pulse. "Are you feeling any strange shivers? Any unusual cold spells or tingling in the spinal column?"

Michael again cocked an eyebrow, wondering what that line of questioning was about. When she cocked an eyebrow right back at him, he said, "Not right now, no." Thinking on it for a moment, he added, "I did have a sensation like that when I came in contact with a strange drug yesterday."

Nodding, Camellia jotted down more notes. "Last question. Have you had any nightmares or night terrors lately? Any feelings of uncontrollable dread?"

"What? No," he said, confusion in his voice. "What does that have to do with anything?" He didn't understand any of what was going on.

"Just the usual questions for someone in your situation," she said. She looked at Michael again for a few more moments and then shook her head. "You're going to be fine, kid, but don't push yourself. You're lucky to be alive."

"Will you please tell me what is going on?" Michael asked, his voice shifting from confused to annoyed. Who the heck was this nurse, anyway?

Shaking her head, Camellia said, "Your contact with that strange drug, as you call it. The doctor wanted to see if you were exhibiting any of the post-exposure symptoms. Anything more, I can't tell you. But the doctor will be in tomorrow to speak with you. For now, just take things easy, get lots of nutrition—low sodium—and stay hydrated." She turned to leave.

He called out, "So who are you? Who are you with?"

She turned and gave him a wink. "I'm nobody. And at the same time, I'm somebody who has a very vested interest in you." And then she was gone.

Sometime later, Michael had finally recovered from the surprise visit by the strange nurse. He had asked the officers outside who the woman was, and the only answer he had gotten other than "my dream come true" and "my next wife" was that she had all the usual credentials.

He had just finished getting his bandages changed with the help of another, more ordinary nurse, when Rodger and Dixie entered the room. Immediately, Dixie was at his side, her arms around him. In her haste, she pressed against his injured shoulder.

"Ow, ow, ow," Michael cried out, pushing Dixie away. "Be careful there, Dix!"

"Oh, sorry, Michael," she said, taking one of his hands into her own.

He saw the worried expression on her face and smiled. She was his closest friend.

The nurse finished washing up and said, "You can visit with your co-workers for one hour, Detective. But then you have to take your medication." She left.

Rodger came around the other side of the bed, looking as tired as ever. "Hey there, partner."

Michael nodded. The two had gone through a nasty scrap just the day before he had been shot. But it seemed the rift between the two had mended. "Hey, Rodger. How's it going, man?"

Rodger shook his head. "Could be better. A lot of new developments in the case. I don't want to burden you with it."

Michael smirked. "Yeah, right. Don't even think for a second you can leave me out of this one, partner." Camellia's warning about taking it easy seemed as distant as her visit. "Catch me up."

Dixie squeezed his hand. "No, Michael, we've got this one. Just rest for now and rec—"

"I can handle it," he said, tension rising in his voice. "Seriously, you two. I've already figured out some things just lying here."

Rodger frowned and said, "Come on, Michael, you've done enough. You don't—"

"Rodger!" Michael shouted.

When Rodger arched his eyebrows, Michael winced and said in a pleading voice, "Please, partner, don't cut me out. I really can help."

Rodger and Dixie traded prolonged glances while Michael anxiously looked from one to the other. Finally, Rodger pulled a chair up next to Michael's bed. "I'll catch you up on stuff. But that's it. I don't do anything more until Ouellette gives you the all-clear. You got me, partner?"

Michael felt a wash of relief. The sudden rush of anxiety was gone, and now that it was, he wondered what had come over him. That kind of behavior was not like him at all.

Over the next thirty minutes, Rodger caught Michael up on everything that had happened over the past twenty-four hours. He recounted the discovery of the bodies of "Blue-Eyed" Marcello and his men in the river. He recounted Richie's information regarding the group that Vincent, Jonathon, and others belonged to—the Knight Priory of Saint Madonna. And he recounted his and Dixie's visit to meet Jonathon and learn that 'Nite Priory' was a misspelling.

Save for asking a few clarifying points, Michael said nothing the entire time.

"So whoever's writing the notes to the old accomplices is using a slang version of 'Knight Priory,'" Rodger said, leaning back in the chair. "At least, that's how I see it. Whoever's doing this—be it one or more people—they want to implicate the original Knight Priory."

Michael frowned. Not only was there a copycat serial killer, there was a copycat Priory? This case kept getting more complex.

"Analytically speaking," Dixie said, "it would be easier for an individual or a small group to carry out these murders than it would a larger group. They'd have to be specially trained military or something to pull off moving around a city without attracting attention. And I really don't think that's what we have here."

Michael rubbed his forehead. He was getting a tension headache. "I think that this plays well into the 'finding out about the past' theory, guys. Jonathon said that when Sam was five years old, they did some voodoo ritual on them, right?"

"Right," replied Rodger.

Michael sighed. There was the voodoo angle again. Even though he was sure there was nothing supernatural actually going on, since such things were not real, it was making the cult theory Sam had brought up even more plausible.

"So what have you been thinking on?" asked Rodger.

With a cocky grin, Michael said, "Here's the summary of it. I think that Vincent committed the original murders to cover for one real murder. Just like the old theory behind Jack the Ripper. Right now, I've got it down to two people—Maple Christofer and Edward Castille. My theory is that one or both were the real murder and all the rest were misleads."

Even as he spoke, Michael knew Rodger might take his comment badly. Edward had been his partner, after all. "Sorry," he added. He still wasn't used to apologizing, but the past week had really changed him from being socially awkward to at least trying to get along with others.

"It's all right," replied Rodger, getting up. He began to pace the room. "I think—and this is just a thought, mind you—that you're onto something. Not necessarily with Edward being the real target, but with Vincent having a real target and everyone else being a ruse. It would make sense. The only person he murdered who had any connection to him was his son, Edward."

Dixie spoke up. "So, then, why did he bury Maple?"

When Rodger and Michael looked over at her, she shrugged and continued, "Come on, guys. Think about it. Vincent never buried his victims. Why did he bury Maple? That doesn't make any sense at all."

"We always figured that it was to dispose of Dallas as well," said Rodger.

Dixie shook her head. "Now that doesn't make any sense at all. Vincent was a remorseless murderer. Why not just kill Dallas? There had to be a reason to keep the boy alive. And there had to be a reason to bury him and his mother."

Shrugging, Rodger said, "I wish I knew. I never knew the Christofers."

Michael gently sucked on his bottom lip. He knew he could make sense of things if he was given a chance to ponder it alone. Filing away all that information to sort through once his friends were gone, he asked, "So, out of curiosity, who is handling the Marcello murder case?"

"Oh, Landry and Rivette," said Rodger.

"Ah, OK." Michael knew those two detectives were competent enough, even if Landry loved eating—all the time—and Rivette collected toys like Transformers and Power Rangers and kept them on his desk. That was no worse than Rodger smoking or Michael obsessively playing word puzzles.

The three chatted a bit more about the cases, making sure that everyone was up to date on the facts, before the doctor came in and informed Rodger and Dixie that they needed to leave so he could treat Michael.

Dixie hugged him again and told him to get lots of rest. Rodger patted him on his good shoulder and told him he'd check back after dinner.

Soon the two were gone.

As the doctor administered his medication, mostly antibiotics and painkillers, Michael asked, "So, who was that redhead who came by earlier today?"

"Redhead?" replied the doctor. "Who do you mean?"

"The nurse," said Michael, wondering why no one seemed concerned that a random person had come into his room. "Camellia, the one who came in to check on me earlier."

"Ah," said the doctor. "Camellia is the personal assistant for one of the hospital directors. She aids him on all of his special assignments." He finished administering Michael's medicine. "There. You're good for the rest of the evening. A nurse—not Camellia—will be by later to give you your dinner. I'm afraid it's a liquid diet for a while, Detective."

As the doctor headed out, Michael asked, "So, who is this director?"

He turned and smiled pleasantly. "Oh, Dr. Lazarus. He's a director for over a dozen hospitals here in southern Louisiana. In fact, I heard that he'll be here tomorrow."

Michael watched him leave. He remembered Dr. Lazarus's last words before they'd parted. He had said, "I'll be keeping an eye on you, Detective LeBlanc. Do your very best."

That combined with Camellia's statements made Michael wonder just what he was getting wrapped up in and what Dr. Lazarus's true intentions were.

It was another thirty minutes before Michael was calm enough to focus on the investigation again. He felt frustratingly close to a breakthrough. Looking through his notebook, he flipped back to Maple Christofer. He couldn't place it, but something about her death seemed vitally important to the original murders.

Dixie had a good point. Why go through the trouble of burying Maple? And why bury Dallas with her?

He recalled that Dallas, locked away in Acadia Vermilion Hospital in Lafayette, was a horribly burnt shell of a man who scribbled the same thing over and over again: "Nite Priory."

Those words tasted foul on his lips. Why would someone deliberately use the same misspelling of "Knight Priory" for murders taking place in New Orleans, which was home to the actual Knight Priory, that Dallas had been scribbling for years while hundreds of miles away?

Michael closed his eyes and visualized the timeline. The only plausible explanation was that someone had been planning these copycat murders for twenty years. Who would have done that? Who would have had the level of personal interest in the original murders necessary to plant seeds so far away, so long ago?

The thought that came next wasn't pleasant. It had to be someone who was directly linked to the original murders. Someone who also had contact with Dallas. There was only one person who fit those criteria.

"Sam." He whispered her name. "Dr. Klein said that Sam had a persona hidden underneath her psyche. He called it 'Sam of Spades.' Could that be our killer? He seems to think so."

He frowned. None of the other evidence supported her being the killer or having multiple personalities. But if you only looked at who was connected to both the original murders and the first use of the words "Nite Priory," she was the only plausible person.

Michael sighed and rubbed his eyes again. He was getting tired, more so than he wanted to admit. Determined to get through his latest train of thought, however, he shook off the cobwebs and focused on his notebook.

"Let's see. Rodger said that in his interview with Fat Willie, he found out that Maple and Dallas were the only ones Fat Willie did not kidnap. So someone else did. Fat Willie thinks it was Vincent."

Michael's brow creased. Vincent might not have been frail, but Michael doubted that he could have overpowered a grown woman and her ten-year-old son without some sort of struggle or drug. But there were no signs of a struggle when they were taken, and the only traces of a drug found were of the paralytic agent used to keep Dallas still while Maple was killed. *So if Vincent did take them, that means they went with him willingly.*

He looked up, repeating those words. "So they knew him. Then . . . then . . ." He gritted his teeth. He was missing something. Something significant.

Leaning back, he sighed. "Rodger said that Edward lost it when he found out that Maple was dead. But we know nothing about Edward's relationship to her. A friend? A relative? A lover? Heck, we don't even know who she really was. I don't know enough about her to theorize, and I'm going nowhere with this."

He decided to try focusing on something else.

Michael flipped to the notes from his interview with Rosemary Boucher in Lafayette. One thing stood out. Rosemary had stated that Magnolia had been murdered. She had also stated that she knew who had done it.

He rubbed the sides of his head, his mind spinning with facts.

He'd already theorized that one of the M&M sisters was Mary Castille—Edward's wife and Sam's mother. Ouellette had said that Magnolia had had health problems, and Rodger had said that Magnolia had died of a heart attack. That added up. *So if people believe that Magnolia died of natural causes, but someone said she was killed, then that means . . .*

His hands dropped. "Magnolia's death was a murder that was made to look like a heart attack. And I can verify that by talking to Rosemary again."

He scratched his head and groaned. "Ugh! This is all so confus-ing. Why is there so much mystery surrounding these twins?"

Michael froze at the word *twins*.

"Whoa, hold on," he said, biting his bottom lip. "What if the twins switched places? Or what if one twin posed as the other? Who-ever married Edward would have access to the Castille fortune, right? What if . . ."

Things were starting to fall into place. It was all theories and pos-tulates, with no hard evidence to back it up. However, if there was one thing he had learned in the past few days, it was to trust his gut.

And his gut told him this: One sister married Edward, and the other twin got jealous because of the Castille fortune. Could she have tried to take the other twin's place? Why not? But for one twin to be-come the other twin, the first one would have had to die. *So, then, what if . . . what if . . .*

The conclusion Michael came to was as horrible as it was plausible.

"What if Marigold murdered Magnolia?"

Chapter 4
You'll Be the One

Date: Sunday, August 9, 1992
Time: 4:00 p.m.
Location: Corner of Tulane and LaSalle
              Downtown New Orleans

"Richie, what the hell are you doing here?" Rodger stood at the coffee stand, hands on his hips, staring incredulously at Richie, who had just finished adding sugar and creamer to a large cup of gourmand coffee.

"Getting a cup of coffee?" Richie said, holding up and pointing to the cup as if it were a courtroom exhibit. He looked hopelessly confused as to why he was getting questioned.

Rodger shook his head. He had clearly instructed Richie to take care of Sam, and there was a definite lack of Sam around. Not only that, but with the recent reports on how "Blue-Eyed" Marcello and his men had died, the information Richie had discovered about the Nite Priory seemed even more important. Rodger couldn't risk Richie making stupid decisions with his or Sam's well-being.

Taking Richie by the arm, he led him a few yards away. "I mean, where the heck is Sam?" he said in a harsh whisper. "I asked you to keep her safe!"

Richie pulled away. "Man, calm the hell down. You need to chill, Detective. Sam's fine. I was just getting some coffee while she got checked out."

Any frustration Rodger felt got overridden by a rising sensation of panic at the mention of Sam being in the hospital. He wanted to demand to be taken to her. Before he could speak, Richie started talking again.

"We were out enjoying ourselves and she got hit with a dizzy spell, the second she's had in twenty-four hours. I think it's the stress, Rodger. It's getting to her, and can you blame her? Anyway, she's fine. She's getting checked out by a doctor right now."

He nodded. "All right. Take me to her. I'll see if she needs any—"

"I don't think that's a good idea, Rodger," interrupted Richie.

Rodger was stunned. He never would have imagined Richie talking to him like that. He folded his arms and glowered. "Well, I don't much like your tone. And I definitely do not like you deciding if I can or cannot see my niece." Even though they had just recently patched things up, he was already back to being "Uncle Rodger."

"Look, Rodger, it's not like that," Richie said in an exasperated tone. "I know you care for Sam. I get that. But, man, you told us yesterday that Ouellette is watching all of us under a magnifying glass. So if you go gamboling up to see her and somehow this gets back to the police . . ." He held out his hands.

Rodger sighed and rubbed his forehead. He hated to admit that Richie was right about anything related to Sam, but it was more apparent than ever that Rodger was too emotionally involved with her—just as Michael and Ouellette had said.

"All right, Richie," he said. "I'm sorry. You're right, I need to back away and let you handle her. I shouldn't have jumped your shit."

"Well, all right, then," Richie said, sipping his coffee in a huff.

"So get back to her! But before you go, I have something I want to ask you." He figured that this was the best time to follow up on the "Nite Priory" versus "Knight Priory" conundrum.

"I have a question, too," Richie said, looking around as if he expected someone nearby to be eavesdropping.

Rodger felt annoyed with him looking around. It was like he was becoming more and more distracted every day.

Finally, Richie said, "It's about Sam. Did either of her parents have any medical problems? I wanna know what to tell the doctor, and Sam doesn't remember."

Rodger hummed softly to himself, his brow creasing in thought. "I think her mother did. I remember Edward saying that she died of health complications soon after Sam was born. I don't know what it was, though. I didn't know Mary Castille."

Richie flicked his tongue over his cup of coffee, licking off a few droplets. "Sam's fainting spell was indicative of a person with heart problems. Any way we can find out whether her family has that kind of history?"

Rodger stared at him. "Jesus, Richie! Heart problems? That's not a small deal, man."

Richie again held out his hands. "Whoa, whoa. You gotta trust me, Rodger. I've got it handled. Believe me, if I thought she was in any danger, I'd let you know right away."

Rodger nodded, taking a deep breath.

"So?"

Rodger refocused on the question. As much as he hated to admit it, Richie might have found a link as to which M&M sister was Mary. If one of the sisters had indeed had heart problems, that one would have had to have been Sam's mother. He was also starting to see Michael's point—Sam's mother was somehow central to the original murders twenty years ago. He was going to have to pass all this on to Michael.

"I'll follow up on that, Richie, and let you know. Now it's my turn," Rodger said. "You said that you researched the Nite Priory the other night and discovered that they were a group of assassins who used cutting weapons and bare hands, correct?"

Richie looked around again, like he was expecting to see one of those Nite Priory members standing nearby. "Yes."

Rodger nodded and folded his arms. His description matched up to what had happened with Marcello's men. "And you're sure it's spelled N-I-T-E, correct?"

Richie sipped his coffee, looking thoughtful. "Yes, that's right."

Rodger nodded again. If Richie had indeed found a source with "Knight Priory" spelled incorrectly, then where he had gotten the information was important. "So you got this information at the local library, right?" he asked.

"No, no, no," replied Richie, shaking his head with considerable vigor. "I got it at Sam's house, in one of her books." He looked around again.

Rodger hardly noticed Richie's paranoid antics. Instead, he felt his temperature drop. *No goddamn way.* Richie had to have found it somewhere else. If the source of the misspelled word was Sam's townhome, it was another nail in her coffin.

He was feeling desperate. "You're sure that the information you came across had it spelled N-I-T-E."

"Yup," said Richie with a nod.

Rodger raised his hands and tried to keep his cool. "And you're sure, absolutely one-hundred-percent sure, that the only place you found this information was in Sam's home?"

"Yup," said Richie with another nod.

"Good to know," replied Dixie's voice from behind them.

Rodger felt his temperature plummet. Turning around, he saw Dixie holding a cup of coffee and sneering. *Oh, no!* He hoped Dixie wasn't about to start in on Richie.

She leaned toward Richie and said, "Well, hello there, Mr. Fastellos. Funny meeting you here."

Richie scowled and motioned back toward the hospital. "I should get back to . . . you know . . ."

"Back to Sam?" she asked, sipping her coffee in a way that looked pretentious. "She's in the lobby waiting on you. I just had a nice long chat with her, since I'm good friends with Rodger and Michael. Really sweet girl. I hope for your sake she's not our killer. She won't be much fun in bed if she's dead."

As Richie noticeably tensed up, his free hand balling up and his jaw clenching, she whistled, showing what could only be called a bitchy smile.

Christ, Dixie. This was not the time to play the psychology game on him.

"Ho ho! Getting mad there, lover boy?" asked Dixie. "Don't worry, I'm sure Sam will be waiting for you. She turned seven shades of red the moment she found out that I knew you. Don't worry, though, I didn't tell her about you only wanting to get in her pants."

Rodger just shook his head. The last thing he wanted to do was undermine Dixie, who had a reputation for being able to make suspects blow their cool and their cover. However, if he ever wanted to get information out of Richie again, he needed to stay on his good side.

Richie made a grunting sound and tossed his cup into a nearby trash can. "I'm outta here, Rodger. It stinks of trailer trash."

"The only trash here is a low-life who thinks he's good enough for Samantha Castille." She glared at Richie as he stormed off. "She's too classy for someone like you. You—"

"Whoa, whoa, whoa. Calm down, Dixie!" He held his hands out. *Dammit.* He had waited too long to say something.

Dixie fixed her glare on him. "Why did you shut me down, Rodger? That son-of-a-bitch made fools of Aucoin and me the other night. How the heck can you defend someone who's probably bullshitting us to protect our number-one suspect?"

Rodger's head hurt. He needed to get them back on the same page quickly. He chided himself for not taking time this morning to explain what was going on with Sam and Richie.

Closing his eyes, he silently counted to five and then said, "Okay, there are some things you need to know if we're going to continue working together. First off, Sam may be a suspect, but she's not under arrest. The goddamn justice system says she's innocent until proven guilty. I'm doing my best to remain objective, despite the fact that she's practically my niece. I know her past and what she suffered better than anyone else. So whether she's the killer or not, I'm going to make sure that she gets fair treatment under the law."

Dixie's expression went from peeved to confused. "Okay . . ."

Opening his eyes, Rodger continued, "Second, I trust my gut about Richie. The guy is an ass and a goof, but I believe he genuinely cares about Sam. So I asked him to keep an eye on her. I'm afraid someone may try to harm her as this thing goes on, just because she's Vincent's granddaughter."

Her expression relaxed. "Go on."

"Lastly," said Rodger, "I believe Richie may have been approached by this Nite Priory voodoo cult we're beginning to suspect. His information about how they kill is too similar to what happened down at the Riverwalk with Marcello to be a coincidence. If I'm going to get this information from him, I need him to trust me."

She folded her arms, tightening her lips and looking at the ground. "You should have told me all this earlier. It would have saved me a lot of groundwork and mistakes."

He blinked. For a moment, Dixie sounded like Michael. It was scary how much alike they were sometimes. They could have made a cute couple if things had been different.

With a soft exhale, she said, "Well, that's that, then. Okay, I'll back off for now. But next time, don't wait to tell me anything. And make sure you tell Ouellette about the Nite Priory thing. Because if you don't, I will. And I really don't want to take a butt-tanning for your bad judgment."

Rodger found himself chuckling at her remark.

She chuckled as well and patted him on the shoulder. "See, you're laughing again. Much better!"

Instantly, he felt better. Dixie was just one of those people who had a way of lightening your mood. People like her gave him hope for the future of the New Orleans police.

"Come on, temporary partner," she said, nodding her head toward the squad car. "Ouellette paged me. We need to get back to the precinct. He wants to meet everyone right now."

Rodger cocked an eyebrow, figuring that she meant her electronic pager. He, like many of the older detectives, usually kept his off. "What did he say it was about?"

"He didn't say what it was," she said. "Just that it was extremely important. There was a lot of background noise. It sounded like the precinct was full."

He didn't like the sound of that.

"So, Dixie, now that you've had a chance to talk to Sam, do you think she's the kind of person to commit serial murder?"

They got into the squad car. Dixie strapped herself in and sat back, looking contemplative. Finally, she said, "If she is the killer, then she's an expert at hiding it. I couldn't get a single read on her that made me feel uneasy." Then she grinned. "And she's well read, obviously intelligent, and likes Hemingway and Frost. Big plusses in my book." She winked.

In spite of himself, Rodger laughed out loud again.

When they arrived at the eighth precinct, however, it was clear that something was going on and that it was quite serious. The parking garage was full, and the sides of the street were lined with squad cars.

"Jesus," Dixie said as they searched for a parking space. "Arsenault's Arsenal is here."

Rodger looked just in time to see the large SWAT vans used by Sergeant Arsenault's team parked in the alley off the street. As usual, they were painted with logos and designs that belonged more in *Full Metal Jacket* than on a police vehicle.

"What the hell happened?" he asked.

Her eyes widened and her voice hushed. "There must have been another victim."

They quickly found a parking space.

Inside, the squad room was buzzing with activity. As they entered, Rodger saw every detective in the homicide division, as well as every uniformed officer he'd ever run across in the French Quarter, along with a number of police from nearby precincts. He even saw the black uniforms of Arsenault's SWAT team. *Jesus, is this a manhunt or something?*

"Let's find Kyle and learn what's going on," Dixie said, her voice thickening with concern.

It took them a few minutes to wade through the crowd toward the desks where Dixie and Aucoin sat. Both were empty.

Someone called out from a few desks away. "Dixie!"

Rodger turned to see a detective in his thirties, wearing a black duster, sporting a goatee, and with hair likely too long for regulation. He looked haggard and anxious and smelled of cigarette smoke.

"Rivette," said Dixie. She looked him over. "You're a mess. What's going on? Is it the Marcello case?"

"No, it's not," said Rivette. "The Marcello case has been put on hold along with everything else."

"What the hell's going on, Rivette?" asked Rodger.

Rivette shook his head. "It's the Ripper case. A third victim was found this morning."

Dixie's eyes wandered down to the ground, her lips silently moving as if thinking out loud. Slowly, a look of horror came over her face. "Where's Kyle?"

Rivette motioned toward where the interview rooms were located. "He's in there with Cathy and Ouellette."

Rodger started to feel sick to his stomach. He had a sinking feeling that he knew what he was about to hear. "No. No goddamn way."

Rivette looked riddled with anxiety as he said, "It was Cheryl."

Dixie's bottom lip immediately started to tremble, tears rolling down her cheeks without even a blink. "I gotta go to him." She rushed off.

Rodger felt his throat tighten. He watched her go, his body twitching as feelings of helplessness wracked him. He braced himself on Dixie's desk and rapidly shook his head. What kind of lunatic would torture a kid to death? How could anyone be so evil?

"I'm so sorry, Rodger," Rivette said, struggling to find the words. "When Aucoin showed up, he had Cathy with him. They'd been looking for Cheryl all night. They went all the way to Mandeville. Ouellette took them back there. Aucoin . . . man, you could hear him shriek all the way across the building."

"You'd scream like that, too, if it was your child," Rodger said, heading after Dixie. He started to imagine what he'd feel like if it had been Sam. He hastily pushed those thoughts away, as if they would kill him.

When he reached the interview room, he was stopped by Ouellette. "Let them be."

Through the one-way mirror, he saw Dixie embrace Cathy. Cathy looked as though she had just been beaten up, her clothes, hair, and makeup in a complete shambles. Aucoin was seated at the interview table and had the pallor of a man told he'd be executed within the hour. He was holding onto his hair like death and staring blankly ahead.

The last time Rodger had felt this powerless, he was watching another human being get pulverized by a machine.

As he saw Dixie go to Aucoin to embrace him, and saw Aucoin start to unhinge, burying his face against her, Rodger heard Ouellette clear his throat.

"Bergeron," he said, snapping Rodger's attention back to the world around him, "I need you to pull your shit together right now and help."

Rodger nodded, looking into the room once more. The three inside were holding onto each other and openly crying. He frowned. He couldn't even imagine the pain Aucoin was in right now, so instead, he pushed those feelings down as deep as they went and focused on the one thing he could do—be a detective.

His emotions buried for the moment, he asked, "What do you need me to do, Commander?"

Ouellette rubbed his hands over his bald head and started pacing. "Find that damn killer before any more people die?"

"I'm doing the best I can," Rodger said.

Ouellette dashed in, his face darkening, and stuck a finger in Rodger's face. "That was rhetorical, Bergeron!"

Rodger shook off the urge to punch Ouellette. He hated himself for even having that urge. It was just like the old case back in the seventies—everyone was starting to claw at one another's throats.

"This is worse than last time," Ouellette said, almost as if he could read Rodger's mind. He flicked a switch and the mirror went opaque, giving Dixie, Aucoin, and Cathy privacy. "Half the police force has convinced itself that Samantha Castille is the murderer. And while I'd love to say that we can arrest her, so far she looks less like a suspect and more like a patsy."

Rodger didn't respond. He still refused to suspect Sam, certain that she was somehow being framed.

"And now Aucoin's gone unhinged and Cathy's had a nervous breakdown. They'll both be heading to River Oaks as soon as Olivier's finished talking to them."

"You're admitting them to the psychiatric hospital?" he asked, thinking that was a bit extreme.

"They want to go, Bergeron," responded Ouellette. "Cathy wants to be admitted and Aucoin agreed to a psych-eval to see if he can still work."

"He wants to work?" Rodger couldn't believe that.

"He wants to wring Sam's neck!" Ouellette's face grew red, his voice deep and threatening.

Rodger backed away. He couldn't remember the last time he had seen Ouellette get this angry. Then he realized that Sam had been mentioned. "Wait, Sam? Why?"

"Christ, Bergeron, don't you ever read the newspaper?"

"Newspaper?" he asked. Then he froze. There was only one reason for the *Times-Picayune* to be brought up now. He felt the blood drain from his face and his knees shake. "No . . . No damn way. Not again. Not two times in a row."

"Read it yourself. It's on the interview prep table," Ouellette said, pointing out a newspaper and the official report from Cheryl's crime scene.

Rodger picked up both the newspaper and the official report. The newspaper featured the morning's story by Sam of Spades, and he compared it and the report side by side. The details were, once again, remarkably consistent. It was as similar as the previous story was to Rebecca Clemens's murder.

He put both papers down. He was sweating profusely. How the hell was the real killer doing this to Sam?

"See what I mean?" asked Ouellette. "She may be innocent until proven guilty in the eyes of the law, but in the court of public opinion, as well as in the eyes of most of the officers here, whoever wrote this story is the new Bourbon Street Ripper. I'm not losing any more cops to this bullshit."

Rodger felt the stress and worry aging him by the moment. "Any more cops? What do you mean?"

Ouellette shook his head. "Officer Guidry found the third body as well. I swear, that girl is going to need years of therapy. She asked to be admitted to River Oaks this morning. She'll likely resign after all this crap."

Rodger sighed, wondering if he should retire after the case concluded. "So what happens now?"

"I get a search warrant for Sam's townhouse," said Ouellette as they headed back to the squad room. "And when I do, we tear that place apart looking for evidence. Then we either arrest Samantha Castille . . ." He turned to Rodger. The look on his face was deadly serious. " . . . or we take her into protective custody before she becomes a victim herself."

Rodger followed Ouellette to the squad room in silence.

There, Ouellette jumped up on a desk and whistled loudly, getting everyone's attention. Standing off to the side, Rodger wracked his brain for theories on how the killer could be framing Sam. It was the only hope he had to hold onto.

Ouellette spoke, his voice carrying effortlessly across the room. "Okay, listen up, people! From this moment on, we are all on the New Bourbon Street Ripper Task Force. This order comes from the very top. Mayor Barthelemy wants this case closed and this son-of-a-bitch caught before another body turns up. So here's what will happen. Bergeron, you and Olivier are partners until this case is over. No Aucoin and no LeBlanc. They're both on the sidelines until I say otherwise."

Several heads turned toward Rodger as he was mentioned. He barely noticed as Dixie came to his side.

"Meanwhile," Ouellette said, "Breaux and Gravois, you two start sifting through the profiles of every person who knew the three victims. See if you can find a link or a common thread."

Breaux and Gravois, two older, seasoned veterans, nodded, Gravois giving the commander a thumbs-up. Rodger remembered that they were particularly good at profiling suspects and victims.

Ouellette motioned toward Detective Rivette and his partner, a big-bodied guy who was eating a hoagie. "Landry and Rivette, I want you to interview the entire Castille family, as well as everyone who has had personal contact with Samantha Castille in the past five years. That includes her friends at the newspaper. And track her movements since the killings started. I want to know what she ate, when she slept, and where she crapped. Lastly, find out as much as you can about Richard Fastellos, the author from Pittsburg she's been hanging around."

Rodger felt sick to his stomach. There was no way this could end well for those who were close to Sam.

Rivette slapped Landry on the arm to get him to put down the hoagie. "We've got it covered, Commander."

Ouellette called out. "Sergeant Arsenault?"

The crowd of officers parted. A tall, dark, and very muscular man in a SWAT uniform with its sleeves ripped off stepped forward. His brutally unattractive, pug-like face sported a scar over his left eye and a scowl that could scare an angel.

Oh, and he made Mad Monty look small.

"Here, Commander," Arsenault said in a voice that could only have gotten more manly if it had made the room shake.

"Good," replied Ouellette, showing no reaction to Arsenault's appearance or voice. "Get all your men and start patrols. From now until this case is closed, you keep every area of the French Quarter covered. Every tourist trap. Every hotel. Every titty bar. Everywhere. I want it all patrolled. You see someone so much as sneeze suspiciously, you take them in for questioning. The mayor has given me full authority to keep the French Quarter safe, and I'm passing it to you and your Arsenal."

Arsenault nodded and popped his head to the side, cracking it loud enough to make people flinch. "Don't worry, Commander. No one dies on my watch unless I kill them myself."

A murmur went through the crowd. For the past ten years, Arsenault had refused promotion beyond sergeant, stating that he wanted to be "in the trenches." Heading up the SWAT team nicknamed Arsenault's Arsenal, he was the guy Ouellette called in when things got out of control. Rodger was impressed but concerned. He wondered if the Arsenal was really necessary.

The Arsenal was known for its impeccable tactics and ruthless aggression, sometimes going overboard on what was acceptable. On more than one occasion, Ouellette, the only person in the city who Arsenault seemed to respect, had to do damage control when the Arsenal got too close to the proverbial line.

"For the rest of you detectives," Ouellette said, looking over the rest of the room, "you have a list of every business and residence in the French Quarter. You and your partner's names are next to a portion of that list. You are to go to all those businesses and residences and ask about the nights in question. Get any information. You see something suspicious, you call in for a search warrant. Connick has people on call just to get those warrants. Contact information is at the top of the list."

Rodger exhaled and looked over at Dixie. She was shaking her head. It was bad if Harry Connick Sr., the district attorney, wanted someone on call just to bother judges for search warrants. It was obvious that fear was starting to override common sense, and that the investigation was getting dangerously close to stepping on the civil rights of New Orleans's law-abiding citizens. *Just like last time*, he thought to himself with a frown.

"So now for the suspects," Ouellette said. "First off, there is an unidentified woman in an indigo hooded robe and what looks like a voodoo skull mask. She is armed with military-grade equipment. Forensics suspects she has a Soviet Dragunov semi-automatic sniper rifle. Since the Soviet Union was dissolved last December, the black market has been flooded with these weapons. This woman has killed two people already, one being a Jefferson Parish deputy. She is to be considered armed and extremely dangerous. If you see her, call for back-up immediately. Do not engage her alone." He turned toward Arsenault. "I repeat, do not engage her alone."

Arsenault tightened up his face, but didn't say anything, just nodding in understanding.

"Another suspect," Ouellette said, "is Samantha Castille, the granddaughter of the original Bourbon Street Ripper. She is a high-value suspect. You are to observe her only. Do not, I repeat, do not make a move against her unless I authorize it beforehand. I want a tail on her constantly until this situation is resolved. Rivette and Landry, you two sort that out."

Rivette saluted. He looked proud of himself for being given so much authority.

Rodger, on the other hand, felt ill. Despite his best efforts, Sam was more a suspect than ever.

Ouellette continued. "Then there is something called the Nite Priory. This name has been attached to letters sent to old accomplices of the original Bourbon Street Ripper. We know nothing about the Nite Priory, and I don't like not knowing anything about them. Ask around, people. It may be a person. It may be a cult. When you gather evidence, look for the words. It's Nite Priory. N-I-T-E P-R-I-O-R-Y."

People scribbled down the name.

"Lastly," he said, "we have an unknown group responsible for the mass murder of Giorgio 'Blue-Eyed' Marcello and his men the other night. Rivette and Landry have been looking into the case. Unfortunately, the security cameras were off. Marcello had been putting pressure on City Hall to arrest Samantha Castille, likely in revenge for bad blood between him and her father. But anyway, whoever did this were expert assassins."

Dixie whispered, "Just remember, partner. We need to tell Ouellette everything that Richie told you. It looks like the Nite Priory really did murder Marcello."

Rodger nodded. He didn't want to focus on it. It was yet another mark against Sam.

As everyone wrote down the information, Ouellette concluded his speech. "So that's it, people! Detectives and SWAT, get going now. The rest of you, help make room for the map and boards. We've got a lot of crap to put up. Okay, everyone, get your asses in gear. Let's put an end to this Bourbon Street Ripper bullshit before Labor Day."

As he stepped down from his desk, the crowd dispersed. About a dozen officers started moving desks around to transform the room into the task force command center.

Rodger motioned for Dixie to follow. They headed toward Ouellette's office.

On the way, they passed Arsenault, who was busy giving instructions to his men. Spotting them, he stepped in their way and said, "I just want to say that I hope you catch the killer before I do."

Having to lean back to lock eyes with him, Rodger asked, "Oh, yeah, why so?"

Arsenault grinned wolfishly and said, "Because if I catch him first, there won't be enough left to stand trial." He blew them a kiss, then smirked at them before heading back to his team.

Dixie whistled and shook her head. "I'm glad he's on our side."

Rodger knew she was trying to lighten the mood, but it didn't help. He was determined to be sour grapes.

Later that night, after reporting everything to Ouellette, from Richie and the Nite Priory to Jonathon and the Knight Priory, Rodger parted ways with Dixie. She wanted to be with Aucoin and Cathy. They agreed to meet again the following morning to continue the investigation.

After leaving the precinct, he headed to Tulane Hospital and visited with Michael for a while. They traded information, especially about Sam's mother and the M&M sisters. Michael appeared to be in good spirits and seemed to be piecing the case together in his head. Rodger left him shortly after his evening medication.

After a boring dinner at a nearby diner, he wandered along Bourbon Street.

Police were everywhere. Arsenault's Arsenal was standing at nearly every street corner. The few civilians out and about the French Quarter were looking around nervously. It was surreal, like the city had transformed into a police state.

Ducking into the bizarrely empty Jean Lafitte's Blacksmith Bar, Rodger sat at a table, the same one he had usually shared with Michael, Edward, or any other detective who would tolerate his company. He opened a tab and ordered a beer.

Two pints later, he was starting to feel comfortably numb. That was when he felt a comforting hand on his shoulder and heard an older man's voice. "Mind if an old timer like myself joins you?"

He looked up and saw the wizened face of his old mentor, Douglas Dugas, who looked congenial but concerned. "Douglas," said Rodger, smiling for the first time in hours.

Douglas, who was a retired and decorated detective, sat across from him.

Even though Rodger hadn't seen Douglas in several days, he could only think of one thing to say. "So, I patched things up with Sam."

Douglas chuckled and said, "I figured as much, Rodger. You were always like an uncle to her. I'm glad for you."

Rodger started to drink his beer and then realized that he was talking to Douglas on Bourbon Street. "Wait, why are you here, Douglas? It's half past real late. I thought you'd be in bed by now."

Douglas waved him off. "When I saw what was happening on the news, Mabel told me to find you and make sure you were OK—else I'd never taste her pound cake again. So I went by the precinct, found out that you weren't there, had a quick chat with Ouellette, and finally figured if there was anyplace you'd be, it would be here getting a drink. Sitting at the same damn table drinking the same damn beer."

Rodger laughed out loud, and then, without warning, began sobbing uncontrollably. Douglas silently watched as Rodger wept into his hand. It took a few minutes before he could speak. "It's all gone out of control again. Sam. That poor girl. She's going to die. Either the police or some vigilante or some mob is going to kill her. And there is nothing I can do about it."

Douglas's lips drew tight, and he got a look of concentration. "Rodger, it's not your fault that Edward died. He knew the risks and made his choices. You couldn't have saved him. You may not want to hear it, but it's true. Edward chose to put himself in harm's way."

Rodger looked into Douglas's eyes, searching for hope.

"However," Douglas said, pointing at him, "Sam isn't making any choices here. Someone else, someone very intelligent and very evil, is making the choices for her. So while you couldn't save Edward, you can save Sam."

"How?" Rodger asked, hoping for answers one more time.

Douglas tightened his fist. "Find the person who's making the choices for her, and stop them. Give Sam control of her life back, so that she can make those choices. You do that, Rodger, and you'll be the one who saves that little girl."

Rodger nodded, his eyes puffy and aching. He felt like someone finally understood. To him, Sam was still that ten-year-old girl, her eyes hollow and devoid of life, who needed someone to save her.

"Come on," Douglas said, getting up. "You're drunk and blubbering like a little kid. That means it's time to get you home. You still living at the apartment with the Rent Nazi?"

Rodger struggled to his feet. "Ms. Parkerson? Yeah, same place. Keys in my pocket."

Looping Rodger's arm around him, Douglas said, "All right, then. Let someone else take care of you tonight."

Rodger had never been so happy to have Douglas as his mentor.

Chapter 5

A Black Hooded Coat

Date: **Sunday, August 9, 1992**
Time: **4:15 p.m.**
Location: **Tulane University Hospital**
Downtown New Orleans

Richie Fastellos was in a bad mood, and he owed it all to Dixie Olivier. With just a few choice comments, she had made every negative feeling he had bubble up to the surface. After storming away, he took a few minutes to calm down in the men's bathroom.

Running cold water over his face, he stared at his reflection for a long time. Looking back was a man as haggard and tired as the woman he loved. His five o'clock shadow was unseemly and his hands were shaking.

He'd now gone more than a day without his anxiety medication, and he'd been going between feeling just fine and having miniature fits of crazy. It didn't help that during his entire conversation with Rodger, he had been sure he was seeing members of the Nite Priory watching him. He wasn't sure if it was really them or his stress making him see things.

Unsurprisingly, he felt the calmest when he was with Sam. It was like she was his new drug. And at that moment, he really needed a fix.

Face and hands clean, Richie stumbled out of the bathroom and into the lobby where Sam was waiting. She was sitting and squeezing her charm in her hands. She flashed a small smile at him as he sat down beside her, then she slid into his arms and rested her head on his chest. He couldn't help but notice how good she smelled and how soft she felt.

"Hey there," he said, already feeling calmer. "You ready to get out of here?"

The doctors had examined her. They had expressed concern over her having two fainting spells in a twenty-four-hour period, but they had found nothing wrong with her. She was prescribed some motion sickness medicine and told to follow up with her doctor. She ended up making an appointment with her psychiatrist, Dr. Klein, for tomorrow.

Richie had only left her in the lobby because she had asked for some fresh coffee. That was when he had run into Rodger and Dixie.

"Yeah," she said, grabbing his waist and holding him close. "Let's go home and rest up before tonight. I'm not going to be robbed of an evening with my boyfriend and my best friend."

He walked with her back to the car, thinking about Jacob. Something about him didn't seem right. Richie got that he cared for Sam, but he seemed almost . . . fake sometimes.

At the car, Richie got in the driver's seat, while Sam leaned over and put her head on his shoulder. "Mind if I rest like this on the way home?"

He kissed the top of her head. "It's probably not very safe."

"I don't care. I need to be next to you."

She stayed like that as he drove home.

A little while later, Richie was in Sam's bedroom getting dressed. His clothes, even though they had been laundered, were starting to show signs of wear.

As she came out of the bathroom wearing a tank top and panties, he said, "Ya know, if we have the time, I'd really like to go back to my hotel room and get a fresh change of clothes."

She let out a short "Ha!" and started rooting around in her dresser. "We should go get you some new clothes. You know, make you look snazzy and sexy." Thankfully, she was in a better mood and seemed ready to have a good evening.

He chuckled. "Really now, Sam? The 'let's have the girlfriend dress the boyfriend' bit? Isn't that completely cliché?"

She stuck her tongue out at him. "Hun, you have a great body, but a complete lack of fashion sense." She winked.

As Sam turned back around to get out her clothes, Richie admired her shape. She had such an amazing butt. He found himself falling in love again. He couldn't get over how strange he felt—no one had ever had this kind of an effect on him before. It was like something in her was feeding off his desire. If he was ever going to believe in succubi or sexual demons or any of that nonsense, it would be because of Sam.

He pushed those thoughts away as she turned to him and held up a black T-shirt with a pair of red lips and vampire fangs on one side and the words "Bite Me!" on the other.

"What do you think?"

He snickered. "Going out in New Orleans in a vampire T-shirt? Sam, how very Gothic of you."

"Oh, hush, you," Sam said, putting the shirt back. After rummaging around for a few more moments, she pulled out a dark purple T-shirt with a skeletal figure wearing a top hat and holding a shovel. The back of the shirt had "Dig My Grave" written on it. She looked at the shirt quietly, her lips pursed.

Richie leaned in and examined it. "Hey, isn't that the dude from the Patterson voodoo tour? The one who digs your grave right before you die? Ya know, Baron Samhain?"

"Baron Samedi," she said, staring at the print. She seemed transfixed.

"Hey, Sam, you OK?" he asked, touching her arm.

She jumped back as if he were hurting her, her bangs sliding over her face, her pupils heavily dilated.

He blinked. *What the hell?*

Sam rapidly shook her head. When she looked back up at him, her eyes were back to normal and her hair was out of her face. "Sorry, just spaced out a bit. That stupid ride really messed with my head. Voodoo. Loa. Barons. Sometimes I think I'm possessed, ya know? It would explain so much about my screwed-up life." She put on the T-shirt. It was a perfect fit.

She had mentioned being possessed so casually that Richie wasn't sure if she was serious or not. He wasn't superstitious by nature and certainly didn't believe in ghosts, but with how she'd been acting lately, he wasn't sure what to believe.

"Well, if you ever want to talk about it, just let me know," he said as he finished getting dressed.

She pulled on some black jeans and nodded but didn't say anything. She was silent all the way to his hotel room at the Ritz Carlton as well, just writing in her notebook with that silver pen, scribbling down notes on her story.

Once there, while he got dressed in fresh clothes—a business casual outfit that looked as good as it did out of place—Sam called Jacob to tell him where they were. Once he was dressed and shaved, Richie looked through his bags once more for any traces of his anxiety medication.

They were all gone. He really had lost his pills. It really had been over twenty-four hours since his last dose of medication.

"Jacob'll be here in a few minutes," she said, resting her hands on his back. "No pills left, huh? Not even an emergency supply?"

"Nothing," he said, his lips tight. He was already feeling his heart rate increase to an uncomfortable level. Just thinking about it upset him. "I'll have to call my doctor in Pittsburg on Monday, get the prescription sent to a pharmacy here, and then go fill it. It's gonna be a major pain in the ass."

Sam laid her head on his shoulder. "What can I do to help?"

Richie nervously clenched his jaw. "Just be with me. I need to work through it. To be honest . . ." He pulled her into his arms. "I've been relying on them way too much. And if I'm going to be a good man for you, I need to stop letting this stuff hold me back."

She leaned up and placed a small kiss on his lips. "Never think that you're less of a man for having that problem. This is all from your abuse as a child, right?"

He kissed back. He hated remembering what his father had done to him, haze or not. It was a painful memory he'd rather submerge with writing, sex, and booze instead of actually facing his problems and sorting through them.

And yet Sam made him want to face his problems, conquer them, and truly live.

"I don't want to use that as an excuse anymore." Richie smiled.

She laughed softly and tousled his hair. "Okay, then. No more excuses. No more fussing about it. We'll get your meds when we can. We'll deal with the bigger issues when we can. Until then, I'll keep you too distracted to go crazy."

He leaned in and was just starting to kiss her with more passion when there was a loud knock on the door.

Richie jumped back like a cat from a vacuum cleaner. "Shit!"

"It's probably just Jacob." Sam opened the door and said, "Hey, Jacob! We were just talking about you."

Jacob entered and gave her a brief hug. He was wearing a leather jacket over a black shirt. His hair was combed back and he looked pretty slick. He reached over and shook Richie's hand. "Hey, Richie, looking good. Not very Nawlins, but good nonetheless." He popped Richie gently on the arm, which stung anyway.

Richie managed a grin. "This is the hip urban dress style in Pittsburg. All the cool people wear it." It was a lie and he was sure everyone knew it.

Sam patted Richie fondly on the bum. "We'll fix you up tomorrow. For now, let's get out of here. I want to eat and then hit the town."

Richie followed, rubbing his arm. Jacob's grip and his "friendly" arm pop were way too strong. *What's this guy's problem?*

In the elevator, Sam and Jacob decided, after a brief conversation, to have dinner at Landry's Seafood House, a Cajun restaurant located on the Mississippi River in the French Quarter. Watching the two collaborate like the long-term friends they were, Richie started to feel like a third wheel. It was only when Sam took his hand and smiled softly at him that he stopped feeling that way.

In the lobby, he was tasked with getting Sam's car out of parking while Jacob took her outside to check out the new chrome on his bike. She showed such interest in Jacob's motorcycle that Richie, who was beginning to think he'd be competing all night for Sam's attention, wondered why she didn't own a motorcycle instead of a car. She seemed to really go for them.

Heh, I guess there's more to Sam's tastes than fine furniture and coffee. He was going to have to really get to know her—what she liked and what she disliked.

The concierge raised his upper lip as Richie approached, as if he smelled something foul. Richie shrugged. He had already offended the concierge several times by vastly under-tipping him and had ended up splashing in the muck of a back alley for it.

"Hey," Richie said, reaching into his wallet and pulling out both a fifty and the parking slip. "I need to get my car out of valet parking, and I don't know where to go. Can you handle that for me?"

The concierge looked at the fifty with what could only be called surprise. "I will have your ride brought around right away, Mr. Fastellos."

Richie walked away with a smirk as the concierge called valet parking. If the fifty hadn't worked, he likely would have clocked him right there. Richie was getting really tired of people walking on him.

Once outside, Richie saw that it was already getting dark. He approached Sam and Jacob, who weren't looking at the motorcycle so much as across the street. Following their gaze, he saw a line of police cars, lights flashing, heading into the French Quarter.

"What's going on?" he asked, approaching the two.

Sam was frowning. "Not sure. Looks like something's going down on Bourbon Street."

Shrugging, Richie went to the doorman and asked, "Hey, bud, what's going on with the police?"

"There's been another victim of the new Ripper," the doorman said, shaking his head. "Mayor Barthelemy got the French Quarter under martial law, it seems. Heard that SWAT and everything is there."

"Serious? Holy crap," said Richie, looking back over at the flashing lights on Bourbon. "Who was it this time? Any idea who the victim was?"

"No idea her name, some cop's daughter," replied the doorman.

Richie's brow furrowed. The only daughter of a police officer that he knew of was the teenage daughter of Detective Aucoin, the one he had seen in the precinct just the other night. His eyes widened as he remembered Sam saying that the next victim in her story was a teenage girl. The two facts clicked together in his head with uncomfortable precision.

No. It couldn't be, could it?

He decided not to stir the pot until he had more information.

Approaching the two as Jacob put an arm around Sam, the cuff of his leather jacket lifting enough to show a skull tattoo on his left wrist, Richie said, "Hey, guys, we're going to need to find a new place to eat. There was another victim last night. The mayor's got the French Quarter locked down."

Both turned to Richie with surprised looks. Jacob immediately backed off. "Let's go to the lakefront. There's a Landry's there as well. My treat, guys. Just follow me."

Richie put his arm around Sam. "You good for this, hun?"

She nodded. "I can't let this ruin my life. Do you know who the victim was?"

Richie bit his bottom lip and looked down at her. She was starting to show signs of stress again. He felt the feverish desire to protect her overwhelm him. Taking a breath, he bent the truth. "The daughter of a cop or something. Some chick in her mid-twenties who goes to Tulane or something. I didn't get the details. It's nothing like your story, though."

That seemed to relax her. As her car was brought up front, Richie took the driver's side. He hoped his fib was accurate. He didn't think Sam could take another coincidence.

Once at Landry's at the Lakefront, the three of them took a few minutes to get situated. Richie was impressed by the lake. From the parking lot, he could look out over it. While he couldn't see the water in the nighttime, he could see lights moving across the horizon far away. It was amazing to see such a huge lake this far south.

As he stood there, taking in the sight, Jacob stood next to him and said, "Impressive, isn't it? You should see it in the daytime."

Richie looked over. "Man, Lake Erie could hold twenty Lake Pontchartrains. This thing is a pond."

As he walked with Sam to the restaurant, he was sure he saw Jacob's face get red. That made him smile.

Landry's was one of those places Richie had wanted to eat at before leaving New Orleans. From the outside, it looked like an old fisherman's bar, the weather-beaten wooden planks a perfect match to the brackish water washing up from Lake Pontchartrain. A pelican perched on a nearby halogen light.

Inside, the restaurant continued the fisherman's bar motif. There were decorations of swordfish, life preservers, and even ship wheels on the walls, interspersed with photographs of local sailboats and commercial fishing trawlers. The high-vaulted ceiling was lined with dozens of fishing nets. The sound system played zydeco music from the local radio station.

It was a busy Saturday night, but somehow Jacob managed to get the three of them a booth within a few minutes of arriving. The hostess who showed them their seat glanced over at Richie, blushed and giggled, and then hurried off.

Sam, seated next to Richie, leaned over to Jacob and asked, "So, what was that about?"

"Oh, our hostess is a fan of Richie's," he said with a grin as he sipped his water. "She's going to get her book and Richie's going to autograph it."

Richie just stared at him as Sam started laughing. This guy was a real piece of work. But if it got them a seat and it helped Sam enjoy herself, he guessed it was OK.

She continued to laugh out loud. "I can't believe you, Jacob Hueber. You really are too much."

Jacob winked at them. "Nah, just looking out for my best friend. And giving her boyfriend a hard time."

Once again, Richie felt confused. He really didn't know what to make of this guy or his intentions.

"So, Jacob," he asked. "You and Sam met in college?"

The hostess came back and showcased a copy of *The Pale Lantern* as if it were her prized possession. As Richie scribbled a generalized dedication to her, he listened to Jacob.

"Pretty much. I knew her from creative writing classes. Even back then, she was a recluse, kept to herself. However, at that time, there was a series of assaults on campus. A nutcase was beating up students who walked around at night. Some of them were hurt pretty badly, too. The cops never did catch the guy."

"Wow, seriously?" Richie handed the book back to the hostess, who scampered off.

Sam's head was lowered and she grabbed Richie's hand underneath the table. "Yeah. Seriously."

Jacob continued, "Anyway, I walked with her at first just to keep her safe, from class to her car. Over time, we got to know each other. And one Halloween, I had two tickets to Anne Rice's vampire ball. I took Sam, who was dressed as Elvira. I was dressed as Gomez Addams. And after that, we became best friends. Right, Sam?"

"Yeah," she said, looking pensive. "Can we talk about something else?"

Jacob got an "oh, crap" expression.

Not missing a beat, Richie said, "Sure, Sam. Let's talk about something else. I think I see the waitress coming."

Jacob ordered for the group, leaning back and playing up the cool act for the waitress—a rather attractive redhead in her early twenties. Richie watched as he finished the order by blowing her a kiss and winking at her. But she rolled her eyes and gave him a glare before heading off. This guy was not fooling anyone with the stud act.

"Oh, Lord, Jacob," said Sam, waggling her eyebrows, "if you pick up another girlfriend, I'm gonna hit you with my breadsticks."

He blinked and looked over at her. She was chuckling along with Jacob. *Seriously?* He couldn't believe Sam couldn't tell that Jacob was being a creep. Was she just blind to him or something?

Dinner was relatively mundane after that, with Sam and Jacob talking about bikes and thrill-seeking. Richie learned that although she wanted to own a motorcycle and would love to do things such as skydiving and hang-gliding, she never did because she always got out of breath. To him, that was just more hard evidence that she had a heart condition she never knew about.

The conversation continued until dessert, when Landry's radio stopped playing music and a newscaster came on.

"Ladies and gentlemen," said the newscaster in a genuinely distressed voice, "we have just received word that Commander Ouellette of the eighth precinct is giving a press conference concerning the latest murder in the new Bourbon Street Ripper investigation, as well as the state of the French Quarter lockdown. We take you live to City Hall."

Richie felt Sam tense up. She took out her shoe charm and rapidly squeezed it. Placing his hand over hers, Richie said, "Let's get the check and go."

"All right." Jacob left the booth to go pay for the meal.

As Ouellette's voice came over the radio, Sam gripped Richie's hand tightly. All around, men were protectively placing their arms around their female companions. Parents were telling children to hush. Everyone was silent as the commander of the eighth precinct spoke.

"Good evening. This is Commander Louis Ouellette of the New Orleans eighth precinct. Today at 4:00 p.m., the body of the third victim of the serial killer known as the New Bourbon Street Ripper was found. The victim was sixteen-year-old Cheryl Aucoin, daughter of Senior Detective Kyle Aucoin. Preliminary medical reports show that she was murdered last night."

Richie felt his blood run cold. It was that very same girl he had seen only a few days earlier.

"You lied," Sam said, her voice seizing. "Outside the Ritz. You said it was an adult. Why did you lie to me?" She was squeezing his hand painfully.

He couldn't respond. It was like someone had sucker-punched his brain and knocked it out. He had seen both Rebecca Clemens and Cheryl Aucoin the nights before they were murdered. *What the shit?*

Ouellette's voice continued. "As of this evening, Mayor Barthelemy is declaring a state of emergency over the French Quarter and the surrounding areas, instituting a strict curfew. Anyone caught outside after 10:00 p.m. will be detained and questioned by the police. This extends to the area surrounded by Poydras, Claiborne, and Elysian

Fields. We ask that all citizens living in that area stay home with the doors locked after curfew."

Richie felt Sam trying to wiggle free. "Fuck you, Richie. Why the hell would you lie to me about that?"

He really didn't want to fight with her. He got up and said, "Let's get outside. We'll talk there."

As they left, he heard Ouellette say, "I've brought in the reserve SWAT team, headed by Sergeant Damien Arsenault, to keep watch over the French Quarter. If you see any suspicious activity, report it to them immediately."

Once outside, Richie turned to Sam to talk. Immediately, she raised her hand to slap him. He flinched and stepped back, throwing up his arms. She then balled her fist up and glared at him

For a moment, he envisioned putting his hands around her neck and squeezing. It would be so easy.

Then he saw the tears in her eyes and the hurt expression on her face. Instantly, his own feelings of anger melted away. He couldn't be angry at the woman he loved, especially not since he had hurt her. "Sam, just hear me out."

"You better have a good story, writer boy," said Sam. Angry tears rolled down her cheeks.

Richie was starting to feel panicked, and knew that without his medication, he'd start having a full anxiety attack within minutes. He took a deep breath. "I didn't know it was a teenager, Sam, just that it was a cop's daughter. When I told you about it earlier, I didn't have all the facts. The truth is that I met the Aucoin girl when the police questioned me the night before. The whole coincidence just freaked me the fuck out. I swear I never meant to lie, Sam. I just didn't know everything. I swear it!"

He knew he sounded desperate at the end. In his mind, he imagined her telling him to fuck off, saying that she never wanted to see him again, and then asking Jacob to take her home. It was enough to make him want to curl into a ball and cry.

When she looked up at him, he flinched, certain that she was about to break up with him. To his surprise and horror, she let out a blood-curdling scream and threw herself at him.

The psycho-fuck?

Richie stared blankly as she hit his chest again and again, the blows intentionally weak.

"I can't take this," Sam cried out into his chest. "I can't fucking take this anymore. Why is this happening? What the hell did I do to deserve this?"

Suddenly, he realized that everyone in the parking lot was staring at them. Some were looking very concerned, others looked almost sympathetic. He put his arms around her, shielding her face from the crowd. He wasn't sure what to do, but it was obvious that she was suffering.

"I can't deal with this, Richie," she said between sobs. "Everything is falling into hell. Even after twenty years, that evil bastard is still haunting my life. Do I have to die for this to end? Because I'll blow my damn brains out tonight, I swear I will!"

Richie tightened his grip around her, trying to quell his own feelings of panic. "Don't say that."

Selfishly holding onto the relief that she wasn't breaking up with him, he said, "It'll work out. I promise. We gotta believe that Rodger and Michael will solve the case and clear your name."

"It doesn't matter," Sam said. She sagged against Richie. "Caroline already said people were going to witch-hunt Sam of Spades if another story matched another murder. I'm dead and you know it."

Jacob came out from where the pay phones were, looking concerned. "Hey, um, what's wrong with her?"

Richie mouthed the word "breakdown" and then said, "We need to get Sam home. Can you follow us, just to make sure she's OK?"

Jacob nodded and said, "Yeah, come on. You drive her. Let's go."

The drive home was eerily similar to the drive home from the Pattersons' voodoo shop. Sam just scribbled in her notebook, muttering, "I'm gonna make up the most twisted shit ever. People getting arms blown off, houses eating people, half the police force getting killed off. No goddamn way all this nutty shit's gonna happen. If I write something crazy enough, then there won't be a coincidence next time."

"Sam, are you gonna be OK?" Richie asked at last, feeling that it was the weakest thing he could have said.

"Just get me home," she replied and closed the notebook. "I need to rethink this whole writing thing. Hell, I need to rethink my whole life." She leaned against the window and closed her eyes.

Sam was asleep by the time they got home, so Richie and Jacob went to unlock her townhome before waking her. But when they got to the front patio, they both stopped.

The front door was open.

"Oh, shit," Richie said. He looked over at Jacob, whose face was starting to show signs of incredulous anger.

"Go back to the car and keep an eye on Sam. I'll make sure it's safe." Jacob took out a keychain with a metal bar attached to it. Saying, "It's not supposed to go down this way," he headed inside looking like he was spoiling for a fight.

Richie paid him no mind. Quickly, he returned to the car.

Sam was waking up. Groggily, she said, "What's going on?"

He leaned in and said, "Wait here, hun. I'll be right back." Kissing her forehead, he locked the door. Then he headed back inside. If this was the Nite Priory and they didn't know that Jacob was a friend, they would slaughter him.

The front hallway was quiet, the lights out. He moved toward the grandfather clock, where Sam kept her father's service revolver. Retrieving it and making sure it was loaded, he crept toward the kitchen in the back of the townhome.

The sound of movement upstairs startled him. With a quick motion, he spun around, looking for a sign, any sign, of an intruder.

Nothing.

Upon entering the kitchen, Richie could only hear droplets of water splashing into the empty porcelain sink. Each of his steps creaked loudly. Each of his breaths was like a bull's. The silence within the townhome was deafening.

At the far end of the kitchen, he saw that the pantry door was slightly ajar. He couldn't remember if they had left it that way. Cocking back the revolver's hammer, he walked forward.

He had never fired a gun before in his life and wasn't sure how well he'd do it. But despite his previous feelings of anxiety, he felt strangely calm now. It was surreal, like someone else was moving him and he was just watching. He wondered if the fear and stress were making him so dissociative.

At the pantry door, he heard what sounded like breathing. Keeping his own breaths shallow, he formulated a plan. He'd throw the door open, point the gun right at the intruder, and tell them to freeze. *Perfect plan.*

Hand on the doorknob, Richie took a deep breath and counted to three. He thought of Sam and reminded himself that should he be forced to shoot someone, it was for her sake. With that resolve, he opened the door.

Nothing. The sound was coming from an air vent in the floor.

"Old goddamn house," he said in disgust, turning around to leave.

In his way was a man wearing a black ski mask.

"Bitch!" the man said before punching Richie in the face so hard he saw Lite-Brites.

With a thud, Richie hit the ground, blood filling his vision and the back of his throat. The revolver flew from his hand. His nose was surely broken and his adrenaline was in full swing. He was vaguely aware that someone was stepping on him. "We're gonna kick your ass, pussy boy. Then we're gonna fuck that murdering whore to death."

Sam, he thought. *I have to protect Sam.*

The last time he had felt this defenseless, the Nite Priory had murdered a crime boss and over a dozen of his thugs. As panic set in, he heard the sound of meat hitting meat, and felt the man get pushed off of him. *Are they here?*

He cleared the blood out of his vision, half-expecting to see them again.

Instead, he saw Jacob fighting the man. His movements were fluid, like a boxer's, and after raining several punches on the intruder, he threw an uppercut that looked like it belonged in a movie.

Richie stared in disbelief. Could everyone other than him fight like an expert?

The man stumbled back from the uppercut and bellowed with rage. "That bitch is dead. Just a matter of time!" He knocked Jacob back and ran out of the front of the house.

"Get Sam!" Jacob yelled as he chased the assailant.

By this point, Richie was able to get up, grab the revolver, and stumble up front. Sam's home office, where she kept her computer, copier, and fax machine, was trashed. Revolver in hand, he stumbled out to the car.

Sam was awake, watching Jacob pursue the man down the highway. The intruder jumped into the back of a pickup truck that was filled with a couple of other guys. The truck zoomed off as they shouted obscenities and yowled out a rebel yell.

Richie helped Sam out of the car. She took one look at him holding the revolver, his face bloody, and said, "My hero?"

He spat out blood. "Jacob did most of the work. I was useless and stu—"

Sam kissed him. It effectively shut him up.

An hour later, the three of them were cleaning up the front of the townhome. Richie had an ice pack on his face, his broken nose throbbing. Jacob was sweeping out the entry hall while Sam was examining her office and study.

While she refused to call the police until she spoke to Kent, she agreed that the incident had to be reported. Richie was glad that she didn't fight that—the threats were rapidly escalating.

"It seems the only thing they took was something from my copier," she finally said.

Richie and Jacob looked up. Jacob tilted and shook his head, saying, "Um, what?"

"What did they take?" Richie asked. He didn't know the first thing about copiers. Looks like Jacob didn't, either.

"I don't know what it was, some device with green and amber blinking lights on it." Sam shrugged. "It's always been there. I figured it was part of the machine."

Jacob shrugged as well and stood up. "Well, don't stay here tonight, Sam. It's not safe. Go to the Ritz with Richie."

Richie smirked and said, "Well, not how I had planned on getting you in my hotel room, but yes, please come stay with me tonight, Sam."

She nodded, rubbing her tired, baggy eyes. His flirtation seemed to go over her head. "Yeah, this is too serious to ignore. Richie, I'll stay with you. Tomorrow, I'll speak with Kent and then file a police report."

Jacob gave her a thumbs up. "Sounds like a plan, Sam."

Richie stood up as well. "So, then, let's go get you packed."

Sam agreed. The three went upstairs.

Thirty minutes later, Sam was loaded up with a suitcase in her car. It was raining now, a light, warm summer drizzle. Once she was settled, Richie headed over to Jacob and his motorcycle.

"Look, man," Richie said, clearing his throat. He had gotten so used to swallowing his pride lately that he was starting to like the taste. "I thought you were a bit of a dick before, but what you did back there was amazing. You really care about Sam. So, in my mind, you're cool. Let's keep Sam safe together, OK?"

Jacob grinned. "That's cool. I kinda thought you were a wuss, but you took a punch to the face like a champ. You've got my permission to date Sam."

He then leaned in and said, "But break her heart and I'll mess you up worse than those guys ever could."

For once, Richie didn't bristle at being threatened. "Get in line." After all, Rodger had made a similar threat.

He shook hands with Jacob just as the rain started to come down even harder. "Take care. It's storming tonight, ya."

"For God's sake, can this night get any worse?" Jacob pulled a large, black hooded coat out of the side compartment of his motorcycle and threw it on. "Later, Richie. I'll call you and Sam tomorrow," he said before driving off.

Richie just stared, watching as Jacob drove off. He had seen that coat before. It looked a bit newer and a bit less tailored, but the shape and color were unmistakable.

That's the type of coat the Nite Priory guys wore.

He looked down, the rain pouring down his aching face, as a theory came to mind that made him shiver. Was Jacob a member of the Nite Priory?

Or was he one of the people the Nite Priory was after?

He looked over at Sam. She was waiting patiently in the car. The rain was coming down in torrents.

Christ. Nothing makes any sense.

He watched Jacob ride off in the distance.

There's no way any of this is going to end well . . .

Chapter 6

The Madness Is Spreading

Date: **Monday, August 10, 1992**
Time: **7:00 a.m.**
Location: **Esplanade Apartments**
New Orleans City Park

"You're kidding me," Dixie said into the receiver of her cordless phone.

She already knew that Rivette wasn't kidding. He might be the kind of guy to pull a few pranks in the precinct, like replacing the sugar at the coffee station with salt or sliding a signed photograph of a Playgirl model into Aucoin's jacket, and he might keep toys on his desk, but when it came to work, he was completely serious—arguably the hardest-working detective in the division.

"I wish, Dixie. I really do," said Rivette. "Gravois took the call before he and Breaux headed out. That witness, Topper Jack, was found with a bullet in his head. Stone cold dead."

Sitting at the dining table in her apartment, her breakfast still steaming before her, Dixie felt her appetite vanish. Now all of Vincent Castille's accomplices, save for Blind Moses, were dead. Dixie recalled that Harry Connick Sr., the district attorney, had offered Topper Jack protection if he provided every bit of information he could about working with the original Bourbon Street Ripper.

"Did you hear me, Dixie? Ouellette wants you and Rodger to check the scene out first thing." He sounded more tired than annoyed. "Maybe you can find something the other guys couldn't."

She tried to take a bite of her breakfast and then put down her fork. She wasn't hungry.

"I heard you. No worries. We got it covered. Now what about the info on Sam I asked about?" She had requested that Rivette get information on Sam's psychological profile.

"Right, right," he said, the sound of shuffling papers overtaking his voice for a moment. "Her psychiatrist is Dr. Lucius Klein. He has a private office on St. Charles Avenue. Did you want the phone number?"

"That and the address," Dixie said, scribbling it down as Rivette gave it to her. "Any chance you know what Sam was treated for?"

"It just lists 'trauma,'" replied Rivette. "Good luck getting a doctor to divulge anything about a patient."

She didn't respond to his comment. Michael and Rodger had already been there. She was certain she knew what she was getting into. "Thanks, Rivette. As always, you've been a great help."

"I live to server, m'lady," he said in a faux British accent before hanging up.

Dixie put down the phone. From across the table, Gino was looking at her, concern on his face, as he paused between bites of his breakfast. When he caught her gaze, he motioned to her plate. "Breakfast is getting cold, Dixie."

Offering him a little smile, she ate a few more bites before she realized her appetite was completely gone. She sighed and then downed her coffee. "Sorry, Gino. I'm not all that hungry. I'll—"

"You're turning on the work mode, honey," he said, offering her a small smile back, and motioned toward the eggs. "Just eat those, then. Protein, Dixie. Will keep you going."

She gave the eggs a dubious look before eating them quickly. She knew he had a point, but it didn't help when she had no appetite. At least he looked out for her.

In fact, Dixie was grateful that so many people in her life had always looked out for her. As she forced herself to drink her glass of orange juice, she remembered how her foster parents used to fuss over her just as much.

While her sister had been placed in the care of a family in New Orleans East, Dixie was fostered by a simple, older couple up in Covington, a town north of Lake Pontchartrain. The area they lived in was relatively rural.

The old couple, Bensen and Millicent Olivier, were conservative and kind and very empathic about the emotional trauma and abuse she had suffered. They went beyond the basics of making sure she was well-fed and clothed. When the state-funded therapy didn't seem to be doing enough, the Oliviers reached into their own savings account and sent her to a private therapist. They also made sure she stayed in school.

When she was fourteen, she found out that her father was dead, having been murdered by her older sister and her boyfriend. She never saw them again. She later heard that the two of them had fled the state, perhaps even the country, to avoid arrest.

A year later, Dixie's mother, who had fallen into drug use and moved in with her dealer, sued for custody of her. The Oliviers fought the battle in court and won, and three months later, they formally adopted her. She then changed her name to Dixie Millisen Olivier—her middle name a combination of their first names.

She came out of her memories and realized that she was staring right at Gino. He was staring back with a comical expression—a pinched face and squinty eyes. She laughed out loud and finished off her orange juice.

"Okay, I've got to run," she said, patting her mouth dry, getting up, and dressing. "Rodger's not returning my phone calls and he's not at the precinct, so I bet he's still sleeping. Aucoin took our squad car with Cathy to River Oaks, so I'm going to take a cab to get—"

Gino casually tossed her a pair of car keys. "Take the Porsche."

Dixie caught them and blinked in surprise. "Baby, you just got it detailed. If it gets scratched, I—"

"It's fine, honey," he said. "You can bring beauty to this ugly city. You take the Porsche." He took another bite of his bagel and cream cheese.

She blushed. Despite not placing a lot of value on material possessions, she loved that car—it was a Porsche, after all. She put her arms around him and kissed his ear. "Thanks. Love you, baby. See you later."

As she left, Gino said the same thing he always said whenever she headed out to work: "I love you, Dixie. I'll be here when you come home."

Thirty minutes later, she was pulling Gino's red convertible with black leather interior onto the curb of Rodger's Burgundy apartment building. As in the French Quarter, the street had a heavy police presence.

A few uniformed officers cat-called as she got out. She tipped her sunglasses and peered at them, raising her eyebrows. One of them recognized her, cleared his throat, and motioned to the Porsche. "Sexy car there, Detective!"

Dixie pushed her sunglasses back up. "Good save there, Officer." She went into the courtyard of the complex.

A few of the tenants were about. The two most notable were a portly man dressed in a jumpsuit labeled "Earl's Plumbing" and a short, elderly, African-American woman who was busy whacking his shins with a cane.

"Earl Mastadon," said the elderly woman, "you is touched by the angels if you think you can go one more day without my rent."

"Oh, come on, Ms. Parkerson," said Earl, skipping back as he got whacked. "With the police everywhere, most folks are too afraid to leave their house, let alone have a plumber come over. I need that money to eat."

"I'll fix you a mess of jambalaya and black-eyed peas," said Ms. Parkerson, patting his stomach with her cane. "You can eat that. Good for you. Get ya to lose that gut. Now go get my rent, Earl! You get going!"

With a few more choice whacks to the shins, she chased Earl away, the portly man quickly waddling toward his apartment. As Dixie approached her, figuring her to be the landlady, Ms. Parkerson spun around and raised her cane as if to hit the detective.

Dixie jumped back, almost reaching for her gun before stopping herself, realizing that the elderly lady was just frightened.

"Lord, save me," Ms. Parkerson said. "You about stopped my heart. Thought I was going to see my dear Fred again. What you want to be scaring an old woman like that for?"

Dixie held out her hands, peeled back her overcoat, and showed her badge. "Detective Dixie Olivier, ma'am. I'm working with Rodger while Michael's recovering. Is he home?"

Ms. Parkerson leaned forward, squinting behind her thick glasses, and examined the badge. A few moments later, she nodded. "Yes, he is, young lady. Come with me and I'll lets you inside."

Dixie followed Ms. Parkerson, who opened Rodger's door with a master key. From inside, Dixie could hear some of the loudest snoring she'd heard in many years. *Yeah, I'm probably violating Rodger's right to privacy about a dozen times over.*

"Thank you, Ms. Parkerson," Dixie said with a smile. "Sorry about scaring you."

"Aw, it's OK," said Ms. Parkerson as she hobbled off. "You just catch that monster what's making this city all crazy. Bourbon Street Ripper, my club foot. Making my tenants late with the rent and all sorts of nonsense . . ."

Dixie shook her head as the elderly woman walked off, still muttering.

Inside Rodger's apartment, which had a dusty smell to it, she saw him sleeping in his easy chair, still dressed in yesterday's clothes. For a moment, he reminded her of Papa Olivier after a hard day's work. However, as she approached him, she saw a glass of half-drunk whiskey on the table next to him.

Dixie scowled, unpleasant memories of her real father and his alcohol-laden abuse bubbling forth. Before she realized what she was doing, she had shaken him awake. "Come on, you old fart. Get your ass up. We've got work to do."

He awoke with a startled yelp and raised his arms defensively. When he saw her, he glowered and rubbed his hands over his face. "Jesus Christ, Dixie! What the hell?"

Still frowning, she said, "We need to get moving. Go clean up. You reek of booze and you're not stinking up Gino's car with it. Go change or whatever. I'll wait outside."

She left as he continued to look surprised and startled. She needed to get out of there before she lost her temper. Seeing people passed-out drunk was a definite hot-button issue with her.

It was close to nine o'clock when Rodger came out, wearing new clothes save for his overcoat, which smelled of Febreze.

In the meantime, Dixie had thought about how she had treated him. She felt awful. "Hey, sorry about how I acted. It was the whiskey. Also, I'm getting on edge with this case. It won't happen again." She knew it wasn't much of an excuse.

He snorted gruffly. "Well, it pissed me off. But we've all been ruffled lately, so I'll let this one slide. Apology accepted. For now, though, just tell me what we're doing."

She didn't immediately respond. Instead, she wondered if the stress of the investigation was taking its toll on everyone. It felt like it was.

"We're heading to Odyssey House," she said, starting up the Porsche. "Topper Jack was murdered last night."

He sighed and shook his head. "First Willie, and now Topper. They're dropping like flies. Isn't this great?"

They entered the lobby of Odyssey House on North Tonti to the sound of angry voices. All around, groups of patients were noisily checking out of the clinic. The orderlies seemed barely able to keep up.

Dixie was just looking for someone to talk to when she heard Rodger groan.

"Oh, God. Not him again."

A balding man with dark splotch of a birthmark on the side of his head approached the two detectives. He was dressed in scrubs with the name tag "Gomer Bernard." He looked like he hadn't slept recently.

"Morning, Detectives," said Gomer, an obvious strain in his voice. "They said you'd be coming over. Where's that partner of yours? The guy with the nice suit?"

"Shot and in the hospital," said Rodger as he motioned to Dixie. "This is Junior Detective Dixie Olivier. She's taking Michael's place for now."

"Pleasure to meet you, Gomer," said Dixie, looking around Odyssey House. The few patients she saw seemed to be anxious. She could hardly blame them. After all, someone had just been murdered there.

"This way, then," said Gomer, heading down one of the hallways. "As you can see, we're losing most of our patients over what happened to Mr. Topman last night."

"Not so much fun anymore, is it, Gomer?" asked Rodger in a distinctly snarky tone.

She glanced over, not sure what bad blood existed between him and Gomer.

"No, sir, this ain't fun. Likely gonna lose my job over it. Doubt I can get a new one after this. Don't know what my wife and kids are gonna do."

Dixie felt kind of bad for him. His life was obviously ruined.

Rodger shut up and looked away, his face showing shame.

In Topper's room, which was sectioned off with police tape, they started looking around. While Topper's body had already been removed, the scene had obviously been combed over by the crime lab unit. All around were little numbered tags where they had taken photos. The blinds to the window were up, and the window had a bullet hole in it. The pillow on Topper's bed was covered in dried blood. The room stank.

Dixie shook her head. "So what happened?"

"About four in the morning," said Gomer as he shuffled about the room, "an orderly heard a loud cracking sound from Mr. Topman's room. When he got in, the window there had a hole in it, and Mr. Topman, he . . ." His voice trailed off as he leaned against a wall.

"Topper was dead," Rodger said, finishing Gomer's sentence. He was already looking over the blood-stained bed and pillow. "Was his head burst like a melon all over the room?"

Dixie remembered from her briefing that Mad Monty's head was blown apart by an explosive round. She nodded at Rodger. They were thinking about the same person—the indigo-clad assassin that had nearly killed Michael.

"No, no," said Gomer with sudden shock. "Not at all. He had a hole clear through his head. Bone, blood, and brains was only on the back wall."

"That doesn't sound like an explosive round," Dixie said. "Then it wasn't the same type of bullet that killed Mad Monty, was it? What about J.L.?"

Rodger stood up from checking Topper's bed and rubbed his eyes. "The kind of bullet that killed J.L. was a normal bullet, I think. But the same assassin who killed Monty killed J.L. I saw her myself both times."

She recalled the reports on the Jefferson Parish deputy who was killed moments before Michael's famous chase. *Come to think of it, why did that assassin kill J.L.?* He hadn't been an accomplice like Mad Monty. He must have just been at the wrong place at the wrong time. *That sucks.*

"Also, the crime lab guys said the angle of the bullet says the shooter was right outside the window," Gomer said, sounding very tired. "But no one saw or heard nothing but that window crack. He musta used a silencer."

Dixie frowned as she looked over the crime scene. Taking a few steps back, she said, "Silencers don't quite work in reality like they do in the movies. There's no way the killer could have fired from street level without someone hearing the shot."

"Detectives, if it's all the same, I'm going to get back to work. We have a ton of patients leaving, and I gotta handle it," said Gomer.

Dixie ignored him, going into "work mode" and focusing on the scene before her. She nibbled on her thumb, as she often did when analyzing something.

She heard Rodger say, "Yeah. Thanks, Gomer. Good luck." Then she heard Gomer leave.

Soon, Rodger was standing behind her, asking, "What do you think, Dixie?"

Dixie hummed to herself. After a moment, she said, "Well, if we just take the hole in the window into account, it's low enough that the shooter could have been standing at street level. But again, someone in the adjacent rooms would have heard the shot."

"Maybe the killer has access to a new type of silencer?" He shrugged. "If it's that indigo assassin, I wouldn't be surprised. Didn't she have military-grade equipment?"

She continued to nibble on her thumb, visualizing Topper's body lying there as a bullet came through the window, penetrated his head, and embedded itself in the wall behind him. Shaking her head, she said, "No. No, that's not right."

"What do you mean?" asked Rodger.

Frowning, Dixie said, "This theory would only work if the bullet travelled through the victim in a straight line. Bullets don't do that. Their path is altered as soon as they enter the human body."

He leaned next to her. "So, what do you—"

"Rodger, I have an idea. Drop the blinds."

Rodger grumbled a bit, but then lowered the blinds. There was a bullet hole in them.

"I knew it," Dixie said. "The orderly must have raised the blinds before the police got here. See the position of the hole? It's lower than the hole in the glass. There is no way the shot originated from the street." Putting the pillow back where it originally was, she took a step back and looked everything over.

"Perfect," she said before lying on the bed.

"Hey, Dixie, what the heck?" Rodger said. "What are you doing?"

"Playing the part of the victim," Dixie said, lying where Topper had been when he had died. She smelled the dried blood as she settled into place. She looked up at the bullet holes, trying to line up the shooter's location.

He snickered. "Really, Dixie? Lying in dried blood? You're one hard-core lady, you know that?"

She said nothing, focusing on the angle of the shot.

"There!" she exclaimed, sitting up, lifting the blinds, and pointing. "Across the street and on the roof of that building. Let's go!"

Rodger shook his head, hands on his hips. "My God, there's two of them."

Dixie blushed as she realized he was comparing her to Michael.

"Only, let's face it, Michael would never get dried blood on his nice suit, or in his hair, for that matter," Rodger added.

She laughed and stood up, trying to dust off the back of her head. "Let's confirm I'm right before you start comparing me to him."

The other building happened to be an old office now used as off-site storage for corporate documents. There was no security, and they didn't run into anyone on their way to the roof. Once there, she went into work mode while Rodger stood by and watched. She was grateful that he, like Aucoin, let her work in peace and quiet.

Hunching at the edge of the building, she again nibbled on her thumb and gazed toward Topper's room. She crept along until she saw the holes start to line up. *That's it! The shooter was right here.* She would have bet her badge on it.

Standing up, she looked around for a rifle cartridge, some bits of hair or cloth, even as much as a thread. All she found were scuff marks on the ground that might have come from a rifle stand. "They covered their tracks and took all the evidence," she noted.

She squatted again and looked along the sightline she'd established. "And they made a shot through a drawn set of blinds in the middle of the night. See the lamp lights? That glare alone would make most people miss the shot. It's either the same person who killed Monty and J.L., or someone with the same type of training. Either way, an expert killer."

He looked over the edge and whistled. "I see what you mean. This is rather improbable—just like the person who killed Monty and J.L. and almost killed Michael."

She stood up and winked at Rodger. "I agree. Odds are very good it's the same person."

"All right. Good work there, Dixie. So, what's next? We aren't due to the Castille mansion for a few more hours."

Heading downstairs, Dixie said, "We'll pick up some coffee on the way to St. Charles. You look like you need it."

He followed her. "Thanks. But why are we going to St. Charles?"

"We're going to meet with Dr. Klein."

After a pause, he said, "Forget the coffee. I think I need a cigarette."

By the time they arrived at Dr. Klein's clinic, it was almost lunch time.

Dixie noted that Rodger was still in a rotten mood, despite having gotten coffee after all and then smoking three cigarettes. She had gotten out of him that he distrusted Dr. Klein when it came to Sam. He thought Dr. Klein was more concerned with using Sam as a guinea pig for his theories on psychosis than with actually helping her. Given that her own experiences with therapists were that they were more interested in fixing the symptoms than the problems, she could sympathize with his feelings.

She also wasn't completely sure about Sam's guilt. After just a few minutes of talking to her at the hospital, she saw Sam as a likeable and personable woman. Someone she could even have been friends with, had things been different. Given everything she had learned about Sam, she figured that the blond woman was either actually innocent or a dangerous sociopath.

Once inside the waiting room, she flashed her badge and asked to see Dr. Klein. To her surprise, she was told that he'd see her right away. She collected Rodger, who had gotten comfortable in one of the waiting room chairs, and went back to the office.

Dixie was shocked by the amount of obsessive order present in the room. Everything was at right angles or lined up with something else. She spotted the short-statured man at the window, hands behind his back, looking out over St. Charles Avenue.

"Dr. Klein, I'm—"

"I know who you are," said Dr. Klein, not turning around. His German accent was immediately apparent. "You are Junior Detective Dixie Olivier, formerly known as Dixie Electra Gateaux of Slidell. You graduated top of your class und are a first-rate junior detective. Your boyfriend is Ginopolis Eliopoulos. Your blood type is B+ und your favorite color is red."

She stood there, stunned. *How the hell?*

After a few moments, she stuttered, "Well, well, Doctor. You know a lot about me. I'm at a loss."

"I make it my business," he said as he turned around, "to find out about ze people I feel are ze most useful to know."

Dixie did not know what to make of that statement. Everything about him felt creepy.

"Dr. Klein, you remember Detective Bergeron."

"I do, indeed," he said, nodding curtly at Rodger. "So why are you here, Detective? This is about ze new Bourbon Street Ripper, *ja?*"

Dixie approached his desk. "I want to talk to you about Samantha Castille," she said, remembering that he got agitated when anyone called her Sam. "Specifically, I want to know more about the personality you refer to as 'Sam of Spades.' You spoke about it at length with my colleague, Michael LeBlanc."

"Ah, yes," he said. "That poor boy who is caught up in ze web of a shyster. I really pity him."

Again, she didn't know what to make of Dr. Klein or his statements.

Rodger was getting agitated. "You're really barking up the wrong tree here. First you spit out crap about Sam and then you start saying things about my partner. You must love pissing me off."

Dr. Klein turned a cold gaze on him. "Her name is Samantha. Und, Detective Bergeron, please remember that you are a guest in my office. If you cannot keep your rude comments to yourself, I suggest you wait outside."

Rodger tightened his jaw. "No, I'll shut up and deal with it. I left Michael alone with you. I sure as heck am not going to make the same mistake twice."

Dixie flashed him a small smile, mouthing the word "thanks." She was thankful to him, for both staying and for behaving. In truth, Dr. Klein made her feel very uneasy. She wanted to interview him and be done with it.

Dr. Klein offered her a seat and then sat down himself. "So, please, Detective Olivier. Tell me what it is you want to know about Sam of Spades."

Rodger remained standing.

"Specifically," she said, flipping to a blank page in her notebook, "we want to know when the Sam of Spades personality first came out and what it has said to you over the years."

"Ah," said Dr. Klein, rhythmically nodding his head as if it were a metronome keeping time. "Well, Sam of Spades showed up in my very first session with Samantha. It vas a very engaging conversation. After the first half dozen or so sessions, Sam of Spades became more dormant, und I started talking to just Samantha."

Dixie wrote that down. "So what did she talk about? Sam of Spades, that is?"

"She talked about how much she enjoyed hurting other people," he replied. "Listening to her speak, it was obvious zat Sam of Spades despised humanity as a whole. She was even personally condescending to me, of all people, acting as if I were uneducated und stupid."

"So Sam of Spades just talked about hating people?" she asked.

"Not entirely, Detective," said Dr. Klein. He leaned forward in his chair, elbows cocked at perfect angles on either side. "Her contempt und hatred for people was tempered by her admiration for Vincent Castille's work. The murders, precisely. Sam of Spades wanted to emulate zat brutality in her own way, saying it was a beautiful work of art."

Dixie frowned as she scribbled down notes. More and more, Sam of Spades was sounding like a violent alternate personality. And yet Michael, in his own notes, was adamant that Sam didn't have a true dissociative disorder. Could Michael have misjudged Sam's psychosis?

"So did the threats about hurting people, making others suffer, and so on, ever actually come to anything?" She figured the answer was no, but she needed to ask anyway.

She wasn't expecting Dr. Klein's response.

"Yes."

She looked at him, confused.

From behind her, Rodger said, "Wait, excuse me? Sam of Spades confessed to murder?"

Dr. Klein shook his head. "Not murder, Detective. Assault and battery."

Rodger was at Dixie's side before she could speak. "I think you better explain—"

"Rodger, please," she interrupted. He had been handling himself so well up until now, and she didn't want him to blow it.

Settling back, he muttered, "This is all bullshit. She'd never hurt anyone. All bullshit."

"I apologize for Rodger's outburst," she said. "This is a very emotional case for him, as you are aware. Now on the matter of Sam of Spades and assault and battery, who did she attack?"

"I wish I knew, Detectives," Dr. Klein said. "I'm not sure when she started attacking people. I would suspect as early as sixteen, after she left ze Castille mansion und started living on her own. I advised Samantha to stay indoors whenever she was suffering from any sort of stress. From vhat Sam of Spades told me, during that time, she'd take control, don a costume to hide her face, und attack random people throughout the French Quarter and Uptown."

"A costume, eh?" said Rodger. "What kind of costume?"

Dr. Klein shrugged. "An indigo hooded robe with a skull mask. Something she got from a second-hand Mardi Gras shop, if I recall correctly."

Dixie sat there, stunned. Without prompting, he had just described the indigo assassin. Could Sam really be her? The one who had almost killed Michael? What were the chances that the two were the same?

Looking over at Rodger, she could see that he was stunned as well, his face pale.

Quickly, she turned back to Dr. Klein. "So is this something I would have read about in the newspaper? I haven't heard anything about a person in this costume attacking people."

"I don't think you'll find much, Detective. Sam of Spades would ambush people in dark alleys und other places where ze lighting was bad. But I would check any story where the victim states to have seen ze skull mask."

Dr. Klein leaned back in his chair again. "Und they stopped several years ago anyway, when Samantha was about twenty-five years old. I started to prescribe very potent medication that seemed to quell Sam of Spades's dominance. I believe the side effects were waking nightmares, but better than random acts of violence, yes?'

Dixie shook her head. This was almost too much. "Another question, please. How many counts of assault and battery did Sam of Spades tell you about?"

"Oh, many dozens," he said, rubbing his goatee. "Hundreds, possibly. I have all my sessions taped, if you wish to hear zem."

Dixie nodded. "That would be—"

"Hold on a minute," Rodger interrupted.

She looked at him, wondering what he was doing.

Poking his finger into his palm, he said, "I know that you cannot divulge privileged information unless there is a clear and present danger to the client or others. Now I may not buy into any of the crap you're spewing about Sam, but if you give us those tapes without a subpoena, then whether they exonerate Sam or convict her is irrelevant. It'll get thrown out in a heartbeat."

Dixie blinked. She was sure that he was trying to protect Sam again, but at the same time, he had a valid point. Indeed, if Sam wasn't given due process, it could make the case very difficult. Defense lawyers loved that stuff.

Before she could speak, though, Dr. Klein spoke in a stern voice. "No, I have told you. The good person's name is Samantha und the bad one is Sam. You must say it properly!"

She looked back at him with a start. His eyes were like coals. She shook her head. *He's already a bit creepy, but that was crazy. It seems like, bit by bit, the madness is spreading.*

She sighed and softly said, "We apologize, Dr. Klein. However, it's true. If there is no clear and present danger, we cannot accept those tapes."

Dr. Klein calmed down. "Well, then, you are in luck. There is a clear und present danger. I do believe that Sam of Spades will surface again very soon, und this time she vill kill someone."

Rodger again seemed stunned. Dixie took advantage of his silence to ask, "How do you know that?"

With a smug expression, Dr. Klein said, "Sam of Spades told me herself when Samantha came in today und quit as my patient."

Chapter 7

The Monster Inside

Date: Monday, August 10, 1992
Time: 10:00 a.m.
Location: Ritz-Carlton Hotel
Canal Street, French Quarter

A few hours before Dixie visited Dr. Klein, Sam looked at her reflection in the bathroom mirror of Richie's hotel room, brushing out the tangles in her wet blond hair. Her bruised eyes and the pencil-thin lines on her face clearly showed her stress.

Yesterday had begun so well. She was in love with Richie, had given herself to him, and was living in a dream world where life was a collection of sweet moments. It was a kind of happiness she had never known before. She wondered if she'd ever know it again.

"Sam," called Richie from outside the bathroom, "Kent said he's available at eleven, but only until noon. Afterward, he's busy the rest of the day."

She didn't reply. She had started shutting down emotionally after her outburst at Landry's, and by the time the break-in at her house had been resolved, she was as unresponsive as the dead. Richie had tried to show her affection, just by holding her gently, but she hadn't reciprocated. She had just lain there.

"Sam?" Richie called, concern in his voice.

Sam gradually looked in the direction of the door. In her heart, she knew that he was doing all he could for her. She valued that. However, the numbness she felt was overwhelming. Upon hearing that her story was once again the same as what had actually happened, she felt like the last of her humanity had burned away. She also felt that within her beat the heart of a monster. And every time she focused on that feeling, she felt that monster grin.

"Sam?" His voice sounded a bit panicked. The doorknob started to turn.

"I'm here. Just thinking," she lied. The truth was that she wasn't thinking about anything.

"Well, don't scare me like that," he said. There was a long pause. "I'm really worried about you."

"I'll be fine," she said. She knew the moment the words left her lips that Richie would know it was a lie.

Richie just said, "I'll have some fresh clothes laid out for you. Then we'll head out to meet your lawyer."

Without replying, Sam looked back at her reflection. The person looking back didn't look thirty—she looked older and more tired. She continued brushing out her hair, yanking so hard that sharp pains tore through her scalp. She didn't mind. Part of her liked the pain. It had been her only constant companion for the past thirty years. People had come and gone. Mostly, though, she'd been alone.

When she finished, she put down the brush and closed her eyes. She remembered that Richie was out there, waiting for her. And later today, they'd meet up with Jacob again. And then there was Rodger, sweet Uncle Rodger, who was doing all he could to clear her name.

Richie. Jacob. Rodger. Three men who loved her in their own ways. With a soft sigh, she remembered that she was not alone.

A few minutes later, Sam was dried off, towel wrapped around her body. She stepped out of the bathroom and looked for Richie.

He was sitting on the edge of the bed and wringing his hands nervously while half-looking at the television. She felt bad for him. The call to his doctor for a new prescription wouldn't go through until Monday. And she could tell, just from watching him rock back and forth, that her attitude was causing him to feel what was likely unbearable anxiety.

"Hey, honey." When he turned to her, she smiled. "I love you. I'll be OK now. I've got you at my side. Let's go put this crap behind us and then get on with our day."

His jaw tightened, but he nodded. She hugged him close. She had to believe that this would work out. *I'm not a killer. Things will be OK.*

An hour later, Sam and Richie were seated in Kent's office.

She noted three things about her lawyer that seemed very different. One, his entire office space had painter's paper down everywhere. Two, he looked exhausted, much more so than usual. And finally, he seemed less than pleased to see Richie, shooting him a few unsavory glances.

"So, Kent, are you moving? Or just redecorating?" Sam motioned around the room.

Kent was cleaning his glasses. "Oh, just some redecorating, Sam. I haven't spruced the old place up since before your Aunt Marguerite passed. Figured it could use a new look and all."

She looked around again. She had grown to like the old feeling of Kent's office. It was one of the few things that had remained the same since she was a teenager. "Well, change is good, for the most part. Speaking of which, how are you? You look exhausted."

He straightened his glasses. "I've been a very busy person. All of my clients have been reacting poorly to the new string of murders. Wills have been updated, estates have been modified. It's been a real mess. In fact," he said with a bit of a laugh, "the Castille accounts are the only ones that aren't making me work late. Ironic, isn't it?"

Sam laughed, too, and then reached for Richie's hand. She squeezed her charm in the other hand. "Well, Kent, I need your legal advice."

Kent arched an eyebrow when he saw them holding hands. "So what's going on, Sam?"

She took her time explaining everything that had happened to her since the copycat murders had started. She told him of the similarities between her stories and the murders. She told him of the threatening notes. She told him of Michael wanting to search the house for ways to prove Sam's innocence. And lastly, she told him of the break-in the previous night.

The entire time she spoke, she and Richie held hands. She squeezed his hand the way she squeezed her charm—it gave her a sense of security.

"So that's the gist of it, Kent," Sam said, finishing her story. She sat back and exhaled. It was draining just reliving it.

He sat back in his chair, peering at her from behind his glasses. His look was a cross between analytical and annoyed. It made her feel apprehensive. Then he spoke.

"It sounds like you're in a world of trouble, Sam," Kent said. "I'll be honest with you. As your lawyer, I don't see any way that you can get out of having your house searched. One coincidence is enough to rouse suspicion. But twice?"

He continued to speak as Sam, who was starting to feel uneasy, squeezed more rapidly on the charm. "Also, the fact that someone broke into your townhome several times is not something that can be ignored. You could have been seriously injured or worse."

She frowned. He was saying exactly what she had been afraid he would say.

"What I advise you to do is what you had planned on doing. You need to file a report with the police. You will want them to come and look at your house to do this. However, the law states that they can only use in court what's in plain sight. So I suggest you take your notes, *all* your notes, for your story, and your manuscript, and hide them. Or, better yet, give them to someone you trust."

"Will you hold onto them?" asked Sam.

Kent chortled and brushed his fingertips over the lapel of his jacket. "Sam, I'd have suggested that if doing so wasn't so egotistical."

Richie spoke up. "Either that, or give them to Rodger."

Kent shot him a nasty look. "I don't recommend that. Detective Bergeron may be your friend. He may even be 'Uncle Rodger.' But he is a police officer."

"I trust Rodger with my life," she said. It was true. Despite all the years of distance between them, in that one moment of reconciliation after visiting Fat Willie, she had felt a complete reconnection with Uncle Rodger.

Kent leaned forward, his tone becoming patronizing. "Sam, I don't mean to preach to you, but I've known you since you were a child. I've always looked out for you and your family, despite the . . . complications of your grandfather being the Bourbon Street Ripper.

Believe me when I say that I want to trust Rodger as much as you do. But remember, this man hasn't been in contact with you in years. He never sent you a single Christmas or birthday card. He didn't even give you a call for your confirmation or graduation. In short, until this copycat murderer showed up, he basically ignored you." He leaned back and held out his hands. "So tell me. Can you trust a man like that to stay true to you now?"

Sam didn't show any outward emotion, but inside, she felt like someone had sucker-punched her in the gut. Rodger had specifically mentioned sending her cards for her birthday and Christmas, her confirmation, and her graduation. That was way too precise to be a coincidence.

"I'll take that under advisement," she said flatly, giving her charm a hard, long squeeze. Someone was stringing her along—either Kent Bourgeois or Rodger Bergeron. And since she felt she could trust Rodger with her life, things weren't looking great for Kent.

Kent arched his eyebrows and then said, "Well, I can only advise you, Sam. I do think that whatever you choose, make sure you clear those items out before you file your report."

Sam nibbled on her bottom lip. "Thanks, Kent. I really appreciate the help." She couldn't hide the suspicion in her voice no matter how hard she tried. Something wasn't right. Someone did not have her best interests at heart.

As they all stood, Kent straightened his glasses again. "Mr. Fastellos, may I have a moment with Miss Castille? I need to go over something confidential with her."

Richie flashed a look over at Sam. She kissed him quickly on the cheek. "Go on. It'll be fine. I'll meet you in the lobby downstairs."

As Richie was leaving, Kent motioned to the charm. "So what's with the shoe? New nervous habit?"

"Good luck charm," she said, holding it up and giving it a jiggle. "A keepsake from Mom."

Kent nodded in understanding. Once Richie had left, he led her to a window. His voice was hushed. "Sam, I don't trust that Fastellos fellow. When he was first here, he told me an outright lie. He said his reason for being here was to buy your townhome. Watching you two together, I can clearly see that he was after something else."

Sam smiled a small, tight-lipped smile. She didn't want to believe that Kent was purposefully trying to throw suspicion onto Richie. Giving her charm a few pumps, she said, "Well, he's my boyfriend."

His expression fell. "Sam, I know you're lonely, but—"

"Whoa, whoa," she interrupted, holding up a hand. "First off, bucko, I'm not a little girl. I'm an adult. I choose who to sleep with. I choose who to be with. Second, you work for me. You may be a friend of my family, but you are still my lawyer. That doesn't give you carte blanche to stick your nose in my love life. Just don't be a prick, Kent. You've been a great asset to my family and to me. And thank you for helping me out during this difficult time. But stay out of my personal life."

Kent narrowed his eyes. His expression was cold. "As you wish, Princess. Now, if you'll excuse me, I have to get ready for a very important meeting."

She left the office, fighting back the urge to say something else. Part of her wanted to apologize, while the other part wanted to tell him off even more. She hoped Kent was just being an over-protective jerk, instead of deliberately trying to sabotage her.

She decided to leave the jury out on him for the time being.

Outside the office, Richie joined her. "Everything OK, Sam?"

Sam took his hand and squeezed it. "Yeah. Let's get going. I have some things that I need to do." In her other hand, she tightly squeezed the charm.

Regardless of what happens with Kent, I need to start cutting the negative influences out of my life.

Once she got home, it took her only a few minutes to collect the sensitive material that Kent had warned her about: her notebook containing all of her notes for her story, her partially finished manuscript of Chapter Three, and her silver pen. All three were placed in a knapsack and put in the back of her car.

Only then did she call the police. The dispatcher said that an officer would be there in a little while.

After hanging up with the police, Sam gave Jacob a call. To her surprise, she got his answering machine. She left a brief message. "Jacob, I'm going to extend my stay at Richie's room for a few more days. We want to have lunch with you once we finish with the police today. Give me a call, OK?"

Hanging up the phone, she saw that Richie was in her office across the hallway. She had instructed him not to touch anything, so he was walking about, hands in his pockets, looking around.

"Find anything?" she asked. It was a rhetorical question.

To her surprise, he said, "Actually, I think you found the important part earlier."

Sam peered at him, confused at his statement. "What do you mean?"

"Well, see this?" asked Richie, pointing out the photocopier. "The area that's disturbed the most is around the copier. Like you said before, someone opened it up and took something out. But the rest of the office just looks like someone just threw everything around."

She blinked and looked more closely at the way things were strewn about. She realized that he had a point. With the exception of the copier, which was methodically opened and dissected, the rest of the room looked like a child had had a temper tantrum.

"So you think that the purpose was to take something from my copier," Sam said, joining him in the room, "and then they just trashed the room to throw us off?"

"That's how I'd write it," Richie said, flashing a grin.

She chortled. He was a successful novelist, after all. "All right, writer boy. Then what was the reason for messing with my copier?"

He got a look of extreme concentration, and then shrugged. "Hun, I got nothing."

Sam laughed out loud and patted him on the lower back. "Well, at least you have a cute butt."

"Not as cute as yours," said Richie with a wink.

Despite what she'd been going through, Sam blushed again. She was just about to lean in to kiss Richie when the phone rang. Hurrying over, she picked it up. "Hello?"

"Hey, Sam," said Jacob. "Sorry, I was busy dealing with my attorney. Ya know, moving money around and that sort of thing."

"Ah, OK," she said, not wanting to think about attorneys after just having such a negative experience with Kent.

"Anyway, you and Richie want to do lunch? How about Acme Oyster House?"

Sam thought about it. She could really go for some Cajun food, and Acme Oyster House was one of the best in the city. "Sounds good. Why not come over? The police should be here any minute. You can give your statement and then we can go eat."

There was hesitation before Jacob said, "You know I don't like the police much. But for you, Sam, anything. Just remember not to mention me kicking anyone's ass."

"Right, right," she said. "Just please come. I need friends near me."

After another pause, he said, "All right, Sam. I'm on my way." He hung up.

She looked up at Richie as he placed an arm around her, thinking that she really needed to try to lean on friends more. She was so used to toughing it out alone, she needed to remember that there were people she could trust.

Jacob arrived just before the police did, and, unsurprisingly, three officers answered the call. The interview didn't take long, with Richie and Jacob doing most of the talking, recounting the events from the previous night. Sam only spoke enough to say that she had been in the car during the incident and to relate how she had witnessed the assailant being chased from the townhome.

The police took down everyone's story and then walked around the first floor of the townhome. Again, she was not surprised that they took a long time, taking photographs and making copious notes. Even though they said it was to catalogue the attack, she was sure that they were investigating her—just as Kent had predicted.

Whatever the police were looking for, they didn't find. After being there a little over an hour, they left.

Sam quickly ushered Jacob and Richie out of the townhome, locked it up, and said, "OK. Let's go eat lunch." She wanted to get out before she went nuts.

Lunch at Acme Oyster House was mercifully quiet, the restaurant only having local traffic. The police presence in the French Quarter on the way there had been unmistakable. Uniformed officers and members of the SWAT team were on every corner. Even more than before, Jacob's comment about New Orleans being a police state seemed a reality.

Sam was grateful that the restaurant wasn't busy. It gave her a chance to take out her notebook and silver pen and finish up her notes on her story. All in all, she was proud of how it was turning out. Now that she had made up her mind to write things that could never happen in real life, alleviating any fear of the third chapter coming true, she had never been so inspired. All that was left was for her to figure out the ending—but she had time for that.

Near the end of lunch, Jacob said, "Hey, here's an idea for tonight. Let's go clubbing. There won't be too many people, since it's a Sunday night, but there'll be just enough to keep up your alibi."

"Clubbing," she said. She smacked her lips in between spoonfuls of seafood gumbo. "That's something I haven't done since I was, what, twenty-four?"

"Twenty-five," he replied with a wink. "We went to House of Blues and Howling Wolf that night."

Sam nodded as she remembered that night. They had gone to the two most popular clubs in New Orleans. She had gotten pretty drunk, and he had knocked out some guy who had tried to feel her up. It was one of the few times she'd ever seen him get violent. She sweated a bit at that memory. "Oh, yeah. Now I remember why I haven't gone clubbing lately."

Jacob chuckled. "Yeah, well, this time it'll be different."

"She'll be OK if I'm with her," Richie said. He was eating jambalaya like a native, gulping down the spicy rice and sausage mixture as if it were candy.

Sam reached down and squeezed his thigh gently. Her man was standing up for her. She thought it was adorable.

Richie said, "But if we're going to do this clubbing thing, I'll need to know what to wear. Last night, you two pretty much declared me a fashion victim."

"True," said Jacob. "While this isn't Ibiza, you'll stick out like a sore thumb if you don't look good."

She smiled to herself as they got into a conversation about Richie's lack of taste in "cool" clothes. This was what she needed. To be with people who really cared about her. Not lawyers and doctors. She needed more friends like these two. When this was over, maybe she would find some more. That Dixie woman seemed pretty cool. And, of course, there was Uncle Rodger.

When she came back to the conversation, Richie was saying, "So, Sam, what do you think? We can hit the shops after your appointment with Dr. Klein?"

She knew she looked lost, because both Jacob and Richie were snickering at her. She stuck out her tongue and then said, "All right, fine. Doctor, then clothes, then clubs. Got it."

The rest of lunch went quickly, with the conversation centering on where to shop for clothing and what clubs to hit that evening. They decided that clubs in the French Quarter would be best, as it would ensure that Sam would be seen by the eighth precinct. She liked the idea of Ouellette's own people being part of her alibi.

It was close to three o'clock when she and Richie walked into Dr. Klein's office. Sitting in the reception area, she decided what to talk about. While she was no longer legally obligated to see him, having only been compelled during the first ten years after her release from Acadia Vermilion Hospital, she still saw him once a month for any necessary changes in medication. But the recent string of events had her re-evaluating what was necessary.

While they were waiting, Richie leaned over and whispered, "So, Sam, I have to ask. This Dr. Klein seems to operate out of a very exclusive location. Is he one of those celebrity psychiatrists?"

Sam was leaning forward with her charm firmly secured in her hand. "In a manner of speaking. Dr. Klein treats a limited clientele, mostly only the rich, old families of New Orleans. He sets appointments whenever a patient needs to see him."

"So he's on call and lets you choose the hours? Lucky you."

She giggled and said, "Hun, at a fifty-thousand-dollar retainer, I think it's more 'lucky him.'"

A few minutes later, the receptionist called out that Dr. Klein was ready to see her, and she headed into the office.

"Ah, Samantha," said Dr. Klein. He had been standing in front of his bookcase, almost as if it were the blocking in a play, when she entered. "It is good to see you again. I was wondering when you would come to see me, what with the recent string of murders und the police investigating you."

Sam shook his hand. Despite everything about him that seemed off-putting, she reminded herself that he did give her what she needed to sleep well at night. "Thank you for seeing me so soon," she said, taking a seat. "The truth is that the medication you've been giving me—well, it hasn't been very effective."

He walked around the desk and took a seat as well, sitting straight, hands on the desk before him at a perfect angle. He sniffed and said, "Ah, I suspected as much. We should increase your dosage, then, *ja?*"

She shuddered at the idea and shook her head. "I think I'm starting to become resistant to it."

With a methodical stroke of his beard, Dr. Klein asked, "Why would you say that, Samantha?"

Sam frowned and said, "My nightmares. They're starting to happen while I'm awake, like they used to. They're the same as before. Dreaming of Grandpa after he murdered Papa. Blood and death everywhere. It hasn't been this way since I was in college."

He pulled his hands into his lap. "Und your memories of that horrible event, when your grandfather murdered your father?'

Every time he asked it, she never knew what to make of that question. It was almost like he was saying that she witnessed the murder, when that clearly wasn't true. "The same as always."

He stared at her for a moment too long. "Well, we may have to try a new medication. It sounds like you are having a rough time of it, Samantha."

She frowned, wanting real advice and not just pills. "Dr. Klein, please," she said, squeezing her charm, trying to stave off the rising anxiety. "Lately, I don't feel quite like myself. I feel like there is something inside me, gnawing at me, clawing to get out. Something that feels downright evil."

Nodding, Dr. Klein asked, "Tell me, Samantha, have you had any periods of blacking out? Have you had any periods of not remembering what you were doing?"

Sam started to sweat. He was obviously insinuating that she had some sort of disorder. But this was the first time he had ever broached the topic so openly. It was unnerving. "No . . . I . . . I mean . . ."

Sam bit her bottom lip. It was getting hard to focus, and her vision was starting to tunnel out. For the longest time, she just stared wordlessly at him, feeling like she was looking down a long hallway. She could barely feel the charm in her hand.

The wave of nausea eventually passed. When she again looked at Dr. Klein, she saw something on his face that she had never seen before—a small smile.

It looked wicked.

"Excellent to hear, Sam," he said.

She stared at her doctor. It had been many years since he had called her Sam, always insisting that she use Samantha. Once again, her vision tunneled out, everything around her feeling distant and unclear. She glanced at the clock and realized that she had been staring at him for over five minutes. She also realized that she had dropped the charm on the floor and stepped on it, grinding it into the carpet.

Dr. Klein nodded sympathetically. "Well, zat was very informative. I am sorry that you are suffering so much, Samantha. I can assure you that I will do everything in my power to fix zis as soon as possible."

"Wait, what?" said Sam, looking around. "What do you mean?" Her feelings of alienation and confusion were overwhelming.

He walked over to her and patted her shoulder. "The war for your mind is almost over, Samantha Castille. Together, we will cure you of ze damage done to you by that terrible man, your grandfather."

He went to the doorway, as he always did when the session was over. "For now, I suggest you break up with zat Richie Fastellos. He is no good for you right now. You need to focus on yourself, not on being in a relationship. And throw zat charm away. Mementos of your mother are not going to help with the anxiety. We will get you a new, better medication, my dear. Science will save you."

Her stomach sank like a brick. She had come to her psychiatrist for help, and instead, she was more confused and upset than ever. Picking up her charm, she said, "Wait, Dr. Klein, please! A few more minutes. There are some things I need to say."

Dr. Klein's eyes narrowed. He seemed honestly annoyed. "What do you vant, Samantha? You are wasting my time. Haven't you learned by now zat I will cure you if you trust me?"

"It's not that I don't trust you," said Sam, desperation growing in her voice. "It's just . . . I've always thought that a healthy relationship was good for someone."

"Ah, zat is true," he said, nodding his head. "But you are not capable of a healthy relationship. You cannot love, not in your present condition. Even now, what you feel for zis Richie is more of a codependence. You must learn to fix yourself before you can be with another person."

She was stunned. Deep inside, a part of her felt like laughing hysterically while the rest of her felt like crying.

"How can you say that?" she asked. "How can stuffing me full of pills be better than finding someone to love, who will love me in return?"

Dr. Klein sighed and got up to pace around her. "You are still suffering from ze same trauma you had when you were ten years old. I have told you many times, Samantha, that this will take years upon years to fix. Today, we have hit a true breakthrough. But before we can move forward with treatment, we must first remove all unhealthy crutches from your life, such as Richie und zat charm."

Sam shook her head. She felt so many emotions: confusion, anger, frustration, anxiety, fear—all rolled into a needle that stuck deep into her heart. *No. There's no way he's unhealthy for me. No way in hell.*

"I can't break up with him," she said. "I love him."

"You do not love him, Samantha," Dr. Klein said, his voice thick with irritation.

"No." Sam was adamant. "No way. I will not break up with him. Throughout all this, he's been the one thing that has kept me sane."

"You are not sane!" His shout reverberated throughout the room. He was right in her face.

She recoiled, feeling as defenseless as when she was a child.

"You are very ill, Samantha," said Dr. Klein harshly, although he was no longer shouting. "You have not been well since your father died. You should be confined to a place where you can be of no harm to yourself or others. But your lawyer made sure zat was not possible. However, do not mistake being free with being healthy. You are very sick, und until we cure you, that sickness will continue to consume you."

Sam wanted to scream. His words hurt because she knew they were true. She was not OK. Deep within, she felt something laughing at her, at the entire situation.

"I've accomplished so much—" she started, her body trembling.

"You've accomplished nothing," he said, contempt in his voice. "I vill speak plainly. You have something evil hidden deep inside you. I've done everything in my power to hold it back. But if I am going to free you from it, you need to give me complete und total control. After all, I am a doctor. I know what's best."

Sam stared at him, her head spinning. Sitting down, she squeezed her charm so hard she felt she might break it.

"Now, if you vant to get better," Dr. Klein said, sitting back down, "just trust me. You will get better, Samantha. We will get through this. We will persevere. Und when the rest of the world sees what we have done, they will know that it was my science zat brought the monster inside you to its knees."

She looked up as he said that. Her mouth hung open. *Monster . . . inside . . . me?*

Any confusion she had about him vanished. Suddenly, she realized why he was more concerned about stuffing her full of pills than listening to her problems. It was never about her care. It was always about the prestige of "fixing" her. *I can't believe it. This guy doesn't give two craps about me. I'm just an academic paper to him. God, I've been so stupid!*

With that realization came a complete aversion to him. She had to cut all ties. She had to get away.

"You're fired."

Dr. Klein blinked and, in an incredulous tone, said, "I beg your pardon. You cannot fire me, Samantha. The state has—"

"That expired ten years ago and you know it," she said, standing up. "Maybe it's time I found a new doctor. You're obviously more interested in keeping me doped up than in fixing me."

He rose. "Now wait just a minute, Samantha. No one else has ze right to treat you. You are my patient. I have earned zat right." His voice, despite the incredulous tone, had a rising touch of panic.

Sam smirked. "Not anymore, Dr. Klein. Last time I checked, this was still America, and I'm still free to choose my doctors."

As she headed to the doorway, he followed her. "No! Wait! Samantha, you must remain my patient. I cannot help you if you stop seeing me. If you leave, ze consequences will be dire. Leave my care, und you will regret it!"

She stopped at the doorway to his office and, without turning around, said, "The only thing I regret, Dr. Klein, is not doing this years ago. I'm sick and tired of being treated like I'm crazy. I'm beginning to think I'm the only sane person in New Orleans."

She walked out on her doctor without looking back. "Farewell, Dr. Klein."

Chapter 8
Everything Is Connected

Date: **Monday, August 10, 1992**
Time: **12:00 p.m.**
Location: **Tulane University Hospital**
              Downtown New Orleans

"So I'm off the case until further notice?" Michael sat in his hospital bed and glowered at Ouellette, who was standing, arms folded, in a most unyielding fashion.

When his commander had shown up, Michael had immediately asked for access to the files on the investigation. He had been less than ten seconds into laying out his reasoning when Ouellette had dropped the bomb—he was officially off the case for now.

Despite his irritation, he could see the creases on his commander's brow, lines on his face. *He never shows stress or age. He must be shouldering a great deal of weight right now.*

"You know I can't risk any information on the case being leaked, to the media or otherwise," Ouellette said. "You want to work on this case? You do it without your notes or any reports."

Michael arched an eyebrow. "Commander, did you just tell me to work on the case entirely in my head?"

Ouellette sighed. "I'm not telling you to do anything. If you think you can solve this case just by mentally sorting the facts, then go for it. Otherwise, you're off until you're discharged from the hospital."

He put his hand on Michael's shoulder. "In other words, concentrate on healing and getting back on your feet. Olivier and Bergeron can handle the rest. You do that and you'll be fine. Trust me."

Michael couldn't believe it. He had really hoped that Ouellette would allow the case files to be brought to him. He was sure he could solve the mystery if only he could get his hands on them.

As Ouellette turned to leave, Michael cleared his throat to get his commander's attention. "Commander, the answer to the case lies in the mountain of notes and files we have on both the original and copycat murders. I am completely certain of that."

Ouellette stopped and looked at him.

Michael sweated. It was a desperate, humbling plea. "If I were allowed to just sort through all of it, every scrap of paper, I am certain that in a few days, I'd figure everything out."

To his surprise, Ouellette smiled at him, something he had never seen him do before. "You don't need to prove your brilliance to anyone, LeBlanc. Just concentrate on recovering. You're not worth much to me, the city, Dr. Lazarus, or any of us if you're dead." With that said, he left.

Michael thought that was odd. Why had the commander mentioned Dr. Lazarus? Did they know each other? Michael leaned his head back and sighed. *Whatever. I don't know if I should even care.*

Alone in his room again, he closed his eyes and reflected on a conversation he'd had with Rodger the previous night. With the cool air of the room washing over him and the gentle hum of the machinery, he found it easy to slip back into the memory of Rodger's visit. It was as if he was reliving it.

"Rodger," Michael had said while finishing up a bowl of soup, "tell me about the M&M sisters. Specifically, tell me about the differences between Magnolia and Marigold. Was one more popular than the other? Were they easily confused with each other? Did they like or dislike each other?"

He had been working on a hunch that one sister had traded places with, or possibly even murdered, the other. And after learning that Sam's mother had likely had a weak heart, he felt he was on the verge of learning which one of the sisters was Mary Castille.

Rodger harrumphed and said, "You know I don't remember all the details. Like I said before, I hated going to that club, what with the likes of Blue-Eyed Giorgio and his gang there. I only went those few times because of Edward."

"Please," Michael said, "I have a hunch that this is all very important. Anything you say might help. Any detail about them, no matter how small."

"Right . . . well, one was definitely more popular," Rodger said, shifting in his seat. "Magnolia was more sought after because she was more gentle and soft-spoken. She had a way of talking that just pulled you in. Marigold, on the other hand, was more passionate and, well, aggressive. She was also the only sister to ever get angry in public."

Michael tilted his head at that. "What do you mean?"

Rodger looked to be in deep thought. "Well, it was on one of the nights I went there. The M&M sisters were at a table with Edward, Giorgio, and myself. Everyone was having a good time until some poor cocktail waitress tripped and spilled a drink right on Marigold's red dress. Marigold lost it. She slapped the hell out of the waitress and called her stupid. It was bad. Edward had to escort her out. Magnolia just sat there looking very embarrassed. Giorgio, of course, sidled up next to her, which made her look extremely uncomfortable." He folded his arms and added, "I ended up escorting Magnolia out. That was probably the closest I ever got to her."

Nodding, Michael hummed to himself and looked up at the ceiling. The contrast between Magnolia and Marigold was stark. "So, Magnolia was popular with everyone, being the sweet one, while Marigold was not?"

Rodger sat up. "Yes. Even Vincent liked Magnolia. In fact, she was the only one he'd allow to sit with him whenever he'd show up at the club."

Michael hummed to himself again, and then exhaled sharply. "So Edward was having a relationship with Marigold, as you remember, but Magnolia was the one with the heart condition. Correct?"

"Correct."

Michael had one more question to ask. "So, just out of curiosity, you said that you didn't go to Edward and Mary's wedding. Correct?"

"Correct. I wasn't invited. I think only the commander went," replied Rodger. His brow furrowed, as if recalling the memory upset him. "In fact, Edward was real weird about it. He refused to say why, just that it was a family matter. He got married at the mansion. That was about nine months before Sam was born."

His eyes widened. "Wait a minute! You think that Mary and Edward got married because of a pregnancy?"

"Yes," Michael said, closing his eyes and leaning back. "I think that Mary got married because she was pregnant with Sam."

His evening medication had come soon after that. Rodger had left, saying he needed to sort some things out himself. They'd promised to reconnect within a day or two.

Slowly, Michael came out of his memories.

He was sure now that Magnolia was Mary Castille. Both had had weak hearts. That meant Marigold, whose real name he didn't know, was Sam's aunt. Magnolia was gentle and refined. She had Vincent's favor. Marigold was too coarse to be allowed to marry into the Castille family.

He wondered what their maiden names were. He shrugged. It didn't feel relevant right now.

At any rate, his current theory was that Vincent had arranged for Edward to marry Mary. However, Edward was actually sweet on Marigold.

Michael opened his eyes and frowned. "This is getting ugly. Marigold and Edward were in love, but Edward was forced to marry Magnolia and have Sam with her. Was Edward sleeping with both sisters? Did he have a child with one but not the other?"

Would that have driven Marigold to murder her sister?

He sighed. There had to be something to this tale of intrigue. Why else would there be so much secrecy surrounding the M&M sisters? "I need to go back and speak with Rosemary Boucher."

A man's voice came from the doorway. "Boucher. Now there is a name I have not heard in many years."

Michael opened his eyes. Standing at the doorway was Camellia. Seated before her, in a wheelchair, was someone who had, to Michael, become synonymous with general weirdness.

"Dr. Lazarus," he said. "Nice to see you."

Dr. Lazarus smiled pleasantly as Camellia wheeled him over. "It is good to see that you are well, Detective. You already know my personal assistant, Camellia."

"Yes, we've met," Michael said.

She chuckled sultrily.

He shook his head. He wished she had just said from the beginning that she was with Dr. Lazarus. "OK, so why are you here?" He looked from one of them to the other and back again. "Camellia asked me some very unnerving questions, and every time your name comes up, I feel like I'm being recruited into a secret order."

Dr. Lazarus laughed out loud and shook his head. "I wouldn't worry about being recruited into any secret orders right now, Detective. I'm not here to do anything but get to the bottom of something that interests me. You recall that I was close colleagues with Vincent Castille, yes?"

Michael nodded and said, "Yes. You claimed that he was very close to you before he became the Bourbon Street Ripper."

"Yes, indeed," said Dr. Lazarus. "After you visited me, I started to look through my old files. Notes taken from many years ago regarding the different research projects Vincent and I performed together. I began to suspect that some of the doors opened by Vincent twenty years ago are still causing problems today."

Michael blinked. "Excuse me, what do you mean?"

"Ah, I am confusing you. My apologies." Dr. Lazarus shifted in his wheelchair as best he could. "Let me start from the beginning."

Michael folded his hands in his lap. Although people being cryptic annoyed the hell out of him, he still believed Dr. Lazarus to be a straight shooter.

"You remember me saying that Vincent and I studied neurology, correct? That we looked for ways to surpass human limitations?"

Michael nodded again.

"Good," said Dr. Lazarus. "And you remember that Vincent believed that with the proper stimulation, a person could perform well beyond normal human capacity, correct?"

Once more, Michael nodded, recalling the conversation from a few days ago.

Dr. Lazarus continued. "Something was driving Vincent to try and best the frailty of human beings. Something was driving him to strengthen the weak and extend life well beyond its natural span."

"You mean Sam Castille?" Michael said. It was obvious that Vincent would want to help her before anyone else. It had already been established he loved her the most.

"Very good, Detective," Dr. Lazarus said. "When Samantha was five years old, she collapsed while playing. She recovered, but the test results showed that she had a weak heart, just like her mother. Some of the doctors believed she would not make it past her tenth birthday. That's when Vincent began to change."

Michael tilted his head. "What do you mean? You told me he didn't start getting reclusive until a few months before the original murders. That was when Sam was ten, not five."

Dr. Lazarus pointed to Michael and said, "Correct. What I mean is this: after that incident with Sam, Vincent started to research ways outside of conventional medicine to strengthen and enhance life."

Michael pursed his lips and fought back the scowl that was threatening to surface. "You mean that voodoo crud?" Even saying the word "voodoo" made him feel dirty, like he was urinating on all logic and reason.

Dr. Lazarus chuckled. "That? Yes, of course. But not just the supernatural. Vincent looked into Eastern medicines, exotic herbs, and even experimental pharmaceuticals. Anything to extend the life of his granddaughter."

Michael's brow furrowed. "I'm not sure how this fits into the investigation of the Bourbon Street Ripper. Or how this fits into Vincent Castille being the original killer."

Leaning in as much as a man in a wheelchair could, Dr. Lazarus said, "What Vincent used was an African incense called the *tkeeus*." There was a hard clicking sound at the start of the word. "I believe you encountered it directly."

Again Michael blinked, but this time it was in shock. "Hold on, Dr. Lazarus, you're talking about that pink stuff that made me . . . act funny?"

Camellia spoke up. "Your report stated that you felt like you could do anything. You felt invincible. Isn't that right, Detective?"

He peered at her. "How did you—"

"We have our sources, kid," she interrupted.

Dr. Lazarus abruptly held up his hand. "Camellia, please. That is enough for now."

Again, Michael felt frustration building within him. Was someone from the police passing information on to others? He was going to have to tell Ouellette about this . . . this weirdness.

Finally, he spoke up. "OK, so Vincent gets this *tkeeus* or whatever and then starts murdering people? Why? Did it induce madness in him?"

"That's what we are trying to determine," replied Dr. Lazarus. "Your answers to Camellia stoked my curiosity. I have some follow-up questions, if I may?"

"Only if I may ask a few of my own," said Michael.

After a moment of a thoughtful expression, Dr. Lazarus said, "Fair enough. But I go first, all right?"

Michael nodded.

Dr. Lazarus settled back and said, "You said you felt invincible. That you could do anything. Was that the only time you felt that way? And if not, when else?"

Michael looked at him for a second and then closed his eyes. He thought back on the time he had chased a gang member—who had tried to kill Topper Jack—across the rooftop of the Odyssey House. "Yes. One time prior. I was chasing someone on a roof and felt like I was unstoppable."

Dr. Lazarus hummed to himself. "Was that sensation as strong as the one you felt when you came in contact with the *tkeeus*?"

Michael thought for a moment and then shook his head. "No. It wasn't as strong."

"Did you feel tired after that first time?" asked Dr. Lazarus.

Again, Michael thought about it. It seemed so long ago. "A little, but I had just run up a fire escape and across a roof, so I figured that was normal."

Dr. Lazarus was silent for a few moments. "Before the feeling of invincibility, did you feel anything else unusual? A tingling sensation? Perhaps in your shoulders, along the back of your neck, or at the base of the spine?"

His eyes still closed, Michael thought back, sorting through his memories of that evening. Then he remembered a definite tingling sensation. It felt almost like exhilaration.

Opening his eyes, he said, "You know, I did feel a tingling sensation along my spine. Both times. It was much stronger the second time around, when I came in contact with the *tkeeus*."

As the other two looked at each other, he asked, "So are you telling me that this drug was being used then, too? How did I get exposed to it the first time?"

"That I am not sure about," said Dr. Lazarus flatly. "By every recorded account, the phenomenon that you experienced cannot be felt without the *tkeeus*."

"It had to have been an external influence, Director," said Camellia. "Someone must have attached it directly to Michael the first time."

Michael didn't know what "it" was supposed to be. He had no idea what Camellia was talking about, and that frustrated him even more. "So what's going on here? Who attached what to me? How does this relate to Vincent Castille or the murders?" He was starting to feel desperate.

Dr. Lazarus shook his head. "You wouldn't believe me if I told you, and I won't say any more until I have stronger evidence. Suffice it to say, Vincent introducing the *tkeeus* years ago changed the playing field, so to speak. This is not just about a serial killer and his victims. This is about something far older and far uglier."

Michael closed his eyes tightly. He felt panicked, like he was once more being left out. Were they talking about occult stuff? Were they talking about the same voodoo cult thing Sam had mentioned? Or was Dr. Lazarus just being cryptic because he had no idea, either?

It took him a minute to relax. He remembered that as a police detective, his job was to solve a murder mystery, not get involved in some crazy conspiracy theory that belonged on a show like *The X-Files*.

When he finally opened his eyes, he saw Dr. Lazarus and Camellia patiently looking at him.

"OK, now it's my turn to ask questions," Michael said. "Dr. Lazarus, you said that you hadn't heard the name Boucher in a long time. What do you mean?"

"Ah, yes, Boucher," Dr. Lazarus said, shifting in his wheelchair and getting comfortable. "He was a boy under my care about the same age as Samantha and Dallas. Julius Boucher. A very troubled boy with an equally troubled mind."

"What do you mean by troubled?" asked Michael.

Dr. Lazarus cleared his throat. "He was incredibly gifted, not too different from Samantha or Dallas. Very creative, with a talent for puzzles. He excelled in word games, especially anagrams."

Michael quirked an eyebrow. "Anagrams? Words that are scrambled into other words?"

"Yes, exactly," said Dr. Lazarus. "Sadly, most of his pathos came from years of mistreatment. He was very badly abused by his foster family, if I recall."

Michael listened, wondering if Julius was the son Rosemary had spoken of, the one she had with Robert and couldn't keep. With the last name of "Boucher," it sounded like he was. "Did Julius know Samantha and Dallas?"

Dr. Lazarus frowned. "Yes, indeed. Poor child became close to them both, especially Dallas. Same age and all that. They played word games together, everything from anagrams to phrases with hidden meanings. Seemed to help with Julius's fits, I recall."

"Fits?" Michael asked. "What fits did he have?"

"Oh, terrible fits of rage," Dr. Lazarus said, shaking his head. "From the abuse he suffered while under foster care. We'd often have to sedate him, right, Camellia?"

Camellia nodded. "He was pretty well behaved around other children, but he'd go into a fit if any adults got near him. One guard had two fingers bit clean off. It got so bad that he was being considered for a lobotomy."

Michael frowned, not so much at the barbarism of the procedure, but at the fact that a lobotomy would effectively remove Julius as a suspect. And how old was Camellia if she was around twenty years ago? She looked Sam's age.

"When did Julius get the lobotomy?" he asked, closing his eyes.

"He didn't," said Dr. Lazarus. "The fire that destroyed most of those blocks occurred before talks of the procedure went anywhere."

"So Julius was killed?" Michael asked, still seeing any leads go up in smoke.

Dr. Lazarus said, "Sadly, yes. One of the many fatalities. It was Julius that Dallas went after to try to save, which resulted in him getting burnt to the point of brain damage, if you recall. Julius's body was never discovered, unfortunately. He and so many others were burnt beyond recognition."

Michael's eyes popped open. "Julius's body was never found?"

Dr. Lazarus nodded. "Like I said before, Detective. The fire was so bad that almost everyone died."

Michael just stared ahead. It was like a plot to a movie, but it made sense. The question was, if Julius's body was never found, was it possible that he didn't die that night?

"Dr. Lazarus, one more question," he said, frantically sorting through the facts and seeing what was missing.

"Of course, Detective. What is it?"

"Did Dallas learn the term 'Nite Priory' from Julius?"

Dr. Lazarus shook his head. "You know, I'm not entirely sure how that came about. Samantha would often talk about the Knight Priory of Saint Madonna. I believe that 'Nite Priory' was a purposeful misspelling. In fact, now that I'm thinking about it, I'm sure of it. It was part of the word games they used to play."

Michael sat back and just stared up at the ceiling. *My God. Could it be that simple?*

It was an hour later, after Dr. Lazarus and Camellia had left, that Michael finished sorting out everything he had learned. He was silent as some nurses changed his bandages and took his readings.

Dr. Lazarus's parting words had been, "Your commander recommended that I keep an eye on you for a future project. So, I'll be watching you, Detective. Do your best." So, the doctor did know Ouellette.

What stuck out, however, was what Camellia had said. "It's important to know when you're out of your league, kid. Just because you can't understand something doesn't mean it can't kill you. Be careful."

Michael couldn't help but wonder if this had anything to do with Fontenot's warning that "the snake is dangerous because it knows."

He sighed and settled down as the nurses left him. He really wanted things to go back to normal. The train to Crazy Town was no longer a fun ride.

Vincent was using some drug called the *tkeeus* to extend Sam's life. This *tkeeus* made people feel invincible and pull off superhuman stunts. That matched what Michael had experienced and what Richie had seen: the Nite Priory, a group of assassins who performed superhuman feats while slaughtering over a dozen armed men.

Michael twisted his lips and snorted. "Wouldn't it be hilarious if that same group was responsible for the serial murders as well?"

Remembering what he just learned about Julius, he suddenly found it to be a lot less funny. Julius had had a rage issue due to his foster parents. What if he was charismatic enough to lead a group like the Nite Priory?

More than ever, things were starting to make sense. The Nite Priory. The *tkeeus*. Julius, Sam, and Dallas. And now the M&M sisters.

Everything is connected.

It was later in the evening, after Michael had finished dinner, that a nurse came in and connected a phone to the wall. "Detective LeBlanc, you have a call. A family member."

He was shaken out of his thoughts. "A family member?" He hadn't heard from his family in quite some time.

Picking up the phone almost gingerly, he said, "Hello?"

"Hey, Michael," came a teenage girl's voice. Like his, it was calm and measured.

A sincere smile parted Michael's lips. "Alexia! How did my little sister know to find me here?"

She let out what could only be called a "giggle snort" and said, "Yeah, right. It's kind of hard not to know that my big brother was shot in the line of duty when it's in the news."

He groaned softly. "You all are getting that story all the way up in Shreveport?" Surely by now all his friends and family upstate knew.

"Don't go thinking for a moment that just because of problems between you and Papa that Mama and I don't worry about you." Her tone was lecturing. He imagined she was wagging her finger at the receiver. "Whatever happens, Michael, you're family. We wanna know what's going on with you."

Michael frowned a little when Alexia mentioned their father.

A Southern Baptist minister, Frank LeBlanc had never agreed with what he saw as Michael's "choices." And just as his father had cut him out, Michael had cut out religion. Only his sister, Alexia, who was devout yet significantly more tolerant, and his mother, who was his mama through and through, remained in contact with him.

He realized he had gone silent.

"Sorry, Michael," she said. "I shouldn't have brought him up."

"It's OK," he said, clearing his throat. "And I'll be fine. The bullet went clean through. Tell Mama I'll be out in a few days."

"All right, then, all's well," said Alexia. He knew that when she said "all's well," that part of the conversation was effectively over, ending on a positive note.

The two of them talked for a little while longer, catching up on each other's lives. He found out that his sister was graduating high school in May with a grade point average high enough to be in the top five percent. He also found out, not surprisingly, that her latest boyfriend had dumped her for not "putting out."

Ever moral, Michael thought with an inward chuckle. He loved talking to her. She was like him in many ways, but underneath her calm and calculating exterior was a genuinely sweet girl. A bit jaded at the mental ineptitude of others, but a sweet girl nonetheless. She was one of those beacons of light in an otherwise dark world.

He spent time telling Alexia the basics of the Bourbon Street Ripper investigation, leaving out anything that was confidential. She asked a lot of questions about the technical aspects of the crimes—not surprising, as she had more than a passing interest in forensic science. By the time they were done, he was pretty worn out but in quite a good mood.

"All right, Alexia. I'll call you and Mama next week," he said, wrapping up the phone call. "I love you, sis."

"Love you, too," she said. "I'll pray for God to watch over you."

Michael hung up, a warm feeling in his heart. Alexia offering to pray for him was the same as a kiss on the cheek.

Well, at least they won't be affected by the ugliness down here. People getting cut up and thrown into the river and . . .

Michael's thoughts went back to the deaths of Blue-Eyed Giorgio and his men. Maybe someone in the Nite Priory had slipped up at the Riverwalk.

Who was handling that case? Rivette and Landry, right?

Dialing the precinct, Michael asked for either of them. In the background, he heard what sounded like a rather intense commotion.

A moment later, Landry picked up. "Hello, Detective Landry speaking. Who's this?"

"It's Michael. Landry, do you have a moment?" Michael asked.

"Um, Michael? Wow, what are you doing on the phone?" Landry asked. "Yeah, I have a moment. Not long, things are about to get crazy in here."

Michael said, "OK, look. I need to know if, when working the Marcello murders, you or Rivette got any witnesses. And if those witnesses saw anyone suspicious leaving the Riverwalk."

"Suspicious?" Landry paused for a moment. On the other line, Michael heard Ouellette ask where Rodger was, and then heard a muffled response from Dixie. What was going on over there?

A moment later, Landry said, "Yeah, here it is. The only witness was Gloria Lambert. That was Marcello's girlfriend. She was found in his limousine, passed out drunk. She only remembers one guy coming out. She said it was the same guy who was taken to have dinner with Marcello a few hours before the murders. She didn't remember any details other than him being Caucasian."

Who the hell was that? "Any security footage?"

"Nothing," said Landry. "Marcello always turned the security cameras off when he had dinner at the Riverwalk."

Damn it, another brick wall. Michael gritted his teeth in frustration.

"What about the Rivergate next door? They're building a casino there and should have cameras up, right?"

Landry said, "Just a moment, Michael." Again there was a pause and some muffled yells. Michael could hear Ouellette calling the squad room to order.

"Sorry, Michael," said Landry. "This is just not a good time. Try calling back tomorrow."

Michael shook off Landry's dismissal and said, "What's going on over there, Landry? What's Dixie doing?"

"Yeah, we need to get going," said Landry. "Dixie cracked the case wide open. We're about to go arrest the prime suspect. Sorry, got to run." He hung up the phone.

Michael was stunned. "Prime suspect? Who are they going to arrest?"

A feeling of helplessness overtook him.

They can't mean . . . Sam?

Chapter 9
Magnolias and Marigolds

Date: **Monday, August 10, 1992**
Time: **3:00 p.m.**
Location: **Castille family mansion**
                  Lake Pontchartrain in New Orleans

By the time Rodger and Dixie got to the Castille mansion on Lake Pontchartrain, it was already mid-afternoon. Since she had wanted to take a break from driving, he drove the Porsche—slowly and deliberately. He knew he couldn't afford to fix even a scratch on a car that expensive.

Dixie, for the most part, just kept her eyes closed. She had said she was preparing herself for the upcoming interview.

He was already prepared to meet the Castille family matriarch, Sam's aunt Gladys. He had his list of questions ready. Nothing would derail the interview today.

A pair of armed security guards met them at the gate, checked their badges, and called ahead. A moment later, the gate opened and he was driving toward the mansion.

And indeed it was a mansion, with the estate as beautiful as a dream: expansive green lawns, bushes trimmed into perfect shapes, and the greenery of willows and cypresses forming a luscious curtain of privacy. All along the driveway leading up to the mansion were rows upon rows of carnations, in bloom with glorious reds, pinks, and whites. Similar flowering plants framed the side of the sparkling white mansion, built in Plantation style, complete with oversized pillars, extended balconies, and a large, sweeping staircase going from the front porch to ground level.

In the center of the horseshoe driveway was a single magnolia tree, young and in full blossom. Rodger remembered that Vincent had planted that tree when Sam was born. It was as old as her, to the day.

He parked the car in the front of the horseshoe.

Dixie looked over the mansion. "Are you sure that everything's in order, Rodger?"

He nodded. "Ouellette set up the interview himself. It's ridiculous the number of hoops you have to jump through to talk to old Madame Castille."

Like everyone else who knew of "old Madame Castille," he was aware of how much of a recluse she was. But it couldn't be helped. All the other Castilles with links to Vincent were dead. There was no one else to ask about Edward's marriage—something that was becoming more and more of a key point in the investigation.

"All right," replied Dixie as they got out of the car. "Think we can get her to open up about Edward's marriage to Mary?"

"I hope so. We have to treat this very delicately." He knew that with one wrong push, the iron gates to the Castille estate would close to them.

As he climbed the large sweeping steps to the Castille mansion, Rodger felt the start of a sweat. While he had only been here a few times during his life, the experiences were impossible to forget. It was here, after all, that Vincent murdered Edward in front of Sam, and that Rodger arrested him and ended the original Bourbon Street Ripper murders.

As they reached the top of the steps, the front door opened. An aged Caucasian man, dressed in a tuxedo and tails, his mouth puckered like he always tasted something sour, looked down at the two detectives.

"You are the two detectives from downtown?" He arched a single eyebrow, and said nothing more.

Rodger took out his badge and said, "Detectives Bergeron and Olivier, New Orleans Homicide, eighth precinct. We'd like to speak to Madame Castille, please. We have an appointment made by Commander Ouellette."

The butler stared down at the two a bit longer before stepping back and motioning for them to enter. "This way, Detectives."

He walked stiffly across the white marble flooring of the foyer, where the Castille family crest, an embroidered 'C' over a coat of arms, was emblazoned.

The foyer alone was massive, two stories high with a gold and crystal chandelier casting radiant light throughout the room. Two staircases swept up to the second-floor landing. Underneath the stairs, a set of double doors led toward the dining room, while to the left and right, doors led to the music room and the drawing room respectively. A scent of musk perfume wafted in the front hall.

Just taking in the foyer was enough to remind Rodger that the Castille family was one of the oldest and wealthiest in all of southern Louisiana. He remembered that Vincent Castille, the eldest brother in a family of three, had inherited the estate from his father, Louis Castille, who had vanished in the African Theatre during World War I, when Vincent was just five years old.

And after Louis vanished, they had all his pictures taken down and locked away. Never did understand that, but Edward certainly loved having a mysterious grandfather. It was always something he liked to brag about.

Rodger came out of his memories and realized that he had stopped walking. Mason was standing at the end of the foyer and clearing his throat in an annoyed fashion, while Dixie was looking at him curiously.

Rodger ignored his embarrassed blush and whispered, "You probably didn't learn this in school, but the Castille family is heavily rooted in the history of New Orleans."

"News flash, Rodger," whispered Dixie back, her tone dripping with sarcasm. "The Castille family is filthy rich."

He smirked quietly and said, "They have a little bit saved up, yes." Still, the wealth of the Castille family always felt foreign to him until he was standing in the mansion. He was far more used to the townhome.

This is all rightfully Sam's.

The butler led the detectives to the right—into the drawing room. Plush red carpet covered the floor, with wooden panels for the walls, and a vaulted ceiling. Oversized windows let generous amounts of sunlight into the room. The central pieces of furniture were two large chairs and two large sofas that looked to be from the Elizabethan period.

The sound of a Chopin piano sonata—beautiful, yet sad—sculpted a restful atmosphere.

Mason announced both detectives. "Detective Bergeron and Olivier here to speak with you, madam and sir."

In the center of the room, sitting on one of the sofas, was Gladys Castille. She was wearing a hand-crafted gray dress and drinking a cup of tea.

Rodger tried not to stare. *Time has not been kind to this woman.*

Her pinched, gaunt face, her sunken eyes, and her thin lips made her look more skeletal than human. Her cold gray eyes were focused on the two detectives. Around her neck was a sizable gold chain and pendant with a photo etching of a pudgy woman in a state of perpetual mirth.

Sitting in a nearby large chair, dressed in a tailored Armani suit, was the Castille family lawyer, Kent Bourgeois. He looked older than the last time Rodger remembered seeing him.

"Well, hello, Rodger," Kent said, heading over to vigorously shake his hand. "How have you been? You look great." Kent patted him on the stomach.

"I'm fine, thanks." Rodger was surprised. He hadn't expected to see Kent there, even though it did make sense that, since the interview had been set via official channels, the family lawyer would be contacted. "You're looking pretty well."

"That will be all, Mason," crackled Gladys, her voice sounding as old and decayed as she looked.

Mason bowed his head before leaving, nose tilted up in the air.

"Who are these people, Kent?" she asked.

"This is Rodger Bergeron, Gladys," said Kent. "He's the detective who captured Vincent. He's an old friend of Edward's. And that young woman is his partner, Dixie Olivier."

"Ah, good. Captured Vincent. Very good," she replied, bobbing her head up and down. "I'm glad you caught my brother, Detective. He was an evil man. Heart full of poison and malice."

"She's lost a bit of her hearing in her old age," Kent said, tapping an ear gently. "Come, have a seat. It's been such a long while. How have you been? How's the murder investigation?" He returned to his seat and motioned for the detectives to sit as well.

"Mr. Bourgeois, forgive me for asking," Dixie said, walking around the room instead, "but are you on a first-name basis with all your clients?"

He wrinkled his brow at her. "Only to members of the Castille family. Remember . . . Detective Olivier, it is, yes? Remember that I have been the trusted lawyer of the Castille family since I was able to practice law. Why, I knew Sam when she was just a baby."

"Well, that's good," replied Rodger, sitting across from him. "Because we're here to talk about Sam. More precisely, we're here to talk about Sam's mother."

"My mother was a very strict woman," said Gladys in a matter-of-fact tone. "If we said anything out of sorts, she'd have us kneel on a bag of rice and say the entire rosary." She nodded her head several times as if answering a question.

Kent leaned over and patted her arm. "Rodger is talking about Mary, Gladys. Mary Castille. Sam's mother, not yours."

Instantly, her voice grew nasty and her mouth puckered even more. "Oh, she was a black widow, that one. A real gold-digger. I wasn't fooled by her sweet charm and frail body. She was a devil. A vixen!" She turned to Rodger. "I told Vincent he had no business with someone like her in the house. But did he listen to me? No, of course not. Older Brother always knows best. Then little Princess comes along and, surprise, surprise, has a weak heart! So what does Big Brother do? Use the powder and get poor Robichaux nearly killed. Mary bats her eyes and turns on the charm and he just falls for it like every other man."

Rodger stared at her, disbelieving what he had just heard. So they had done something to Sam when she was a little girl. The rest of her statement sounded like incoherent rambling.

Gladys continued to rail, "And Edward! Poor, misguided Edward! Bad enough that he was a policeman, such a vulgar profession, but to marry a harlot and a whore? Such a disgrace!"

"You just called Mary Castille a whore," said Dixie, still pacing near Rodger. "Was she flirting with both Vincent and Edward? Was she sleeping with both of them?"

"I hardly think that is an appropriate question," Kent said sharply, sitting up in his chair and staring at her with disapproval.

Dixie pursed her lips and mumbled, "Sorry. So, Madame Castille, why do you refer to Mary as a whore?"

"Oh, they both were," Gladys said, hands shaking as she sipped her tea. "Those harpies had their claws reaching for the family fortune. If it wasn't one, it was the other."

Rodger was still trying to sort through everything she had said when Dixie again spoke up. "Madame Castille, when and where did Edward get married?"

Gladys looked up at her. The nastiness was gone, and in its place was a grandmotherly grin. "He married her here in the mansion. We use the ballroom because the light in it is so pretty. This was right after he found out she was with his child. Oh, you should have seen how angry Vincent got. Oh, the scandal of it all! Why, my dear departed sister, Marguerite—she fainted six times that day." She clasped the pendant around her neck and sighed.

Rodger's brow furrowed. Something about what she had said seemed incorrectly worded. He wondered if it was intentional, or if it was the ramblings of an old woman.

"Wait, Madame Castille," he said. "So, Vincent got angry at Edward for marrying Mary? Why would Vincent be angry that Edward married the mother of his child? Was it because she was of low birth?"

"No, no, no," Gladys snapped at him, her white face getting red in seconds. "Edward didn't marry the mother of Vincent's child. What kind of question is that? Are you making fun of me, young man? How dare you!"

The strain in her voice made him flinch. He hadn't expected his question to get so badly misinterpreted, but that's what seemed to have happened.

"I think that's enough for today," Kent said, holding out his hands. "Gladys gets confused easily if you don't speak in clear, short sentences. I won't have you upsetting her."

"Madame Castille." Dixie leaned on the back of the only vacant sofa. "How many weddings were there in that ballroom?"

"Oh, we've only had one recently," Gladys said in a most conversational tone. The malice was gone as if it were never there. "And it was such a lovely affair, we—"

"I really must insist that you desist," Kent said, standing up and putting a hand on her shoulder. "Again, you are confusing her with large sentences. You have to be concise and slow."

Gladys smiled shakily and he patted her shoulder. "Detectives, why don't we pick this up later in the week? On Thursday? If you send me the questions in advance, I can advise you on how to ask them. That way, you won't risk confusing her."

Rodger, who been silent, stood. "Thanks for your assistance, Kent. We appreciate you taking the time to see us. We'll be in touch with any follow-up questions. Have a great day."

As they shook hands, he noted that Kent had been keeping his left hand stuffed in his pocket the whole time. *What is he hiding?*

Dixie looked confused as Mason was called for and they were ushered outside. Once they were heading to the car, Dixie confronted Rodger. "Why did you stop me back there? I thought we were past that?"

"It's simple," he said as he tossed her keys to her. "Kent was stonewalling us. Someone has been stopping me from speaking to Sam for twenty years. Someone has been making sure we don't get the facts surrounding Castille family affairs, such as Edward's marriage. All morning, I've had a feeling it was Kent who was doing these things."

They both got inside the car.

"Now I'm certain of it."

Dixie whistled. "So you think Kent is our killer?"

Rodger hummed to himself, trying to organize his thoughts. "He's definitely hiding something. In her own way, Gladys was trying to help us. Kent didn't want us to hear what she had to say. Maybe he's not the killer, but he's involved. My gut says so."

As Dixie started up the car, she got a thoughtful look on her face. "From what Gladys said, it almost sounds like those sisters both got married. Also, she made it sound like there was another wedding recently. Maybe a cousin of Sam's or something? Any way we can follow up on any of that?"

She acts more like Ouellette than a detective at times, he thought. *Her natural leadership skills are really starting to come out.*

"I'll see about getting the wedding license for Mary and Edward," he said. "I'm not sure about the whole bit about having a wedding recently. There are very few members of the Castille family alive that I know about. Well, there are a lot of distant relatives with the Castille name, but none of them would matter when it comes to this. Just Sam and Gladys. Like you said, maybe a few cousins?"

As Dixie drove, she nibbled on her thumb, tension showing on her face. "Possibly. Shake the family tree and see what falls out. For now, I'm thinking of sorting through our information on the Nite Priory. If it's all a ruse, like Jonathon said, then someone is using the Knight Priory of Saint Madonna in order to keep us off their trail."

Rodger nodded and said, "So what do you want to do?"

Dixie's lips curved into a smirk. "Drop you off at your apartment and get back to mine. I have a hot meal, a hot shower, and a hot guy waiting for me. Then I ponder my way through this Nite Priory crap."

He couldn't help but chuckle at her statement. Having had only the briefest and most fleeting of relationships himself, he had never experienced the all-consuming romance she had with Gino. It was utterly alien to Rodger, who would rather spend his evenings wrapped around a nice bottle of whiskey or a fine cigar.

"All right, then," he said. "Take me home. I need to make some phone calls, anyway. Then before heading to the office tonight, I'll go tell Michael what I learned from this utterly revealing interview." His voice dripped with bitter sarcasm.

She laughed.

Outside of his townhome a little while later, as Rodger started to get out of the car, Dixie unexpectedly hugged him and said, "Rodger. You're a damn good cop. Don't let anyone say otherwise. Not even you."

He smiled with a little uncertainty. He wasn't sure what was bringing this on.

She must have picked up on his unease, because she said, "Hey, just giving a friend some love. You look like you need it."

He hugged her back almost anxiously. "Yeah, well . . . not too much love. Else Gino will get jealous."

Dixie winked. "Ha! Well, if you were thirty years younger, Gino might have a reason to be jealous."

Rodger paused again, his smile fading. He wasn't sure what had just happened. He was about to say something when she poked him teasingly. "Come on, old man, it's a compliment. Learn to take them, because you'll get a lot more when you catch this killer."

He smiled again. This time, however, it was genuine. He hadn't been complimented much before, and in the past few days, two women and his partner had given him considerable compliments.

As he headed into his apartment complex, he found himself wishing that there were more people in the world like Dixie, Sam, and even Michael. People who, once they got to know you, did their best to make you feel good about yourself.

Once inside the inner gates, he heard the voice of his landlady, Ms. Parkerson, calling out to him. "Rodger Bergeron, there you is. I needs to speak with you."

He waited for her to catch up to him. He wasn't sure what she wanted. He had already paid her this month's rent. "What can I do for you, Ms. Parkerson?" He tried to sound as congenial as possible, but he was pretty exhausted.

"There's a package waiting for you," she said, holding it right up under Rodger's nose.

He flinched away from the box, his nerves on edge.

"I held onto it in case someone tried to mess with it. Looks important. It's from Angola. Figured you'd want me to keep it safe."

He exhaled and gratefully took it. "Thanks. I'll go ahead and open it inside."

"No problem," Ms. Parkerson said.

He started to walk off and was halfway to his door when she called out again. "Rodger, wait a minute!"

Rodger turned around, trying to maintain an outwardly cheerful disposition. He really wanted to just disconnect from people for a while. "Yes, Ms. Parkerson?"

Her voice became lower and more serious. "You gonna catch that killer soon, right? Like last time?'

He blinked. The strain on his landlady's face was the same as on everyone else's in the city. *This case is hurting so many people. More than just the victims and their families are suffering.*

He put on a sincere smile and saluted. "I'll do my best, Ms. Parkerson. I'll do my best."

Rodger went inside his apartment.

He put the package from Angola on top of a pile of mail and then picked up the phone. There was something he needed to take care of before he got sidetracked by another development in the case. He dialed a number he knew by heart.

A moment later, a sweet elderly woman picked up. "Hello?"

"Mabel, it's Rodger," he said, glad to hear her voice. In the background, he could hear the sound of excited yipping and growling. "Sounds like Boudreaux is having a good time."

"Oh, hello, Rodger," said Mabel, sounding pleased to hear from him. "Yes, Boudreaux is very excited. Mommy just baked some cupcakes, and he's deciding which one he wants."

Rodger chuckled. The Dugas family's Shih Tzu loved everyone in the world except him. But he was the closest they had to any children now that their son was up in Chicago. Mabel positively spoiled Boudreaux.

"Would you like to speak with Douglas, hun?" she asked. "He's watching the news. I won't watch. Horrible story, the murders are."

"Yes, please. Thanks, Mabel. And pet Boudreaux for me."

There was the rustle of movement, along with the sounds of a news broadcast in the background, and then Douglas's voice was saying, "Hey there, Rodger. I was just watching Ouellette and Connick talking to the press. Seems that Arsenault arrested Bobby Hebert for drunken and disorderly conduct."

Rodger stifled a cough. "He arrested the Saints's quarterback? Does he want to get fired?"

"Arsenault's a thug," Douglas said with disgust. "Always has been. But Ouellette and Connick know they need him when things go south. Still, half the city is calling for his blood and the other half thinks he may have saved the upcoming season!" He laughed so hard he started coughing.

Rodger laughed along with him. Pride for the Saints, and hopes that they'd one day win the Super Bowl, was something he naturally felt as a New Orleans native.

But sadly, it was irrelevant to the investigation.

So he said, "Well, Douglas, I didn't call to talk sports. I need to know if you still have contacts at the Orleans Parish clerk of court."

There was relative silence as Douglas hummed thoughtfully on the other end. "I think my friend Derek still works there. Why? What do you need?"

"I need to get the Castille marriage license from when Edward married Mary."

"Ah, OK," Douglas said. "I can arrange that. So the wedding was in the sixties. Do you know where it took place?"

Rodger recalled what Gladys had mentioned. "Yes. The Castille mansion. Private ceremony."

The sound of the television was muted, and Rodger heard someone scribbling. Then Douglas said, "So, marriage license from the sixties. Took place in the Castille mansion. Got it!"

"Thanks, Douglas," Rodger said, feeling like he had taken care of something important. "I appreciate it."

"No problem, Rodger," replied Douglas. His voice lowered a bit. "Just come over for dinner some time. Mabel misses having you over."

Rodger hummed to himself. "All right. As soon as this is done, I'll come over for dinner. Take care, Douglas. Good night."

He hung up the phone. He had just started to get up when it rang again. He blinked and picked it up, figuring that it had to be Douglas calling back. "Hey there, what's—"

"Roger? It's Sam." Her voice sounded upset, like she had been crying.

He sat at attention. "Sam? What's going on? What's happening?" In the background, he heard the sound of a shower. "Is everything OK? Is Richie treating you well?"

"What?" Sam asked. "No. I mean, yes! Richie's fine. I just . . ."

She took a deep breath. "I need to talk to someone. Someone who was there. You know, when my father . . ."

Rodger felt his palms and brow start to sweat. "What's going on, Sam?"

"I quit Dr. Klein today, Rodger," she said, sniffling, her voice sounding labored.

He didn't say anything. He knew that because of his interview earlier.

Fortunately, she continued without a response from him. "I just can't take the bullshit anymore, Rodger. I feel lied to by everyone. I don't even know if I'm sane anymore." She sniffled again and blew her nose. "I've even started to think that I'm somehow possessed. Like there's something evil inside me. Isn't that crazy?"

Rodger thought back on what Gladys had said about a ritual performed on a girl with a weak heart. He figured that was Sam. While he didn't particularly buy into the supernatural aspects of voodoo, appreciating only its cultural impact, he'd seen enough recently to make him question his own beliefs. "Not entirely crazy, Sam. Not entirely."

"And more than that, Rodger. I think . . . I think I saw Grandfather do something. Something horrible. I think I saw him murder. It's like a stained glass image just behind a layer of fog . . ."

Rodger closed his eyes, a few tears rolling down his cheeks. He wanted so badly to tell her that she did indeed witness Vincent murdering Edward, but he couldn't bring himself to say it over the phone. She deserved to hear it face-to-face.

"It's banging in my head!" she cried out. "Grandfather, Dad, torture, murder, loa, voodoo, everything is just pounding in my skull. I feel like I'm losing it. I feel like I'm going mad!"

Rodger made several shushing sounds until she had calmed down enough for him to speak. "Sam, do I need to come over there?"

Sam sniffled again and said, "No. Richie and Jacob are taking me out. Richie and I are about to go out clothes shopping. I just . . ."

There was a long pause as she sobbed silently. "I just need to know that I can trust you. I've been betrayed and hurt so much recently. Uncle Rodger, I can trust you, right?"

She had him at "Uncle Rodger."

"Yes," Rodger said, wiping away his tears. "Yes, of course you can trust me. I've got your back, Sam. Don't worry. I'm going to clear your name. I'm not going to let you die."

There was another sniffle before Sam said, "Thank you." Her voice sounded completely grateful.

He was about to speak when she added, "Richie's done showering. Rodger, I'll call you tomorrow, OK?"

"OK," he said, exhaling deeply. "Take care, Sam."

He spent the next couple of hours ordering take-out, eating his dinner, and then relaxing in his chair. It was past eight o'clock when he finally got up and shuffled over to the mail. On top was the package from Angola. It was from Charles Daigle, Assistant Warden of Angola, and Rodger's contact when he and Sam had gone to visit Fat Willie.

Opening the package, he read the letter from Charles:

> Dear Rodger,
>
> I found these letters in Fat Willie's cell while we were cleaning it out after he died. I hope that they can help you.
>
> Sincerely,
>
> Charles Daigle

Rodger sat down and looked through the letters curiously. A lot of them were from females he didn't know nor want to, who apparently found Fat Willie sexy and desirable. Some of the letters were written in language so foul, he was sure that even Ouellette would blush. However, amongst the smut, Rodger found one letter that stood out. It had been sent during the beginning of summer that year:

> Mr. Willie,
>
> Yes, as you mentioned, I am interested in writing an article about your story for the Times-Picayune.

The editor I write for, Mr. Hueber, has expressed interest as well. I find it fascinating that a tale as depraved as yours has never been made public.

So, Henrietta Babineaux was the only woman you know of who ever conceived from one of your "parties"? And you said her name is Virginia? I am anxious to know where this Virginia is located, as I would like to interview her as well.

If you can provide that information, I will have a good starting point. I will look forward to your next letter and when we finally get to meet.

Sincerely,

Nick

"Who the heck is Nick?" Rodger stared at the letter before folding it up. He then went to hunt down a glass of whiskey.

A moment later, a thought hit him. It was as subtle as an elephant on a unicycle. Taking out the letter, he read through the names again.

"Henrietta Babineaux."

He'd heard that last name before. In fact, he couldn't forget it.

"Virginia Babineaux."

Rodger's eyes widened as he realized the significance of the letter. *Virginia Babineaux, otherwise known as "Virgin Baby," was the copycat killer's first victim. And Henrietta Babineaux was Dr. Castille's first victim. The mother and daughter were both first victims.*

He looked at the date again. It lined up perfectly in the sequence of events leading up to the killings. His hands shook as he read the name on the bottom of the letter once more.

"Nick."

The revelation was so overwhelming that he was forced to sit down. Finally, a name could be linked to the murders.

"Could this guy be the killer?"

As those words left his lips, the phone rang.

It was Dixie.

"Rodger? We need to meet with Sam tonight. It's important."

Chapter 10
When You Come Home

Date: **Monday, August 10, 1992**
Time: **7:00 p.m.**
Location: **Esplanade Apartments**
          New Orleans City Park

With a loud, throaty moan, Dixie fell forward, the strength in her arms suddenly giving out. For a few precious moments, she knew nothing but oblivion. She floated down an endless river where there was no worry and no stress—nothing but the feeling of complete release.

Then she was aware of the warmth above her, the scent of sweat filling her nostrils, the clash in temperatures of hot body heat versus cold air. She was aware of the soft bedsheets underneath her, damp with perspiration. And finally, she was aware of sensual repetitive kisses to her shoulder blades, back, and neck.

Turning her head as the kisses traveled up to her face, she met those lips with her own, kissing back until her senses fully returned, the trip into the blissful abyss concluded.

Lying half on top of her and half beside her, with just enough of his weight on her to press her against the bed, Gino kissed her several more times. His dark eyes looked into hers. His deep, sensual voice asked, "Again, Dixie?"

Dixie smiled. It was a secret smile she gave only him. She could feel the love radiating from him. It was like the warmth of the sun. But the reality of a serial murder investigation that wasn't solving itself began intruding.

Giving him a small peck on the lips, she said, "I'd love to, honey, but I need to get back to work. Let me shower off."

As he rolled over, she slowly sat up, enjoying the afterglow. After a few minutes, she slid to her feet and took the sheets with her, covering herself in a modest fashion. Behind her, she could hear her lover stretch and yawn.

"I'll make some coffee, Dixie. I need to get back to work as well."

Walking stiffly, she stepped into the bathroom, looked in the mirror, and saw that her hair was a matted mess. *Oh, well. I needed to shampoo, anyway.*

The warm water felt good as it poured over her, washing away the sweat from the hour of love-making. Unlike the past few mornings, she didn't ponder things too much in the shower, nor did she revisit her past. Instead, she mentally prepared herself for work.

Getting out of the shower, Dixie dried off and then put on her robe and slippers. From the front of the apartment, she heard the television and smelled fresh coffee brewing. With a final stretch, her mobility restored, she walked up front.

OK, OK. Enough playing. Time to work.

As she entered the kitchen, she looked at Gino at the coffeemaker. He was wearing only his boxers and was humming along with the television to the opening theme to *Night Court*. His dark olive skin was in delicious contrast to his light green boxers.

Dixie blushed as she watched him. Sometimes, she couldn't believe her luck. It was as if someone had taken the hero from a romance novel and breathed life into him. Even after five years of living together, looking at him could still take her breath away.

"Hey there, beautiful," he said.

She realized she had been staring at him. Cheeks still flushed, she looked away and cleared her throat. "Hey, hun. Shower's free."

As he walked past her, he offered her a mug of fresh coffee, prepared sweet and light. "Then I better go get cleaned up."

Before Gino left, however, he leaned in and whispered, "Save me some coffee."

As he walked off, Dixie shivered a little. He was the only man she knew who could make "save me some coffee" sound sexy.

Sipping her coffee, she headed to the dining room table. Spread across its surface were her notes from the investigation and copies of every important piece of evidence taken so far. There were the notes she and Rodger had compiled on the case, photographs of the crime scenes, and photocopies of everything from receipts to facsimiles. And lastly, there were photocopies from Michael's notebook.

On the other end of the dining table was Gino's electronic word processor. It looked so lonely all by itself.

She looked over all the information on the table. The task seemed positively daunting. She wished that Michael was out of the hospital and helping out. She had had many occasions to work directly with him and felt that the two of them made a great team.

About a month ago, they had pulled an all-nighter at his apartment in the French Quarter. Not only had they closed the reporting on over fifty cases, but they had also cracked several new ones. It had been like a tag-team. She had analyzed each scene for raw information, then Michael had figured out the puzzle. That night had ended with the two of them getting rip-roaring drunk at a Bourbon Street pub. The following day, she had woken up back at Michael's apartment with a hangover and a feeling of great accomplishment.

She looked at the task before her. *Well, Michael isn't here. It's up to me to solve this case now.*

She nibbled on her thumb.

As she scanned the documents, she came across something that looked a bit odd. One of Michael's notes, amidst a page of dates and timelines, simply said, "Check other restaurants. Commander's Palace turned up negative."

Getting the oddest sensation that she had seen something like that before, Dixie flipped through her copy of Michael's notebook. Near the beginning, she found what she was looking for.

Of course! Michael marked it down right here. During the original Bourbon Street Ripper murders, Vincent Castille treated himself to an expensive restaurant meal after every killing, both as a reward and to establish an alibi. Places like Commander's Palace, Arnold's, and Café Giovanni. If the copycat killer is trying to emulate Vincent, perhaps he's doing the same thing?

Circling Michael's note about the restaurants, she checked the rest of the notes for a follow-up to that theory. The search turned up empty.

She leaned back and sipped her coffee. "Wow, I can't believe something like this was overlooked. This is part of profiling the murderer. So unless the Nite Priory really is behind the murders, we could potentially use this to help identify our killer."

She triumphantly finished her cup of coffee, feeling as if she had done a rather solid bit of detective work. "I may not be a Michael LeBlanc, but I've got what it takes."

It was times like this that she was glad she decided to become a detective.

Ever since Dixie saw her father nearly beat her sister and mother to death, she had wanted to be a police officer. Her adoptive parents, the Oliviers, had been supportive of her, although they clearly wanted her to choose a less dangerous profession. She joined the police academy right out of high school. From the moment she graduated, she was set on being a patrol officer, wanting to work on the streets to prevent incidents like what had happened to her.

In fact, she initially rebuffed the idea of becoming a detective. However, that changed one night when she answered a call at the Fischer Projects, one of the most rundown and dangerous housing developments in New Orleans. A ten-year-old girl had witnessed her drunken father beat her mother to death and then run away. Dixie wanted to help figure out where the man had gone, but all she could do was collect evidence and pass it to the homicide division. It was that incident that made her realize that she had to go a step further with her career.

So she enrolled in a community college and, going to school during the day and working at nights, got her degree in criminology in three years. After putting in numerous applications for the scant open detective positions, she lucked out and was accepted by the eighth precinct. On her first day in the homicide division, she was paired up as the junior partner of Kyle Aucoin.

It was the beginning of her new life as a homicide detective.

Gino's strong arms wrapped around her, making her exclaim, "Hey!"

His hair was still wet and he was wearing a robe. He looked over her shoulder and asked, "So, have any new leads with the case, Dixie?"

She waved him off. "Case work, baby. You know I can't share anything with you, or the evidence won't be admissible." She winked playfully at him.

"Right," he replied, taking her empty cup back to the kitchen and pouring her some fresh coffee. "Just like the case you had last spring when I recognized a photograph of the killer and that helped you arrest him. Completely inadmissible."

Dixie stuck out her tongue. "Oh, hush, you! The truth is, I feel like I'm on the verge of a major breakthrough, and I need to focus. Undisturbed."

He chuckled. "I think I liked the 'inadmissible evidence' bit better, Dixie. Don't worry. I've got a lot of work to do as well. Producers want a finished script by Wednesday morning."

She nodded.

He came over to the table and handed her the cup of coffee, looking at her papers again for a long moment.

Giving him an annoyed look, Dixie shooed him away. "Stop that! Go do your own work, you annoying man. Go, go!"

With a gentle chuckle, Gino sat down at his word processor. While the machine booted up, he put on a pair of reading glasses. His vision was fine, but the glasses kept down the eyestrain. Once the machine was ready, he slipped in a floppy disk. A few moments later, he started typing.

She watched him work. She didn't mind the reading glasses. She actually thought they were kind of cute. After a few moments, she asked, "So, honey, what are you working on now?"

"I cannot tell you," he responded. "My publisher will discard my manuscript if I reveal anything about it to my girlfriend."

Hearing him say that so stoically in his Greek accent, with those little reading glasses on, made her burst out laughing. Any tension that she had felt melted completely away.

He just smiled at her and went back to typing.

Once she had calmed down, Dixie looked back at the notes, particularly the ones on the Nite Priory. When she looked at the theory as a whole, she didn't know what to make of it. It seemed like a most grotesque concept—a secret organization devoted to murdering like Vincent Castille, possibly even a fanatic voodoo cult. And they seemed to have links to the original Knight Priory of Saint Madonna.

That or they're deliberately trying to implicate the real Knight Priory.

That theory was just as plausible as Jonathon's statement of "I do believe the killer is playing the police."

She took a mental step back. *My best chance to sort out the Nite Priory is to compare the locations of the murders with the locations of the kidnappings and try to find routes a group of people could take without being seen.*

She took out a map of the French Quarter and wrote "Nite Priory Routes" at the top of it.

After marking down the locations for each kidnapping and murder, she started tracing routes throughout the French Quarter. She traced the main streets, side streets, and alleys, plus the dozens of winding paths through the courtyards every building seemed to have. She even looked at the sewer system, which was not deep enough to effectively use, seeing as how New Orleans was below sea level. With the routes plotted out, she leaned back, chewed gently on her thumb, and went into work mode.

Immediately, Dixie noticed three things.

First, each of the murder locations was in a building that had been abandoned for a long time. *The equipment used in the killings would take a while to set up. The killer must have purchased these locations ahead of time.*

Second, each kidnapping location was in a fairly public area. *None of the victims could have been taken by force, like with Vincent using Fat Willie. Even taking a drugged victim would arouse suspicion.*

Third, every kidnapping had taken place during the French Quarter's peak hours. *Witnesses would remember seeing the victims with a large group of people. So the Nite Priory has to be small. No more than three to five people.*

She was so engrossed in thought that she nipped down on her thumb a bit too hard. She mouthed a silent "ow" and shook it off.

As Dixie performed her analysis on the map, she stole occasional glances over at Gino, who was diligently working on his latest manuscript. Her eyes softened as she watched him work. As beautiful as he was on the outside, it was his inner beauty that had won her heart. Among everything else, he was always waiting for her when she came home.

Her cheeks flushed. Despite not being into soap operas or romance novels, she read everything he wrote. She was also the first person he knew who had figured out his pen name.

If you took the short forms of his first and last names, you had "Gino Eli," which is a good short name, but easy to trace back to Ginopolis Eliopoulos. However, if you simply went one key down on the keyboard from the letter *I*, you went from "Gino Eli" to "Gino Elk." Instantly, you have people thinking of the larger cousin to the deer instead of the quiet Greek man down the hall.

Simple, yet genius. But that was his style, to pick the solution that was so obvious, no one thought of it.

Dixie returned to the map, tracing the victims' routes with her finger. *So, there's no way any of the victims could have been forcibly taken. Every route would require crossing a highly populated main road at some point. So the victim had to willingly go with the killers.*

She compared her notes on the murders with her analysis. *That means it would have to be someone the victims trusted. So maybe it's a small group, like a bunch of partygoers, who chat up the victim and have her go with them? Then they bring the victim to an isolated location and kill them?*

Her brow tightened. The more she looked at everything, the less she liked the Nite Priory theory. *Even that would attract attention. If it's just one person, one killer, who's charismatic and harmless-looking, wouldn't that work? So each victim is approached by one person who is very personable, chats her up, and convinces her to go with them. It's the French Quarter, so no one is going to pay attention to a woman walking off with someone so long as they look like they're having fun.*

She leaned back and looked up at the ceiling. *The charming solitary killer theory is much more plausible than this murder cult theory.*

And didn't Jonathon say he thought the killer was playing the police? She exhaled deeply. "I only have a hunch to go on here, but what if the Nite Priory is a ruse?"

"Anagram," said Gino as he walked by.

Dixie felt her brain slam against a brick wall. She looked blankly at her lover. "Ana-what?"

He sat down, put on his reading glasses, and said, "Anagram."

Dixie's brain had frozen. *Anagram? What's that?*

It took a few more seconds for her to remember. "Oh, right. Where the letters in a word are rearranged to make another one."

Smiling at her, he nodded. "Yes. Exactly. That phrase. Nite Priory. It's an anagram."

Taking out another blank piece of paper, she wrote "Nite Priory" at the top. Her hand shook as she started rearranging the letters.

"It is a trick used by writers," Gino said as he continued to type, peering through his reading glasses. "Also secret agents and spies, people in secret groups, even newspapers. That's how you get the word puzzles. Lots of people use them." He chuckled.

As Dixie worked, trying to make sense of it, Gino continued, "That one is a good anagram, but too similar to one that already has been used. It was in that movie we saw last year. What was it called? Ah, yes, *The Silence of the Lambs.*" He gestured dismissively and returned to typing.

She didn't hear that last bit. She was too busy staring at the middle of the page, where the efforts of her furious descrambling revealed two words that made her blood run cold.

Iron pyrite.

She felt her face pale. "Fool's gold."

Gino took off his reading glasses and rubbed his eyes. "Yes. A misdirection. A lie. But like I said, not very original. Been used already."

My God, I was right. That's exactly what Jonathon meant. This whole Nite Priory thing is a lie someone created to throw us off the scent of the real killer. And it's worked. Someone has been playing us.

Leaning back, Dixie rubbed her eyes as well, groaning in quiet discomfort. "Whoever is misdirecting us is likely the killer."

It was a rhetorical statement, but he responded anyway. "That's what I'd say, Dixie."

She grabbed her notebook and flipped through it, looking for her record of who had mentioned discovering written evidence on the Nite Priory. When she found the page, she just stared at the note, her mouth tightening.

Richie told Rodger that it was a book at Sam's townhome. Jesus . . . we've been played by that bitch. And to think I almost actually liked her.

Dixie stood up so quickly it made Gino scoot back. She grabbed the cordless phone and dialed work.

A tired voice picked up. "New Orleans eighth precinct, Bourbon Street Ripper task force, Detective Rivette speaking."

"Rivette, it's Dixie," she said as she went into the bedroom, dropped her robe, and started getting dressed. "I need you to call every fine dining restaurant in town and find out if anyone of interest spent money on the nights of the murders. Anything out of the ordinary. Anything!" She clasped on her bra.

"Restaurants, what?" He sounded surprised. She heard him shuffling papers around. "Dixie, it's almost nine o'clock. Most restaurants will be closing soon."

Her voice rasped with irritation. "Then you better start calling. Oh, and Rivette, if Rodger is there, do not—I repeat—do not say anything to him until I arrive." She still wasn't sure that Rodger could be objective about Sam's guilt.

Dixie hung up the phone and threw on the rest of her clothes, securing her badge and gun as well. She then brought the phone up front and headed over to Gino.

He had his glasses back on and was nonchalantly typing as if her behavior was routine.

She put her hand on his shoulder. "I need to run, honey. See you later."

He smiled as he typed. "All right. Go get the bad guys." He leaned up and the two kissed briefly but firmly.

"Love you, honey," she said as she headed toward the front door of the apartment.

The last thing she heard from Gino was the same thing she heard every time she had to run off to work: "I love you, Dixie. I'll be here when you come home."

When Dixie got to the precinct, Rivette was still making calls to restaurants and Ouellette was going over the day's patrol with Arsenault. Landry was nearby, cleaning out the coffee pot. Rodger was nowhere to be found. *He must still be at home.*

"Olivier," Ouellette called out as she arrived, "you mind telling me why you have Rivette calling every restaurant in town that serves blackened catfish and bananas Foster?"

She had come prepared, assuming he would question her. She slipped out the paper with Michael's notes on the dinners. "Michael and Rodger forgot an important angle, Commander. Vincent Castille used to treat himself to a fine dining experience after each murder. We need to look for three instances of the same person spending a lot of money on food each night of a murder."

After listening, he looked over the paper. "All right, but from now on, run all changes in the investigation by me first. I had Rivette searching for connections between the three victims."

"Yes, sir," replied Dixie, glancing at Rivette. "Sorry about that, Scott."

He waved her off, furiously scribbling down information in a notebook.

Ouellette continued, "Also, Olivier, don't forget that you are currently Bergeron's partner. Where the hell is he?"

"I dropped him off at his townhome several hours ago," she said. "He said he was going to go over his notes and get some rest before tonight."

Ouellette didn't seem too pleased. His tone started rising. "Do you people forget how to follow orders? Olivier, call Rodger and tell him to get his ass over here right now." He turned back to Arsenault, ignoring her.

Dixie felt the conversation spiraling out of control. So she took a deep breath and loudly exclaimed, "The Nite Priory doesn't really exist. It's a ruse by the killer!"

All conversation in the squad room stopped, except for Rivette, who was cursing in Creole.

Turning around, Ouellette eyed her dangerously. "What are you saying, Detective?"

She didn't flinch. Unfolding her worksheet with the Nite Priory anagram, she handed it to him. "We've been had. 'Nite Priory' is an anagram for 'iron pyrite.' Fool's gold. A similar trick was used in *The Silence of the Lambs*. Commander, someone has been signing the notes to the accomplices with 'Nite Priory' because they were counting on us wasting our time focusing on it."

Ouellette looked at the paper, his eyes narrowing. He looked like he was getting more pissed than usual.

Arsenault looked over Ouellette's shoulder and said, "Well, I'll be damned. If that ain't the shit to end all shit. Good work there, Dixie."

Just then, Rivette hung up the phone and headed over. "Hey, guys. Listen up! You all are going to love this."

He held out his notebook, the page covered with incomprehensible scribbles. "On the nights of all three murders, someone spent a tidy sum on dinner. On the night of Virginia Babineaux's murder, someone ordered a lobster dinner from Arnold's for delivery to their house. Just so you know, Arnold's doesn't deliver to just anyone. On the night of Rebecca Clemens's murder, that same person racked up a two-hundred-dollar bill at the Ritz Carlton hotel restaurant. And on the night of Cheryl Aucoin's murder, someone racked up an even higher bill at Muriel's in Jackson Square."

Ouellette looked at him. "Who are these bills charged to?"

"Samantha Castille," Rivette said.

"You see, Commander?" replied Dixie. "Plus, Richie Fastellos reported that he found written evidence of the Nite Priory, spelled N-I-T-E, in Sam's townhome."

She counted off on her fingers. "So, her stories match the murders, she's treating herself to meals the exact same way her grandfather did, and she's the only one with written information about the Nite Priory. All the while, she's putting forth the act of being emotionally distraught. She's been playing games with us the entire time."

Rivette spoke up. "Sounds like she's one of those schizophrenic types, doesn't it?"

Ouellette cocked his head at him, glaring.

Rivette cleared his throat and looked flustered, then turned away while muttering that he was just throwing out a theory of his own—all the way back to his desk. As he sat down, his phone rang. He picked it up and started talking.

Dixie thought she heard him say Michael's name.

Turning back to her, Ouellette said, "Well, this is good circumstantial evidence, but until we get something hard, there's no way the DA will issue an arrest warrant."

"Then I've got your smoking gun," came a crotchety and disenchanted voice from the squad room's doorway. Morton Melancon, the coroner, limped in, holding up a folder.

"What's with the limp, Morton?" Dixie asked, feeling concern for the old coroner.

"Gout, it flares up in this humid summer weather. Don't worry about it," Morton responded curtly before presenting the folder to Ouellette. "Here you go. We lucked out on poor Miss Aucoin."

"Please tell us that the killer left something on her that we can use," Ouellette replied as he flipped it open.

"Well, more like inside her," Morton said, carefully leaning against a desk.

As Ouellette looked through the file, Morton said, "There was some skin tissue in the victim's chest cavity. Looks like your killer scraped his or her hand a little. Not much, but enough to give us the cells we need for a DNA test."

"This is fantastic," Dixie said, looking at the report. It was a medical report with DNA charts and more terminology than she cared to sift through. "If we can get a DNA match, we've got our killer."

Ouellette nodded in silent approval. "So now we just need probable cause to force Samantha Castille to give up her DNA. Something that can't be refuted."

"Already got that for you, too," replied Morton with a derisive sniff. "I had a hunch, so I ran a few comparisons. I found a very close match. Only problem? It's someone who can't be the killer."

"Oh, why not?" asked Dixie.

"Because he's been dead for twenty years," he said. "Vincent Gilles Castille."

Ouellette raised an eyebrow at Morton. "Melancon, are you telling me that Vincent's DNA was inside Cheryl Aucoin?"

Shaking his head, Morton replied, "More like his direct kin. A child or grandchild."

Ouellette closed the file and handed it to Landry. "Landry, take this to the DA. Wake his ass up if you have to. Unless Edward Castille has found out a way to come back from the grave, our killer is Samantha Castille. Get a search warrant for her townhome in the Garden District."

"Yes, sir," replied Landry, taking the folder and heading off.

Ouellette turned to Dixie. "Contact Bergeron. Have him set up a meeting with Sam to discuss the Nite Priory. Choose someplace secluded, away from the general populace. Once we've taken her into custody, we'll see about getting a court order compelling a DNA test."

Nodding, she started to head off before stopping midstride. Something nagged at her conscience. "Commander, about Rodger. Do we tell him the truth? About Sam being the prime suspect?"

Ouellette shook his head. "That's a negative, Detective. We need him to contact the suspect, but he has proven himself biased. We can't let him risk the operation out of sentimentality. Do I make myself clear?"

She bit her bottom lip, but she would do as she was commanded. She didn't want to lie to Rodger—they had spent the past few days building up their friendship. However, Ouellette was right. In the matter of Sam Castille, Rodger couldn't be trusted to remain objective.

"Rivette," said Ouellette, "help Melancon back to the lab, then get your ass back here."

Rivette hung up the phone mid-sentence before helping Morton out of the room.

Dixie looked for Rodger's phone number. *Rodger, I am so sorry . . .*

Ouellette again jumped on a desk and called out to the room. "OK, everyone, listen up! We going to head out and give Detectives

Bergeron and Olivier cover during this operation. Samantha Castille has a history of mental illness. You are to consider her extremely dangerous. If she shows any signs of hostility, do not—I repeat—do not hesitate to open fire."

He turned to two other detectives. "Breaux and Gravois, once Landry comes back with that warrant, take him and Rivette and search her townhome. Tear the place apart. We're looking for anything the district attorney can use when the case goes to trial."

The two detectives nodded in understanding.

Dixie closed her eyes and picked up the receiver. *So sorry you fell for the trickery of that psychotic bitch . . .*

Ouellette continued. "Arsenault, get your SWAT team ready. We'll need them in case the indigo assassin shows up."

Arsenault sniffed disdainfully. "Hell, the suspect might be the indigo assassin, for all we know."

Please forgive me . . .

Looking around the room, which was rapidly filling, Ouellette said, "Once again, I cannot stress how dangerous the suspect may be. Make sure you're wearing your vests." Finally, he approached a wall of suspects' photos. "Our prime suspect and the target of this operation is . . ."

Dixie dialed Rodger's number.

Ouellette slapped his hand onto the photo of Sam. ". . . the granddaughter of the original Bourbon Street Ripper—Samantha Castille!"

Chapter 11
Another's Eyes

Date: **Monday, August 10, 1992**
Time: **6:00 p.m.**
Location: **Gargoyles Gothic Shop**
                      Decatur, French Quarter

"Richie Fastellos? Is that really you?'

Richie, holding hands with Sam, turned to see a portly woman with a ruddy face and an armful of shopping bags. She was coming toward them with a massively friendly smile and all the grace of an elephant. He returned the greeting with a nervous grin and a curt nod of the head.

He had no idea who this woman was.

"Don't you remember me?" the large woman said as she invaded Richie's personal space. She smelled of strong, cheap perfume, offsetting the clove-laden scent of Gargoyles. Her wide mouth was outdone only by her wider stature, taking up the entire aisle and blocking Richie's only means of escape—unless you counted curling up into a ball and crying. "I was at your book signing a few days back."

Richie felt trapped. It was pretty obvious from the way she was out of breath that she had rushed into the store after him. He also felt about a dozen sets of eyes upon him. The woman, who was wearing an "I Love Bourbon Street" T-shirt, seemed as out of place in Gargoyles as Richie did, her tourist style clashing with the rows of leather and vinyl garments, spiked collars, chained leashes, and items of clothing made entirely out of belts.

Still, his training from his publicist, Gordon, kicked in, and Richie kept up a congenial grin. "Nice to see you again." *Someone, please save me.*

"Oh, come on, Richie," she said, pressing the conversation as one would pressgang someone into military service. "You have to remember me. After all, we talked a whole two minutes on the symbolism of Detective Montoya's simultaneous mentor and stalker relationship with Junior Detective Paddington."

He just stared at her, and she stared back, awaiting a response as if they had been having the conversation all afternoon. He hardly recognized the characters from his own book, *The Pale Lantern*. This woman's sudden approach and subsequent tête-à-tête had been that disarming to him. A full-blown panic attack was forthcoming.

Sam spoke up hastily. "I felt that the relationship was subtly more antagonistic than the reader would first suspect. Very similar to Dr. Lector and Agent Starling, but with less regard for formality."

Starling? What's a starling? Richie thought as he felt her squeeze his hand. It took him a few more moments to realize that she was saving him from social embarrassment.

Then a light bulb went off, and he remembered who this large woman was.

"Oh, I remember you—the woman who was impressed with the way the two detectives played off each other as both friends and enemies, right?"

She smiled again, shifting from foot to foot. "That's me. As I said before, I love your work. I can't wait for your next novel to come out. I am just simply stoked!"

He nodded, keeping up his expression. From the corner of his eye, he saw Sam turning to the side, covering her mouth politely, her shoulders shaking mightily. *Lord, make it tough on me, eh, hun?*

"So who's this, Richie?" the woman asked, motioning to Sam, who came to attention. "I didn't know you had a girlfriend."

Richie came very close to saying "Sam Castille" and proudly introducing her as his girlfriend. He stopped himself when he realized that they were the center of quite a bit of attention in the store. *No . . . I need to be careful. People will recognize the name.*

"No, this is my cousin, Linda . . . Blair . . . Witch. Linda Blairwitch!"

Sam looked up at him with widening eyes.

Keeping up his public smile, he let go of her hand and grappled her head. A moment later, he was giving her a noogie, her arms flailing helplessly.

"We're really close friends, practically grew up together. She lives here, and we haven't seen each other since my book tour began, so I thought I would spend the weekend with her," Richie said.

The fib seemed to work. Sam wiggled free and made a fussing noise, fixing her hair and saying, "Really, cousin? We're not kids anymore. Don't do that again!"

The large woman nodded with obvious approval.

"Well, I shouldn't keep you, then," she said, adjusting her armful of bags. "But it was darling seeing you again. I'll be sure to come to your next book signing. Ta, ta, Richie! Au revoir!" And she waddled out of the shop, staring and giggling at him the entire time.

As he stood there and twitched, Sam stood beside him, arms folded, leaning against him as if he were a hitching post.

"So . . . cousin . . ." she said with a smirk.

Despite the social anxiety Richie was feeling, he laughed and put his arm around her.

Gargoyles was a shop specifically designed for Gothic clothing, and while he couldn't care less about the style here, she seemed to love it. They had been there only thirty minutes and already she had found her ensemble for the evening—a pair of black hip-hugging leather pants, a black vinyl tank top that zipped in the front, a pair of black boots lined with buckles on the sides, and black fingerless gloves.

He had waited outside the dressing room, and when she came out, hair down and cascading over her shoulders, he thought that not only was she the most beautiful woman he'd ever seen . . . she somehow managed to look like a blond Sarah Connor from the *Terminator* sequel.

"What do you think?" she asked, striking a dramatic pose.

"Going for the Gothic rebel there, eh, Sam?" Richie quipped.

Sam blew him a raspberry and went over to the front cashier, wrapping up her hair in her trademark ponytail. "I'll take all this. And I'll wear them out," she said. One minute and what must have been a horrendously high credit card charge later, she was back with him, holding a bag with her old clothes. "Your turn!"

Richie grimaced, fighting back the tingle of nervousness. "I told you, hun. I'm not really into the Gothic look." He had mentioned it twice earlier in the day.

Sam's shoulders dropped and for a moment, she looked away. "Oh, right, well . . ." Then she looked back at him and shrugged. "Look, Richie, I'm going like this and Jacob's going to be decked out in his leather biker gear. If you can't dress like us, then dress in something that will at least look good."

"That's the problem, Sam," he said. "I honestly don't know the first thing about fashion. I mean, my only impression of what's hip is John Travolta in *Saturday Night Fever*." He bit his lower lip.

To his surprise, she burst out laughing. After a few seconds, she snorted and said, "Richie, Baron Samedi dug disco's grave so many years ago, I bet he's forgotten doing it."

Richie frowned. He was starting to feel picked on by her. It was making him feel extremely uneasy.

However, before his anxiety could bubble forth, she leaned in and kissed him. She lingered for many seconds, and he felt her sweet, hot breath wash over his lips. When she leaned back, she said, "I know what to get you that will make you look butt-fine gorgeous. Come on!"

Sam walked out of the store. He followed her with his eyes, taking in the beautiful way the leather pants hugged her hips and rear.

He heard the store clerk, a bald guy with more tattoos and piercings than clothing, say, "Cousins, my ass."

"Piss off," Richie said under his breath.

On the way out, something caught his attention. He saw a person playing with a flogger, the kind used for BDSM play. He was wearing a black hooded coat that covered all but his mouth. The person was frowning at Richie and smacking the flogger against his hand. Richie blinked, shook his head, and looked again, but the person was already gone, the flogger back in place.

Holy shit . . . he thought, remembering the night at the Riverwalk. *The Nite Priory is watching me. Why are they frowning? What do they want?*

When they got outside, he saw a few more people in black hooded coats watching from an alleyway. The coats looked a bit different, and the people wore pull-over masks that looked like Halloween costumes—he noticed a skull and a clown. One of them was sitting on a motorcycle.

The hell is going on here? Richie was starting to get more than a little anxious.

Sam took him to her car, loaded up the bags, and told him where to drive. With the Riverwalk a crime scene and the French Quarter under curfew, there was only one real option—The Shops at Canal Place, an indoor mall.

It took her only a few minutes to get him into a men's clothing store and pull several sets of clothes off the rack—pairs of colored slacks, button-down shirts, several jackets, and a few sets of shoes. She also pulled a couple pairs of sunglasses from a display.

As she dragged him by the hand toward the back of the store, he said, "Really, Sam? You don't need to come with me. Just tell me what to try on and—"

"Just shut it and follow," she interrupted, pulling him to where the dressing rooms were. None of the employees were there, and after making sure they were alone, she pushed him into the dressing room that was farthest back.

Wow, she's gotten bossy something fierce.

Putting the clothes on the hook, Sam looked him over and said, "Hey, sweetie, can I see your belt for a second?"

The way she said that made Richie arch an eyebrow. "Why, are you going to spank me with it?" He started to remove his belt, albeit a bit cautiously.

She waved her hands dismissively, saying in a sweet voice, "No, no. Nothing like that. I'm just going to tie your hands up over your head."

He had just removed his belt when her words registered. "Wait, what now?!" Before the reality of what was happening hit him, she had taken his belt and was wrapping it around his hands.

He instantly felt his anxiety spike. "Sam! What the hell's gotten into you? This isn't some gam—" His protest was stopped as she covered his mouth with her hand.

"Shut up," she said, glaring, her bangs coming loose and going to either side of her face. "Just shut up before someone hears you."

Richie closed his mouth and stared at her. This was the second time today that she seemed like a totally different person. Feeling incapable of moving, he stayed silent as she looped the belt around the cross bar above the stall. His hands were now secured above his head. He felt uncomfortably vulnerable.

Leaning in, Sam whispered, "Now listen here, Richie. Tonight is going to be my first night out in years. You may not realize it, but you're doing everything you can to ruin it for me. So, one way or another, you're going to be accommodating of me tonight."

He nodded. Something in her eyes looked dangerously unhinged. *Is she really starting to lose her shit?*

Leaning up, she nipped his nose and said, "So, let's play dress up Richie Fastellos, OK?"

He nodded again.

Over the next several minutes, she held up the articles of clothing to him as if playing with a paper doll. It took her a while to settle on a set—a pair of white slacks, a dark red button-down shirt, a white jacket, a pair of white shoes, and a pair of red-lensed sunglasses.

"There," Sam said, looking over the clothing. "Looks good, doesn't it?"

Richie sighed. His arms were getting tired, and he was no longer having fun. His anxiety was swelling, and he wanted to just sit down for a few minutes. He really didn't want to be around her right now. He wanted to be alone.

Maybe she's the one who needs to be on medication instead of me?

"Looks great," he said at last. "Now please untie me."

She looked him over as if appraising a cut of expensive meat. Giving him a sultry grin, she leaned in, her hand resting on his crotch. "Not yet, I think . . ."

He looked around, his pulse starting to rise as she lowered herself to her knees, unfastening his pants. "What? Seriously? Here in the dressing room of a store? You've got to be kid—"

His protest was cut short by the blissful sensation of her lips upon him. *Oh, God, I'm dating a crazy chick,* was the last thing he thought before succumbing to his carnal desires.

The sun had already set when Sam and Richie left the store. She paid for his new clothing, which he was now wearing, his own clothing dirtied on the dressing room floor. Both were quiet as they got into the elevator, avoiding each other's eyes.

What's going on with her? He watched her lean against the other side of the elevator. One part of him was hurt at the way she had just used him. The other part was concerned for her.

However, as the elevator continued down, he realized she was looking back at him. She was squeezing her charm once more. Her face looked tired and anxious. "I'm sorry," she said softly. "I think I'm really messed up."

Richie felt his heart melt again, any suspicion of her gone. If she was leading him on, he was falling for it. "Come here," he said, just as softly, opening his arms.

Sam slid into his embrace. She sighed heavily. "Richie, hun, what's going on with me?"

"I don't know," he said, kissing the top of her head. "I really don't know."

As he held her, he wondered if he had problems, too. Despite the depths of his feelings for her, every time they made love, he ended up feeling like he was committing a vile sin. And as soon as they finished, he felt disgusted with himself.

He didn't know what to make of it. He just wanted to be near her. It was almost an obsession.

They exited the elevator into the parking garage. With the exception of Sam's car, it was completely empty.

She didn't say anything as she unlocked the trunk. Richie bit his bottom lip. He didn't know if she was going to break up with him or not. Pushing others away seemed to be how she dealt with stress.

I'll try talking to her when we get back to her townhome. I'm sure it'll be OK.

He had just tossed his bags into the trunk when the sound of several motors echoed through the parking garage. From the street level below, six motorcycles roared up, skidding on the concrete as if they were drift racing.

Each motorcycle was colored black and accented with dark purple. On the sides of the motorcycles were designs of skeletons and skulls. Each rider was wearing a black hooded coat, their faces covered in various pullover cloth masks—a skull, a snake, a clown, a hockey mask, a shark, and a devil. All of them were making hollering sounds as they peeled out, spun around, and surrounded Sam and Richie.

Richie stared at the riders, his eyes wide. *What the hell?!*

Sam looked around, confused. "Richie? What's going on?"

He had seen these coats before. They had been outside Gargoyles, watching from the alley. And up close, he could see that they were different from the coats of the Nite Priory. Different design and different material.

He believed he knew who they were.

"These are the guys who are framing the Nite Priory," he called out. *This has to be them, the ones the Lady in Red wants me to find.*

The six riders stopped hollering, got off their bikes, and closed in on the two of them. Each one was brandishing a length of chain, a pipe, a bat, or some other similar weapon.

Sam hurried to Richie's side, grabbing his hand. "Come on, let's get out of here. I don't think these guys are messing around."

Richie glared at them, his eyes narrowing. A part of him felt utterly insulted. *A fucking biker gang? The group causing this shit is a fucking biker gang?* After all he had witnessed, including his ordeal at the Riverwalk, to find out that it was a lousy gang behind everything was like being slapped in the face.

"Zat them, Nick?" asked Clown Mask.

Richie recognized the voice. *The guy from Sam's townhome! The one who attacked me!*

Devil Mask pointed at Sam.

"Little Sam Castille and her faggot boyfriend," said Skull Mask. "Can we fuck them up, boss?"

Sam tightened her grip on Richie's hand. "Let's make a break for it, Richie."

Again Devil Mask pointed at them, menacingly swinging his lead pipe around.

"Maybe we can fuck the bitch," said Snake Mask. "She looks pretty hot. I'll bet she's tight as hell, too."

Richie felt himself bristle and Sam tense up.

Devil Mask spoke in a low guttural growl. "Just hurt 'em!"

"You heard the boss," said Hockey Mask. "Let's show this psychotic bitch what happens to people who torture and murder in our city."

As the riders closed in on them, Richie bolted, taking her with him and heading up to the top of the parking garage. The riders gave chase, three on foot, the other three getting back on their bikes.

"If we can make it to the top of the garage," Richie said, still running, "there should be an entrance back into the mall. We can get security or someone to help us."

"Right," replied Sam, barely keeping up with him.

The sound of the motorcycles roaring through the garage was deafening. It made Richie's ears hurt. He fought to keep down his nearly choking anxiety as he tugged her along. He had to keep it together for her sake.

As they neared the top of the garage, one of the bikers, Hockey Mask, rode past them and skidded to a stop, blocking their path. He smashed his chain to the ground as if it were a whip.

Richie stopped abruptly, with Sam bumping into him from behind. She gasped and fell to her knees. He was about to help her up when a powerful impact knocked him to the ground. Pain exploded in his back as Devil Mask rode by, having nailed him with his pipe.

Snake Mask drove past and grabbed Sam by her hair. She cried out, desperately holding on as he dragged her to the top of the ramp, joined by Hockey Mask and Devil Mask. While Devil Mask watched from his bike, the other two grabbed her arms.

The other three riders were almost upon Richie. He tried to get up, only to have Clown Mask kick him in the gut so hard his vision momentarily went out. Then Skull Mask and Shark Mask were raining down fists and boots, beating him until he curled up into the fetal position, covering his head.

Devil Mask whistled loudly.

Richie groaned as Clown Mask pulled him up to his knees. Skull Mask stood in front of him, dancing from side to side and slapping him mockingly in the face. Meanwhile, Shark Mask stretched leisurely and then headed up the ramp to where Sam was being held.

Making chopping motions to his own crotch, Skull Mask continued to mock him. "Fucking faggot! You can't handle our stuff. We're gonna smack your bitch dooooown." Richie had no idea what this guy meant. He seemed like a mental degenerate.

Skull Mask then kicked Richie in the stomach so hard he doubled over.

The two riders restrained him, one kneeling on his back and the other holding up his head, forcing him to watch. He felt like he was going to throw up. His stomach churned with anxiety. He hadn't felt this helpless since Marcello's men had nearly killed him.

Devil Mask just stood by, his arms resting on the pipe over his shoulders, surveying the scene. He was obviously the leader.

"Let's see how wet this bitch is, guys," said Shark Mask as he stuck his hand down the front of Sam's pants. "Holy shit, she's soaked down her—"

She spat in his face. "Get your hands off me, you freak!" She kicked at him, missing as he recoiled.

He wiped away the spit and cried out, "Stupid bitch!" Rearing back, he punched her in the face. Blood flew from her lips and nose. Her head rolled limply to the side.

Richie wailed. "Noooo! What the hell! She's a woman, you coward!" He tried to stand, only to be pinned back down.

"Shut up," said Skull Mask as he held Richie's head steady. "Watch us fuck your bitch. Watch us fuck your nasty bitch. Oooooh! We're gonna ruin her!"

Again, Shark Mask punched Sam, this time on the other side of her head. It lolled once more, her hair coming loose from its ponytail. Her bangs fell over her face.

Richie felt sick. His heart and head pounded. His eyes were glazed, and every breath seemed to grow heavier and heavier.

"Good job," said Hockey Mask, as she went limp in his arms. "Now let's get this bitch's pants off and—"

Sam's head whipped up. Her lips, which were covered in her own blood, were in a cruel grin. With a guttural bellow, she flipped back so abruptly that the riders let go. As she flipped back, she kicked Shark Mask in the chest. He flew nearly five feet.

Everyone, even Devil Mask, watched in shocked silence as he hit the ground in a heap.

Richie just stared. The pounding in his head and chest vanished as a coldness overcame him. "Oh, my God."

Landing gracefully, Sam reached back and pulled her ponytail holder out, shaking loose her hair, still with only that sick grin showing. "Let's play, boys." Her voice had a deep, resonant reverb.

What. The. Hell. Richie's brain froze. He had never heard anyone talk that way before.

Hockey Mask and Snake Mask rushed at her.

Hockey Mask swung his chain so hard the air whistled. Catching it with ease, she pulled him close, kneeing him in the stomach. As he crumpled over, she elbowed him on the back of his head. He fell to the ground. She now had the chain.

Skull Mask swore and then sprinted up the ramp, swinging his baseball bat and yelling obscenities.

Richie again tried to stand, but Clown Mask continued to pin him. For the moment, he was forced to watch Sam fend off her attackers by herself.

It wasn't like she needed the help.

Snake Mask swung his bat at her, but she caught it with the chain and disarmed him. She then jabbed him in the face with it several times before picking him up and throwing him at Skull Mask.

The two crashed in a pile. Skull Mask's bat rolled on the ground.

Clown Mask got off Richie and sprinted up the ramp. Sam picked up the two bats. As he swung his chain, she ducked underneath and hit him twice in the midsection. He fell to the ground in a heap.

She stopped right in front of Richie. Two of the riders were getting back up while Devil Mask started up his motorcycle. Richie looked up at her face. He could see into her eyes.

They were bloodshot. The pupils were heavily dilated. The irises looked cloudy. Those were not the eyes of Sam Castille. They were another's eyes.

He asked, "Who—who are you?"

Her sick grin persisted as she said, "The doctor called me Sam of Spades, little boy."

Richie didn't understand. Sam of Spades was Sam's pen name. *What the hell is going on?*

By now, Shark Mask and Skull Mask were back up and charging her, Shark Mask flicking out a butterfly knife.

She charged and then jumped over them, flipping. She came down on them with her weapons, and they hit the ground with pathetic cries. The knife slid across the concrete floor.

The sound of an engine's roar ripped through the garage as Devil Mask rode past her, swinging his pipe half-heartedly. She ducked with ease.

As he passed Richie, he swung again.

Richie stumbled out of the way and saw Devil Mask making his escape. He was about to sprint after him when an aluminum bat flew right by. Sam had thrown it.

Even though Devil Mask was dozens of yards away, the bat hit him in square in the back with a loud thud. He swerved, grabbing at his back in pain, and nearly fell off the bike before riding away.

Richie shook his head. "Good God, what the hell just happened?" He cautiously looked over at Sam.

Her head was still down and her hair was still over her face, only her cruel grin showing. She picked up the butterfly knife, closed it up with an expert flick, and pocketed it. Stalking up to Shark Mask, the rider who had tried to rape her, she raised the bat and said, "Give my regards to the Lord Baron . . . on your way to hell!"

She swung downward with lethal force . . .

. . . and stopped short of hitting the cowering rider in the head when Richie yelled, "NO!"

The bat hovered an inch above Shark Mask's face. He was shivering and blubbering. All around, the riders were either groaning in agony or gurgling in a stupor—a morbidly beautiful sound. Every one of them would likely end up in the hospital.

Richie thought it was amazing that no one was dead.

Slowly, Sam stood. Her head tilted up and her bangs parted off her face. He saw the look in her eyes—it was the Sam he knew and loved.

"What the hell did I do?" she asked weakly, her voice now normal. Tears streamed down her cheeks.

He started toward her. He wanted to hold her and feel her close to him.

As he neared, she swung the bat. "Don't touch me!"

He jumped back.

She looked at the bat in her hand and dropped it, her lips starting to tremble. It clanked to the ground loudly before rolling down the ramp. Stumbling, she fell to her knees, lowering her head. Her arms and shoulders shook.

"What the hell is happening to me?" Sam asked, looking up. Her face was wet with tears. "Goddamn, Richie! What's going on?"

Again, Richie rushed to her side. This time, she didn't push him away. She just held herself and shivered. He wrapped his arms around her and held her close, stroking her hair, her arms, and her back.

"What's happening to me?" she said repeatedly. "God, what's happening to me?"

"I don't know, Sam," he said, burying his face in her hair. She smelled like the Sam he was familiar with. "We'll find out, OK? We'll get you to a doctor and find out."

"I'm not crazy," she said again. "I'm not crazy, Richie. I swear I'm not."

"I know, honey," he said softly, kissing the top of her head. "I know you're not."

But he wasn't so sure. *If she's not crazy, then what else could it be?*

Chapter 12
Confrontation at the Wharf

Date: Monday, August 10, 1992
Time: 10:00 p.m.
Location: Napoleon Avenue Wharf
Port of New Orleans

It was ten in the evening, and Dixie was at the Napoleon Avenue wharf, the part of the city near the warehouse district where cargo boats would load and unload off the Mississippi River. Nearby, Rodger smoked a cigarette, looking both tired and grumpy. Dixie couldn't blame him. He had been told that they had come here for a secret meeting with Sam, and yet the place looked like it was set up for a sting—which it was.

The area had been specifically cleared out for the operation. Normally, it was completely blanketed by large, metal, rectangular cargo containers. For now, however, a large circular space had been prepared, the containers stacked high on all ends to provide an enclosure. A few containers were even placed inside the open space to give adequate cover in case a fire fight broke out. Nearby, an obscenely tall crane loomed over the area. The only two gaps in the enclosure lead to either Napoleon Avenue or right over the pier and into the Mississippi River.

As she absentmindedly adjusted her safety vest, which was under her overcoat, Dixie surveyed the area. Ouellette wasn't taking any chances with arresting Sam Castille. *It's like he's prepared for a fight.*

"So what gives, Dixie?" Rodger asked as he finished his cigarette. Tugging on his own vest, he sniffed the nighttime air with a look of discomfort. "You really expecting that indigo assassin to come here?"

"Things are too dangerous at this point to mess around with safety, Rodger. We need to wear the vests just in case."

It had taken very little convincing to get Rodger to wear his safety vest. Dixie had only had to mention the indigo assassin who had nearly killed Michael. What had taken more effort had been convincing Rodger to call Sam up at her townhome and ask her to come to the wharf to discuss the Nite Priory.

I didn't want to lie to Rodger. He's not a bad cop. He's just too taken in by Sam's charm. Heck, I almost was. You just don't realize how manipulative someone like her is until it's too late.

If not for the sudden flood of evidence, such as the skin cells in Cheryl's body, Dixie felt she might still be taken in by Sam. Those thoughts set her teeth on edge.

"I don't see why we have to meet Sam out here in this humid weather," said Rodger, leaning against a metal container and rubbing his eyes.

Dixie didn't tell Rodger that the very moment Sam left her townhome to come to the wharf, four detectives and about a dozen uniformed officers entered with a search warrant to remove any and all evidence found. "It's really best that we meet her out here. I don't think her townhome is all that safe anymore."

The truth is that Ouellette wants Rodger right here where he can be watched. If he was at Sam's townhome, he might try to mess up the detectives there. At least here, in front of me and being watched by Ouellette, he won't do anything stupid to compromise our case against Sam. At least, that's what I want to believe. And Ouellette is certain, too, that when push comes to shove, Rodger will choose being a cop over being Sam's uncle. I have to trust the commander with this decision.

Rodger looked around the wharf. "I know. And I agree. It's just that Sam's been through so much. And when I called her, she didn't even pick up. Richie did. He wouldn't go into details, but he said that something happened to them earlier and that Sam was a nervous wreck." He shook his head. "Dixie, I have this bad feeling that someone attacked them."

Dixie frowned. She didn't trust the ground Richie Fastellos walked on. To her, it just sounded like another "Poor Sam" story. She tried to push away the negative thoughts and focus on getting Sam to confess and consent to a blood test.

Headlights appearing just around a stack of metal containers signaled the arrival of Sam's car.

While Dixie couldn't see or hear the other police, she knew they would be ready. Three snipers, one even on top of the large crane, would keep the area covered for the duration of the sting.

Sam's car pulled into the clearing and stopped. Richie was in the driver's seat with Sam in the passenger's. She was leaned against the window, her eyes closed as if sleeping. Richie gently shook her and she sat up. The two looked at each for a lingering moment before getting out of the car.

Dixie looked over the couple's outfits. Sam was dressed in black leather with a red plastic charm dangling from her belt, while Richie was in a dirtied white suit. To Dixie, they both looked ridiculous, especially Richie's red-tinted sunglasses, which he was wearing at night. She closed her eyes and took a deep breath.

All right, time to play the part of the concerned friend.

She put on a smile. She had convinced Ouellette to allow her to try to talk Sam into surrendering, as opposed to the SWAT team rushing in like Arsenault wanted. Ouellette had insisted on the safety phrase "tonight is too hot to handle." One utterance of it, and Arsenault's Arsenal would swarm the area like locusts.

Sam and Richie joined hands in front of the car and headed toward the two detectives, stopping a few feet away. Keeping up her pleasant expression, Dixie noted that Sam looked drained. *Good. If she's exhausted, it might be easier to get her to surrender.*

Well, enough pondering, Dixie. Let's get this started.

Dixie cocked her head toward Sam. "You look like crap, Sam. You gonna be OK to talk?"

She nodded.

"Sam, are you and Richie OK?" Rodger asked. The concern in his voice was apparent.

Dixie sighed softly. Well, a little conversation before jumping into this couldn't hurt.

"Not really." Richie removed his sunglasses and placed them in his jacket. "Unknown people have been leaving threatening letters at Sam's townhome. The other night, someone broke in. We filed a report on that. And tonight, a group of masked people attacked Sam and I. We barely escaped."

Dixie and Rodger traded looks.

"What the hell, Richie," said Rodger. "Why didn't you tell me about all this?"

Dixie didn't say anything. Two attacks and a break in. People were suspecting that Sam was the killer. They were starting to take matters into their own hands. *We need to end this soon.*

While Rodger and Richie started talking about their suspicions that someone at the *Times-Picayune* was leaking that Sam was a suspect, Dixie looked Sam over. Dammit. She couldn't get a read on the other woman. Was she really some kind of sociopath?

Sam's eyes slid in their sockets and met her gaze. Her lips curved into a small grin. With her pasty skin, she looked like porcelain.

What the hell is going on with her anyway, the creepy bitch?

"Dixie, do you think Ouellette will take Sam into protective custody?" asked Rodger.

Dixie glanced over at him, getting pulled back into the conversation. She hadn't been paying attention. She decided to just play along for now, until she could take back control of the conversation. "Probably," she said. "I'm sure we can ask him."

"Would you like that, Sam?" asked Richie. "The police can—"

"Not Ouellette," Sam said, snapping her head up and looking around. It was like she had been actively participating in the conversation the entire time. "I don't want anything to do with him at all. Anyone but him."

Dixie blinked. What the hell was Sam's problem with the commander?

However, Sam now seemed to be fully engaged in the conversation. "So what did you call us out for, Dixie?"

Getting back into the mindset of the game, Dixie said, "I'm here to discuss the Nite Priory. I did some digging of my own and discovered something really important about them." Dixie felt all eyes at the wharf upon her. That was fine. She was about to play hardball with a serial killer.

"Oh, what did you find out, then?" asked Sam. She folded her arms, tilted back her head, and stared down her nose.

Dixie decided that it was time to stop beating around the bush. Something about Sam's shifts in mood, something about her expressions, just made her feel uneasy. She felt certain that the longer this whole thing was drawn out, the higher the chance of a bad outcome got. She needed to stop playing around and start accusing this condescending bitch.

Looking directly into Sam's eyes, she said, "They don't exist. They're bullshit."

The air at the wharf dropped two degrees.

Rodger spoke up first. "Wait, we're talking about the Nite Priory spelled N-I-T-E, right? You're saying that group doesn't exist?"

"Correct," said Dixie. "They're not real. They're fake."

Sam laughed nastily, sneering at her. "What do you mean they're not real? Of course they're real, dammit. Richie—"

"No, Sam, they're not." She produced the paper with the anagram on it, handing it to Sam. "As you can see, 'Nite Priory' is an anagram for 'iron pyrite,' which is fool's gold. It's a sham. A lie. A misdirection."

Sam looked at the paper with genuine disbelief. For a moment, there was a glimmer of recognition in her eyes, and then it vanished as she shook her head. She handed the paper to Richie. "I don't freaking believe this. Never in a million years would I have figured that out. Did you know this, Richie?"

He looked like someone had slapped him across the face. He shook his head. "No. No, that can't be right. I've seen them. I've seen the Nite Priory. I've seen them and I've met them."

Rodger bellowed, "What the hell? You saw them, Richie? You lying son of a bitch! You told me you found them referenced in a book in Sam's townhome."

Dixie couldn't help but smirk. After how he had played her and Aucoin a few nights ago, it was satisfying to see him caught in a lie.

Sam backed away from Richie, looking upset. She squeezed the plastic charm several times. "Richie?" Her tone was one of disbelief. "You lied to Rodger about this? You told the police that you found information about the Nite Priory in my home? Why? Why would you do that to me?"

"I just . . . I just . . ." Richie's voice was already faltering, and he was starting to gibber.

Dixie felt disgusted. *Your boyfriend is pathetic, Sam.*

"Just shut the hell up, Richie," Sam said, anger and hurt coating her voice. "Just don't talk to me. You're such an asshole!"

As Richie covered his face, Dixie moved in for the kill. "It gets worse, Sam, I'm afraid. Not only is the Nite Priory fake, but we found someone who treated themselves to fancy dinners right after each murder. Just like Vincent did."

Sam arched an eyebrow at her. "Oh? Like Grandpa did? Who's that?"

Dixie flashed a little smile. "You, Sam. Care to explain that one?"

Rodger turned to her. "Wait, what now? Dixie? What's this about Sam and dinners?"

Dixie did her best to tune him out, knowing that it was only a matter of time before he realized what was going on. For the moment, she concentrated on the suspect. "I'm waiting, Sam."

Sam shrugged. "I don't have anything to explain, Dixie. I treat myself to delivery from certain places when I'm hungry and working on my stories, because I can afford them. I went out to eat with Richie when we first met, and then I went on a date with him two nights later. What more is there?"

Dixie was disgusted. Sam wasn't even trying to hide it. "So you admit to having a similar modus operandi as your grandfather. You acknowledge that the Nite Priory thing is bullshit. You still can't account for your whereabouts during the times of the actual murders." She shook her head. "I'll be honest with you, Sam, it doesn't look good."

Sam stared at her in disbelief, her expression starting to darken. "It's not enough that I'm a suspect—I'm being accused? Rodger, is this true?"

"That's what I'd like to know," said Rodger, folding his arms and glaring at Dixie. "What's going on here?"

Dixie refused to look at him. She knew that in all probability, it would be a long time before he'd speak to her again. "Right this very moment, Sam, we're tearing your townhome apart looking for something to link you directly to the murders. We will find it. And when we do . . ." Thinking of all the innocent victims and the lives this case had ruined, Dixie's anger burst forth in the most vicious thing she could say. "When we do, it's a short ride on a steel gurney to the death chamber."

"No, no, no, no! I can't believe this," Richie cried out, grabbing his face and stomping around in a circle. His expression was a mixture of anger and anguish. "This is completely ridiculous. Sam has nothing to do with those murders. Nothing! Look, I'm sorry about lying about the Nite Priory, but I saw them kill Marcello and I got scared and—"

Rodger punched him across the jaw and he hit the ground. Sam gasped and jumped back, her hands over her mouth. Rodger's eyes were wild looking, a man barely keeping himself together. "Shut the hell up, you dumbass!" His voice was strained. Turning to Dixie, he asked, "Are we here to arrest Sam?"

Dixie looked at him. His expression was dark, and that made her start to feel anxious. His moment of truth—whether he would choose his duty or his niece—was uncomfortably close. She stood her ground. "Yes, Rodger. That's what I intend to do."

Rodger narrowed his eyes dangerously. "Ouellette told you to keep me in the dark, didn't he? So, tell me, is there hard evidence against Sam?"

Her heart rate increased, for Rodger's expression was uncharacteristic and a little frightening. Her voice cracked some. "Yes, Rodger. Yes to both."

Rodger nodded. "Fine, then."

Looking at Sam, he said, "I'm sorry, Sam. For now, I think you need to come with us. I'm sure it will get sorted out." He looked around the wharf. Dixie figured he was piecing together that this was a sting and that the area was crawling with officers.

He looked back at Sam. "Right now, I want you to get on the ground and put your hands on top of your head. Surrender. Trust me, right now it's the best thing to do."

Dixie said nothing, but on the inside, she sighed with relief. At this critical moment, Rodger chose to be a cop instead of Sam's uncle. *Thank you, Rodger.*

Sam, who had been looking around, uncovered her mouth. "So you're going to arrest me, Rodger? I thought you believed me." Her voice sounded like a hurt little girl's. She continued to squeeze the plastic charm at her waist.

The strength in Rodger's voice cracked. "I do believe you, Sam. I always will. But right now, you're in a very dangerous, unfriendly place. The only reason we're arresting you is because . . ." He looked over at Dixie, prompting her.

"DNA evidence," Dixie said coldly. She could sense how much those words hurt Rodger, his face tightening as he looked away. It made her hate Sam even more. "DNA found in Cheryl Aucoin's body. Skin cells. Once we arrest you, Sam, we'll get a sample and compare your DNA to those cells. It'll match. And then that's it. You're done."

Sam bit her bottom lip and wrinkled her brow. She looked like a child who had just been scolded.

Dixie shook her head. *When you strip her of all her manipulation, Sam Castille is pretty disgusting.*

"You found my DNA in the victim, then?" Sam asked, looking away from everyone else. She then shrugged and looked back into Dixie's eyes. Her voice was cold and emotionless. "Fine, I'll give you a blood sample right now."

Dixie was still processing that when Sam made her move.

She reached into her pocket and whipped out a butterfly knife. With a few flicks of the wrist, she opened it up. Light glinted off the shiny metallic blade.

Holding the knife, she said, "In fact . . ."

Oh, shit, Dixie thought, certain Sam was about to stab her.

The key phrase she had agreed on with the SWAT team caught in her throat. She let out a strained cry and reached for her gun. She was about to shout the phrase and fire when Sam slashed with the knife.

What Dixie saw next made her entire body seize in horror.

Sam's forearm was bright crimson as blood dripped from the long cut she had made. "In fact . . . take all you need, Detective!" She held up her bleeding arm. Her voice was no longer cold and emotionless. It was firm and commanding, like she was giving an order.

"I have had enough of this shit," she said, her voice projecting with an anger released after years of suppression. "I am fucking tired of it. Every day of my life for the past twenty years, I have lived with the shadow of my grandfather looming over me like a curse. I don't sleep, and when I do, every dream is a goddamn nightmare. I close my eyes and I suffer like my grandfather's victims suffered. That's been my life, Detective. Pain and misery!"

Dixie's eyes were wide, her shoulders and hands shaking. She was frozen in Sam's gaze. It was unnatural how that gaze held her captive, like a predator and its prey. *Insane! She's totally insane.*

Sam held out her bleeding arm. "The only people who have ever given me a chance have been these two men here and Jacob. And I sure as hell don't want them to get pulled into the miasma of my fucked-up family."

She walked toward Dixie, blood dripping from her arm, pattering on the ground like raindrops. Her voice got deeper and more menacing. "So go on, Detective Olivier. Take my blood. Match it to the killer if you can. Lock me away. Execute me. I don't give a shit anymore. It'll be an escape from this hell I live through. I'd welcome the cold embrace of death instead of the torture of life."

All of Dixie's confidence about Sam's guilt was thrown to the wind. Was Sam a sociopathic killer? Was she a tortured soul? Was she suffering from an insanity she'd had since childhood? Dixie didn't know anymore. Sam's behavior was incomprehensible. Real people didn't act this way.

Sam went on, "You want to be the one to take down the Bourbon Street Ripper? You want that? Go on! His princess is right here. Take her, if you dare!" She pushed her injured arm forward, splattering her blood on Dixie. "What are you waiting for, Detective? Arrest me! I surrender!"

Dixie felt Sam's hot blood splash on her face. She cried out, panic penetrating her heart for the first time in years. Sam's sudden psychotic break brought back vivid memories of how her father had abruptly snapped. Images of her father beating her big sister played out in bone-breaking reality. For every drop of Sam's blood on her face, she saw, heard, and felt every one of those blows.

Then the deep, booming voice of Sergeant Arsenault rang out. "Freeze! On your knees or I'll blow your fucking head off, bitch!" He was heading into the clearing, holding an automatic shotgun on Sam.

Rodger's eyes got wide and he rushed toward Sam. "I've got the suspect covered. I've got her covered! Sam, listen, please drop the weapon and surrender."

Snapped out of her flashback, Dixie stepped away, putting distance between herself and Sam. She felt, for the first time in her life, that she was looking at a real case for the insanity defense. Any certainty that Sam was a cold-blooded and manipulative killer was gone. For now, she was only certain that this situation was rapidly spiraling out of control.

"Back the fuck off, Bergeron," Arsenault boomed at Rodger. "This crazy bitch is in my sights. She'll never hurt anyone again. She needs to get on her knees and surrender!"

"Sergeant! Stand down!" Ouellette said over a loudspeaker. "Bergeron has the suspect covered. Stand down!"

"Yes, sir, I'll stand down," Arsenault roared back. "As soon as this psycho-bitch drops her weapon and gets on her fucking knees. You told me to make sure no one got hurt, and that's what I'm doing, Commander."

Dixie stared at him. The lighting at the wharf made him look even more menacing. She couldn't tell if his threats were real or a feint. She had heard stories of his over-use of force, but even this seemed too much.

"Arsenault, stand down—that is an order," Ouellette boomed over the loudspeaker again. "Bergeron, for fuck's sake, take Samantha into custody. Do not let this get out of control!"

Dixie drew her pistol and pointed it at Sam. "Please, Rodger, get the knife from her. Sam, listen to me, please. If you don't drop that weapon right now, this officer is going to kill you. Please, for God's sake, drop the weapon."

Richie moaned and started to get up. His expression was decidedly deer-in-the-headlights. "Sam? Rodger? What the hell is going on?"

Meanwhile, Rodger had slowly approached Sam. When she saw him, her gaze softened. He reached out for the knife, but she jerked her hand back. He spoke in a low and controlled tone as he said, "Sam, listen to me. We have to arrest you. Please don't fight back. This is serious. They will kill you. Please don't make Edward watch his daughter die like this."

"Yeah, little Sam," taunted Arsenault. "Don't make Daddy watch you die like a bitch. Now drop the knife and get on your goddamn knees before my trigger finger gets too itchy and I blow your brains out by accident!"

Dixie was horrified. Arsenault was throwing gasoline onto a fire. "What the hell is wrong with you, Arsenault? We've got it under control. We've—"

Sam's voice once again got deep and menacing. And it started to reverberate in an unnatural way. "You have nothing, Detective ."

Dixie snapped her head over to look at Sam.

Her eyes were cloudy, her pupils were dilated, her face was even paler, and she was tilting her head to the side. She was also staring at Arsenault with a condescending smile. It looked like she was sizing him up. "This one needs to learn its place," she said, flipping the butterfly knife and catching it by the blade. "Perhaps I should throw this into its eye? Or maybe its throat? Would that shut it up?"

Arsenault grinned widely. "That's assault against an officer. Big mistake, bitch."

As he pumped his shotgun, Sam cocked her arm back, ready to throw.

Oh, God, no . . . Dixie felt her stomach drop. Any second now, the sound of gunfire would fill the air.

Instead, it was a scream.

"Aaaaaaaaahhhhhhhhhhhhh—" came a voice from above.

The scream had come from the sniper once positioned on top of the crane. When his body hit the ground, it folded in half like a lawn chair, making a sickeningly wet sound accompanied by blood splattering. Some of it splashed on Arsenault's face.

Dixie looked at the top of the crane. So did Arsenault. So did everyone else.

A figure holding a rifle and dressed in an indigo hooded robe with black gloves and a skull mask had also leaped from the crane. Arsenault looked up just in time to have the indigo assassin land on his face.

The impact was so hard that Arsenault's face caved in, making a sound similar to crunching ice. The indigo assassin bent her knee as she landed on him, using his body to absorb the shock of the fall. Pushing herself off, she did a forward flip and landed a few yards away.

Dixie was stunned. Somehow, the indigo assassin had jumped from the top of the crane and landed precisely on a target the size of a basketball, all without any harm to herself. No human being could do that.

Arsenault was gurgling on his own blood and struggling not to fall. His face was caved in; an eye had popped out and was hanging by the nerve. With what must have been a monumental force of will, he raised his shotgun toward the indigo assassin.

A shot fired out, the sound resounding throughout the wharf.

The indigo assassin, while still facing Dixie and the others, had just pointed her rifle backward and shot Arsenault in the head. The rounds must have been explosive, because there was nothing left of it. Arsenault's lifeless body fell back, hitting the edge of the pier and flipping into the water.

Dixie stared. What she had just seen was impossible.

As she recovered her senses, she realized that the members of SWAT Team Alpha were coming out, weapons trained on the indigo assassin.

Ouellette called out. "Team Bravo, answer me! Team Charlie, answer me! Team Delta! Snipers Two and Three! Someone, anyone, fucking answer me!"

Oh, my God. She killed them all. All the other SWAT teams. While everyone else was preoccupied with us, she was killing all of them. That's why no one is answering.

The indigo assassin cocked her head toward the approaching police, and then did a back flip, going several yards into the air. SWAT Team Alpha opened fire.

Dixie watched as the indigo assassin began a series of flips, rolls, and other acrobatic moves. They were moves no normal human could perform, dodging bullets while firing the rifle with one hand. In less than a minute, every member of SWAT Team Alpha was either dead or writhing on the ground in agony, limbs blown clear off.

Once again, she felt helpless as she watched the carnage unfold. *What kind of monster is this?* She didn't say anything until Ouellette's voice had died down. Then she asked no one in particular, "Who . . . who is this person?"

While Sam seemed to have returned to normal, her expression was still grave. She put away the butterfly knife. "I believe that's Blind Moses."

"What?" Rodger said, shocked. "That's Blind Moses?"

Richie was also in shock. "Violet said Blind Moses would seek you out soon, Sam. Shouldn't we leave?"

Sam didn't answer. Instead, she stepped toward the indigo assassin. "Blind Moses, I presume?"

The assassin nodded. Her white skull mask looked just like the design on Jonathan's oxygen mask. *A voodoo death mask?*

Blind Moses pointed her rifle at Sam, holding the weapon in one hand. Her aim was rock-steady. Dixie knew enough about firearms to recognize that no human being had either the strength or control to accurately aim a rifle with one hand. But Blind Moses was doing just that.

This person wasn't human. Sam had no chance. Dixie felt a sudden surge of fear for her. "Stop!" she shouted, putting herself between the two. She pointed her weapon at the assassin. "Blind Moses, is it? Put your hands up where I can see them."

She wasn't sure where this sudden courage was coming from. It felt instinctual. Sam, suspect or not, was clearly being threatened by a superior foe.

Sam gasped. "Dixie, stop! What are you doing?"

Dixie held her gun on Blind Moses, her hands starting to shake. "What am I doing? My job, Sam. You may or may not be our killer. But like everyone else, you deserve fair treatment under the law. This Blind Moses seems to have no intention of letting you leave here alive."

She wasn't sure what was going on anymore. What she had just seen Blind Moses do defied all logic and reason. Too many things were happening too quickly. However, she was certain of two things: she was an officer of the law, and Sam wasn't the one who had just murdered dozens of police officers. *Sam, we'll sort you out later. Right now, it's my job to protect you.*

Blind Moses started walking toward them both.

"I said stop," she commanded again, cocking back the hammer of her gun.

Blind Moses continued walking forward, lifting her rifle and pointing it at her.

"Detective Olivier, stand down," Ouellette's voice cried out over the loudspeaker. "Do not get between Blind Moses and Sam. Do you hear me? Stand down. That's an order!"

Dixie didn't back down. "Protect and serve, Commander. I can't ignore that." Her hands were shaking, her aim was unsteady. She was so scared.

She inhaled deeply through her nose, then exhaled through her mouth, focusing. Her hands stopped shaking. *On my honor, I will never betray my badge, my integrity, my character, or the public trust. I will always have the courage to hold myself and others accountable for our actions. I will always uphold the Constitution, my community, and the agency I serve.*

Dixie's aim centered on Blind Moses's heart.

"Last chance, Blind Moses. Drop your weapon and lie on the ground." Her voice was strong and controlled.

Blind Moses continued to walk forward, rifle pointed at her.

She clenched her jaw. This was it. Her trigger finger started to squeeze.

From behind her, Sam gasped out, "Dixie, no!"

I'm so sorry, Gino. Dixie thought of the dark-skinned beauty that had waltzed into her life and taught her how to cherish every precious moment. She saw his smile, his eyes, his love, as he told her he'd be waiting.

I won't be coming home tonight.

Two shots fired, the sounds resonating throughout the wharf.

Chapter 13
The Good and the Bad

Date: Monday, August 10, 1992
Time: 11:59 p.m.
Location: Napoleon Avenue Wharf
     Port of New Orleans

In her first meeting with Dr. Klein, Samantha Castille had said nothing, as had he. For an entire hour, they had sat and stared at each other across his office desk. To her, it had been a surreal experience, as if she had been watching a movie of the two of them just staring at each other. At the end of the hour, he had leaned forward and said, "Zis vas a very informative session, Samantha. I thank you."

The second session had been much the same: the two staring at each other, him tapping his fingers together while studying her, and her sitting in her day dress, staring wordlessly up at him. It had been the same for the third session, then the fourth, and then the fifth. Each time, at the end of the session, he would thank her, saying it had been "very informative."

On the sixth session, she had finally spoken, asking, "I don't want to be here anymore. When can I stop coming?"

His answer had been, "Ven you are better."

When she had asked when she'd be better, he had said, "Ven it is only Samantha I am talking to, und no one else."

As the months and years went on, she started talking more and more. She started talking about school, and about becoming a writer, about how much she loved Auntie Marguerite and hated

Auntie Gladys, and even about living on her own after her sixteenth birthday. However, in a session one afternoon in April of 1979, she got a reaction she had never gotten before.

"I'm thinking of shortening my name," Samantha had said. "I want to call myself Sam."

Dr. Klein had gone ballistic. He had stood up and exclaimed that he had spent too many years with Samantha for her to throw away everything that they had accomplished together. His face had been so red and his voice had been so loud that she had had to cover her ears. He had then immediately prescribed a round of rather strong barbiturates for the terrified seventeen-year-old girl.

After that incident, things went smoothly so long as she never referred to herself as "Sam" in front of him. Every time she did, he would get furious, to the point of yelling at her for ruining "all the hard work they'd done." Then he would prescribe another round of stronger medicine.

She hadn't been sure what she was getting out of the sessions. Oftentimes, they'd stare at each other without saying a word.

Finally, one day, she had asked him why she couldn't call herself Sam.

His response had made no sense. "Because you are Samantha Castille, not Sam. Samantha was victimized by her murderous grandfather. Samantha is a good girl who wants to live a normal life. That is who you are. Samantha. Not Sam."

But outside of her sessions with Dr. Klein, Sam had never gotten those surreal, distant feelings. Not until the night of August 10, 1992. First, when she was being attacked in the parking lot with Richie, and later when she was being accused by Dixie at the wharf. Both times, Sam had felt as if she were watching things happen instead of being in control.

Therefore, when Blind Moses appeared and destroyed the SWAT team, Sam felt what little hold she had on reality melt away. The past twenty years, the waking nightmares, the constant insomnia, the ever-increasing prescriptions, and the confusing sessions with Dr. Klein—everything came crashing down at once.

She had just stood there, transfixed, for most of the fight.

But when Dixie stood between her and Blind Moses, it jarred her back into reality enough to appreciate the gravity of the situation. Watching as Dixie faced off against an obviously superior foe, she cried out, "Dixie, no!"

Violet had said that Blind Moses would seek her out. This meant that she was the real target, and that Dixie was risking her life to protect her. Suddenly, she was terrified for Dixie's life.

Stop! What the hell are you doing?

Both Dixie and Blind Moses fired at the same time. However, Blind Moses twisted to the side and dodged while Dixie did not. Sam felt herself get distant again.

Dixie, no!

In the blink of an eye, she pushed Dixie. It was just enough to keep the bullet from striking her chest, and instead it struck her left elbow, promptly exploding. Hot, red blood, chunks of muscle, and bits of bone splattered everywhere. What was left of her arm fell to the ground.

Dixie screamed in agony. Both women were knocked to the ground.

Sam rolled several times and slowly got up. Her body hurt all over from the impact, but despite her own pain, she rushed to Dixie's side.

Dixie was holding what was left of her arm, shaking as she tried to squeeze the stump. There was enough pressure that the blood squirted past her fingers, coating Sam's face, hair, and chest.

"Help!" Sam cried out, trying to help Dixie hold back the lethal bleeding. "She's bleeding out! Help us!"

In a moment, Rodger and Richie were at their side. Richie's face was pale. Rodger seemed to be on auto-pilot, taking off his belt and telling Richie to remove his jacket. It looked like they were making an improvised tourniquet.

All the while, Dixie stared up into Sam's eyes. Sam's heart pounded in her chest as she looked wildly back at her, not sure what she could do to help save her life.

Dixie's eyes showed sincere regret. "I'm sorry, Sam." She then went limp, her eyes closing.

"Dixie, no!" Rodger screamed. "Commander! We need a bus now! Dixie's dying!"

Sam's heart rate slowed. She felt Dixie's blood on her face. She also felt a nearly uncontrollable urge to start harming anyone around her. So she focused on Blind Moses, who shouldered her gun and stared back. The two faced off against each other.

"So, then, Violet was right. You're here for me, aren't you?" Sam asked softly.

It was obvious that Blind Moses heard her, because she nodded. Her hearing was somehow heightened.

"What do you want with me?" Sam asked, still speaking just as quietly.

Blind Moses said nothing. She just made a slashing motion over her throat.

"You want to kill me?" Sam asked, not at all surprised. "Why not just do it already?" She felt she knew the answer to that as well.

Blind Moses pointed to herself, then to Sam, and then made a fist and shook it.

"I see. You want me to fight you one on one. You want to defeat me. You want to best me." Sam reached down and squeezed the shoe charm that dangled from her belt.

She felt several things at once. She felt a tingle, like every nerve was shivering. She also felt an even more intense craving to inflict harm on others. But beyond that, she felt something even stronger—a deeply rooted hatred for Blind Moses. It was as if the next logical action was to leap on her and rip her throat out with her teeth.

It was a similar feeling as when she had confronted Violet Patterson, but exponentially stronger. She felt as though her life could not continue if she didn't fight against Blind Moses and win. With a few flicks of the wrist, she popped out the butterfly knife once more.

"Very well," she said in almost a whisper. "We fight to the death. But leave everyone else out of it. This is between you and me."

Blind Moses nodded again, pulling out a rose-colored capsule from a pocket. She pantomimed breaking it open and then tossed it to Sam.

Sam caught it and sniffed. It had a distinctive fruit smell. "You want me to inhale this?"

Blind Moses nodded once more.

Sam became aware of the shouting behind her, followed up by Ouellette saying, "Let me see her. Dixie? Oh, my God."

Richie shouted, "Sam! What the hell are you doing? Get back!"

She turned to look. The remaining police were lining up, pistols and rifles at the ready. Ouellette was standing to face her and Blind Moses.

Smiling softly at Richie, she said, "I love you." She gave her plastic shoe charm one more squeeze.

She faced Blind Moses and then cracked the capsule open. Instantly, pinkish-red powder billowed up. She inhaled deeply, getting her lungs full of it. A moment later, she dropped to her knees as every part of her body lit up in pain.

Holding herself, Sam screeched as she felt her head pound with agony. She felt an electric shock rip down her spine, every nerve in her body firing off at the same time. Her heart beat so fast it felt like it would burst, and her senses went into overdrive.

She could see the fibers on Blind Moses's clothes. She could hear the heartbeats of everyone around her. She could smell the lingering gunpowder from the shots fired. She could taste the microscopic blood particles still floating in the air and clinging to the humidity. Those headaches, which had been plaguing her all her life, felt as if they were encompassing her entire being.

Rodger cried out, "Sam! What the hell! What have you—Sam! No!"

Then she felt her sense of self get pulled into the very back of her mind as if by another mental force, only allowing her to watch what she was seeing and doing. This time, she knew that someone else was in control. She watched as she removed the wrap from her hair, her ponytail falling out and her blood-matted bangs covering her face.

Ouellette called out, "Get ready to open fire on Blind Moses. Samantha Castille, get down or we will open fire on you as well! Do you hear me? Samantha Castille, get down now!"

Sam wasn't sure what was going on. Her voice was deeper and had an unnatural reverb to it. And she was no longer in control. Someone or something else was speaking through her. "There is no Samantha."

She watched as she stood and peered at Blind Moses from behind those bloody bangs. "I am Sam." She felt a sick, cruel grin spread over her face.

Blind Moses hoisted her rifle in preparation to fight.

She felt herself look back at Ouellette. She felt her teeth bared like fangs. She heard herself say, "You may call me . . . Sam of Spades."

Ouellette's eyes widened. "Open fire, now!"

Sam felt herself smirk and then felt herself somehow force adrenaline to rush through her system. All around her, the world slowed down to a crawl. The cries of those behind her were incomprehensible slurs, the sound of the arriving ambulance was a whale's song, and the police gunshots were corks popping off wine bottles. Only Blind Moses moved at her speed.

What is going on here? What's happening to me?

Blind Moses dashed at her, and her body did likewise. All around them, bullets from the police whizzed by sluggishly, as if going through water.

Why, why can't I control my own body?

Blind Moses fired upon her, three successive shots. Sam's body bent back, the bullets flying inches from her nose.

I . . . I can dodge bullets? That's impossible! No one can move that fast.

Sam's body flung herself forward and cut at Blind Moses, who dodged and knocked the butterfly knife out of her hand and into the air.

The police continued shooting at them. While most of the bullets whizzed past, one knocked the plastic shoe charm from her hip.

No! Mother's charm! Another bullet grazed her thigh. She mentally cried out in pain, even though she was unable to move.

Then she heard a different voice speak, the one that had spoken out loud earlier. It spoke within her head—all her body did was grit its teeth.

"Shut up, you stupid little girl!" said the voice, thick with frustration. It was deep and rumbling but still sounded female.

Sam's body punched Blind Moses into the air with an inhuman level of strength.

However, Sam hardly noticed that, as she was too shocked by the other voice and its response. She could only assume that this voice belonged to the other presence she felt within her. It felt like this "other" did not care for her one bit.

Who the hell are you? she asked the voice.

"*Sam of Spades. Now shut up and let me concentrate!*"

Sam of Spades, in control of Sam's body, flew up with Blind Moses, catching the butterfly knife. As Blind Moses started aiming the rifle, she moved to push it away.

Bullets from the police still buzzed past them.

Sam of Spades? Sam thought. *That's my pen name. What do you mean?*

Sam of Spades wavered in her actions, as if the inner dialogue was causing her to hesitate. "*Your doctor gave me that name. And gave you the pen name. Idiot!*" Sam of Spades pushed the rifle to the side just as it fired. Three bullets flew past Sam's head.

But that doesn't make any sense, Sam said to the voice. *How can it be that you're here now, after all these years?*

Sam of Spades landed and looked up, focusing on the pistol attached to Blind Moses's hip. She made a grab for it, but was knocked back when Blind Moses kicked her in the chest.

Sam flew back, pain exploding inside her, crying out.

Her body slid back from the impact, then caught herself. Sam of Spades said, "*You're distracting me from the fight. Shut your mouth and enjoy the ride.*"

Sam shrieked hysterically in her mind, *No! Answer me! How can you be in my body now?*

"*I'm not new, you pathetic child,*" said the voice. "*Remember all those times you've blacked out? Or stared blankly?*"

You mean like earlier tonight in the parking lot? And in all my old sessions with Dr. Klein?

"*That's always when I've been in control.*" The voice sounded distracted as Sam of Spades rushed in at Blind Moses, stabbing repeatedly and pushing her back as the assassin parried each blow with the butt of her rifle.

Why have I never been aware of you until now? Sam was terrified. She felt she no longer owned her own body.

Blind Moses thrust the butt of her rifle toward Sam's shoulder.

Her body ducked out of the way while a few stray bullets from the police cut some strands of her hair. *"Hell if I know,"* said Sam of Spades. *"Probably that pink stuff."*

Are you a part of me? Sam asked, fearful of having a split personality.

Sam of Spades stabbed upward at Blind Moses's gut.

The assassin caught Sam's wrist, stopping the knife.

The momentary distraction was enough for Sam of Spades to grab the pistol. She then fired the pistol at Blind Moses, who dodged by flipping backward and kicking at Sam's head.

Sam's body jumped back, avoiding the kick as Blind Moses landed from the flip. The two paused a moment to regroup as the police reloaded.

"I doubt it. I'm nothing like you," said the voice, dripping with disdain. *"I don't remember anymore. Those drugs Dr. Klein fed you muddled my memory. And they usually kept me trapped inside, but whenever you'd get too stressed, I'd get a chance to come out and play. Remember that rash of assaults at your college? That was me."*

Sam was stunned. *I . . . I attacked those people? Have I killed anyone? Tell me, please!* She felt growing desperation.

Only Ouellette's voice came through the haze, barking out orders.

"No, those drugs always limited my time in control and inhibited my rage," said the voice. *"But recently, shit has gotten real enough that those drugs aren't holding me back. Besides, I . . . I really hate this bitch. I don't know why, but I've never felt so compelled to kill anyone before."*

I don't understand! What are you? Sam asked the voice. Things had never been so confusing.

Sam of Spades dove at Blind Moses, who bounded back toward some cargo crates, firing three shots at her. She dodged by spinning to the side.

"I told you, I don't know," the voice said angrily. *"Dr. Klein is convinced that I'm a darker version of you, another personality. He thinks you created me to deal with all the trauma you suffered. Hell if I know for sure."*

Sam of Spades sprinted toward the cargo crates as Blind Moses jumped on top of them. With a powerful leap, the blond woman soared high into the air, flipping over Blind Moses. Both fired at each other.

This isn't possible! she cried out. *No one can jump that high.*

Blind Moses dodged to the side, a few bullets grazing her robe. One of her own three bullets came inches from Sam's head.

"I can do things with this body that a weakling like you never could," said Sam of Spades, her voice once again thick with disdain. *"You can't even face what really happened to your father."*

Sam landed in a secluded area surrounded by those cargo crates.

Blind Moses jumped high into the air, the moon behind her. While airborne, she fired three shots at Sam.

Wait, what do you mean? Sam asked. *What about Papa?*

Sam of Spades bent like a reed. The first two bullets whizzed past. The third, however, grazed her pants, slicing her skin like it was a hot knife through butter. Sam felt pain that she could do nothing about.

The voice grunted. *"See? If you keep distracting me, we're going to die. This bitch is not joking around. She's trying to kill us."*

Sam of Spades stood upright as Blind Moses started to come down, poised like a scarecrow, the moon looming behind her. The skull mask glistened. For a moment, Sam saw into Blind Moses's steely blue eyes. She saw only remorselessness.

Tell me what you meant about Papa! Sam felt indignant. *All my life, I've been plagued by nightmares and half-memories of what my grandfather did. Tell me what happened!*

Blind Moses kicked down at Sam, who dodged as Blind Moses landed, missing. The impact made the ground crack.

The voice started to laugh. It was a cruel and unpleasant sound. *"You can't handle it,"* Sam of Spades said. *"You locked that memory away inside of me. Dr. Klein said it would destroy you. You're too weak to deal with it."*

No! I want to know. I don't care what happens, Sam said.

"Fine, then! If you're that intent on destroying yourself, be my guest," said the voice, thick with frustration. *"Here is that memory you've locked away for so very long. Enjoy it and adios, Princess!"*

A white light started to appear before Sam, like a movie projector that was out of film.

Sam of Spades threw her knife at Blind Moses, who caught it effortlessly.

The white light encompassed Sam's consciousness completely.

When her vision returned, Sam still felt like she was watching her life. Now it was like everything was grainy and old, like an 8 mm film. She was in Vincent's study, wearing a pretty day dress and sitting on his lap.

"Can you do that, Grandpa, really? I don't have to be afraid any-more?" she asked, her eyes widening.

"For you, my darling Sam," he replied, hugging her, "I will do anything. No matter the cost."

Then the scene shifted, and Sam saw the world through ten-year-old Samantha's eyes.

Vincent was stepping away from her, holding a needle. She was sitting in a comfortable chair in the middle of what looked like a me-dieval torture chamber. Her body was completely immobile. It wasn't hard to infer what had just happened.

No . . . Grandfather injected me with something? I couldn't move? I was trapped within my own mind? Is this when I started locking myself away from reality?

Vincent, stepping back with empty syringe in hand, said, "Now you will get what you have asked for, my dearest Sam. And Magnolia will rest in peace."

He walked over to an operating table, where a bound and gagged Edward Castille lay. He took out a shiny silver pen and scribbled notes, appraising his work. "Now, this is the important part, Sam. Always take notes. It helps you organize and remember. Everything happens as you desire when you take proper notes."

Clearing his throat, he began. "Subject is Caucasian male, forty-two years old, six foot even, and two hundred ten pounds. Name is Edward Castille."

Taking a scalpel, he said, "We will start with the removal of the tendons of the left elbow."

For Samantha, and for adult Sam, the show was very long and very gruesome. Tendons were cut, muscles were excised, veins and arteries were pinched off, joints were severed, limbs were removed, and wounds were cauterized. During the entire process, Vincent was as clinical as possible, explaining his actions as if he were giving a lecture. Edward screamed constantly into the gag, kept alive and conscious with a combination of circulatory, respiratory, and intravenous machines located to the side of the table—all the miracles of medical science used to prolong his life . . . and his suffering.

When Edward was nothing more than a breathing torso, Vincent removed the gag and said, "The subject will now apologize to Samantha for what he has done."

Edward locked eyes with hers. "I love you, Samantha! I love you, my little magnolia!"

She sat still the whole time, unable to move, unable to blink. Her eyes were wide and staring even as Vincent opened her father's chest with the Y-shaped cut of an autopsy. Edward finally died when Vincent cut out his heart with a scalpel and forceps.

He held Edward's heart up and said, "Do you see what I've done for you, Sam? Isn't it wonderful, Sam! Isn't it wonderful?"

At that moment, Rodger came bursting in and arrested him.

And then the memory was done, and Sam was watching her body fighting Blind Moses as it had before.

Sam of Spades, whoever or whatever you are, I remember now. I was forced to watch my grandfather murder my father. I was so terrified. I don't know if I created you to deal with things, but I did use you to lock away that memory. I'm sorry.

What she had witnessed had, indeed, disturbed her to the core. However, the feeling that remained wasn't hatred or rage, nor was it despair. It was resolve. A powerful resolve to put an end to the madness that had plagued her life since childhood. Finally, Sam was ready to face being a Castille—the good and the bad.

Blind Moses was throwing the knife back at Sam. The voice in control of her body was too distracted to dodge in time. The knife embedded itself in her shoulder. The pain was immediate.

The voice cried out in agony. *"You're still here? That's just great, Princess, but I'm kind of busy right now. So shut the hell up! You can't handle this kind of reality."*

Blind Moses did a cartwheel and kicked at Sam. Her body blocked, but the impact made her fly back against a cargo crate. The pistol flew out of her hand.

Sam felt her resolve strengthening. With every second, she felt more and more disgust at how she had spent a lifetime running away from her problems. She was tired of running.

No, Sam said to the voice.

"What did you say?" The voice was low and intense.

I said no! I can handle this.

Blind Moses rushed forward with a powerful and precise kick that connected to Sam's chest, knocking her back.

"Every time you've gotten too stressed, I've come forward. I am definitely stronger than you!"

Sam felt that might have once been true, but she was determined not to be weak anymore. *You're wrong!*

With the internal debate going on, Sam was almost defenseless. Blind Moses started to hit her with a series of punches and kicks that made her cough up blood, turning her abdomen into minced meat.

"You think you can push me back, little Princess?" said the voice, deep and guttural. *"I'd like to see you try. Anyway, you get rid of me, and you're killing us both."*

I doubt it, Sam thought with sudden indignation. *I might die here today, but I sure as hell won't go back to living with my head in the sand. I'm a Castille. I saw my grandfather murder my father. I've got a mountain of problems. But one of those problems will not be watching my body move on its own. If I win only one battle today, it will be to push you back down where you belong!*

Sam of Spades threw up a wild block and pushed, knocking Blind Moses back.

Blind Moses kicked, knocking Sam once more against the cargo crate. Taking a few steps back, she then cartwheeled, aiming both feet at Sam's chest.

Sam could tell that this blow was potentially lethal.

Whether I made you, or whether you're something else, this is my body. You want to lend me your power to kill Blind Moses? Fine, but I'm the one in control. From this day forward, for the rest of my life, I'm in control. I will never lose control of my body, or my life, again. Do you hear me? I control my life!

As Sam said that, she pushed everything she had forward, as if clawing through a forest of tangled briar weeds. The pain in her head was excruciating, and she felt this other presence pushing back with claws and fangs. Sam screeched internally as she ripped through the tangled briar, pushing past years of self-doubt, insecurity, and fear. Every ounce of what Sam was pushed forward until she was once again experiencing the world, instead of just observing it.

And then she was in control.

Blind Moses's attack was suddenly stopped in midair as Sam caught her by the ankles. Sam caught a brief glimpse of her own eyes in Blind Moses's mask.

They were no longer hollow, no longer devoid of life.

They were no longer filled with rage, cruelty, or ugliness.

They were full. They were strong.

And they were her own.

"I'm going to kick your ass, Blind Moses," said Sam. Again she grinned. But this time, it wasn't with cruelty. It was with confidence.

Chapter 14

Blind Moses

Date: **Tuesday, August 11, 1992**
Time: **12:15 a.m.**
Location: **Napoleon Avenue Wharf**
               Port of New Orleans

Sam felt absolutely incredible. She was in control and yet had all the power of Sam of Spades. She felt as if she could do anything—it was a sensation of complete invincibility. She knew she could defeat Blind Moses.

After catching Blind Moses's kick, she spun her around by her ankles and threw her into the side of a cargo crate. Blind Moses landed with a hard impact.

Immediately, Sam felt time speed back up to normal. She heard Ouellette shouting. She saw flashing red and blue lights everywhere. She knew that even once she defeated Blind Moses, she'd still have to contend with the police.

Fine. I can handle them.

She grabbed the knife embedded in her shoulder. The intense desire she felt to kill her opponent made her animosity toward Violet seem like child's play.

Blind Moses started to get up, leveling her rifle at Sam.

Sam smirked. *It's on now, you bitch.* With a hard yank, she pulled out the knife. Fresh blood poured from the wound. The moment she saw it, she willed herself back into the state where time slowed down. Once again, every nerve in her body tingled, the world slowed to a crawl, and every sense became acute. She could see, hear, and feel every detail around her.

Sam picked up the pistol. She already had it leveled at Blind Moses while her opponent was still aiming the rifle.

"Bang," she said, firing off two shots.

Blind Moses's eyes widened for a moment. She swiftly threw herself to the side in a spin. The bullets whizzed past her. As soon as she landed, she ran out to the open part of the wharf. Sam gave chase.

Once out in the open, Sam saw that an ambulance had arrived and that EMTs were on Dixie. She also saw that dozens of police cars had arrived, and that the uniformed officers were setting up a perimeter around the area where they were.

As soon as Ouellette saw them, he ordered the officers to back away. He stared intently at Sam.

She gritted her teeth, momentarily locking eyes with him. *He'll let us fight it out and kill each other, and then he'll arrest whoever survives.*

Anger flared up inside her, although she didn't know why she hated him so much.

Rodger and Richie were running toward the fight, but they moved so slowly, they might as well have been crawling.

Sam focused on her opponent again just as Blind Moses aimed at her and fired off three shots.

She jumped into the air, flipping. She heard the bullets fly underneath her. She then drove both feet into Blind Moses's face, letting loose with a ferocious yell.

Blind Moses let out a yelp of pain and fell back, sliding along with Sam almost standing on her face. The two traveled to the edge of the pier.

Sam hopped back and aimed her gun. Again, a surge of hatred for Blind Moses bubbled up to the surface. Aiming at her opponent's head, she pulled the trigger.

However, Blind Moses was already attacking. She kicked up, knocking the pistol out of Sam's hand. The bullet hit the metal cord holding the crane's payload. It started to fray. The pistol flew upward and landed on the crane's scaffolding. Blind Moses flipped up to her feet.

Sam brandished her knife and growled. "You'll pay for that."

Blind Moses shrugged, and the two charged at each other, Sam stabbing.

Blind Moses parried again with the butt of her rifle, knocking the knife way up and into the Mississippi River.

This time, however, Sam was ready. "My turn!" Doing a back flip, she kicked the rifle out of Blind Moses's hands. It also flew up into the crane's scaffolding.

Blind Moses jerked her head toward the rifle as it flew away. She then looked back at Sam.

Sam shrugged.

Blind Moses shook her head and pointed up.

Sam looked up. The cord holding the crane's payload, a large bundle of metal poles, had broken. They were falling down upon both of them.

Her shoulders dropped. *You gotta be kidding me . . .*

Both of them jumped back as the metal poles landed with a deafening crash.

One of the shorter poles bounced toward Sam, who caught it, spun it around, and held it at the ready. Grinning at Blind Moses, she again motioned for her to come. "Just bring it."

Instead, Blind Moses grabbed a pole about her height and sprinted toward the crane. She used it to vault up and land on the lattice. With a series of jumps, pole still in hand, she started to ascend the scaffolding toward where the guns lay.

Rushing forward, Sam jumped to the side and rolled as the rest of the metal poles crashed to the ground. She was vaguely aware of Richie and Rodger hurtling out of the way but was too focused on the fight to notice anything else.

Reaching the base of the crane, she noticed that its sides were studded with large rivets, about the size of the nubs on rock-climbing walls. Without losing any momentum, she jumped and stepped on the first rivet. Pushing up, she ran up the side of the crane, using the rivets as steps.

The two arrived at the scaffolding at the same time.

"Blind Moses, face me!" Sam cried out.

Blind Moses turned and saw that Sam was armed. She slammed her pole down on her knee, breaking it in half. She then brandished the two weapons and approached.

Sam chortled. *Neat trick. I'll have to try that with her face.*

Rushing forward, they entered into a flurry of blows, each trying to overpower the other. Sam kept spinning her pole around to keep Blind Moses at a distance, while Blind Moses used her twin weapons to try to overpower Sam. As they clashed, their weapons hit so hard and fast that sparks flew.

Sam grinned as she fought. Despite it being a duel to the death, she had never felt more alive.

She swung downward, but Blind Moses caught the pole with both of hers. Sam pulled back before she could be disarmed, realizing that they were both too evenly matched. For a moment, she wondered if Blind Moses had something similar to Sam of Spades within her. It was like they were two sides of the same coin.

Sam knew she would never beat her with skill. She needed to psyche her out.

Suddenly, the solution came to her. Three bullets. Blind Moses always fired in sets of three. Sam could use that against her.

As the two of them entered yet another flurry of melee attacks, Sam maneuvered so that the pistol was behind her and the rifle was behind Blind Moses. It was time to feint.

With a loud shout, Sam swung her pole into a powerful down-ward strike again. Blind Moses effortlessly captured her weapon, and this time, Sam let the assassin disarm her. With a series of back hand-springs, she landed next to the pistol. Blind Moses took the bait and flipped back to the rifle.

Quickly, she counted the bullets in the clip. Four bullets. This fight was hers.

Standing, she held the pistol out and faced Blind Moses, who had leveled her rifle and was preparing to fire. They were standing on oppo-site edges of the scaffolding. The moment of truth would arrive within seconds. *I can do this. I can definitely do this. I am unstoppable.*

Finally, Blind Moses fired: one, two, three shots.

Sam focused, watching the bullets traveling toward her chest. Time seemed to slow down even more, and she felt her hand being completely steadied. She felt Sam of Spades focusing all of her power into her, willingly lending it instead of resisting. Sam knew she had already won.

Bang! Bang! Bang! Bang!

Sam fired off all four bullets. The first three collided with the bullets from Blind Moses's rifle. The fourth kept going.

Sam looked into her enemy's steely eyes and smirked. *Bye-bye, bitch.*

Blind Moses's eyes widened as the fourth bullet struck her chest, the impact throwing her back and off the crane.

Time continued to move slowly for Sam as she ran toward the edge of the scaffolding. She watched as Blind Moses fell to the ground, hitting it with a sickening impact. Blood gradually pooled around her.

Sam breathed a sigh of relief. Locating a ladder, she slid down to the base of the crane. She then willed the power within her to subside.

Time returned to normal as she approached Blind Moses, who lay supine on top of a blood splatter. More blood pooled around her head. Tossing the empty pistol to the side, Sam got down on one knee in front of her.

Blind Moses twitched and gurgled, looking up at her with steel blue eyes.

Sam was only partially surprised that Blind Moses still lived. At this point, very little could surprise her.

She looked at Blind Moses's skull mask. It was smooth, likely porcelain, and definitely a voodoo design. It was badly cracked. Without any ceremony, she tugged the mask off.

It was Violet Patterson.

Sam wished that Richie had been wrong. But it answered so many questions.

"Violet," she said. "So it was you."

"Princess . . . it looks like you won," replied Violet in a weak voice. Her gaunt face was covered in blood.

"God, Violet," Sam said, shaking her head. "I didn't want to kill you. Why did you do this? Do you hate me that much?"

It was partially true. She didn't want to have the desire to kill Violet, but she had felt it since meeting her again the other night. It was irresistible. She had felt that the two of them had to fight, and that one had to kill the other.

Violent started to laugh, but it quickly dwindled to a pained chortle. Spitting out some blood, she said, "You have no idea how much I loathe you, Princess. If you knew, you would have killed me years ago."

Rodger and Richie, supporting each other, limped over to them. Richie exclaimed, "How the hell did a blind woman do all this?"

Sam didn't pay them any mind.

"Tell me why," she said, desperation in her voice. "What did I ever do to you, Violet?"

Violet gave a snort. "Who is loved by the king of the castle? Who? The princess? Or the dog?"

Sam winced at Violet's words. It was true that she was the one person Vincent loved the most. But to think that he treated Violet so horribly . . .

Violet shook as her breath began to fail. "And whose life is valued only so long as she remains useful? Surely not the king's heir."

"Violet," Sam murmured, tears in her eyes, "I had no idea Grandfather was using you, abusing you. Even back then."

Violet nodded weakly, tears shimmering in her eyes, too. It was the first time Sam had ever seen her cry. "I was his dog. Every day. Went where he needed me to go. Killed who he needed me to kill. Never a kind word. Never a thank you. Nothing but the next task. All while you got everything and did nothing for it. I loved him, Princess, with all my heart. And all I got in return was a vengeful hag and a lifetime of frailty and pain."

"That's too cruel," Richie muttered.

Violet's lips curled into a sneer. "Cruel? You're one to talk."

"Violet Patterson, are you the new Bourbon Street Ripper?" Rodger asked.

Violet shook her head. "No. I simply did what my master asked, as always. Take care of the people from before. Finish what was started twenty years ago. Tie up the loose ends."

She started coughing a series of long hacking coughs. Blood coated her teeth. She turned her head and spat a wad of bubbling blood to the side. "The storm that's on the horizon, Princess, will make what's happening now seem like a fairy tale. Be prepared . . . for hell."

Rodger shook his head. "Violet, who is your master?"

Violet's lips had started to turn blue. It took her great effort, but she muttered, "In our store. In the King's hat. My letter is there. It will explain everything I know."

Rodger nodded. Richie rubbed his mouth.

"Violet, I am sorry," Sam said, her tears flowing freely. "I never saw how much you suffered. Please forgive me. Please."

"Samantha," Violet muttered softly, her eyes glazing over, "I . . . I . . ."

And then Violet Patterson, alias Blind Moses, passed away.

Sam had just closed Violet's eyes when she heard someone cock a gun right behind her. Eyes flashing up, she saw Richie recoil in horror and Rodger's hand drop to his pistol.

She heard Detective Aucoin's voice behind her. "Samantha Castille, you are under arrest for the murders of Virginia Babineaux, Rebecca Clemens, and Cheryl Aucoin."

Her shoulders twitched. Her nerves tingled once more. Her body trembled in an impending release of violence. *I could kill him. It would be so easy . . .*

"Go on," Aucoin said behind her, his voice trembling with unbridled rage. "Just give me a reason."

Sam looked up at Richie and Rodger. Their expressions were fearful and anxious. She knew she couldn't fight. If she resisted Aucoin, whether she killed him or he killed her, it would hurt the two of them. She couldn't hurt them anymore. Resting on her hands, she lowered her head and muttered, "I surrender."

With her adrenaline high finally gone, she felt immense pain within her body. Her guts hurt. Leaning forward, she vomited up some blood and felt herself weakening. Staying conscious was getting more and more difficult. Looking at the puddle she had spat up, she saw blood from her arms and chest trickling down and mixing with it.

It made a macabre pattern on the ground. *Oh, crap. I think I'm bleeding out.*

She saw Commander Ouellette heading toward her, barking at Aucoin to stand down.

Looking back at Richie, she locked eyes with him. She wanted to say she loved him, but she couldn't speak. It was like every spark within her was going out, one at a time.

Someone, please help, Sam thought as Aucoin stepped to her side. His gun was still pointed at her head, and he was arguing with Ouellette and Rodger. She couldn't make out the words. *Someone, help me. I think . . . I think I'm dying.*

Her body gave out, and she fell forward, landing beside Violet. Looking at the peaceful face of her dead rival, she coughed up more blood. She managed a small, shaky smile.

You killed me after all, Violet.

She heard Richie yell her name. She heard Rodger shout for the EMTs to come.

She felt weaker and weaker, until her mind was within a body that couldn't move. She was aware that the EMTs had arrived and that she was being rolled onto a stretcher. She could just make out the words "cardiac arrest" before her hearing shut down. The world was getting darker, and she could barely see Richie at her side. As one of the EMTs pulled him back, she could feel herself being lifted. She saw the interior of an ambulance, and then her vision went dark.

Her last thoughts were, *Funny. Shouldn't I hear the old Baron digging my grave?*

Chapter 15

Farewell, Sam

Date: Tuesday, August 11, 1992
Time: 5:30 a.m.
Location: Tulane University Hospital
                  Downtown New Orleans

Sam was no longer lying on her back. She was no longer dying. As the feeling of floating passed, she was aware that it was a beautiful May spring day, that she was in the Castille mansion, and that it was many years ago.

Samantha, at ten years old, was heading down the hallway toward her grandfather's study. The sound of birds singing was melodiously joined by the buzzing of bees. The cloth of her brand-new dress rustled as she half-walked, half-skipped. In her arms was a brand-new porcelain doll which she had named Marie—a gift from her grandfather. Marie was wearing a similar dress to her own.

Stopping outside the entrance to his study, she smoothed out her dress and adjusted the barrettes in her hair. She wanted to look her absolute best for him. Then, putting on her cutest expression, she walked inside, beaming like a ray of sunshine.

Vincent was sitting at his desk and sobbing into a handkerchief.

In all her ten years, even when she had been injured in a riding accident or when her father had been stabbed while making an arrest, she had never seen her grandfather cry. So upon seeing this, she walked over and gently touched his knee. "Grandpa?"

He jerked a bit, obviously surprised, then looked at her. "My sweet Sam," he said, pulling her into his lap. "Sorry you had to see me like that." He looked tired and old. He had never looked that way before, and that worried her.

"Grandpa," Samantha said, reaching up to hug him and laying a soft kiss on his cheek, "what's wrong, Grandpa? Why are you crying?"

Her small body got enveloped in warmth as he hugged her back, holding her tightly. She just closed her eyes and held onto him. She didn't know what was wrong, but she wanted him to feel better.

After he pulled back from the hug, he said, "Your grandfather lost someone very important to him, Sam, and it hurts. It also scares him."

"Why's that?" Samantha's bright blue eyes looked up at him.

"Because I thought I'd go first," Vincent said, running his fingers through her hair. "I'm an old man. But life, it ends so easily. And losing this person made me realize that I could lose you in the blink of an eye. That is what makes the pain so much worse."

She hardly understood what he meant, but she knew that seeing him in pain made her very upset. "What if I promise not to die, Grandpa? What if I promise to live forever and ever?"

Of course, to her, "forever" meant a very long time. She didn't want to see her grandfather suffer anymore.

He dried his eyes. "Live forever, Sam? Yes. Yes, that is what I want for you as well."

She threw her arms around him and said, "I want us all to never be afraid of dying. I don't want to be afraid, either." Because now that she was thinking about death, which she almost never did, she was afraid, too.

Vincent tilted his head and looked at her. "What did you say, Sam?"

Looking at him nose to nose, Samantha said, "Grandpa, I said I wish I could live without being afraid of dying." She rubbed her small nose against his larger one.

He wrapped his arms around her once more, whispering, "Your father does love you, Sam, so very, very much."

Not understanding why he said that, she just hugged him again.

When he stopped hugging her, tears were traveling down his cheeks. "All right, Sam, we have a deal. I'll find a way to help you live a life without fear, without the fear of death."

She thought that was a wonderful idea and, holding out her pinkie and interlocking it with his, made a pact with her beloved grandpa.

Vincent said, "Now, I just need to figure out how to do that." He winked at her.

Samantha giggled. "Can you do that, Grandpa, really?"

"Well, I can try," he said with a grin. "A friend of mine, one who has seen many of the world's secrets and who I trust completely, gave me an idea I could follow up on. Similar to how I strengthened that little heart of yours." He gently tapped right over her heart. "We'll see if Grandpa can't find a way to keep the old Baron from digging your grave, OK?"

She again had no idea what he was talking about. She shrugged.

"Now, go run along and play," Vincent said, setting her on her feet before patting her back. "Grandpa has work to do."

"OK, Grandpa," Samantha said as she started to head back out to the hallway.

"Oh, and Sam?"

When she turned back to him, he smiled. "I love the new dresses. They fit you and Marie very nicely."

She beamed sunshine and rainbows at her grandfather.

The sunshine through the window got brighter and brighter until it flooded her vision completely. The sound of birds singing and bees buzzing was replaced by a monotonous beeping sound. And the sweet comfort of a spring afternoon was replaced by an aching, all-encompassing pain that felt muted only by medication.

Sam never opened her eyes; her vision just returned. She was aware that she was in a hospital room, and that the room had a number of people in it, all of whom were currently blurry. She was also aware that the presence that called itself "Sam of Spades" was deep within her, but felt weak and subdued.

But what she was most aware of was that she couldn't move. She tried to move her eyes and failed.

Immediately, a feeling of panic rose in her as she wondered if this was death. After feeling her body breathe a few times, as well as an annoying itch on her butt, she realized she was, indeed, still alive. She was just paralyzed.

She was groggy as if still waking up. Fighting back more panic, she took what she could from her field of vision. Her left arm had an IV drip in it, and her left wrist was handcuffed to the bed. Her right wrist was also cuffed. Both arms were dressed. She felt similar dressings down her midsection and thighs.

Handcuffs? I'm under arrest?

Then she remembered what had happened at the wharf. Her duel with Violet. Violet's death. Aucoin arresting her. It all came right back.

Oh. Oh, shit. This is not good.

Her hearing returned. At first, the words were a jumble. But they soon evened out into speech.

"We still don't have enough evidence to guarantee a conviction, Ouellette. You'll have to do better than this."

She focused on the person speaking. He was an older white gentleman in a business suit. She remembered seeing him somewhere before. He was standing next to Ouellette, who looked annoyed. She also saw Rodger talking off to the side with a doctor. Lastly, she saw Aucoin leaning against a wall. His face got red when the lack of evidence was mentioned.

"Not enough evidence?" Aucoin's tone was incredulous. "Her manuscript in the newspaper? Chapter Two of her story? Teen girl gets whacked next. The details were on target with what happened to my daughter! How is that not proof?"

Ouellette held out his hand. "That's enough out of you, Detective. Don't forget that you barely passed your psych-eval. I could put you on leave like that." He snapped his fingers.

Aucoin glared at him.

Ouellette glared right back and said, "Go out into the hallway and cool down. Better yet, go wait with Gino in the lobby. Olivier will be out of surgery later. She's going to need you."

As Aucoin left in a huff, Sam wondered what had become of Dixie. She really hoped the detective lived.

The man in the suit asked, "So, then, how is Detective Olivier doing?"

Ouellette folded his arms. He looked grim. "She'll live, and thank God for it. We were seconds away from losing her. Unfortunately, the attacker used explosive rounds. Her left arm was blown off at the elbow joint." He shook his head. "She'll be getting outfitted with a prosthetic when she recovers."

"Will she be kept on the force?" asked the man in the suit.

Ouellette looked annoyed. "That depends entirely on her. Anyway, my question to you, Mr. Connick, is what do you intend to do about Miss Castille here? This woman, despite being a suspect, put down a dangerous assassin who wiped out a good chunk of my division. I don't think our friends will be so quick to prosecute her now."

Holy shit! That was Harry Connick, the DA.

Mr. Connick put his hands on his hips. He shook his head. "First off, Commander, I decide who my office prosecutes—not anyone else and certainly not you. Now, I have every intention of charging her the moment your office gets me some hard evidence. When will the coroner have the analysis of her DNA done?"

Sam remembered bleeding everywhere. She could only hope that the DNA test would exonerate her and put an end to this madness.

"Soon," Ouellette replied. "I have Melancon doing a rush on it. Meanwhile, I have to figure out how the hell a single blind woman managed to kill over two dozen highly trained and heavily armored SWAT members. You talk about wanting answers, Mr. Connick. Well, that right there is what I want to know!"

Connick motioned toward the door with his head. "Let's go talk about that, Louis. I want to hear how the whole thing went down. So will the mayor's office."

A uniformed officer came in. He was holding a plastic bag. Inside were her red plastic charm, her notebook, and the silver pen.

Hey! Those are mine. You have no right to take them. Sam boiled in frustration at being unable to interact with the world.

"Commander," said the uniformed officer. "We found these in Sam's car. They're the notes for the mystery she was writing. What do I do with them?"

Give them back to me!

Ouellette thought for a moment. "Give them to Bergeron. It's his case now."

Motioning to Connick, he said, "Let's go get some coffee."

Connick nodded and left the room.

Ouellette started to follow, then stopped. He looked into Sam's eyes for a few seconds, then shook his head as if bitterly disappointed. Then he left.

She wondered what that was about, and why she always felt so angry every time she looked at him.

The uniformed officer handed Rodger the packet, then left.

Rodger looked Sam over before asking, in a hushed voice, "So, Doctor, you really think she may never recover?"

Never recover?

The doctor, a middle-aged man with some fat on his face and a severely receding hairline, shook his head. "It's too early to tell. To be honest, Detective, I'm surprised that she's still alive. The sheer amount of internal trauma she's suffered is beyond what a human being can normally survive. As it is, I've contacted one of our directors to come and see her later."

"Would that be Dr. Lazarus?" Rodger asked.

"Indeed. He specializes in strange cases like this. For now, you can see that she's completely unresponsive." The doctor waved his hand over her face. "She blinks at regular intervals, but she doesn't respond to any stimulus. As it is, we're going to need to do an EEG to see if there is any brain activity."

Rodger approached Sam. The lines on his face were heavy. His anxiety was evident. His hand touched her gently. "She's in there. I know she has to be, Doctor."

I'm here, Rodger! I'm alive and I'm here!

She didn't care that he had known, all these years, about her witnessing Edward's murder. He had been showing mercy by saying nothing. She couldn't hate him, not with how he was looking out for her. His love for her was unquestionably apparent.

He rubbed her hand gently for a few minutes, a paternal look in his eyes. "So then, Doctor, any idea what made her act so . . . incredible? It seemed—well, I'll just say it—superhuman."

The doctor shook his head. "I wish that I knew the answer to that. Again, this is something Director Lazarus will have to look into. He's taken a keen interest in both the pink powder and Miss Castille's condition. But as to what happened? I have no idea."

"Most likely zat substance is a highly experimental drug that unlocks a person's physical potential," said a German voice from the doorway. "Und likely Blind Moses received it from the same person who armed her."

Sam felt her stomach drop as the diminutive form of Dr. Klein entered the room. He was eyeing her like a wolf eyes its prey. *Oh, God, not him. Anyone but him!*

Dr. Klein turned to the doctor and added, "And I would caution against letting that charlatan Dr. Lazarus see Samantha. He vill only bring quack theories into what is already a difficult case."

"He's one of the hospital's directors," replied the doctor. "I can't just refuse him admittance."

"So who the hell let you up here, Klein?" Rodger asked with vocal hostility.

"I contacted him," replied the doctor. "While you and the other detective were arguing, your commander asked me to contact Dr. Klein for a statement on Miss Castille's psychological situation."

"One I intend to give," replied Dr. Klein indignantly. "Since Samantha saw fit to fire me earlier, I can no longer protect her from herself."

Sam felt sick to her stomach.

He puffed out his chest. "I have already spoken to Mr. Bourgeois, und we have come to an agreement. I will divulge the tapes of my conversations with Sam of Spades. Und I have over two hundred hours of taped sessions. In return, I will be allowed to treat Samantha once she is acquitted on an insanity defense."

Oh, God, no, Sam thought in terror. She would rather die than go back to that man.

Rodger clenched his jaw angrily. "You're assuming Sam will even be formally charged."

"Samantha!" Dr. Klein said forcefully. "I have told you a hundred times, her name is Samantha!"

"Gentlemen," said the doctor, clearing his throat. "I have to look out for the welfare of Miss Castille, who is currently my patient. So, if you raise your voices around her again, I will have you both escorted off this floor."

Dr. Klein and Rodger both mumbled apologies. The doctor nodded and moved in front of Sam, obscuring her vision.

Shit! Sam thought. *Move out of the way!*

"She won't be found guilty, Dr. Klein. She's no killer," said Rodger.

The doctor shined a light in her eyes, leaving behind little dots in her vision.

Dr. Klein harrumphed. "I agree zat Samantha is not a killer, but her other self, Sam of Spades, is remorseless."

The doctor placed a stethoscope against her chest. He moved it around, listening to her breathe.

"Yeah," said Rodger. "Well, good luck offering testimony at a trial that's not going to happen. As soon as that DNA comes back clean, Sam's going home."

"Samantha, not Sam!" said Dr. Klein in a forceful and rude tone. "Und the DNA will match. Of that, I am certain. She will be arraigned, found not guilty by reason of insanity, und I will finally be free to treat Samantha as I see fit."

Sam felt sick. It seemed that both Kent and Dr. Klein were actively working against her.

She could hear Rodger sigh. "You are out of your mind if you think that Samantha, or Sam, or whoever, is the killer."

"It is understandable to be angry, given your emotional investment, Detective," Dr. Klein said, sniffing. "But at least Samantha is going to get ze treatment she needs. The other one was not so fortunate."

Other one, Sam thought to herself. *Is he talking about Dallas?*

She vaguely remembered Dallas and another boy, whose name she couldn't recall, during her time with Dr. Lazarus—a memory that had resurfaced along with the ones of her grandfather. *We played word games. Dallas and that other boy really seemed into the game, especially Dallas.*

Within her mind, she gasped. *Is that where the term 'Nite Priory' came from?*

Sam's thoughts were interrupted as the doctor pushed her head around in several positions, examining her at length, before getting back in front and scribbling down notes.

He moved away from her field of vision. She could see Rodger angrily pacing while Dr. Klein stood there, full of himself. *Dr. Klein . . . I really hate you.*

"All right, listen," said Rodger, rubbing his face. "If this thing goes south, you keep her from death row. Sam of Spades may be a murderous psychopath, but Samantha Castille is the kindest, gentlest person I have ever known."

Rodger! Sam mentally wailed. *How can you even think that? Sam of Spades never killed anyone. Right, Sam? Sam?*

Deep within her, she could feel the other presence. It felt distant and subdued. Maybe her injuries had made Sam of Spades go dormant. It felt almost like the presence inside her was lending her strength.

"I agree," replied Dr. Klein, looking at her. "But she is too far along in her life to integrate her two personalities. For her to be cured, we must destroy Sam of Spades und free Samantha Castille."

It's not like that at all, she angrily thought. *It's not a multiple personality disorder. It's something else. You've been treating me for a disorder I don't have. No wonder I'm so messed up.*

Rodger grabbed his collar. "I don't know what you mean by 'destroy Sam of Spades,' but let me tell you something. You hurt one hair on her head, and I'll—"

The uniformed officer from before burst in. "Detective Bergeron, we need you down in the lobby. Right now!"

Rodger was still holding Dr. Klein's collar, who glared furiously up at him. He let go, roughly patting Dr. Klein's jacket. "What's wrong?"

"It's that guy you brought, Richie," explained the officer. "He and Aucoin started arguing when the suspect's DNA came back positive. Aucoin's taken off his badge. They're about to come to blows!"

Sam's mind hit the skids. *What?! My DNA is a positive match?!*

Rodger stared, and then shouted, "It's positive? Sam's DNA? This is bullshit! Where is Melancon?" He quickly followed the uniformed officer out of the room.

The doctor finished his notes and said, "Well, this is going to be a damn long night. I'll be right back, Dr. Klein. I need to get a nurse to check Miss Castille's temperature."

Dr. Klein nodded to the attending physician, who then left. Slowly, he turned to look at Sam. Then, one step at a time, he walked toward her.

Oh, God. She felt a terror from which she couldn't escape. *Get the hell away from me!*

Leaning in, he said, "Are you in there, Sam of Spades? Did you hear that? You are ze killer. Just like I told you. You see, I know you, Sam. I know all the horrible things you have done, what you want to do."

He touched her face. His fingertips grazed her lips, the curve of her cheeks. "Every sordid detail of your darkest fantasies, you shared with me. Beauty through pain, you called it. To think zat after all has been said und done, you are nothing more than a cheap copy of the original Bourbon Street Ripper."

Dr. Klein leaned in until his rancid breath ran over Sam's left ear. "What a waste of talent. We are all very, very disappointed."

Leaning back, he looked into her eyes. "I have to admit, Sam, you are a fascinating subject. When this trial is over, und you are given to my custody, I will study you and learn every aspect of you, and then I will hurt you. I will use every technique I know to hurt you until you are gone forever from zat poor little Samantha's mind. Beauty through pain, just like you said. It will be exquisite, my little Sam. I look forward to every single second."

He patted her leg and started walking out. His tone of voice changed. "Sleep well, Samantha Castille. And do not worry. I will rid you of Sam of Spades. When ze pain is over, you will be a good little girl again. You have my word on that."

He stopped at the doorway and glanced at her. His eyes were like two hot coals, and his lips were curled in a cruel smirk. "And . . . farewell, Sam . . ."

Sam watched as Dr. Klein left, mentally crying out, *Oh, God! He's insane!*

Although Sam of Spades was still unresponsive, she could feel that the other presence was equally terrified.

The sickened feeling was gradually replaced by a crushing depression. It was already over. All that was left was for the district attorney to formally charge her. DNA was not something that could be refuted. It all seemed so painfully clear. She was a monster and never knew.

My DNA matches. Whether it's this Sam of Spades thing or something else or . . . I don't know.

She wanted to die.

God, is it possible? Is the new Bourbon Street Ripper . . . me?

Chapter 16
Boudin and Bandages

Date: **Tuesday, August 11, 1992**
Time: **8:30 a.m.**
Location: **Ritz-Carlton Hotel**
                Canal Street, French Quarter

The steam rose from the Styrofoam cup in Richie's hands, the winding vapors finding their way from the hot liquid to waft over his tired face. It was black with a bitter smell to it, yet the warmth felt undeniably good. The steam was like a gentle caress, and considering how the past several hours had gone, it was a welcome sensation.

He had been in the hospital lobby, waiting for news on Sam. Sitting beside him had been a darker-skinned guy named Gino, who he quickly found out was Dixie's boyfriend. While he didn't feel much like conversing with anyone, mostly from having a swollen jaw where Rodger had knocked him out, having someone else there in a similar situation made it more tolerable.

Things went downhill when Aucoin came down to the lobby. Immediately, Gino got up to go talk to him about Dixie. Alone and feeling isolated, Richie stewed over Sam's arrest. The evidence was damning, but not enough to guarantee a conviction. From the bits and pieces Richie overheard, everything hinged on a DNA sample found inside the most recent victim.

Suffice it to say, tensions were extremely high.

What finally caused things to snap was when an old guy named Melancon, the coroner, met with the district attorney and Ouellette and Aucoin in the lobby. Richie caught the end of the conversation, just as Melancon handed a file over to Ouellette and the district attorney said, "We'll set the arraignment date."

Right after that, Aucoin shouted across the lobby, "Hey, writer boy! Just want you to know your psycho girlfriend's going down for serial murder. Hope you enjoy banging a corpse."

A powder keg went off inside Richie. With a boiling rage unlike anything he'd felt before, he leapt up and lunged at Aucoin, ordering him to take off his badge and fight him like a man. Aucoin obliged, and the only thing that kept them from tearing each other apart was several uniformed officers restraining them both.

Rodger showed up at the tail end of the confrontation, escorted Richie out of the hospital, and drove him back to his hotel. By the time Richie got to his room and passed out in his clothing, it was four in the morning.

Richie had slept hard until Rodger had woken him by banging on the hotel door. He had just sat on the edge of the bed, staring at the wall, while Rodger used the room's coffee machine to make him a morning cup of coffee.

Holding the cup, he tried to wake up and come to terms with everything that had happened. He liked the way the steam rose over his face. It reminded him of Sam. Looking over at Rodger, who looked like he hadn't slept a wink all night, he asked, "So, um, am I under arrest? Ya know, for assaulting Detective Asshole?"

The left side of his face sported a nasty bruise from where Rodger had hit him. It hurt badly, but he had no intention of pressing charges. Reflecting back on his behavior at the wharf, he knew he deserved it. He had let his anxiety get way out of control.

Rodger shook his head, shifting in the desk chair. "No. Ouellette figures you've been through enough. He will send you back to Pittsburgh if you so much as go near that hospital, Sam, Dixie . . . hell, pretty much if you leave this room, you're done."

"Whatever," Richie said, sipping the coffee and then going back to letting the steam wash over his face. "To be honest, Rodger, I just don't care about anything anymore. I feel numb inside. This is . . . this is too much." He had fallen desperately in love, and then the world had turned into shit. Nothing he'd ever written had been that bleak.

Rodger harrumphed, looking at him in a manner that seemed almost judging.

Feeling another rush of emotion, Richie curled his lips. "What, jackass? You gonna bust my chops, too?"

To Richie's surprise, Rodger didn't react to his outburst. Instead, he just shrugged and said, "I have nothing to say to you about some things, and a lot about other things. But right now, as it stands, I need your help. Michael is off the case until Ouellette says otherwise. Dixie is likely to be out for who knows how long. Aucoin's been temporarily suspended. And everyone else is trying to balance the workload of all the detectives that died last night. For better or for worse, you're all I've got." He sat up and clamped his hands on his knees. "So here I am. You say you love Sam? Good. Here's your chance to prove it. Help me save her life."

His speech caught Richie's attention. Looking intently at him, Richie saw past the tired, old, beat-up senior detective. Looking into Rodger's eyes, Richie saw a fire—slow-burning but steadily growing. "I'll help," he said. "What do you want me to do?"

"I have a few things you can do while I continue the investigation," Rodger said, reaching into his overcoat. "Sam's going to be arraigned tomorrow at noon. So that's how long we have to find the real killer."

Richie shook his head and asked, "How can they arraign a woman in a coma?"

Rodger pulled out a small notebook and flipped through it. "Her EEG showed brainwave activity. She's in what the doctors call Total Locked-in Syndrome. That means that Sam is alive in there and is aware but is incapable of communicating with the outside world. Likely, the judge will just enter a plea of 'not guilty' for her."

Richie felt his heart ache. Looking down into his coffee cup, he saw tears drop into the liquid. "My poor Sam. My poor, poor Sam." He looked up and rubbed his nose. "Any idea what caused this?"

Rodger just stared back at Richie, shaking his head. "Other than her and Blind Moses doing stuff you only see in the movies? Well, she did lose a lot of blood. And has severe internal trauma. The doctors are still amazed she's alive. They're saying that by all accounts, she should be dead."

Richie chuckled and rubbed his nose again, sniffling. He didn't have the strength or the will to even make a quip, much less argue. "I mean, how did Sam do that stuff? She thinks she's possessed. Last night was a pretty good argument for that."

Rodger leaned back and shrugged. "God, I don't know. That pink stuff is what the Knight Priory called the *tkeeus*. I've got almost no leads on it. The lab report said it's an incense of the guava and mango plants of West Africa, but there's some unknown compound in there, one they can't identify. Dr. Klein is convinced it's some wonder drug. Myself?"

He closed his eyes for a second before sighing. "Everything about me that is a police detective does not believe in voodoo. But I've lived in New Orleans my whole life. A lot of people place faith in it. It's as much a part of this city as Mardi Gras and the French Quarter. Hell, the Knight Priory of Saint Madonna seemed to combine the beliefs of Catholicism and voodoo. So if you're asking me if last night was any evidence of either woman being possessed by something?"

He opened his eyes and leaned forward. "Let me answer you with a question. How the hell did a blind woman assassinate over a dozen trained, heavily armed SWAT team members? And how did she snipe Mad Monty or Topper Jack? How did she fight Michael and nearly kill him?"

Richie couldn't answer that question. Just like he couldn't answer how Sam was able to run up the side of a crane. "Maybe that *tee-kees* stuff lets the blind see?"

Rodger held out his hands, shrugging. "You tell me. Logic and reason are rapidly getting thrown out the window. Anyway, I can't focus on an enemy that I can't see or hear. If there is something spooky going on, what can I do? There's no precedent for policemen to investigate ghosts. And I know one thing's for certain. It wasn't a ghost that murdered those women. It was a human being. And I aim to prove that that human being wasn't Samantha Castille."

Richie drained his coffee. "What do you need from me?" he asked.

Rodger opened the small notebook and said, "You mentioned that you and Sam visited the Patterson sisters, correct? Then Tania Patterson knows you. I need you to get that letter Violet spoke about, the one in the 'King's hat.'"

Richie shrugged. "Makes sense. Anything else?"

"Yes. I need you to speak with Jacob Hueber of the *Times-Picayune*. You know him. Sam's best friend. Find out the flow of people who got Sam's manuscripts. Our hunch is that the real killer is associated with the newspaper."

Richie made a face and sighed. He didn't know what to make of Jacob. He liked him well enough, but it was like Jacob was hiding something. And the way he had seemed fake for that brief moment at Landry's Restaurant was unsettling.

Not to mention he had the same kind of coat as the biker gang that had attacked him and Sam. *You can get something like that at any Gothic or punk shop, but that's a helluva coincidence.* He didn't want to believe that Jacob would actually hurt Sam, but something definitely wasn't right there.

All that aside, he wanted to help Sam. "All right. Will do. Anything else?"

"Yeah," said Rodger. He leaned in, his eyes narrowed, his voice low. "This is the most important part, and the part that can get both of our asses in trouble if we're caught."

Richie sat up when he saw the serious look in his eyes.

Rodger pushed a small piece of paper into Richie's hand. "I need you to go to Lafayette and talk to this woman. Rosemary Boucher. I want you to talk to her about the day Magnolia died. And I want you to ask about her son, Julius Boucher. That part is really important—Julius Boucher. Remember it."

Richie blinked and looked at it. The address on it was not in Rodger's handwriting. It was probably Michael's.

"Julius Boucher? Got it." He waved the paper.

Rodger looked very serious as he nodded. "Michael and I believe that what Rosemary tells you could very well crack the case. I'd go myself, but I won't be able to make it there today. I'm still trying to get in touch with Jonathon Russell about the Knight Priory, so I need to stay in town. He was trying to remember something about the *tkeeus*. Something important."

"Fine, fine. I'll need to rent a car, though," Richie said, getting up and tossing the empty coffee cup away.

With a metallic clink, Rodger slapped a set of keys on the wooden surface of the hotel room's desk. "To Sam's car," he said with a smirk. "I have a friend at the impound."

Richie smirked back and said, "I'll get freshened up and head out."

An hour later, Richie stood before the entrance to the La Croix Voodoo Shoppe in Jackson Square. He was about to go inside when he saw a "Closed" sign on the door. The displays were darkened. He tried to peer in through the window, but it was no use. The interior of the store was too dark.

For a few moments, he stood at the doorway, thinking of how he could get inside. Then he heard a voice behind him say, "May I help you?"

Turning, he saw Tania Patterson, dressed in formal black clothing with a small purse over her shoulder and holding a Bible. To him, it was a very strange thing, seeing a woman who owns and operates a voodoo shop dressed in obvious Christian attire. Looking past her, he saw crowds of people coming out of the St. Louis Cathedral.

Oh, that makes sense. Must have been morning service.

Smiling at her, Richie said, "Hey, I was wondering if I could come in a minute, Tania. It's, um . . . Well, it's rather complicated."

"I'll bet," replied Tania, unlocking the door. As she walked past him, he noted that her eyes were puffy and had dark circles underneath them, like she had been crying most of the night. She had to have found out about Violet. He couldn't imagine what that must have felt like.

"You're Miss Samantha's friend Richie, right?" she asked as she entered the store. She turned on a few lights, bringing the room out of darkness.

"Yes, that's me," he replied, looking around. The store seemed very different during the day. It was still nice, but without the full effect of the music, incense, and mood lighting, the interior wasn't very inspiring.

She put down her Bible and purse, then leaned back against a wall. Rubbing the area around her eyes, she said, "So, what brings you here, Richie?"

He didn't know where to begin. He wasn't completely sure if she knew what had happened to her sister. He also wasn't sure if she knew that Sam had killed her. For the man who was able to out-talk a lawyer and two detectives, he felt utterly stuck for something to say.

Finally, Richie just asked, "Tania, do you know about Violet?"

Still rubbing her eyes, Tania shuddered a little. "Yeah. I identified her body early this morning. I decided I would offer some prayers at mass. Her service is on Thursday." There was a momentary choke to her voice.

"I'm really sorry," he said, feeling like he was giving a canned response. After all, Violet had killed dozens of police and tried to kill Sam. Richie wasn't exactly sorry that she was dead.

Looking at him almost crossly, she shook her head. He felt awful, figuring that his tone must have sounded pretty insincere.

She started heading up the stairs. "I was going to have some tea. Want to join me?"

"Sure, I'm right behind you." He followed her upstairs.

Thirty minutes later, Richie was on his second cup of tea, enjoying the smooth flavor of Plantation Mint. To him, the taste was sublime, like being home during the summer and playing out in the nearest creek. It brought back comforting memories. Memories that seemed like they were taken from a picture book.

"You seem to really like that tea," Tania remarked as she poured him another cup. She had since gotten out of her finery and into a skirt and blouse. With her hair pulled back, she looked like the girl next door, if not for the reddish puffiness under her eyes. And she was smiling gently, with a little sadness. It was a pretty smile.

Ya know, she's not bad looking. He felt that she had ended up with the better deal.

He thanked her for the tea, and then he got down to business. "Tania, I hate to ask you something about your sister, but, well, Sam's in serious trouble, and her life may depend on something Violet had in her possession."

She seemed to slow down, her soft smile slowly waning. "It's come down to that, has it?"

He blinked, shaking his head. "What do you mean? Come down to what?"

Tania leaned back in her chair, tapping the side of her teacup. "I suppose that since I'm one of the few left alive, and no one knows that I know anything, it's probably safe to talk."

Richie stared at her, wondering what she was talking about. This sounded really serious.

She shook her head, her expression pained. "Have you ever lived with a secret that was so awful, you did your best to block it out of your head?"

Despite trying not to, he recalled his father beating him and his mother with that spade. "Yeah. I do."

She said, "It's not a long story, but I've kept it inside all my life. Mama took it to her grave. I'd like to tell it to you now, Richie, if you'll listen?"

He nodded and sipped his tea, focusing on her.

Tania began her tale. "As you can probably guess, growing up working for Vincent Castille wasn't exactly wonderful. Even before he started murdering, he was always a bit creepy. When that society would get together, they'd do all kinds of things in the mansion basement that would make everyone in the house feel uneasy."

"Society?" Richie asked. "You mean the Knight Priory of Saint Madonna?" He looked back down at the now-empty teacup.

"That's them. Vincent and his sister, and Russell, Robichaux, Ouellette, Thibodeaux, Paris . . ." Her voice trailed off. "Mama . . ."

He looked up, blinking in surprise. "Your mama? Miss Patterson was a member of the Knight Priory?"

"Well, not exactly," she said, looking away. "The Priory always believed in voodoo, but at some point, Mama was asked to help them with their ceremonies. She became like a priestess for them. So, anyway, back to the story. One night, Vincent did this special ritual. Mama was there. So was Violet.

"I remember hearing Mama talk to Violet the day of the ceremony. Apparently, they had already done it a month before. And apparently, even though there were some snags, it was a success. Vincent was positive that the next ceremony would be flawless. So Mama wanted to use one of us."

Her voice lowered as she said, "Violet was born blind. The ritual was supposed to give her her sight back."

"So what happened?"

She looked up, tears running down her cheeks. "Instead, it changed her into something ugly. It made her mean. It made her sickly. You saw her a few nights back! She's been this bitter, hateful, hollow shell her whole life. All because of what they did to her that night."

Richie sat back, closing his eyes. Suddenly, it all made sense. The Knight Priory had messed around with something they shouldn't have. Whether it was really loa or just strange drugs wasn't important. They had tried it with someone—likely Sam—and it had worked. Then they tried it with Violet, and something went wrong. So Vincent turned Violet into his dog. No love. No thanks. Just use and abuse.

He sighed and opened his eyes. "So while Sam was Vincent's princess, and given the best of everything, Violet was turned into—"

"Nothing more than a rabid beast," Tania said, nodding. Her voice became vitriolic. "My sister became something horrible 'cause of that man. As the years went by, Violet became colder and colder, meaner and meaner. She'd have a hard time focusing on anything other than her tasks. She'd hardly eat. She'd hardly sleep. She'd often space out for hours at a time. That monster robbed my sister of everything beautiful."

Richie was taken aback. He didn't want to delay things any more. And it was obvious that she needed to grieve. "Tania, before your sister died, she mentioned a letter in the 'King's hat.' Do you have any idea what that means?"

For a long moment, she was silent and in deep thought. Finally, she stood up. "One moment, Richie. I'll be right back."

As Tania left, he leaned back and closed his eyes. It was all so much to process. If his hunch was right, and Sam had been put through the same ceremony as Violet, what was the point? Was there really such a thing as voodoo and loa? Or did this *tkeeus* do something else to those two girls?

Either way, the Knight Priory is really screwed up. I guess that's why the Lady in Red wants me to help find out who's framing them.

Richie opened his eyes, realizing that he hadn't seen the Lady in Red in days. And apart from the one glimpse of a hooded man in Gargoyles, Richie hadn't seen anyone from the Knight Priory, or Nite Priory—Richie wasn't sure which spelling was right anymore—since they had saved him from Marcello.

"Here you go," she said, coming up the stairs. She held an envelope in her hand. "In the King's hat. My sister, if anything, has a sense of humor."

"So where was it?"

"Baron Samedi's top hat," said Tania as she rubbed the edge of the envelope against her lips.

Richie took a moment to recall the dark ride he and Sam had gone on a few nights before. "Baron Samedi?" he said, then snapped his fingers as he remembered. "Right, he's the king of the loa. And the belief is that you only die when Baron Samedi digs your grave, right?"

She smiled softly. "That's right. Baron Samedi's job is to usher all souls from the realm of the living to the realm of the dead. So the belief is that no matter how injured or sick you are, until the old Baron digs your grave, you won't die."

"Creepy stuff," he replied, reaching for the letter.

As he did, Tania snapped her hand back.

He scowled in annoyance. "What gives? Hand it over, Tania."

She got a dangerous look in her eyes. "First off, tell me how my sister died. The police wouldn't tell me. Only that it was an accident. But I don't believe that. What really happened?"

Richie's scowl persisted. He didn't really want to get into the events of last night. However, he felt he had to be honest in return. "All right, then." He locked eyes with her. "She tried to kill Sam. They used something called the *tkeeus*. It made them do some crazy, super-human shit. They were like two lunatic superwomen. It was like they were driven to kill each other. They kept going until Sam finally won."

Tania looked away. He could see tears forming in her eyes again.

"She died well," he said, keeping his gaze fixed on her. "It was pretty close until the very end. The police are baffled by how a blind woman could do it. So there you have it. Sam killed her. Your sister said that one day, they'd fight, and they did. Sam won. Violet's dead."

He knew he was being a total prick, but he didn't care. He loved Sam and he hated Violet. He couldn't hide that, not even from someone as sweet as Tania.

"Marinette and Bwa-Chech," she said softly.

Richie blinked. "Mari-who-chech?"

"Marinette and Bwa-Chech," she repeated, her voice bitter. "They're two twin loa. Hags, actually. Vengeful spirits who thrive on pain. But they are also enemies. No matter what is happening, the two will always find a way to be in conflict. To fight to the death."

He narrowed his eyes at her. He wasn't sure what she was getting at.

Finally, Tania snorted and tossed the letter to him. "It's just what you said, Violet and Miss Samantha being compelled to fight. Reminded me of the hag sisters' story. I guess, in the end, it is what they wanted it to be. Like Marinette and Bwa-Chech, they both wanted to fight to the death. My sister lost, and now she's dead."

Standing up, she said, "You have your letter. Now please leave. I hope it helps you save Miss Samantha. But as for me, I want to bury my sister and my past with the Castilles. So I beg you, after today, don't come looking for me. And tell Miss Sa—Samantha to stay out of my life as well."

Picking up the letter, Richie gave her a nod. "All right. I'll leave you alone, then. Thanks and take care."

She didn't say anything in response even as he left.

Once outside, he walked briskly back toward Sam's car. Only once he was seated and had the car running did he open the letter. At first, he thought it was in some sort of cipher made of raised bumps. Then he realized that it was in Braille. "How the hell am I going to read this?"

He decided he'd let Rodger and Michael figure that one out. He still had to stop by Jacob's and then drive all the way to Lafayette.

When Richie arrived at Jacob's apartment, it was close to lunch time. He rang the doorbell. A few moments later, Guidry answered the door in shorts and a tank top. Her eyes were still red and puffy. She looked like she hadn't slept in days. "Oh, hi, Richie," she said. "What do you want?"

He sniffed the air, expecting to smell enough pot to give him a contact high. Instead, he smelled the most wonderful, flavorful food. "I need to speak to Jacob. It's about Sam."

She looked at him for a few moments before calling back into the apartment. "Jacob, hun. Richie's here. Wants to talk about Sam."

He heard a muffled reply from someone he assumed was Jacob. Then Guidry let him into the apartment.

"Hey there, Richie," Jacob called out from the kitchenette. "Emilie and I are making boudin. Do you want some?"

Richie, in spite of himself, bobbed his head in a ridiculous manner. "I don't know what boudin is, but it smells scrumptious. I'm in!"

Jacob laughed and motioned for him to come over. "You can help me season the meat while Emilie prepares the casings."

Richie noted that Jacob was hunched over the stove and standing kind of strange. A few minutes later, Jacob explained that he was recovering from a weight-lifting injury.

Richie learned that boudin was a Cajun sausage made of pork cutlets and pork rice dressing, similar to dirty rice, stuffed into a pork casing. While it was quite an involved process, he had arrived near the end of it. Jacob seemed grateful for his help. Guidry seemed completely subdued the entire time, never making eye contact with him.

In less than ten minutes, he was eating something that tasted, to him, like a delicacy.

"That was incredible," he said as he popped the last link into his mouth. He honestly felt bad about how much he had enjoyed the meal while Sam was still in trouble. A part of him loved the dish as if it had been his favorite since childhood. "Sometimes, I wish I had been born in Nawlins."

Jacob snickered. "Ah, we'll turn you into a Cajun yet, Richie. You're already saying New Orleans like a native."

Richie chuckled. It was nice to feel like he belonged. *Maybe when this mess is over, instead of moving away with Sam, I'll move here and live with her.*

Guidry finished eating in quiet and then curled up next to Jacob, not saying or doing much of anything. She continued to avoid any eye contact with Richie. She looked like she was thoroughly depressed.

"So, what can I do to help Sam out?" Jacob asked, as he leaned back and drank some iced tea with lemon.

Richie, who had caught him up on Sam's situation, said, "I need to know the names of everyone who handles Sam's manuscripts when she brings them to the *Times-Picayune*."

Jacob looked thoughtful and nodded his head slowly. "That's a big request, dude. Caroline would fire me faster than you can blink if she knew I gave that information out."

Richie nodded back. He understood and valued the protection of privacy. "I know I'm asking a lot of you, man. But Sam could die if we don't clear her name."

Jacob held out his hands. "No, no, man, I get that. I'm just thinking how I can pull off not getting caught. I mean, if any of this gets back to her . . ."

He didn't have to finish his statement. Nodding, Richie said, "I'm only interested in saving Sam's life. Same with Rodger. We don't care about anything else."

He and Richie locked eyes for a bit. Finally, Jacob sighed and said, "Be right back." Getting up, he went to the back of his apartment, holding his back the whole while.

Richie sat in awkward silence with Guidry.

Finally, she said, "So, Detective Bergeron isn't suspecting anyone else, is he? I mean, no leads or anything on who might be framing Sam?"

Richie, who had been looking at his shoes, shook his head. "No, nothing. That's why I'm looking."

"Right, right. Just asking," she said, looking over at the window.

Finally, he asked, "Are you still working?"

Looking over at him, she shook her head. "I'm on paid leave for a couple of months. I had a nervous breakdown after discovering Cheryl's body. I found each of the victims. Virginia. Rebecca. Cheryl. Three bodies in a row. God, I'm never going to want to go to the French Quarter at night again." She sighed heavily.

Richie stared at Guidry for a long time. She glanced over only once, but otherwise refrained from making eye contact. *What is she hiding?*

Finally, he asked, "Officer Guidry . . ."

"Call me Emilie," she said.

"Emilie," he said. "I need to use the restroom. Where is it?"

"Use the master bathroom," she said, obviously distracted. "My, um, unmentionables are hung up in the guest bathroom. Just go down the hallway. First door on your left is the master bedroom. It's through there."

He arched his eyebrows at her mentioning her underwear, wondering if that was a New Orleans thing or a Cajun thing or what. Shrugging it off, he headed through the hall to the back. To the right was an office, where Jacob sat at a desk, scribbling on a sheet of paper.

Quietly, Richie went left, into the master bedroom.

He stared at Jacob's bedroom. Between the king-size bed, the television with laser disc player, and the stereo system, it was obvious that Jacob was a regular spendthrift.

He quickly headed into the master bathroom, where a garden bathtub continued to paint a picture of someone who loved to live well. As he relieved himself, he wondered just how much Jacob's trust fund was worth.

As he washed his hands, Richie eyed a set of bandages rolled up and sitting on the sink counter. *Oh, yeah, Jacob burnt himself last week. That sucks.* He picked up the bandages and looked them over. They were made of a hard, durable material. *Crap, that must have been a hell of a burn.*

He rubbed his thumb over the bandage. To his surprise, it hurt. Looking more closely, he saw a small piece of metal barely sticking out of the bandage. His thumb had a small white streak on it where the skin had come up.

That's odd. Why have a piece of metal there? Scraped some skin right off. He found some moisturizer to rub into his thumb, put away the bandage, and then headed back up front.

Guidry was watching television, which was showing news about the new Bourbon Street Ripper case.

Richie looked over at the screen. "Have they mentioned Sam's arrest yet?"

Guidry shook her head. "Ouellette and Connick will want to sit on that until this evening. They're talking about the shooting at the wharf, though, and saying that they do have a suspect in custody."

Richie gritted and ground his teeth, fighting back the rise of anxiety. Once she was named the killer, Sam would never live a normal life again. She was running out of time.

"Here's your list, Holmes," Jacob said, coming out from the back and handing a folded piece of paper to him. "Just please, please, pleeee-ase do not let Caroline find out I gave this to you."

"I won't," Richie said, putting the paper away. "And thanks."

"No problem, dude," said Jacob, clapping him hard on his back. "Anything to help Sam's beau."

Richie shot him a thumbs up. "You know, I need to head to Lafayette and talk to someone. Would you like to come with me? I sure could use the company." The alternative was driving all alone, and that sounded awful.

"Nah, I can't," Jacob said. "I need to take care of some work stuff tonight. You know how it goes, a serial murderer and it doesn't matter if I'm on vacation or not—I'm working."

"Sounds awful. Sorry, man," said Richie.

"Besides, won't Detective Bergeron go with you?" Jacob asked.

"I wish," Richie replied, feeling his anxiety bubble forth. He felt compelled to just talk. "He's going to some dude's mansion. Some rich guy named Jonathon Russell. Supposedly a big clue to the real killer or something."

Jacob grinned. "You don't say, do ya? Well, best of luck to Detective Bergeron!" He then gave Richie a playful punch on the arm.

"Don't worry, though, once Sam's name gets cleared, the four of us will go out and really tear the town apart."

Guidry looked over, frowning. She didn't seem to like the idea at all. As soon as she saw that Richie had caught her gaze, she looked away.

Richie smiled, liking that idea. "Sounds like fun, man." Maybe his suspicions of Jacob had been wrong. He really seemed like he cared about Sam.

"Let's make it a date." He gave Jacob a hard yet playful pat square on the back.

Jacob winced as if in terrible pain, and, for a moment, looked like he was going to take a swing at Richie. His fists tightened and his face contorted in anger.

Richie took a step back. *What the heck?* It was like Jacob was holding back a ton of rage.

Then Jacob laughed heartily and smacked him on the arm again. "Be careful, dumbass," he said in a merry tone. "I pulled my back muscles lifting weights, remember?"

Damn. I forgot. Wait . . . a hurt back and a black hooded cloak . . . Richie's throat went dry. An unpleasant thought was forming. *Holy shit!* What if Jacob was the leader of the biker gang that had attacked him and Sam? Could all this cheer and friendliness be a ruse? Could this guy really be some kind of nut job?

Noticing that Jacob was staring at him, his eyes narrowing, Richie quickly stammered out a response. "Shit! Sorry about that."

Jacob recovered quickly. "Don't worry about it." He laughed again. It sounded a little too forced.

Richie had to get out of there before Jacob figured out that he was on to him. Richie pushed down the anxious feelings that kept trying to bubble upward. He couldn't figure out where he was getting these suspicions, but they were too strong to ignore.

Jacob showed Richie out. Once they were alone, he said, "And Richie, um, keep things quiet about Emilie, OK? Her boss thinks she's checking into River Oaks. But I don't want her to go to that nut house. I think what she needs is a vacation away from this city and a good therapist." He winked. "Know any good ones?"

Richie put on his best fake smile, winked back and said, "Not Dr. Klein."

Inside, however, he was far from smiling.

Jacob had to be connected to the murders. He was sure of it. But how?

Chapter 17
It Had to Be You

Date: **Tuesday, August 11, 1992**
Time: **12:00 p.m.**
Location: **New Orleans Police Department**
                 Precinct Eight, French Quarter

After he left the Ritz-Carlton, Rodger went back to the precinct to check on the status of Sam's arraignment. It certainly felt like everyone was in a rush to arraign, try, and convict Sam. Rodger was just amazed that no one had leaked Sam's name to the media. *Ouellette must have a heckuva gag order in place,* he thought as he entered the squad room.

It was a mess from hosting the now-dismantled task force. Detectives Rivette and Landry, along with some uniformed officers, were cleaning up. Rodger saw that, among the trash that was everywhere, several desks had vases of flowers on them. The sight made his throat tighten. It looked like the SWAT team wasn't the only department with heavy casualties.

"Blind Moses," Rodger said to himself. "A woman driven by a hatred that ran so deep, she lost sight of her goal. If any one of us had ever seen so much as a glimpse into Violet Patterson's heart, what would we have seen? Would we have seen the shadow of the real monster that hides in the dark? Or would we have seen a reflection of the monster in our own hearts?" He found himself wishing Michael was around. His partner loved his occasional poetic moments.

"You should write that down, Bergeron," said Ouellette's voice from behind him. "Maybe after you retire, you can become a writer, too."

As Ouellette walked past him, Rodger chuckled. "Nah, this story has enough writers." Seeing that Ouellette looked tired, if not withdrawn, he followed him to his office.

"What do you want, Bergeron?" Ouellette asked.

Rodger closed the door and leaned against the frame. "Actually, I was about to ask you that same question, Commander," he said, folding his arms. "You seem less antagonistic and more contemplative than usual. And you're not busting my chops for once."

"Yeah, I don't much feel like busting any chops right now," Ouellette said, motioning for Rodger to sit down. Ouellette pulled out a bottle with a black label and two glasses. "Was about to have some Jack Daniels. Join me?"

"Um, sure," Rodger said as he took a seat. Ouellette hadn't shared a glass of whiskey with him since Douglas was still on the force. "Thanks."

"No thanks needed. I figure it's time that I start sharing a glass with you like I did with Dugas," Ouellette said, pouring a quarter glass for each of them. He slid one glass over to Rodger, then raised the other. "To old times."

"To old times," Rodger said. He took a sip of the whiskey. He would have preferred it with ice. *How does Ouellette drink this stuff room temperature?*

Ouellette sipped his whiskey, closing his eyes for a few moments, and breathing in the scent of the whiskey from the glass. "So the mayor's going to do a formal inquiry of the entire department, as well as assess my ability to lead."

Rodger sat there, blinking. He didn't know what to say.

Ouellette leaned back and shook his head. "Over two dozen cops lost their lives last night, Bergeron. Un-fucking-believable. I'll be lucky if I'm just allowed to resign."

Rodger's brow knitted. "There's no way you can be held respons—"

"Bullshit, Bergeron," Ouellette said firmly, almost raising his voice. "Bullshit. The buck stops with me, and you know it. Even if you and Dixie and Aucoin and everyone else who's still alive testify on my behalf, do you think City Hall's going to let this go? Every single officer in Arsenault's Arsenal was killed. Several of my detectives and uniformed officers were killed. There's no way, short of a miracle, that I'm not going to lose my job."

Rodger felt sick to his stomach. Despite Ouellette always being up his ass about something, he had a great deal of respect for his commander. Ouellette had been in this position since Rodger was a rookie over thirty years ago, and there was very little Ouellette loved more than his precinct.

Ouellette looked away, as if he couldn't look Rodger in the eyes. "The damnable part, Bergeron, is that I don't believe we have the right person in custody."

For a brief moment, what Ouellette had said skipped past Rodger's mind. Then it hit him. "What a minute! You don't believe that Sam is guilty?"

Ouellette snorted and shook his head. "Not for a moment. Call it an instinct, Bergeron. I was sure of her guilt until I saw her fighting Blind Moses. Now I know she's innocent."

He paused for a long, long moment, as if he were reliving a memory. Then he sighed. "Anyway, here are the thoughts I'm sharing. For a supposedly sociopathic murderer, Samantha Castille—Sam, as you like to call her—went out of her way to not hurt anyone. That fight was about those two and those two alone. It was a duel. But a sociopath wouldn't care if there was collateral damage. Sam kept the fight away from everyone else. Not to mention, she risked her life to save Dixie's. And in the end, she surrendered. We both know she could have gone on, killing Aucoin and everyone else who stood in her way." He smirked. "Well, except me." He clinked the side of his glass.

Rodger hadn't thought about it, but Ouellette's points made sense.

Ouellette took another sip of his whiskey. "Besides, if Sam is the killer, and the killer contacted each of Vincent's old accomplices, why did Blind Moses try to kill her?"

"Good point," said Rodger, who felt a bit ashamed. He had been so convinced that he and Richie were the only ones certain of Sam's innocence that he hadn't considered that others might feel the same way.

"Well, that last bit wasn't my thought on the matter," said Ouellette. "It was Olivier's. She's also convinced that Sam is innocent. As soon as she woke up from surgery, she was begging me to put her back on the case. Had to have her ass sedated, she was so upset over accusing Sam."

Rodger felt his spirits start to lift. "However, if Sam is innocent, then who is the killer? Why was Sam's DNA found inside Cheryl's body?"

Ouellette finished off his whiskey, then held out his hands in a shrug. "You tell me. You're the detective."

Rodger laughed at that. It was the first time he ever recalled Ouellette making a joke. Finishing his own whiskey, he said, "Then I best get to it. Thanks for the drink, Commander."

He was at the door when Ouellette said, "Just a minute." Rodger turned and looked.

Ouellette rubbed his mouth and nose, leaned forward on his desk and said, "You're without a partner. Olivier is recovering from having half her damn arm blown off. Aucoin's been suspended. Rivette and Landry are on clean-up detail. Better get all the case files to LeBlanc. He keeps crying about how he's got nothing to do."

Rodger blinked. A smile slowly parted his lips. "Yeah . . . yeah! Hey, thank you, so—"

"If you get mushy one more time," Ouellette said, pointing a finger at him, "I will come over there and kick your ass out the door."

Rodger was still smiling as he saluted. "Yes, sir!"

He stopped by his and Michael's desk to get the notes. He also made a point of asking Rivette and Landry to put any other materials from the case in boxes as well. Both detectives, who were grateful to get out of one aspect of cleaning, gladly helped out.

He busied himself with putting together all the notes to take to Michael. Within an hour, he had several boxes, along with the ones from Rivette and Landry, ready to bring to the hospital. Michael would have plenty of reading material. That was for sure.

He was waiting for a dolly cart and chatting with Rivette, who was sweeping up some spilled coffee grinds, when his phone rang. Picking it up, he heard an old, creaking voice say, "Is this Rodger Bergeron?"

"Yes, this is Detective Bergeron. Who is this?"

"It's Russell. Jonathon Russell."

Rodger couldn't believe his luck. "Russell, good to hear from you," he said, sitting down and flipping open his notebook. "I was just about to come over and check up on those leads you gave me."

"Yes. I know."

Rodger cocked his head in surprise. "Excuse me? You knew? What do you mean, you knew?"

"That's not important," Jonathon said. Rodger detected strain and anxiety in the old man's voice. "Look, I need to speak with you. I finally remembered something important."

Rodger got ready to write down notes. "OK, I'm listening. Go ahead."

"No good," said Jonathon. "I need you to come here, after dark. I don't trust the phone lines. Never have. Never will."

Rodger chortled nervously. "What, you think someone is tapping your phone lines?"

Jonathon's voice was stern. "Perhaps. Do you think no one is tapping yours?"

Rodger didn't say anything to that. Either the old man was paranoid or things were getting even more bizarre.

"Look, Detective, please, just come over tonight after dark," Jonathon said. "What I have to tell you is very important. I don't know if it will help you solve your murder investigation, but it will put a lot of things in perspective. Remember the information about the *tkeeus* I told you and that lady detective the other day?"

"Yes," Rodger said. "You told us that Vincent learned about the *tkeeus* from somewhere, and that after he used it on Sam, the Knight Priory started to change, and now it's more of a political group than a secret society."

"That's correct," said Jonathon. There was a pause as he breathed into his respirator. "Well, what I remembered is how Vincent learned about the *tkeeus*."

Rodger blinked. "Go on."

"Someone gave it to him. Someone who had used it themselves. That's what set everything in motion. Well, I remembered who it was. I remember who gave Vincent the *tkeeus*."

Rodger was almost on the edge of his seat. "So who was it?"

"It's too dangerous for me to tell you over the phone. His ears are everywhere. Trust me, Detective, it's big. Come see me tonight, OK? I'll tell you then. For now, watch your back and be careful. That's all I've got to say." Jonathon hung up.

Rodger sat there for a minute, holding the phone to his ear and disbelieving what had just happened. All Jonathon had needed to do was say a name over the phone and that would have been it.

"Man, I am just getting sick and tired of people doing that," he said.

"You and me both," said Rivette. Rodger turned to see him leaning against the broom, waggling his eyebrows. "So what's this about 'turkeys'?"

Rodger kicked the broom out from under Rivette.

He soon got the files to his squad car, made it to Tulane Hospital, and got the files up into Michael's room. He then spent about an hour catching Michael up on what had happened the previous day, including the decision to let him work on the case from the hospital. Michael seemed unsurprised.

"It's because Ouellette knows he's going to be suspended or worse," he said. Still in his hospital gown, he looked as though he wanted to be anywhere but there. However, the doctors wanted to keep him one more night.

Rodger nodded in agreement. "I feel bad for Ouellette, taking the heat for us like that. I think we owe it to him to find out what's really going on, don't you?"

"I feel the exact same way," Michael said, tapping his fingers on a notebook Rodger had given him. "It's a real shame that the commander's being blamed for what was obviously a situation that's spiraled out of control."

Rodger was pleasantly surprised to hear Michael say that. A week ago, he would have been significantly colder, saying something like "that's the burden of leadership" or "Ouellette knows what comes with being in charge."

Michael's come a long way. I'm really going to enjoy working with him again.

"Anyway," Michael said, "Sam is innocent. Of that I am certain. The DNA must have been planted. All you need is a few skin cells. I'll sort through what you've given me as best as I can. What I really need is all the notes from this and the original case and about a day of uninterrupted time with them both."

Rodger harrumphed. "Think you could solve the case with just the notes and your mind, eh, partner?"

Michael grinned assuredly. "The answer to this case is in that mountain of notes we have. I'm certain of it."

Rodger chuckled and got up, patting Michael on the arm. "Well, start with this foothill here. Let me go and see what I can learn. I need to follow up with Douglas on the Castille marriage licenses. Then I need to head over to Russell's mansion and find out what he knows about the *tkeeus*."

"The *tkeeus*," Michael said, closing his eyes. "Rodger, I have a bad feeling that the *tkeeus* is dangerous. You said there was an unknown compound in it. What if it's hazardous? I can't believe in that occult nonsense, but I can believe in a formula that makes a person superhuman. And it could have unknown side effects."

"Well, there's no telling, partner. Hopefully the crime lab will learn more in time. All I know is that it did make you and Sam do some pretty superhuman stuff."

Shaking his head and opening his eyes, Michael said, "Like I said, everything I believe is based in science and fact. There is no room for superstition. But people like Dr. Lazarus are making me believe that there's hidden potential inside all of us. If the *tkeeus* can unlock that potential, wouldn't that be worth killing over?"

Rodger blinked. Michael had just hit an angle he hadn't considered. "You think that the murders are about the *tkeeus*."

"Not about the *tkeeus*, no," Michael said. "But I wouldn't be surprised if the murders, both the original and the copycat ones, and everything that's associated with them are a result of Vincent learning about it." He winked at Rodger. "Just a hunch. You're rubbing off on me, partner."

Rodger felt good about Michael's new attitude. Patting him on the arm again, he said, "Well, rub some of that superior intellect off on me, because I can't figure how the *tkeeus* fits into this at all."

"Can't do it," said Michael, folding his arms. "Too hopeless." He was smiling. It wasn't an insult.

Rodger had a good laugh. It was a welcome break.

It was almost dinner time when he arrived at Douglas's house in Marrero on the West Bank. As soon as he waded past the flamingoes and garden gnomes to the front door, he rang the bell. Immediately, he heard the sound of Boudreaux, the family Shih Tzu, barking with insane ferocity. Remembering that the dog could not stand him, he called out, "It's me, Douglas. Better keep Boudreaux back or I'll have to arrest him for assault."

Douglas must have just made it to the door, because Rodger heard him say, "Ha, ha, ha! He got you there, Boudreaux! Come on, you. Let's go see what Mommy's doing. I'll be right back, Rodger."

As he waited, Rodger reflected on how Douglas had found him in a bar a few nights ago, depressed and drinking himself into a stupor. Douglas's pep talk had really lifted his spirits. He was hoping that his old mentor could do it again.

Douglas opened the door and welcomed him with a strong handshake. "Hey there, Rodger! Good to see you. I wasn't expecting you so soon."

"Well, I wanted to follow up on the marriage licenses," Rodger said, heading inside.

Douglas arched his eyebrows and said, "You could have called. Try again, Rodger. Come on, what's the real reason?"

Rodger hesitated a bit, trying to come up with a good excuse. Finally, with a smile, he playfully popped Douglas on the shoulder and said, "OK, old man, you got me. That invitation to dinner was too much to pass up. And I've been lonely, so . . ." He shrugged. Douglas had him dead to rights.

"Ha, ha!" Douglas pointed at him, then patted him on the back, and then led him into the main room. "Come on, let's get you washed up. Mabel's about ready to serve. So, I heard the police made an arrest. Can you tell me who it is?"

Rodger grimaced a bit and said, "Yeah, about that . . ."

It didn't take long for him to catch Douglas up on what had happened, leaving out the sensational parts—like the epic confrontation at the wharf. Mabel, who had served fried chicken, mashed potatoes with gravy, steamed broccoli, and fresh rolls, didn't want the investigation to be a dinner topic, but Douglas kept asking questions. Finally, Mabel, in a huff, announced that she wasn't going to participate, and contented herself with feeding Boudreaux. Whenever he wasn't quietly eating whatever morsels were given to him, the Shi Tzu sat in her lap and glowered at Rodger.

"So Samantha Castille is the prime suspect, and none of your fellow detectives believe it?" asked Douglas.

"Or Ouellette," said Rodger as he took another chicken leg. Although he had washed up before eating, his hands and face were already pretty greasy. That was just what happened when you ate Mabel's fried chicken.

"Or Ouellette," Douglas repeated, nodding in agreement. "Well, you can toss my name in the hat there, too, Rodger. I don't believe the girl did it."

Rodger helped himself to some more mashed potatoes. The food was amazing, but it was no surprise. He had come to expect that of Mabel. She was a natural cook who, like most New Orleans natives, liked to eat good, home-cooked meals.

"Honestly, if I were going to favor anyone, it would be someone who stood to gain from Sam's imprisonment. Or her commitment. Or her death," said Douglas thoughtfully, poking disinterestedly at the steamed broccoli.

"Come again?" asked Rodger.

Douglas waved his free hand in the air. "Her money, Rodger! Her money. She's wealthy beyond words. Lady Gladys Castille may be the one living in the mansion, but it was all willed to Sam by Vincent. Who gets all that money if she dies, or is otherwise declared ineligible?"

Rodger stopped eating and looked at him. This wasn't the first time someone had mentioned it, and it made sense. "So you think that the murderer is really after Sam's money?"

"Possibly," said Douglas, shrugging. "And why not? Seems as good a reason as any to kill someone. Isn't money the root of all evil?"

Rodger harrumphed. "Well, I'll look into it, Douglas, but I tend to think that you need a bit more crazy and a bit less greedy to kill people the way the Bourbon Street Ripper does."

Douglas didn't seem to have any argument there. He quietly ate some broccoli and made a face.

"About those licenses," Rodger said.

Douglas looked grateful for the break from eating broccoli. "Oh, that's right. So I called my friend Derek and got the search started for licenses filed in the seventies. It's going to take a few days. Nothing to be done about that." Douglas cleared his throat and drank some iced tea.

Rodger felt his shoulders drop. It seemed like another dead end.

"However, he did find out that there was a marriage license filed from the Castille household not very long ago," Douglas said. "A few weeks before the murders started, in fact."

Clank!

Rodger's fork hit his plate. He stared at Douglas in disbelief. Suddenly, his mentor's hunch about the murders being about money didn't seem so far off. "Who was married?" he asked.

Douglas shrugged. "Don't know."

Again, Rodger's shoulders dropped. "Oh."

Douglas winked. "But I did get a copy of that license sent to your precinct. Depending on how quickly Derek processed it, you may get it tonight."

Rodger felt a sudden urge to jump up and head back to the precinct. He fought it back, though, and decided to do it before going to see Jonathon. After all, Sam wasn't going to be arraigned tonight.

"So, there it is," Douglas said. "As for the older license, from when Edward got married, you'll get that in the mail in a few days."

Rodger nodded and said, "Thanks, Douglas. This means a lot."

The rest of the dinner conversation was about the upcoming Saints season, the fishing down in Grand Isle, and plans for the Christmas season. He was pleased to find out that Douglas and Mabel were planning on staying in town for the holidays, instead of visiting their son and his family up in Chicago. That meant he'd have people to visit with over the holidays.

As soon as that thought came, he recalled that he and Sam had also reconciled. For the first time in over twenty years, he felt like he had his extended family back—Douglas, Mabel, Michael, and Sam.

I'll save you, Sam. I'll be the one to save you.

He felt good as he finished his dinner.

"You'll come back again after this horrible business is over, right?" Mabel asked, handing him a Tupperware container of chicken, mashed potatoes, and her famous pound cake.

"Oh, come on now, Mabel," said Douglas, "you don't need to fuss on Rodger like that."

"I don't mind it," Rodger said. It was the truth. Mabel was like the sister he'd never had, and she had always made him feel welcome. "She bakes the best pound cake in New Orleans."

"See there? He loves my pound cake. More than you do, Douglas," Mabel said to her husband. She then feigned a whisper to Rodger. "Douglas really misses you when you're gone."

Douglas cleared his throat, signaling that it was "time to go."

As Rodger turned to leave, he heard the stampede of tiny feet and a loud, high-pitched bark. Then he felt a sudden weight on his overcoat moving side to side. Seeing Douglas and Mabel with a mixture of shock and amusement on their faces, he looked down and saw Boudreaux swinging from his overcoat by a mouthful of fabric. The dog was staring up at him and growling.

He believed he had finally figured Boudreaux out. He winked at the Shih Tzu. "Don't worry, Boudreaux. I'll be back soon."

He stopped by the precinct to see if the most recent marriage license for the Castille family had been delivered. It had not. He gave instructions for the letter to be rushed to Michael when it arrived. While he was at it, he asked Detective Rivette to find out the details of Sam's inheritance and to send that information to Michael as well.

Douglas, you old goat. If you end up being right, I'll buy you a beer.

It was well after nightfall when Rodger arrived at Jonathon Russell's mansion. With the exception of the gas lights at the front gate, the entire outer wall was darkened. When Rodger found the front gate open, however, he immediately cut the lights to his car. Jonathon did not seem like the type of person to just leave the light on and the gate open.

Rolling slowly up to the house, Rodger looked for any signs of life. An array of lampposts outside were lit. A few lights were on inside, mostly on the second floor. Other than that, the mansion was dark, with the front door open.

Front door open! This doesn't look good.

His gaze lingered for only a moment before he cut the engine and put the car in park. Keeping his eyes on the front door, he picked up the squad radio and called the police dispatcher.

"Eighth precinct operator, over," said the dispatcher.

"Detective Rodger Bergeron. We have a 62-R in progress with a possible 30," Rodger said, giving out the codes for residential burglary and possible homicide. "Requesting back-up at Russell estate, 1040 Lakeshore Drive. Over."

The radio crackled. Then the dispatcher came back and said, "Affirmative. Dispatching back-up to your location. Over and out."

Rodger hung up the radio and weighed his options. On the one hand, it would be prudent to wait for back-up. On the other, Jonathon could be in danger, or even dying, right now. Rodger didn't want anyone else dying on him, especially not someone who had important information.

Taking out his gun, he made sure there was a full clip. Then he got out his flashlight, put on his bullet-proof vest, and headed up to the front of the house.

Standing at the front door, he listened. Inside, he could hear a vinyl record playing "It Had To Be You" by Django Reinhardt, likely over the mansion's PA system.

Now that's just plain creepy, thought Rodger as he headed inside.

"*It had to be you . . .*"

The front hall was illuminated by the outside light, but otherwise the first floor of the mansion was dark. He could see the bottom of the staircase and a few doors leading to side rooms—but that was it. The only other light was a dim, flickering one coming from somewhere on the second floor.

"Yes, it had to be you."

He snuck through the front hall, his feet sliding quietly on the floor. As he moved, he shined his light on every shadowed part of the room, gun ready and finger on the trigger. If his fight with Mad Monty had taught him one thing, it was to never let his guard down. Rodger would not be ambushed like that again.

"I wandered around and finally found the somebody who . . ."

When he got to the stairs, he saw a person leaning against the banister of the second floor landing. The flashlight couldn't illuminate the details from that distance, but the person was taller than the average. Keeping his weapon trained, Rodger called out, "Who's there? This is the police. Identify yourself!"

"Could make me be true, could make me feel blue . . ."

The person didn't answer. Keeping his back to the wall, Rodger slowly crept up the staircase, flashlight and gun trained on the figure. When he reached the second floor landing, he saw who it was. "Oh, no . . ."

"And even be glad just to be sad thinkin' of you."

It was the butler, Reggie, dead. He had been tied to the railing and shot several times in the chest. His eyes were open and glazed over, and his jaw was slack. Considering what Rodger had seen in the past two weeks, this was a relatively tame death, but no less cruel.

"Some others I've seen might never be mean . . ."

"What a disgusting thing to do to another human being," he said, closing Reggie's eyes. He didn't do anything else, leaving the rest for the crime lab to do their analysis. But this didn't bode well for Jonathon, so Rodger headed toward the study.

"Might never be cross or try to be boss . . ."

The going was slow, because with all the lights out, there were dozens of places where an attacker could be hiding. Rodger kept his eyes, flashlight beam, and gun trained on them all. It took several minutes to reach the doorway to the study, where lights flickered inside.

"But they wouldn't do . . ."

Slowly, he opened the door to the study and looked inside. The flickering light was coming from a desk lamp. He could see the silhouette of a figure behind the desk, seated in the large wing-back chair. Cautiously, he crept inside, checking the blind spots of the room for an ambush. There was none.

"For nobody else gave me a thrill."

By now, his heart was pounding. While he wished that he had gotten to the estate earlier, the thought of finding another dead body didn't faze him. He had seen too much recently. So with a quick inhale, he shined his flashlight on the figure in the chair.

"With all your faults . . ."

Jonathon was dead, shot in the chest several times. His eyes had been gouged out and his nose had been cut off. The body parts lay on the desk before him, right next to the large red button.

"I love you still."

Rodger fell back against the wall and covered his mouth to muffle any sounds. It looked like someone had shot Jonathon and then mutilated his dead body. He was both disturbed and perplexed. *That's not the way the Bourbon Street Ripper is operating. Who did this?*

"It had to be you . . ."

Then he heard the hammer of a gun click. His blood went cold.

"Wonderful you."

Coming out from behind the desk was a figure in a black hooded coat. He was wearing black gloves and a pull-on mask with the imprint of a devil. He was also holding a .45 automatic pistol.

"It had to be you . . ."

Rodger stood face-to-face with the masked figure. Both had their guns pointed at each other.

"Oh . . . it had to be yooooooou!"

Rodger and the masked figure pulled their triggers at the same time. The sound was deafening.

They both fell.

For a couple of seconds, Rodger couldn't move, having had his breath knocked out by the bullet's impact. His ears rang with the echo of the gunshots. As he lay there, frantically trying to intake air, he saw the masked figure struggle to his feet. That bastard also had a vest.

Rodger continued to struggle to sit up as the masked figure came around with his gun pointed at him. Rodger was helpless as the intruder pulled the trigger several times.

Nothing happened. The masked figure pulled the trigger a few more times and then smacked the gun in frustration.

Out of bullets. Good. Rodger was going to enjoy arresting this son-of-a-bitch.

By then, Rodger was on his knees and trying to stand. His hearing had returned, and he saw the masked figure slipping behind the desk, frantically looking around for an escape. There was a lack of calmness in him that felt out of place for a serial killer. This couldn't be the guy.

Rodger and the masked figure locked eyes, and then the masked figure looked down at the large red button on the desk. "Oh, no, you don't!" shouted Rodger, leveling his gun at the masked figure's chest.

Before Rodger could get off a shot, the masked figure smashed his hand down on the large button. Immediately, red lights started to flash within the room. Throughout the house, a loud klaxon horn started going off.

Rodger covered his ears. He could barely hear himself think.

The masked figure jumped over the desk and ran toward the doorway. Rodger shot at him several times, but the sound of the horn was too distracting. He wasn't able to get off a good shot. The masked figure was gone before Rodger could stand.

By the time he was on his feet, loosening the vest so he could breathe, the horn had stopped and the red lights had changed from flashing to solid. He looked around, staring wildly. Something about this situation seemed extraordinarily bad.

Then he heard, from within the house, the sound of machinery whining as it came to life. It came from everywhere—the walls, the floor, even the ceiling. Looking about with an anxious gaze, he recalled the last machine he had had an encounter with. It hadn't gone very well.

What the hell did Jonathon build in his house?

As if answering that question, the wall behind him slid open. Jonathon's desk, corpse and all, glided into a safe room lit with blue lights.

Rodger rushed for the safe room only to have the wall shut so fast, he hit his nose. As he stumbled back, he heard another clicking sound, and he turned just in time to see the exit slam closed. Whatever machine was active, it had trapped him in the study.

Then he heard a loud crashing sound. Hundreds upon hundreds of long metal spikes burst from the ceiling. Slowly, they started to lower. He was transfixed and in complete disbelief.

When he finally grasped that he was in some sort of death trap, all he could say was, "You've got to be kidding me!"

Chapter 18
Concerning Rosemary's Child

Date: **Tuesday, August 11, 1992**
Time: **6:00 p.m.**
Location: **Home of Rosemary Boucher**
               Lafayette, Louisiana

It was nearly six in the evening when Richie arrived at the dilapidated home of Rosemary Boucher. He had heard of people living in such rundown rural homes, but he'd never seen it. He wasn't sure which turned him off more: the sound of dozens of dogs barking or the smell of dozens of dogs' droppings.

As he knocked on the door, he went over what he was supposed to talk to her about—her son, Julius, and the night Magnolia was murdered. He had even brought a notebook and pen with him to take down notes.

When she answered the door, he was taken aback by how worn-out she looked. Between the lines on her face, the faded light of her eyes, and the wrinkles over her brow, she looked like she had seen everything. She was dressed in a pair of black shorts and a loose black shirt with a pair of pink lips on the chest. She was holding an unlit cigarette and looked like she didn't care about anything.

"Hello," Richie said, offering his most charming smile. "I am, well, my name is Richie Fastellos. Michael LeBlanc sent me."

Nodding, Rosemary lit her cigarette, blew smoke to the side, and said, "I figured one of you would be back. Come in, Detective."

She thinks I'm a cop. Well, that could work in my favor.

He followed her inside, watching as she walked to a nearby couch where five or so dogs sat. There was noticeable cellulite on the backs of her thighs and protruding veins on the sides of her calves.

Man, this woman is spent. Hard life, I guess.

Looking around the house, Richie saw the sheer number of dogs and made a face. He wasn't fond of dogs. The smell of their dander always made him nauseated and gave him a sinus attack. He wasn't sure if it was an actual allergy, but he knew that too much exposure to dogs messed him up.

"Take a seat, Detective," Rosemary said, sitting on her couch between a toy poodle and a bulldog. She motioned to a large wing-backed chair. "How is Michael doing?"

"Truth be told, Michael's recovering in the hospital. He was injured in the line of duty," he said, taking the offered seat. He was trying to sound as official as possible.

Shaking her head, she said, "That's a shame. Real nice kid. Easy to look at, too, even though he's on the other side of the fence there." The embers of her cigarette lit up as she took an exceptionally long drag. "Tell me why you're here, Detective."

Richie looked Rosemary over. The bags under her eyes weren't like Sam's, from lack of sleep. The woman looked high on something. And all around both of them, the dogs were gathering, panting and shaking off dander. Sighing, he sat back in the chair. Already, he could feel the back of his throat starting to tickle. He really disliked dogs.

He forced himself to focus on his task. "Right before Michael left, you had mentioned that Magnolia was murdered. I'd like you to tell me all about it." He brought his fingers together in what he hoped was a contemplative look.

She smirked with amusement and crossed her legs. Richie tried not to stare at them. Her age was ruthlessly noticeable. Puffing on her cigarette some more, she said, "Magnolia was a sweet girl, but she always had heart problems. She called it a congenital heart defect. During their act, Marigold would go out into the audience while Magnolia would stay on stage. Poor thing. It was amazing that she was able to have a child."

"That would be Samantha Castille, right?" he asked.

Rosemary took a long drag off her cigarette and nodded.

Magnolia was Mary Castille. It was no longer a suspicion, it was a fact. Ignoring the itching starting in his nose, he asked, "So, then, if Mary was Magnolia's real name, what was Marigold's?"

She paused for a moment and furrowed her brow. "Lord, Detective, it's been twenty years. Started with the same letter as Mary. Marie, perhaps? Martha? Minnie?"

How can you forget a person's name like that? He frowned and then sneezed, the itching spreading to his eyes. He knew his body. He'd start feeling nauseated soon. "And did Marigold have a child?"

Rosemary shook her head and inhaled the rest of her cigarette before leaning back and blowing the smoke up at the ceiling. It reminded him of a factory's smokestack in Pittsburgh. "That I don't know. Only Magnolia's child was ever talked about, being that she was a Castille. But if Marigold had a kid, it was at the same time as her sister. They were only gone for an extended period of time once, and that was right before Samantha was born. So if Marigold had a child, then both sisters were expecting at the same time."

She lit up another cigarette just as Richie finished his notes. "It's always possible that Edward got both women pregnant."

He looked up so fast, he nearly got whiplash. "Why would you say that?"

Shrugging, she said, "Hun, I know men. The M&M sisters were beautiful. Magnolia was sweet and quiet, Marigold was lively and energetic. Now anyone with eyes could tell that Edward and Marigold was already an item. But when that slimeball Blue-Eyed Giorgio started cozying up to Magnolia, Edward scooped her up as well. And it was obvious that Marigold did not like having to compete with her own sister."

Richie snapped his fingers. A lot of theories started falling into place. "Rosemary, do you think that Marigold murdered Magnolia out of jealousy?"

She grinned in amusement and blew smoke right toward him. The smell of the cigarette mixed with the stink of the dogs was almost overpowering. "Hun, I don't think Marigold wanted Magnolia dead. But I do believe it was both Marigold and Edward who killed her."

For a moment, Richie just sat there and registered what he had heard. "Wait a minute! Time out! Why would Edward kill the mother of his own child?"

Rosemary put out the cigarette and leaned forward, her elbows on her knees. "Listen closely, Detective, because I have never told anyone this story before. The night Magnolia died, she mentioned that her medication tasted funny. She wanted to get Dr. Castille, Vincent, before taking it. However, Marigold said they were in a hurry, and so Magnolia took it. Except for one pill, and when they went on stage, I swiped it."

He anxiously bit his bottom lip. "So what kind of a pill was it?"

"Nicotine, hun. And you don't give nicotine pills to someone with a heart condition," she said, leaning back and giving him a wise nod.

He sat back and looked at his notes. Nicotine pills? He was no doctor, but he was pretty sure that an overdose of those would make a person's heart rate soar. He coughed a few times, his throat itchy. "So, why do you suspect Edward as well as Marigold?"

With a sly look, she said, "Because whenever the M&M sisters had a nighttime performance, Magnolia had an extra batch of pills delivered to her. It was always Edward who would deliver those pills. Who else could switch them out?"

Richie shook his head slowly. "Why haven't you ever said anything?"

Rosemary shrugged. "Detective, someone in that group of elitists, the Knight Priory of Saint Madonna, paid me a lot of money to keep quiet. I figured if anybody ever needed to know, they'd hunt me down. Just like you did."

He quickly wrote that down, figuring Michael and Rodger could use that information. "You mentioned Vincent Castille. So he knew the sisters?"

She ran her fingertips over her robe and concentrated a bit before saying, "Yes. Although Dr. Castille clearly liked Magnolia more than Marigold. He'd always ask for her whenever he'd visit. And it was Vincent who ran to Magnolia's side first when she collapsed on stage that night. He tried to revive her."

He sighed and rubbed his eyes. The glut of information was a lot to absorb, and the dog dander was really getting to him.

She lit another cigarette, then looked him up and down and asked, "You OK, hun?"

"It's the dog dander," Richie said, finishing up the notes. "I never could tolerate it. I'm going to have to jump to the next question and then wrap this up."

Rosemary chortled and said, "Dog allergies, huh? Poor kid. What else did you need to talk about?"

"I wanted to talk about your son, Julius," he said. "We learned that you had him with Robert, then gave him up. What can you tell me about him?"

That seemed to get a reaction. Her eyes cast down, she brought the cigarette to her lips, taking another long drag. The ember went out, and she dropped the nub into an ashtray on the coffee table. "Julius," she said. "My precious baby."

He waited for her to begin.

"My baby came along during a time when I couldn't have children, on account of working at the Jean-Lafitte Theater. I knew he was Bobby's son, and not just because Bobby was the only one with me at the time. He had his daddy's eyes, you see. Those deep blue eyes. And he was so full of personality and charisma, and very smart. He had a mind for puzzles and creativity to match. I was certain my precious Julius would end up like his daddy, a true killer." Her tone was longing.

Richie nodded, remembering that Robert Fontenot was the "Black Bayou Boatman," a rather notorious hit man for the Marcello family. Strange that she'd want to have her child grow up to be an assassin. Richie tried to imagine what kind of a party they'd have thrown after "little Julius" made his first kill, and shuddered.

Rosemary sighed. "Or so I'd like to believe that's how he turned out. I was unable to keep him. If old Carlos Marcello had learned that Bobby and I'd had a kid, I'd have lost my job. I suspect Marcello would even have forced Bobby to break off our relationship. I couldn't have that, you see. I needed that job, I needed Bobby. So I gave my precious Julius up to foster care."

Richie just stared at her, his jaw clenched, his heart pounding. Something about what she had said had triggered every anxious nerve in his body. *Whoa! I'm freaking out!* He wanted to wring her neck.

He inhaled and exhaled several times, even though the smell of dog was starting to make his head hurt. With an effort, he calmed down. He was glad his mom had loved him and looked out for him. He resolved to visit her at the home when he got back to Pittsburg.

He leaned forward, his voice still more accusatory than he intended. "Well, you did give him up, and he was taken to Acadia Vermilion Hospital."

Rosemary nodded ever so slightly, still gazing down. When she looked back up, she wiped away tears. She took the last cigarette out of the pack and lit it. "Yes, Detective. And there ain't a day go by that I don't regret it."

Richie glared at her. She had given up her child, her precious little boy, and now she regretted it? He had no sympathy for her. "And you do know that he died in the same fire that almost killed Dallas Christofer, right?"

Snorting out smoke, she shook her head. "No, Detective. My baby didn't die that night. He sent me a letter from Houma a few weeks after the fire."

He blinked. "What? He's alive? What did the letter say?"

Rosemary puffed on her cigarette. "It ain't much. He just told me he was alive and some nice old woman had picked him up. Told me her name—Beaux or something. Then he told me he'd never see me again, but not to worry. The wording was a lot colder than my baby used to speak, more distant, but I know it was him. Mother's intuition."

Richie just stared, not believing what he was hearing. This could blow the whole case wide open.

"Do you still have the letter?" he asked.

She nodded.

"May I see it?" he asked, coughing a painful, scratching cough.

"Sure, hun. It's in my bedroom. I'll go get it," Rosemary said with a smile, putting out her last cigarette. "Also, I'll see if I have anything for those allergies. You look like shit."

Richie shook his head as she went to the back of the house. *Un-freaking-believable.* If Julius was still alive, he could be the guy. He could be the killer. And Jacob was helping him . . . somehow.

Richie sat back and waited, trying to ignore the dog smell and his growing queasiness.

As the minutes passed, he felt himself getting more and more nauseated. The room was starting to spin, and the compulsion to vomit was growing. His eyes were watering and his throat was terribly scratchy. When he looked at his watch again, fifteen minutes had passed. The house was silent.

What the hell was taking her so long?

Standing up, he called out. "Rosemary! Hey, you back there?"

When there was no answer, he stumbled toward the back end of the house. He didn't see the dogs and figured they were all up front. On his way to the back, he passed two doors, one to a bathroom, and one closed and labeled "Eustace's Pad."

Finally, Richie got to the end of the hallway and stood at the doorway of the master bedroom. Rosemary sat on the far side of the room, at her vanity. The curtains were drawn and the room was dark, save for a single vanity light.

Jesus, what is wrong with this broad? He was about to hurl all over her living room, and she was putting on makeup?

Holding back the desire to snarl at her, he walked over and put a hand on her shoulder. Giving her a gentle nudge, he said, "Look, Rosemary—"

Her head rolled back, revealing that her cheeks had been split, giving her a freakish smile. Her throat was slit, and her vanity was covered in blood that was beginning to dry.

He squealed. "Oh, God, *what the fuck!*"

Stumbling back, he took Rosemary with him. She landed in his lap, blood getting all over his clothes. As he pushed her off him, he saw a letter in one hand and a high heel in the other. The heel had blood on it, as if she had fought against her attacker.

Richie grabbed the letter and ran. For the moment, his head and stomach didn't hurt him—he was way too terrified.

As he rushed out of the hallway and into the front room, he tripped on something large and heavy. With a sharp cry, he landed on the carpet. It was wet, sticky, and warm. What the hell?

Looking up, he saw the face of the bulldog staring right back at him. As he quickly backed up, he saw that it was only the head. The rest of the bulldog's body was off to the side. With another cry, he scooted back, pressing against the large object that he had tripped on. It felt furry and damp.

He was shaking in fear. Almost against his will, he looked back and saw the full body of a Rottweiler, its stomach cut open. He choked on his own vomit and stared in horrified fascination. Then he saw something moving in the Rottweiler's gut. Against all common sense, he reached out and opened its stomach cavity.

With a yelp, the toy poodle, now matted in blood, ran out. Its little stomach was split open, and its tiny intestines, caught somewhere within the Rottweiler, were unraveling as the small dog ran. Shivering in fear, the terrified toy poodle disemboweled itself as it sprinted toward the protection of the sofa. It made it halfway underneath, whimpering and crawling pathetically, before collapsing and dying.

Richie threw up, shivering just as the small dog had right before it died.

He looked around the front room. All Rosemary's dogs were dead or dying, the silence broken only by their whimpers and whines. All the electronics were off. The house was dark, hot, and stifling.

Half crawling and half hobbling, he made it to the front door and threw it open.

Standing at the entrance was a Cajun man with a ruddy face, a big nose, and massive muscles. In one hand, he held a large hatchet, in the other hand, a dead jack rabbit. His eyes were rolled back and glazed over. Dried blood was caked around his mouth.

Richie cried out once more. Somehow, his fear-addled mind managed to wonder if this was Eustace. Richie stumbled back and fell onto the sofa. Eustace teetered and then fell forward with a thud. A hunting knife stuck out from the back of Eustace's head.

Richie took leave of his senses, yelling, "What the fuck is going on here?"

The last of the noises from the dying dogs tapered off, leaving the room in total silence. As he got up from the sofa, he was overcome by a feeling of dread. Almost against his will, he looked over toward the kitchen. That was when he saw them.

The Knight Priory.

The last time he had seen them, even though he knew them by their misspelling, he had been grateful. They had saved him from Marcello's men. This time, however, they seemed no better than butchers. They terrified him.

He took a step back and felt someone behind him. Turning around, he came nose-to-nose with a hooded figure. Gasping, he backed up into another. They both grabbed his arms and restrained him. The room was filled with those hooded figures. They said nothing.

Then Richie heard the sound of heels. The crowd of hooded figures parted and he saw, sauntering toward him, the Lady in Red.

She looked very cross.

"Richard Fastellos," she said. "Author of *The Pale Lantern* and *Darkness Rising*, an up-and-coming author with a promising career." Her hand, smooth but frightfully cold, touched his face, stroking his cheek as a mother would her child's. As before, there was no emotion to it, just the physical act.

"Lived in northern California until his tenth year, when his father nearly beat him and his mother to death with a garden spade. Then moved to Pittsburgh, Pennsylvania. There he went to college—even graduated top of his class—and after holding down many odd jobs, he began his career as a writer." Her hand stopped at his chin, her thumb slipping over his lips. "And—oh, yes. One more thing."

She whipped around and kicked him right in the chest with her heel. He flew back against the wall and landed in a heap. Blood dribbled out of his mouth from where he had bit his tongue.

"He's a complete disappointment," she said, slowly advancing on him.

Richie struggled to breathe, coughing hard enough to make his head throb and his vision blur, until he spat up blood. He felt himself get picked up and pinned to the wall.

The Lady in Red removed a small, shiny object from underneath her dress. It was a scalpel.

She flashed it in front of his face. "You know what's lovely about a scalpel, Richie?"

His eyes focused on the instrument, his body trembling.

"It's small enough to conceal, and yet you can go deep enough to cut nerves and sever tendons." She flashed the blade from side to side, twirling it between her fingers. "It's a terrible irony, isn't it? Something that can give life can also take it. This is the legacy of humanity, Richie, to be able to both heal and harm with the same hand."

Richie finally had enough breath to speak. "What do you want from me?" Blood trickled down his chest from where she had kicked him.

The Lady in Red narrowed her eyes at him. "I want you to figure out who's framing my organization, boy. Who the hell thinks they can frame us, the Knight Priory of Saint Madonna?"

"It's another group," he cried out, his voice getting hoarse. "They dress up just like you guys, black hooded coats and everything!"

She rubbed the blunt end of the scalpel over her lips in a sensual manner. "Who are they?"

"I don't know their names!" Tears were running down his cheeks and snot was running from his nose. "They call themselves the Nite Priory, spelled N-I-T-E. It's an anagram for fool's gold. They're just a bunch of biker thugs. I don't think—"

Moving faster than he could blink, she slammed the scalpel into the wall less than an inch from his eye. He pissed himself, causing the two men holding him to shake their heads in disgust.

"I don't want you to think, child." She glared at him. "I want you to tell me who they are."

Richie trembled as he stared into the Lady in Red's eyes. The sensuality was gone, replaced with the remorseless gaze of a killer. She had gone from composed to cruel in a matter of moments. He couldn't move, like a rabbit caught in a trap.

"I only definitely know of one person involved," he squeaked out. He knew he was sentencing this man to a horrible death. "Jacob Hueber."

She smiled at him, her white teeth almost like fangs. "Thank you, little boy." Leaving the scalpel in the wall, she walked to the sofa. "Drop him."

The men holding him let go, and he fell to the ground.

As he crumpled into a heap, she sat down on the sofa and patted her knee. "Come here, Richie. Crawl to me like the dog you are."

Richie lowered his head, too terrified to disobey, and crawled across the room toward the Lady in Red. His arms and legs were weak, he stank of piss, and his dignity was long gone. When he reached her, he said, "Please don't kill me."

It was all he could think of to say. Anything to stay alive.

Sighing softly, she rubbed his head as if he were a dog. "I won't kill you. You've proven useful after all. Now all you have to do is tell me where Jacob Hueber lives, and you get to keep your miserable life."

He looked away, feeling both disgusted at himself and sickened at the situation. He could barely keep his voice from trembling as he spoke Jacob's address.

Lifting up his chin, she looked at him appraisingly. Her expression hardened as she sniffed. "You smell like piss, boy. Go get cleaned up. The hallway bathroom. Throw those rags you're wearing away. I'll have some fresh clothes laid out for you."

As he struggled to his feet, the hooded figures giving him a wide berth, he asked, "Just one thing I want to know, please."

The Lady in Red raised one eyebrow.

"Why did you kill Rosemary?" Richie asked. His voice was heavy. He didn't like Rosemary one bit, but it made no sense to massacre her, her son, and her dogs. "What did she do to deserve this kind of death?"

Her lovely red lips again parted, showing a very white set of teeth. "Oh, Richie, you should know the answer to that. She knew who murdered Mary Castille. But she sat on that information for money. You realize that the original Bourbon Street Ripper murders might have been solved more quickly if she hadn't?"

That was true. If Rosemary had gone to the police with her information, they might have followed the trail leading to Vincent. "So you have a traitor in your midst. Someone in the Knight Priory who paid Rosemary off," he said. The smell of his own stink was starting to make him nauseated. "Are you going to take care of that person?"

The Lady in Red's smile grew until it looked both unnatural and sinister. "We're going to remove that person from existence."

Chapter 19
Never Off Duty

Date: **Tuesday, August 11, 1992**
Time: **7:00 p.m.**
Location: **Tulane University Hospital**
                Downtown New Orleans

Dixie wanted to scratch her left hand. That would have been rather amazing, as it was no longer there. The doctors referred to it as phantom pain. She referred to it as annoying. Even with the pain medication, she still couldn't escape the sensation.

Looking up at the ceiling of her room, she counted the tiles, trying to pass the time. She had gotten out of surgery earlier that day. It had gone well. The doctors were able to pinch off her arteries and veins before she bled to death, then cut away at the jagged and damaged bone, smooth over the stump with flesh, and sew the whole mess up without a single complication.

More than half her left arm was gone, but she was alive.

She'd be here for at least a few days, if not a week. She wouldn't even get fitted for a prosthesis for another month. *Face it, I'm screwed. I'll be lucky if Ouellette doesn't make me get on disability.*

Gino had gone back home to get some personal belongings so he could stay overnight. Outside her room were two uniformed guards. Ouellette had only come in once to make sure that she was OK, saying they'd talk about her future later.

Dixie wasn't sure what the future held for her.

Despite everything that she had been through, however, she felt proud. When the moment of truth at the wharf had come, she had supported Sam because her gut had told her that the blond woman wasn't a cold-blooded killer. Maybe there was something evil inside her, like another her, but the person Dixie knew was not a heartless sociopath. She had gone out of her way to protect everyone else.

"Oh, Sam," she said to herself. "What demons lurk inside you?"

"It's Samantha, not Sam!"

Dixie blinked in surprise, looking at the entrance to her room. At the doorway was someone who looked tired and yet somehow still completely full of himself. It was Dr. Klein, Sam's psychologist. It was someone she didn't really care to see.

She eyed him as he made his way to the side of her bed. He had purpose in his eyes.

"May I help you?" she asked the approaching doctor.

Looking down at her, he tightened his lips and nodded slowly. "Yes, Detective, I believe you can." He motioned to a nearby chair. "May I?"

Dixie looked away. Something about this guy was really disconcerting. She just didn't want to be around him. "This is a private floor. Go away before I call for the guards."

Dr. Klein sat down. "I wouldn't try my patience if I were you, Detective. I have had a very trying day. Und besides, your boss, Ouellette, has given me permission to talk to you. You can call him if you like and verify it."

As she looked back at him, he added, "I want to talk about Samantha Castille with you for a moment. Und then I want to talk about you. Then I vill be gone."

She looked him up and down, wrinkling her brow. "The commander let you up here? Seriously? Fine. What do you want to know?"

Smiling a vicious little smile at her, he said, "Samantha Castille, as you know, is the killer. She'll be arraigned in the next few days. I wanted to know if you had a chance, while dealing with her, to see Sam of Spades in action."

Dixie narrowed her eyes. "I don't believe that Sam is the killer. I do—"

"Samantha," Dr. Klein said, his voice rising, his face darkening. "How many times must I tell you people zat she is Samantha. Sam is the other part of her und that is the killer."

She shook her head, both her uneasy feeling and her contempt for this man growing every minute. "I have my reasons for believing that she is innocent, Dr. Klein. But to answer your question, the only time I have ever met that 'Sam of Spades' was at the wharf."

That seemed to please him. He again nodded and said, "That fight was not the first time Sam of Spades has harmed others. Remember how I told you before about the times in the past where Sam would take control and force Samantha to harm innocent people."

Dixie closed her eyes. The reminder only added to how conflicted she felt.

Her face must have shown her feelings, because Dr. Klein grinned triumphantly. "Ah-ha, you see! You doubt her as well. It is an unpleasant feeling when you stop und realize that someone you know could be a cold-blooded murderer."

She was getting sick of him. "Whatever you say, Doc," she said, looking up at the ceiling. The pain medication was affecting her ability to focus on the conversation anyway. "You wanted to talk to me about me?" she asked.

"Ah, yes," he said, leaning forward just a hair. "I am very interested in you, Detective. You have figured out some very useful things about this investigation. I am most pleased by how you did."

It was the second time he had made her feel like he was scouting her—the first time they'd met, in his office, he had already known a great deal more about her than he had any business knowing. "Um, thanks. But what do you want?"

"What I want is for you to come work for me when this is over," he said, resting his hands on his knees. "I could use someone with your level of analytical ability, und I think you could benefit from ze prestige of working for me."

She blinked. She couldn't believe this guy. *Is he for real?*

"Of course, you will have to leave the police department," continued Dr. Klein, "but I can provide much better benefits than the city of New Orleans ever could. I have several influential colleagues who would have need of your intellect. In fact, the entire group could use someone like you. But primarily, you will work for me."

"What would I do?" Dixie asked, almost afraid of the answer.

"Why, you'd hunt down serial killers like Samantha for me, so I can treat them. You see, I am working on some very important research, und I need more people like Sam of Spades to complete it."

Looking back up at the ceiling, she ground her teeth. *The utter gall of this prick.*

"Well, sleep on it, then," he said, patting his knees and standing up. His voice suddenly lowered, becoming menacing. "Just remember that I know a lot of powerful people. Don't think for a moment that you can refuse me und walk away like nothing ever happened."

Her eyes were once again wide as he left the room. If her one arm wasn't so weak, she'd have started biting her fingernails. Instead, she just sucked on her bottom lip, staring up at the ceiling and reviewing both the proposition and the threat.

Dixie was like that for a while. When she finally heard someone else enter the room and saw who it was, she instantly felt herself relax and her smile return.

It was Gino.

"Hey, beautiful," he said. He looked tired and his eyes were red, like he had been crying most of the day.

"Hey, handsome," she replied, feebly trying to lift her one good arm to him. She still lacked the strength.

He put down an overnight bag before coming to her side. He stroked her face, holding her remaining hand protectively.

She looked up at him, searching for any sign of revulsion. She couldn't find anything but love. Then she was repulsed at herself for even thinking otherwise.

For the first year of their relationship, Dixie had kept waiting for the other shoe to drop. She kept expecting Gino to get impatient with her for being on call, or for him to get frustrated as the sexual aspect of their relationship progressed at a snail's pace. She didn't even let him kiss her until they had been dating for a month. But he patiently waited and accepted things on her terms.

On the eve of their one-year anniversary, she finally gave herself to him. It was a night she would never forget. Not only was he gorgeous, but he was more gentle and loving than she ever could have hoped for. He seemed to know she was a virgin, and carefully guided her with unyielding patience. As the days progressed, and as she became more confident, they traded caution and temperance in their lovemaking for passion and sensuality.

But throughout all that, he always did things on her terms, when she wanted it.

So when he offered her a chance to move in with him, she took it. Despite her hectic schedule, from being on call at all hours to leaving their Cancun vacation early to help with the new Bourbon Street Ripper case, he always accepted the relationship on her terms.

"What's wrong?" Gino asked.

Dixie realized that she was weeping.

"Sorry," she said as he wiped away her tears. "I am so stupid. For a moment, I really thought you'd leave me now that I am not a complete woman."

To her surprise, he laughed. He then brushed away the last of her tears. "Yes, if you think that, you are very stupid. But you are not stupid, are you?"

Dixie felt like such a heel for even thinking it. "I am so sorry, Gino. I am—"

Gino silenced her with a gentle kiss.

A while later, after the doctor had examined her, Dixie was lying back while Gino sat beside her. He was reading and she was trying to think. The pain medication was really muddling her thoughts, and she lacked the strength to nibble her thumb.

I can't really do much anymore, can I? She wanted to help Michael, help Rodger, and even help Sam. But what could she do?

She didn't realize she was scowling until her boyfriend cleared his throat.

"You seem frustrated, Dixie," he said, looking at her from behind his reading glasses. "Do you want to talk?"

"Yeah," she replied, trying to keep her spirits up. "I'm depressed. I wanna help Michael and Rodger. I wanna help Sam."

Gino continued to gaze at Dixie from behind his glasses. "Why don't you?"

She huffed and scowled. "I can't concentrate. My mind's a jumble. I don't know where to start."

Removing his glasses, he looked into her eyes and said, "Dixie, honey, you just survived losing your arm. Maybe you are over-doing it? Get some rest. The others will figure it out. Sam will be fine. She's no killer."

He said that with such conviction that she found herself starting to really believe it.

"You just rest, Dixie. Get better," he said in a very serious tone. "I love you, but you always push yourself too hard. Stress and exhaustion. Not a good marriage."

Dixie blinked at what Gino had said. "Not a good what?"

"Not a good . . . marriage?" he replied hesitantly. "That is the American expression when two things don't match well together, correct?"

She didn't reply. She was dumbstruck that, once again, her boyfriend had turned the investigation on its head with one simple statement.

Marriage. Oh, God, of course! Gladys was trying to tell us about a wedding!

They had suspected that it had to be someone in the family they didn't know about, but what if Gladys herself had gotten married? How would that affect the Castille estate? Could someone stand to inherit the entire fortune if they married Sam's great-aunt?

Gino cleared his throat, bringing her out of her thoughts. He was still looking at her, his expression still serious.

Dixie smiled once more and said, "You're right, Gino, that is the correct term. And I do need to get some rest. Sorry."

He smiled back at her, put his glasses on, and returned to reading.

She sat there for a few minutes more, mulling over her revelation. She was certain that it was important. She had to get a note to Michael and Rodger.

Leaning up, she called out for one of the officers in the hallway. As Gino gave her a suspicious look, she grinned back apologetically and shrugged. "What can I say, Gino? I'm never off duty. I'm always a detective."

He rolled his eyes and returned to reading.

Chapter 20
Rodger's Really Bad Day

Date: **Tuesday, August 11, 1992**
Time: **8:00 p.m.**
Location: **Russell family mansion**
              Lake Pontchartrain in Slidell

The spikes from the ceiling lowered slowly enough that Rodger had a moment to contemplate his fate. It was as unbelievable as the stuff he had seen with the *tkeeus*. Recalling that he was nearly killed by a different machine only a few days ago, he could only think of one thing to say: "How many times is this going to happen to me?"

His ponderings did nothing to slow the descent of those rows upon rows of spikes. He hurried to the locked door. Peering through the keyhole, he saw the hallway outside, also bathed in red light. *If I can just jimmy the lock open!*

As a last resort, he could shoot the lock, but that had as much of a chance of jamming it as it did of breaking it open.

Rodger hurried through the room, looking for something like a letter opener or a paper clip. As the spikes continued to lower, he realized to his dismay that those things would likely have been on the desk—which was now in the safe room.

Just as he was about to go try his luck with shooting the lock, he saw something that gave him an idea. A pair of pliers. Grabbing them, he looked for something hard and heavy. His eyes fell upon a poker near the fireplace.

Looking up, he saw that the spikes were more than halfway down. He had to hurry.

Returning to the door, he got to work. Quickly, he took all the bullets out of his clip. Next, he used the pliers to yank the slugs out, discarding them across the floor. Then, he poured the propellant from all of the bullet casings into one, packing it down as much as possible. He wasn't sure if this would be enough to have the effect he hoped for.

Rodger heard a cracking sound and saw the spikes penetrating the furnishings of the room with no sign of stopping. He didn't have time to second-guess himself. Taking the improvised explosive, he pressed it into the keyhole against the lock. He could already feel the spikes scratching the top of his head. He was running out of time.

Grabbing the poker, he said a quick prayer. Then he swung it at the bullet as hard as he could. Instead, he hit the door, scratching it.

"Shit," he shouted and swung again. This time he hit the doorknob.

"Come on! Dammit!"

Rodger started to feel the spikes poke at his head again. Getting on one knee, he focused on the bullet's primer, took three deep breaths, and swung, letting out a guttural yell.

With a loud *bang*, the casing exploded, taking the lock with it.

Just as he felt the spikes poking him again, he kicked the door opened and slid out into the hallway.

For a few moments, he laid there on the wooden floor, the red glow of the warning lights all around him. Taking in great gulps of air, he wondered just what kind of nutcase booby-traps his study with a spiked ceiling.

"At least that's over. Now to get out of here!" Rodger went down the hallway toward the landing on the left. He was almost there when he felt a sudden motion beneath his feet. With a grunt, he fell right on his face. *Jesus! Did the floor just move on me?*

He scowled. "I am done with this stupid shit." He got up and was about to keep going when bars shot up from the ground, separating the landing from the hallway. He could see Reggie's corpse on the other side of the bars, and he was cut off from the stairs.

What the—? He couldn't believe it.

Then he heard another clicking sound. The floor underneath him jerked again, and he fell to his ass with a yelp. In moments, the entire hallway had turned into a fast-moving conveyor belt trying to take him past the stairs and further down the hallway.

Rodger grabbed the bars next to him, stopping himself from flying down the hallway. Looking toward the end of the hallway, he saw that the wall had opened up, revealing an eerily familiar vicious-looking shredding machine.

"Oh, what the fuck? Again?!" He couldn't believe it. It was like Jonathon Russell and Mad Monty had teamed up to get him. The flashback of being chained down on that conveyor belt, heading feet-first into Monty's machine, was overwhelming. He frantically looked around for a way to get through the bars, but it seemed hopeless. He was too big. And there were no other doorways nearby that he could get through.

As his grip weakened, he felt that he had once again failed. He had failed to save Edward from Vincent. He had failed to be there for Sam as she had grown up. He had failed to stop Michael from getting shot. He had failed to keep Sam from getting hurt. This was just another failure for an old loser well past his prime.

Maybe the world will be better off if I die.

Rodger's hands slipped and he slid down, grasping the corner of the landing with his fingers. With nothing left for him to grab onto, it was just a matter of time before he was flung down the hallway into the shredder. Morbidly, he wondered if it would be a quick death.

Then he remembered something Douglas had said just the other night, something that meant everything to him: "You'll be the one who saves that little girl."

He remembered breaking down the door into the torture chamber underneath the Castille mansion. He remembered seeing what was left of Edward, with Vincent proudly holding up his son's heart and grinning madly. He remembered seeing little Samantha sitting there like a doll, with her hands on her lap, staring blankly ahead. Even though she didn't remember witnessing the death, her eyes forever reflected her loss of innocence—eyes devoid of life.

I have to save that little girl. She needs me!

Rodger looked up at his tired, old hands, gritted his teeth, and cried out, "I can't die now! Until I save Sam, *I will not die!*"

With a primordial roar, Rodger pulled himself up and linked his arms around the last bar on the landing. The moving wooden floor shredded his pants and then tore at his skin. He ignored the pain. Grabbing his pistol, he started to hit the wood molding of the landing next to the last bar, cracking it off bit by bit. Soon he had a gap large enough to pull himself through.

He got caught by his belt—not unexpected, considering his weight. He quickly undid it and threw it aside. The belt hit the shredder with an awful clank as he squirmed through the gap. As he did so, the jagged wood caught on his already damaged pants and shredded them. With the remaining fragments falling right off his legs, Rodger ran down the stairs.

Unsurprisingly, they flattened into a slide. As he slid down, a trap door at the bottom opened into a pit. It was lined with jagged spikes.

"Of course it is . . ."

Grabbing onto the railing, he stopped himself from falling into the pit by just a few inches. His shoulders yanked in their sockets. He cried out in pain. "Son of a bitch!"

With great effort, Rodger pulled himself up and rolled over the railing, falling down to the foyer floor a few feet below. He lay there for a few moments, catching his breath. He was wheezing. *If I survive this, I'm going to cut down on the cigarettes and pick up exercising.*

The front door had been broken off its hinges, likely by the attacker who had killed Russell.

It was time to get out of there before another trap sprang.

He rushed forward. His legs ached terribly, and every part of him burned with effort. As he approached the front doorway, he roared one more guttural yell and leaped.

He felt the hot August air rush over his face. He heard another click as he flew out of the house and rolled down the front stairs.

A guillotine blade dropped down the front doorway, missing him by mere inches.

Rodger landed on the front lawn and lay there motionless. It felt like every muscle, every tendon, and every bone ached. He waited for another click to sound, for another machine to turn on, for some additional signal that he was still in danger.

All he heard was the guillotine blade retracting.

He closed his eyes and lay there for a long time. In the background, the sounds of the Russell mansion death traps quieted down. He was finally roused by the blinking red and blue lights of the back-up he had called for earlier.

Sitting up, he felt like he had been through a war.

I think I've been through enough bullshit to last me a lifetime, he thought as he lit up a cigarette and sat there, in his overcoat and boxers, smoking on the front lawn. *As God is my witness, I will never be frightened by anything again.*

When the police finally arrived, led by Rivette and Landry, Rodger gave them a brief rundown of what had happened and a warning about the death traps in the mansion. Rivette and Landry, despite being grateful that Rodger was alive, couldn't help but make cracks about him wearing only his boxers. Jokes about him being a flasher helped cut down on the tension of the evening.

Luckily, he had clothes in his car—the dirty ones from when he and Sam had gone to Angola.

"So you've got everything?" Rodger asked after finishing his initial report. He figured the real report would probably read like a horror movie.

"Yeah, I got it all," Rivette said as he finished jotting the notes down. "Likely the entire house is trapped. If we're unlucky, the only way to disarm the traps is in that safe room you mentioned in the old man's study. Fun times all around."

"Probably should cut the power to the whole house," Landry added, making his way to the front door.

Rodger nodded in agreement. "That's probably a good idea, guys. Just cut the power and make sure there's no backups running. That house will eat you."

Rivette started giving orders to some of the uniformed officers. They had already sectioned off the entire mansion as a hazard zone.

Rodger figured that the two detectives would be busy with this all night long. This house of traps would likely cause quite a stir throughout the city.

"Hey, guys," said Landry from right outside the front door. He was peering into the dark house. "I think it's calmed down inside. I think—"

His words were cut short as the guillotine blade came down again, slicing the buttons right off his shirt and barely missing his flesh.

Rivette stared in horror.

Landry fell back on his butt and started screaming.

Rodger put out his cigarette. "Dumbass."

It was 9:30 when Rodger got back to the precinct. His everything still hurt, and he was still shell-shocked over the whole incident. All around, the floor was quiet, none of the detectives were at their desks, and Ouellette's office was dim. Rodger sat at his desk with a heavy thud.

He had almost gotten himself killed and was no closer to solving the case. Furthermore, the identity of the person who had given Vincent the *tkeeus* had died with Jonathon.

"What a fucking night," he said, closing his eyes and leaning back in his chair. He could just go to sleep right there at his desk. *I should. I should just lean back, put my feet up, and—*

His phone rang.

His eyes shot open. Nearly falling back, he picked up the phone. "Detective Bergeron. Richie?" He had told Richie to call as soon as he was done in Lafayette.

"No. It's me," said Michael.

Rodger sat up more. His partner's voice didn't sound weak or even tired. Instead, it sounded all business, like the Michael he knew. "Michael, I—hey, how are you?"

"I'm fine, Rodger," Michael said. His voice then dropped. "Look, can you come pick me up?"

Rodger knotted his brow. The last thing he wanted to do was go anywhere. "Michael, not to be rude, but I almost died a little while ago. Again. So I'm not too enthused about getting up again. I really just want to sit here for a while and, you know, be grateful I'm alive."

Michael exhaled quickly and said, "Look, I'm sorry you almost died again. But this is important."

That got Rodger's attention. "What's going on? What happened?"

Michael's voice sounded strained, as if he were trying hard to contain his excitement. "I did it, Rodger. I solved the case. I know who framed Sam!"

Chapter 21

A Break in the Case

Date: **Tuesday, August 11, 1992**
Time: **8:30 p.m.**
Location: **Tulane University Hospital**
             Downtown New Orleans

Blind Moses,

Years ago, you aided our master, Vincent Castille, in his great experiment. Even after his death, the special talents he bequeathed to you are strong, and it is our belief that you are now more powerful than ever before.

We know that you seek retribution against those who aided in the downfall of your master, just as we seek retribution against the person who undeservedly received the Castille family birthright. Work with us, and we will extinguish the lives of the people you hate the most.

A copycat killer will soon begin a reign of terror in New Orleans similar to Vincent's. These murders are necessary for us to complete our plans. Do not attempt to stop these killings.

Enclosed is a list of names. These are your targets. For the first four names, make sure that they are eliminated as soon as you are able, so that they will not reveal anything to the police. For the rest of the names, you are to eliminate them when the copycat killer finishes off the last victim. You will know who that is when the time arises.

You will find a cache of military-grade weapons in an abandoned apartment on the corner of Chartres and Barracks Street in the French Quarter. The cache should be more than enough to see you through these tasks.

Do not eliminate the detectives who are assigned to this case until the murders are over. Their involvement is necessary to our plans. You may engage them in self-defense, but do not kill them.

Under no circumstances are you to ever directly engage Samantha Castille. She is ours.

We appreciate your compliance in this endeavor, and we promise your satisfaction. For your cooperation, we will also ensure that your sister, Tania, remains unharmed and uninvolved.

Sincerely,

The Knight Priory of Saint Madonna

It was earlier in the evening, before Michael called Rodger, when he put down the letter to Blind Moses, which had been translated from Braille.

In his lap were several sets of notebooks, all open. On and around his bed were stacks upon stacks of papers. In the hospital room were several boxes of papers—all notes on the copycat murder case. Michael was sure Ouellette must have pulled some serious strings to get this to happen.

He shook his head and looked at the list of names. The first four names were Topper Jack, Mad Monty, Fat Willie, and Robert Fontenot. Then there were the names Rosemary Boucher, Giorgio "Blue-Eyed" Marcello, Louis Ouellette, Kyle Aucoin, and Rodger Bergeron.

So there it is . . . Whoever was doing this, whether they were a group or an individual, was using the Knight Priory name. They used the real name for Blind Moses and the fake name for the others. *This is stupid. It feels like a damn child's game.*

He stretched and yawned. "But people have been dying out of order since the start of this fiasco. So I don't know what to believe about Blind Moses's 'hit list' anymore. What bullshit."

He looked up at the clock in the hospital room. In thirty minutes, it would be nine o'clock and time for his final medication. Afterward, he'd be able to check out at any time, even though the doctors had recommended he stay one or two more days. Michael felt fine. He had been in the hospital for three days and was making a remarkable recovery, which he attributed to having a clean gunshot wound and a lot of luck. He was going to be more careful in the future.

Most of the day, he'd been poring over every document he had on the case, including the letter to Blind Moses that Richie had recovered. From what Rodger had said, it seemed Richie had really stepped up to the plate and become helpful.

Well, they say love makes you do strange things, Michael thought to himself, chuckling inwardly. He'd never been in love. His few crushes had caused such great problems with his father that he had simply shut down that part of himself. The only people he truly cared about were Rodger, Dixie, and his little sister, Alexia.

He shook his head to clear his thoughts, going so far as to slap himself on the face a few times. He was starting to lose focus. He knew that he was tired. But he also knew that he needed to figure something out tonight—Sam was due to be arraigned in the morning.

Focusing on the paperwork, he looked over the various notes that he, Rodger, Dixie, and Richie had taken. He even had Sam's notebook for her mystery notes and the silver pen she always wrote with.

And then he had a note from Dixie, delivered by an officer over an hour ago. It read: "Kent stopped us from asking Gladys about weddings. If Gladys was married, would ownership of the Castille estate transfer to the husband?"

Michael felt that she was on to something pretty important.

Looking over all the notes, he started to feel his eyes hurt. He rubbed his brow and sighed. "So much information. But the answer to this case is in that mountain of notes. I'm sure of it. It's no longer about finding out information, it's about deducing the answer from what we know."

Taking out his own notebook, he reviewed the facts.

Someone was killing people in the exact same way that Vincent Castille had. The victims were unrelated to each other. The first victim, Virginia Babineaux, was lured to her death at Ursuline and Dauphine. The second victim, Rebecca Clemens, was abducted on her way to the drugstore and taken to Pirate Alley. The third victim, Cheryl Aucoin, was last seen at O'Flaherty's Irish Pub on Toulouse but was murdered all the way north on Burgundy. Only Virginia was kidnapped and murdered in the same area. The other two were lured from their point of abduction to the place they were murdered.

The junior detective furrowed his brow. *Why take the victims so far? And how? How do you get someone like Cheryl Aucoin over eight city blocks away?*

Unfolding his personal map of the French Quarter, Michael marked off all the known locations. There was no way anyone could drag a girl with them that far and not have someone notice. And O'Flaherty's would have been too crowded to kidnap a teenager. So whoever kidnapped Cheryl had to have been someone she trusted.

Michael blinked and looked up. "Someone she knew . . ."

Quickly sifting through his notes, he pulled up Dixie's impressively assembled biographical data on Cheryl Aucoin. "Sixteen years old. Was a junior at Chappell High School. Average GPA. Favorite musician was Marilyn Manson. Favorite books were supernatural romance. Hobbies included poetry, motorcycles, cemeteries, and photography. Ah, a Gothic girl. Was dating a college student. Whoa!"

Putting down the notes, he nodded to himself. "Rebellious and dated college guys. She was a cop's daughter, so I can't see her being completely stupid and going out with just anyone. So whoever lured her to her death must have known her through her boyfriend."

He flipped through Dixie's notes and found the name of Cheryl's boyfriend. "Gregory Billot. Senior at the University of New Orleans School of Science. Sheesh, talk about robbing the cradle." Michael noted that Gregory was majoring in computer science.

Looking back at his notes, Michael continued to lay out the facts. Sam's DNA was only found in the third victim. Skin cells from the hand. For both the first and second victims, no DNA evidence was found. The only thing connecting Sam to the second murder was her story. And there was nothing connecting Sam to the first murder.

Closing his eyes, he thought, *Skin cells from the hand. You can get that easily. Just a few cells would be needed to positively identify the DNA.* If Sam was awake, he would just ask if anyone had scratched her hands recently. He opened his eyes and put that thought aside for the moment.

He then focused his attention on Sam's published stories in the *Times-Picayune*, reading them very slowly. He noted that they were extremely well written. He had always liked Sam's old stories—the Mortimer Branston stories—but the writing wasn't this good. It was like this project had inspired her.

Michael frowned. Now that he had carefully read both stories, he saw that while there were some stark similarities, the details weren't as exact as the media was making it out to be. In fact, Sam's story didn't include a lot of details.

"All the killer would need to do is get a copy of this manuscript. Then they could fill in the details themselves." He put the newspaper clippings away.

With a sigh, he picked up the list of people at the *Times-Picayune* who had physical access to Sam's manuscripts before print—the list Richie had gotten from Jacob. It was about a dozen names, including Jacob's and Caroline's. None of the names stuck out. But someone at the *Times-Picayune* had to be involved. There was no conceivable way for anyone else to have access to a copy of Sam's manuscript in order to fill in the blanks.

He stopped writing. *A copy . . .?*

Quickly, he organized all his notes and very carefully got out of bed, making sure not to detach either the monitoring equipment or the IV drip. Soon, he was opening a box stuffed with police reports. He took out the report of the police search of Sam's townhome.

A few minutes later, Michael found what he was looking for: the report on Sam's office equipment. There had been a module missing from Sam's photocopier. Computer forensics said that that brand of copier had one module that could hold either extra memory or a tele-communications modem. So it had to have been one or the other.

He snickered. "Extra memory, my butt. Someone had a modem in Sam's copier. That's how they got Sam's manuscripts. I'm certain of it."

Excitement was growing inside him. If his hunches were correct, then he was homing in on the guilty parties.

"Ahem, Detective?" said his nurse from the doorway. It was nine o'clock. Time for his medication.

Michael blushed and slid back into his hospital bed. "Sorry."

She administered his medication and took his readings. While she did, he said, "I need to make a phone call or two. Important to the case."

She nodded, got him some slippers, and helped him out of bed. He leaned on the pole holding his IV drip as the nurse helped him hobble along the hallway to an empty nurse's station.

"You can make the calls here, Detective," said the nurse with a congenial but tired smile. She looked like she'd been working a long shift.

Flashing a small, handsome smile of his own, Michael said, "Thanks. Do you mind giving me some privacy?"

She paused and got a thoughtful look. Then she said, "I'll go take care of a few more patients and then come back. Just be quiet. If the doctors find out . . ."

"It'll be our secret, but thanks. And I understand. I'll stay put here until you get back," Michael said.

Once she had left, Michael dialed the precinct. He hoped that Rodger would be there, but he doubted it. He recalled that his part-ner had a very full plate today.

Someone picked up. "Eighth precinct, Detective Rivette speaking."

"Hey, Rivette, it's Michael. Do you have a moment?"

Rivette replied with a loud yawn.

Michael held the receiver away in disgust. "Rivette, this is serious," he said, trying to keep from losing his patience.

"Sorry, man," Rivette said. "The commander has about half a dozen of us on clean-up duty. Landry and I still have to get back on the Marcello murders. And—hey, aren't you still in the hospital?"

"Yeah, I am," Michael said, holding back a snarky comment. "I just need some information, Rivette. Then you can go to bed."

"Fine, fine," Rivette replied. It sounded like he was getting out a pen and paper. "What do ya need, you slave driver?"

Michael began. "I need to know who installed Sam's office equipment. A complete paper trail, from ordering to delivery to installation. If there was pre-assembly, I need to know that, too. I want to know who pays for it, how often there is maintenance, etc. I am specifically interested in Sam's photocopier. The forensics report here says it can have extra memory or a modem. I want to know if it had either."

Taking a breath, he waited for Rivette to catch up. He heard scribbling.

"OK, anything else?" asked Rivette.

"Yes," said Michael. "I need to know the last time it was maintained, who did it, and what was done. I need—"

"Whoa, whoa, whoa! Slow down, Speedy. We're going to need subpoenas for that," replied Rivette. "You're basically asking me to get records on all business dealings with Samantha Castille. I'm sure her lawyer will have a field day with that."

Michael thought hard about that. He hated to admit it, but Rivette was right. *The only thing covered in the search warrant was Sam's townhome. But there has to be a way to do this legally.*

A moment later, he hit upon the answer. "All right, here's what we do. Just get the names of the companies that handled, delivered, or installed Sam's photocopier. If you can get who owns those companies, even better. We can question them. Then pull the LUDs for Sam's townhome. I am specifically looking for outgoing calls on the 6th and 8th. Call me back with them."

"Right," said Rivette, scribbling. "OK, I'll call you back tonight if I find anything. Otherwise, your ass can wait." He chuckled.

Michael was glad for his recent experiences giving him a little perspective. A week ago, he'd have taken offense to that. "Thanks, Rivette. Get some rest when you do," he said as he hung up.

For a few minutes, he sat there, waiting for his nurse to show back up. When he finally heard footsteps, they were accompanied by a familiar female voice.

"Yes, Director. I've already contacted Abel. The final tests have come in positive."

It was Camellia, Dr. Lazarus's personal assistant. She was talking into something that looked very similar to a cordless phone receiver.

Michael didn't know why, but he quickly hurried into an alcove of the nurse's station. He wanted to trust Dr. Lazarus and his people, but they were a little too secretive for him.

"I'm afraid it's a complete match," Camellia said. "It confirms our suspicions that the *tkeeus* is nothing more than a catalytic agent."

What are they talking about? Michael thought to himself. *Who are they talking about?*

Camellia paced back and forth. "No, sir. Detective LeBlanc refuses to take any hints regarding the *tkeeus*. He's certain it's just a drug. With all due respect, both Abel and I think it's a waste of time pursuing him."

Michael listened intently, wondering what he was missing.

"Yes, sir," said Camellia, her voice getting softer. "We've analyzed surveillance video from the wharf. And we've performed all the spectral analyses and EMF tests on her. There is a definite presence there. We're certain of it."

Michael's eyes widened. *I bet they're talking about Sam!* He wasn't sure if they were testing Sam for brain wave activity or if this was more of that supernatural bunk they had hinted at earlier.

The footsteps stopped right by him. Michael's heart pounded in his chest, and he felt a cold sweat. He was sure he'd be discovered.

Camellia's voice returned to normal. "I understand, sir. . . . Yes. Right now, Dr. Klein is moving to get custody of her. He's using that attorney's help. We're trying to block him, but one more incident where she exhibits abnormal behavior, and we're certain she'll be remanded to his care."

"Yes, sir," Camellia said, her footsteps picking up again. "I'll contact Abel and tell him to get her into your custody. Since she was a previous patient of yours, that should give us some latitude. . . . I understand. I'll pull back and let the detectives finish their investigation. . . . As you command, sir."

A moment later, the footsteps were gone.

Michael stood there for a long time, sweating. He couldn't shake the feeling that he had just overhead something very important.

"Hello, Detective," came the voice of his nurse. She was standing behind him, arms folded. She looked cross.

Michael grinned nervously. "Back to my room, right?"

A few minutes later, he was back in his hospital room, back in his bed, and once more alone. Closing his eyes, he started to think things out again.

Why would Dr. Klein be pushing to have Sam committed? Did he really want to make a case study out of her that badly? Or was there another reason?

Opening his eyes, he recalled what he had just overheard. "Camellia said that it was Dr. Klein and 'that attorney.' 'That attorney'? She can't mean Kent, right? Surely Kent has nothing to gain if Sam is committed?"

Flipping through the notes Richie had given him, Michael found some on Sam's last meeting with her lawyer. "Richie doesn't know the details, but that meeting didn't go well. Would this Kent guy betray Sam?"

Getting up again, he crept over to another one of the boxes, carrying the IV with him. In the box was a copy of the Castille estate files. While he hadn't seen any use for it yet, suspecting Kent was enough of a reason to look through them.

It took him a while to sort through the documents before finding the clause he was looking for. *Right here.* The section was drafted after Sam was committed with Dallas to the Acadia Vermilion Hospital, right after Vincent's arrest.

He read through the document carefully. It stated that if Samantha Castille was ever declared legally insane, either by commitment or by being found not guilty by reason of mental disease or defect, or was convicted of a capital offense, all ownership of the Castille estate would be transferred to the next of kin.

Michael blinked and put down the document. "Next of kin? Says here that Gladys is the only next of kin. Vincent's sister and Sam's great-aunt. Now, I wonder if—"

"Ahem, Detective?" said his nurse, once again at the doorway. She held up an envelope. "You got a letter from the clerk of court. Also, would you like me to unhook you? You don't really need the drip anymore."

His ears burned. "Yeah, can you?"

As the nurse unhooked the IV, he closed his eyes in thought.

It had to be someone who could benefit from Sam's commitment or conviction. It seemed like only the great-aunt stood to gain anything. But Rodger had said that Gladys was an old woman who was barely coherent.

Michael opened his eyes. "But Dixie mentioned that when they brought up weddings, Kent shut the interview down. If Gladys got married and Sam had to forfeit her inheritance, Gladys's new husband would stand to benefit."

Suddenly, the picture was coming into focus for him. And it was ugly. As the nurse left, he picked up the envelope. It was from a guy named Derek Malone and was labeled "Marriage License."

He opened the envelope. One look at the names on the marriage license confirmed his suspicions.

Kent Bourgeois and Gladys Castille.

"The son of a bitch married his way into the Castille family," Michael said. He had never felt such disgust before. "Dixie was right. The bastard has put himself right in line for all of Sam's inheritance."

"Excuse me, Detective," came the tired voice of Michael's nurse. She was standing at the doorway. "Someone named Rivette is on the phone for you at the nurse's station. Take your time. I'm going on a coffee break."

His hands shaking, Michael hurried to the phone. "Whatcha got for me, Rivette?" he asked, barely containing his excitement. It was exhilarating to be on the hunt again.

"Wow, Michael, you hit the nail on the head with this one." Rivette sounded excited as well.

Michael couldn't wait any longer. "Come on, Scott, just lay it on me."

"All right, all right, bud," Rivette said. "The company that manages Sam's office equipment is called Office Electronics. Sam is a priority customer, so the installation and maintenance for her equipment is always handled by their operations manager. Some guy named Gregory Billot."

Gregory Billot, Michael thought, inhaling quickly. *Cheryl Aucoin's boyfriend!*

Rivette continued, "I pulled his record, and he's got three prior arrests for possession. Cocaine, mostly. He got off on all three charges. His lawyer is bank-rolled by a guy named Irving Jennings."

"Irving Jennings?" asked Michael. He had never heard that name before.

Rivette chuckled. "It's not just that. Seems that Mr. Jennings has been paying the legal defense costs of several ne'er-do-wells for years. They all belong to a motorcycle gang whose theme is black hooded coats. Guess what they're called?"

Michael's eyes widened. "What?"

"Why, they're the Rippers, ladies and gentlemen!" exclaimed Rivette. His tone had taken on that of a game show host. "OK, the last one is a real kicker. You'll never guess who their leader is—the guy Irving's bailed out the most times."

Michael thought for a moment, then said, "I have no idea. Who?"

Rivette chuckled again. "Check this out—it's the son of Samantha Castille's lawyer."

Michael's jaw dropped. "Kent . . . has a son?"

"Well . . ." Rivette said, the eagerness gone from his voice, "I think he's Kent's son. Although Bourgeois is a pretty common last name here in the bayou." Rivette said "bayou" like "bye-yoo."

"OK, OK," said Michael. "So who is this alleged son?"

"His name is Nick Bourgeois," said Rivette. "He's called the Demon Rider of Bourbon Street. Kinda has a Sweeney Todd thing going on, eh?"

Michael's head was spinning. *Nick! The guy from the letter to Fat Willie! Holy shit, I was right! Nick is Kent's son. That bastard Kent is out to screw Sam.*

"Anything else?" he asked, sitting down.

"Just those LUDs," replied Rivette.

"OK, what about them? Anything out of place?"

Michael could hear Rivette rifle through some papers. "Honestly," said Rivette, "there are two calls from Samantha Castille's townhome that don't make sense. Both are on the target dates. One is very early on the morning of the 6th and the other is on the afternoon of the 8th. But here's the thing: the 'call from' number is not the same as the house number. And it was transmitting data, not voice."

A modem! Faxes! Slowly, Michael stood up again. Both times matched up to when Sam had made copies of her manuscripts. "Where did those calls go to?" he asked, his excitement growing.

"Ah, to the Inn on Bourbon Street," said Rivette. "I have no way of knowing which room, though."

"No, no, that's fine," said Michael, excitement continuing to grow within him. "Listen, can you get Ouellette on the phone? I think I'm about to break the case."

"Break the case?" asked Rivette. "What do you mean? Isn't Sam the killer? Isn't she being arraigned tomorrow?"

Michael didn't feel like explaining things. He was too caught up in his thoughts. "I'll explain later. Just let me speak to Ouellette, please."

"He ain't here, man," said Rivette. "Just me and Landry, and we're about to take a smoke break."

Michael heard Landry in the background. He sounded excited.

"Or not," said Rivette. "Sorry, man, we've got a call down at Lake Pontchartrain. Gotta run!"

Michael felt frustrated. "Ugh. I'll see about getting in touch with him myself. Thanks a lot," he said sarcastically, and hung up. Almost immediately, he regretted acting like an ass to Rivette, who had been helpful so many other times. *I'll have to apologize when I see him again.*

After a moment of thought, he called the Inn on Bourbon Street.

A woman picked up. "Good evening, thank you for calling the Inn on Bourbon Street. This is Viviane. How may I help you?"

"Yes," said Michael, keeping his voice low. "This is Detective Michael LeBlanc, New Orleans eighth precinct. My badge number is 3276."

There was a pause before Viviane asked, "Yes, Detective. How may I help you?"

Michael nervously tapped on the side of the phone. "I need to know if any of your rooms are wired to receive faxes."

"No, Detective," replied Viviane. "Only our business center is . . ." Her voice trailed off. A moment later, she said, "Oh, my apologies. I see here that someone did pay for an extra phone line."

Michael's pulse quickened. *That's it! A second phone line so that faxes won't interfere with calls!*

"Which room is that?" he asked. "Who's staying there?"

There was a pause, and then Viviane replied, "It's Room 205. An older gentleman named Irving Jennings has been staying in that room for several weeks now."

As the name sank in, Michael broke into a sweat. *Oh, my God. The guy who has been bankrolling the Rippers gang!*

Clearing his throat, he asked, "How much longer until he checks out?"

"Let me see," replied Viviane, her voice accompanied by the clicking of computer keys. "He's checking out tomorrow morning."

Michael processed the information in silence.

Several seconds passed before Viviane asked, "Is there anything else, Detective?"

"No. Thank you." He hung up the phone.

For a few minutes, he sat there with his face in his hands, wondering who Irving Jennings was. Quite suddenly, a thought popped up.

What if Irving Jennings was Kent Bourgeois?

Even though it was a bit of a leap, he felt he was right. Kent had the finances to bankroll the Rippers. He could bail his son out of trouble without implicating himself. And if Sam went down for murder, and Kent was married to Gladys, wouldn't that put him in a position to get the Castille family fortune?

Kent and Nick are behind the murders to frame Sam and get her money. Whether they're doing the killings themselves or hiring someone else, they're behind it.

Michael nibbled on his bottom lip. The only question was, how did Julius Boucher fit into this? Was he part of Nick's gang? Was it another alias? The fact that "Nite Priory" was derived from "Knight Priory," and that it came from the hospital Sam, Dallas, and Julius were at, had to be important. But how did the word game and Julius fit into this?

But Julius aside, as far as Michael was concerned, he had blown the case wide open. And to get the final bit of proof, the person calling himself Irving Jennings needed to be apprehended.

Picking up the phone again, he called the precinct. No answer. Frowning, he called Rodger's apartment. No answer. Then he called Dixie and Gino's apartment. Not surprisingly, no one answered.

Dammit, he thought, *where is everyone? Dammit, I wish I remembered people's pager numbers!*

Rubbing his eyes, he called his commander at home. *Please pick up!*

Two rings later, he heard a sleepy Ouellette answer. "If you're not the mayor, or don't have the best excuse in the world for waking me up, whoever you are, I am going to kick your ass all over the city."

"Commander, it's Detective LeBlanc," Michael said, his tone authoritative. "I broke the case. I know who's really behind it. It's not Sam."

There was silence before Ouellette said, "Tell me."

Michael spent ten minutes laying out his trail of logic.

When he was done, Ouellette asked, "And you're sure of this?"

"I'm positive. They're in Room 205 at the Inn on Bourbon Street, using the alias of Irving Jennings. I'll meet with Rodger and apprehend them."

"That's a negative," Ouellette said. "I'll contact Bergeron and get a team together. God, I hope you're right, LeBlanc." He hung up.

Michael sat there holding the phone. Just like that, he had been dropped from the case again. *What the hell is that about?!* He found himself getting more upset every passing moment.

After all I've been through with this case, how can he just throw me to the side? I deserve to apprehend this son of a bitch!

Picking up the phone, he tried the precinct once more. This time, he got Rodger.

It took very little effort to convince him that Kent was the villain. It seemed that Rodger already had serious issues with the Castille family lawyer. When Michael brought up going to apprehend him, however, Rodger protested.

"If Ouellette thinks you need to stay out of this one, then it's for your own good," Rodger said.

Michael held back his rising temper. "Man, that's bullshit! You know I can handle this, Rodger. I'm fine. The wound was clean, and it's almost healed."

"I don't think it's that, buddy," Rodger said. "I just think the commander is worried about you."

"Then bring a vest!" Michael stopped as he realized he was shouting.

Rodger sighed. "Partner, I've been through shit tonight. I told you I almost got killed by some lunatic's funhouse. I don't think either of us should go in there. Let's let Ouellette handle it."

"Come on, Rodger." Michael was starting to feel desperate. "For all the shit we've been through? For all the heartache we've suffered? Don't we deserve to be the ones to put an end to this?" As he stopped talking, he realized that he was near tears. He had not felt this deeply in a long time. He had forgotten how painful it could be.

Rodger was silent for a long time. Finally, he said, "Yeah. Fine. But we do this by the book, partner. I'll bring the vests. You bring your gun. We work out a plan so one covers the other. We go in, we apprehend, we wait for backup. No deviations."

While Michael appreciated the irony of Rodger saying that things would be done "by the book," he was nonetheless very grateful. "Thanks, buddy. I appreciate it."

"Ugh," groaned Rodger. "Just don't get hurt again, Michael. And this better be the end of it. These two better be the killers."

"They are." Michael hung up the phone.

Even as he went to his room to get dressed, he fought back any doubt. This had to be the end of the case. "I'm sure of it."

Chapter 22
No Reason To Kill

Date: **Tuesday, August 11, 1992**
Time: **9:00 p.m.**
Location: **Home of Rosemary Boucher**
                Lafayette, Louisiana

"Come on, kid," said the gruff voice of one of the hooded figures just outside the bathroom door. "The Lady's waiting. You don't want to be here for too much longer."

"I'm coming! Fuck, I'm going as fast as I can," Richie said as he finished drying off. He didn't completely blame the Lady in Red for hurrying him along. He had taken close to thirty minutes to clean up, spending half the time crying in the shower and nursing the wound she had kicked into his chest.

What the hell had he gotten himself into? Now he was party to two different sets of murders.

He wondered if he had just gone completely mad. It would be better than being in the company of people whose favorite method of killing involved disemboweling. Furthermore, they had taken Julius's letter to Rosemary before he could read it. All he had seen was the name "Annie-Mae Bernard" and the phrase "Don't try to find me."

By the time he was finished showering, he knew he had to talk to the Lady in Red. He needed to get some answers, for Sam's sake. Even if it got him killed, he needed to question the Lady in Red, and he needed to do it now. He pushed back the feelings of anxiety as hard as he could.

Outside the shower, Richie found a set of jeans and a shirt which he recognized as one of his spare clothing sets from the Ritz Carlton.

Great! They had gotten into his hotel room and brought clothes all the way to Lafayette. *Love it! I'm being stalked by a psychotic noir bitch and her murder gang.*

As he exited the bathroom, the overpowering smell of petrol hit his nostrils, the fumes soaking into his clothes and hair.

"Ugh, what the hell?" he said, stumbling out to the front room. Several of the hooded figures were drenching the house in gasoline, coating the corpses of the dogs, Eustace, and even Rosemary, who had been dragged up to the front.

One of the hooded figures said, "You should probably clear out— the Lady's waiting for you."

As fast as he could move, Richie fled the house. As he approached the entrance of the driveway, where Sam's car was waiting, he saw the Lady in Red standing there, arms folded and watching everything. As he joined her, she looked him over, sniffed, and shook her head with disdain.

He smelled his hands. They reeked of gasoline. *Ugh, I hate that smell.*

"Where the heck is your car?" he asked, out of breath.

"Vans are around the corner in the woods," she replied. She raised and then dropped her arm. The hooded figures who were pouring gasoline into the house pulled back. One of them lit a match, flicked it inside, and set the entire house ablaze.

As the glow of the fire cascaded over Richie's face, he said, "OK, so, before you leave, I have some questions."

The Lady in Red was watching the house burn.

Clearing his throat, he added, "Considering that I'm getting pulled more and more into this insanity, I feel I'm owed at least a few."

Without looking at him, she said, "Fair enough. You have three questions."

"All right, fine," he said. "So are you the actual Knight Priory of Saint Madonna? Are you the same group Vincent was in charge of?"

"Sort of," she said. "We're their descendants, or what's left of them. Twenty-five years ago, Master Castille performed a set of rituals that ruined the original Knight Priory. So now we exist to help interested parties take care of certain problems."

He arched an eyebrow at her. "Huh?"

The Lady in Red blew a kiss to Richie. "We kill people, little boy."

He exhaled and nodded. It was exactly what he had been expecting to hear. He was surprised, however, to hear her call Vincent "Master Castille." It was as if, right after the link between her group and the old Knight Priory was made, she suddenly had reverence for him.

Everything he was learning was conveniently helping the Lady in Red's story make more sense than everything else. It was like she was predicting his questions and changing her story to answer them.

He sighed. "So then, why are you so fixated on me solving this crime? I mean, there are others far more brilliant than me."

She smirked and looked away from him before continuing. "Boy, do you ever lack faith in your investigative abilities. Anyway, the real reason is that you're an outsider. You haven't been part of the sickness that infects this city."

He blinked and stared blankly.

Sighing, the Lady in Red patted Richie's face gently, as one would a puppy. "You see, New Orleans has been sick for a long time. It all started when Master Castille became the Bourbon Street Ripper. The madness of the city, it gets to you after a while. You get pulled into it. You become just as crazy as the rest of the city."

Turning away from him to signal the hooded figures, she said, "So I saw you, recognized you, vetted you, and decided to use your silly ass to sniff out the problem. Now that we know who the problem is, we can take care of it."

The figures started to clear up the equipment and prepare to leave.

He sighed. He felt tired. He felt used. Again, she had given him the answer he expected, and he felt like she was saying it just to satisfy him. *I want to get back to Sam. Wait! That's it! Sam!*

Richie got in front of the Lady in Red. She looked at him crossly as he shook his head. "Oh, no! You answer this last question. Why are you so interested in Sam?"

Arching her eyebrows, she said, "Are you really that ignorant? Samantha Castille is the ultimate goal to everything. You need to keep her safe until the very end, Richie. Just like I told you."

"But why?" he asked.

Her pouty red lips curled into a sneer. "Sorry, kid, but you're out of questions."

He scowled, really starting to dislike her. At least she seemed obsessed with keeping Sam alive . . . but why would the Knight Priory have such an interest in Sam?

Putting her hands to her mouth, the Lady in Red whistled loudly. The hooded figures started to fall back, rushing out of the yard and leaping into the brush. Three of them walked over to where they were.

"But—" Richie started to protest, only to be stopped by the Lady in Red covering his lips with her fingers.

"Shhhh . . . stop talking," she said softly, her voice like melted butter. "You're cuter when your mouth is closed."

He blinked and kept his mouth shut.

She smirked again. "Anyway, we want you to watch the finale of this sordid tale. So if you'll just let us take you there, then you can go back home to Samantha."

"Wait, what?" He shook his head. "No, not at all. I don't wan—"

Again, she covered his lips with her finger. Sighing, she said, "Seriously, Richie. Shut up. I'm putting a lot of effort into this whole thing, and you're starting to annoy me. Trust me, you don't want to annoy me."

Taking a step back, she looked behind him and nodded. He realized a moment too late what was about to happen. The impact to his head came hard and fast, and he was unconscious before he realized it.

Richie knew only blackness for a while. Slowly, the sounds of the wind and the bump of a car's tires on the highway roused him. He was in the passenger side of Sam's car, strapped in securely, with the Lady in Red driving and the three hooded figures in the back. He grabbed his head and groaned in pain.

"Feeling OK, Richie?" asked a deep reverberating voice.

He saw the Lady in Red. It looked like her eyes were glowing. Peering at him, she said, "Did we hit you too hard? Can you hear me?"

"What the fu . . ." He shook his head. "You look all messed up."

"He says we look messed up, boss," said one of the hooded figures, his voice deep and reverberating. Richie looked in the back seat. What he saw made him scream.

The three hooded figures were looking at him. The faces underneath the hoods were more visible, and they looked monstrous. Flesh was decayed, teeth were sharp like fangs, and jaws were several times bigger than normal. He cried out and turned around, his vision getting blurry.

"You hit him too hard," said the Lady in Red, laughing with a deep, echoing voice. He turned to her and started to speak, but she grinned at him until her mouth was the length of her face, her teeth numerous. It was like the Cheshire cat from *Alice in Wonderland*, only horrible.

He screamed again and passed out. It was too much.

When he awoke again, he was aware of three things. One, he was lying on the sofa at Jacob Hueber's apartment. Two, he was once again covered head to toe in blood. Three, there were a number of dead bodies lying around him. He recognized them: black hooded coats, a snake mask, a zombie mask, and even a clown mask. The biker gang.

The bodies were eviscerated and cut into pieces just like Marcello's men.

Richie shrieked. His throat was starting to hurt.

The Lady in Red called out from somewhere. "Christ, Richie, will you please shut up!"

He looked around, his eyes adjusting to the light. It was a massacre. The Lady in Red was at the bar, sitting on a stool and drinking a highball. All around the room stood hooded figures. She was the only one not covered in blood.

He sat up and looked at himself. He was even more coated than at Rosemary's house. "Why the fuck am I covered in blood again?!"

She snorted. "Sorry, kid. No matter where I put you, you end up getting sprayed down like a puppy getting a bath. It's kinda cute."

Richie got up, making a face. As he walked over to her, he saw two hooded figures standing by a skinny, terrified-looking guy in a black coat. Something was stuffed in his mouth as a gag. Richie recognized the coat as the kind the biker gang wore, the one that attacked Sam. "Who is this?"

"Ah, don't remember him?" the Lady in Red asked. "Go ahead, boy, take the gag out. You'll recognize him then."

He inhaled deeply, struggling to keep his composure. As he reached for the gag, the guy recoiled from him. Finally, he just snatched the gag out of the man's mouth.

Immediately, the man squealed in terror. "Don't kill me, man!"

"Shut up," ordered one of the hooded figures, kicking the man in the face hard enough to knock out teeth.

Richie didn't watch the brutal display. Instead, he was fixated on the gag. It was a mask. A skull mask. *This guy was the one who beat me up and taunted me while his friends tried to rape Sam!*

"Figured you'd want to talk to him," said the Lady in Red. "He's got a name. And a very interesting story. Go on, ask him."

Turning to the cowering man, Richie gritted his teeth. He was furious with the group of riders for what they had done to him and Sam. He kicked the man in the gut several times. "Tell me who you are! Tell me who the hell you are!"

"You're crazy," the man cried out. He retched as Richie kicked him. "Wait! Stop! No more! My name is Greg. Gregory Billot!"

Richie felt a torrent of rage open inside him. All that anger about Sam being attacked, nearly getting violated, and then almost dying at the wharf—it was all too much.

"What did you do?" he cried out, kicking Gregory again and again. "Tell me, you sorry sack of shit!"

Gregory continued to blubber, begging Richie to stop, and telling him how insane he was acting. Richie kept kicking, telling Gregory that if he didn't start talking, he'd really show him crazy. After a dozen or so solid kicks, Gregory was starting to spit up blood. That's when he said he'd confess everything.

Richie kept his foot ready, just in case.

"I helped screw over Samantha Castille," Gregory said, crying into the wooden floors of the apartment. "I installed a modem in her copier, so that our boss could read her manuscripts. I swear, though, we were just supposed to steal her work. I didn't know the boss was the Ripper, man. None of us did."

The Lady in Red shrugged toward Richie. "I don't believe him, but then again, I wouldn't trust anyone who gave Cheryl Aucoin to the new Bourbon Street Ripper."

Richie turned on Gregory, the desire to pummel him into paste growing. "You did what to that poor little girl?"

"I already told you, man," Gregory cried out. "It was an accident."

"You didn't say shit to me," Richie said, kicking him in the groin. A part of him relished the violence. He'd always fantasized about beating someone up, and now he was doing it. While he felt pangs of remorse, he also felt years of pent-up rage coming out. He could almost see the face of the man who had hurt his mother.

"Tell me what you did to Cheryl." He felt his throat tighten around his words.

Gregory continued to sob like a little girl. "I fucked her. All the time, man. Made her shoot pictures with me. Talked her into thinking her cop daddy was an asshole who didn't love her. I made her my little toy."

Richie ground his teeth. *Fucking pervert.*

Gregory looked up at him, his lips quivering. "Cheryl was hot, in and out of bed. And Nick wanted a taste. Wanted to play with a young'n. Told me that he'd hook me up with enough blow for a month if I let him have Cheryl for one night. Christ, I didn't know he'd fucking kill her."

"Blow?" Richie asked. Then he realized what Gregory meant. Again, he seethed with anger. "You sold out a sixteen-year-old child for cocaine? And you call me crazy?!"

Yelling angrily, he continued to kick. When he finally realized what was happening, two hooded figures were pulling him back. Gregory looked badly beaten.

As the adrenaline wore off, Richie started to feel even more disturbed by his actions. The pangs of remorse grew. He felt like he was going to vomit. The smell of blood was thick.

"So that's it for him," the Lady in Red said. She looked into his eyes. "Do you want to kill him? Or should we?"

He blinked and shook his head. "No, no! Don't do that. Come on, he confessed. Let's drag him to the police. There's no reason to kill him."

"No reason?" she said, her voice suddenly deep and guttural, like a beast's. "No reason to kill him? Need I remind you that not only have these people aided and abetted the new Bourbon Street Ripper, but they hurt your true love, Samantha Castille. And they are responsible for a sixteen-year-old child being tortured to death."

And then, just like that, she had her composure back. Her lips pouted as she said, "Trust me. Even the death we gave Blue-Eyed Giorgio was gentler than what Cheryl suffered."

He looked at her and then at Gregory, who was eying him wildly. Shaking his head, he said, "I can't watch. You do it, but don't make me watch."

The Lady in Red sighed. "Disembowel him."

As Gregory started to beg for mercy, shrieking, "You're fucking nuts," and as the hooded figures converged on him, Richie closed his eyes. He heard the most awful sounds and smelled the most awful smells, but he refused to watch a human being die that way.

When the sounds finally died, Richie looked. Seeing Gregory with his intestines strewn about was disturbing, but Richie felt desensitized to the violence. Instead of throwing up, he just shook his head. "I need to clean off."

Richie passed through the master bedroom on the way to the bathroom. Lying on the bed, bound and gagged but alive, was Officer Emilie Guidry. He stared at her for about a minute while she stared back, her eyes wide with terror. He felt numb to the scene. "Be right back, Emilie," he said, going to shower off.

About fifteen minutes later, he was dressing in Jacob's clothes.

The Lady in Red cleared her throat at the doorway. "You shouldn't leave those there." She nudged her head at his bloody clothes, smirking. "Police might think you witnessed a multiple homicide."

He sighed and picked up the clothes. They were stained in blood. She offered him a plastic bag, chortling. "You, kid, would make a horrible murderer . . ."

"Thanks," Richie said as he staggered into the bedroom. He honestly didn't know what to make of the Knight Priory anymore. Part of him was still thankful for their help, but the rest of him was absolutely mortified by their recent actions.

Motioning to Officer Guidry, he said, "What about her? What did she do?"

"She is responsible for framing Samantha Castille for murder," the Lady in Red said. "She took the skin samples her boyfriend collected and planted them inside Cheryl Aucoin."

She rubbed Guidry's hair, fondling it as one would check the texture of department store clothing.

Richie stared into Guidry's eyes. He could see the remorse and fear. In that instant, he realized what she had done. He remembered his visit to Jacob earlier that day. He remembered the rough bandages with metal that had scratched his own skin. Suddenly, the plan seemed all too obvious.

Those bandages were outfitted with some kind of metal scraping thing. Jacob must have used it to get some of Sam's skin cells. Then he gave them to Emilie, who put them in Cheryl's body for the medical examiner to find.

He felt like a fool for not figuring it out sooner.

"So what about Jacob? Is he dead?"

"No, not yet," replied the Lady in Red, continuing to stroke Guidry's hair. "He's out. When he comes in, we'll descend upon him like wolves."

Richie nodded and motioned back to Guidry. "And her?"

The Lady in Red leaned down and sniffed at her. "We'll kill her, same as the others, of course . . ."

Guidry's eyes got wider, and she started struggling harder. She thrashed so violently that she hit the underside of the Lady in Red's jaw, causing her head to snap back. Shaking off the hit, the Lady in Red got a murderous look in her eyes.

"Wait!" Richie covered Guidry's body with his own. She was crying fearfully into her gag and trying to push him off.

The Lady in Red just looked at him. Leaning back, she wiped a trickle of blood off her chin from where she had bitten her own tongue. "Boy, you have ten seconds to explain yourself to me."

His heart pounded in his chest. As much as he hated Guidry, he knew her testimony could save Sam. "She's a cop. If you kill her, the cops will be all over the Knight Priory. Do you want that when you're so close to your revenge?"

This seemed to calm the Lady in Red. Adjusting her jaw once more, she sat down on a comfortable-looking chair in the corner of the room. Flipping back her long blond hair, she said, "So, then, boy, what would you do with her?"

Richie's mind raced. He knew he needed to get Guidry out of there if he wanted to save her life. He also knew he needed to get her to testify to the police in order to save Sam. *But I don't want to piss these psychopaths off.* So far, he was on the good side of the group, but he felt that one wrong move would make him a target.

He leaned down and whispered to Emilie, "Just play along."

"What was that?" The Lady in Red sounded cross. "No whispering, boy."

"I told her to start praying," he lied. "I . . . I want to kill her myself."

Immediately, Guidry started to thrash about like a fish, screaming into the gag.

The Lady in Red laughed. "Beautiful, little Richie. Just beautiful!" She motioned to the bedside table where a knife was embedded in the wood. "Go on. Kill her."

Richie was sweating hard. He knew he was gambling with both his and Guidry's lives. "No, no, too much here. I wanna take her someplace else. An alleyway. Something dirty like the whore she is . . ."

The Lady peered at him.

He held his breath, certain that she'd snap her fingers and point, and then, within moments, there wouldn't be enough of him left to bury.

Instead, she started to snicker. "Yes. Yes, indeed. Very nice. Very wonderful."

He kept up his fake smile.

Guidry had closed her eyes and was rocking back and forth, praying.

"Go ahead, then, but please don't think we're done." The Lady in Red's expression was serious as she rose.

Richie slid back as she crawled over him. He could smell her perfume, her skin, her sweat. She smelled like death.

With a throaty "mmm," she leaned in and bit his ear, her voice eerily sensual. "If you're wrong . . . and Jacob Hueber is not the new Bourbon Street Ripper . . . I'll come back for you."

He felt his junk shrink in his shorts.

She slid until she was staring him in the face. Her expression was pure cruelty. "And depending on my mood, little boy, that could be the worst day of your life."

Leaning down, she nipped the tip of his nose in a manner that felt like complete domination. "So don't even think about leaving town until I say you can. OK, sweetie?"

Richie nodded. As she got off him, he was grateful he hadn't drunk anything in hours. Otherwise, he was sure he'd have pissed himself again.

A few minutes later, he was walking outside with Guidry, who was still gagged and bound. The Lady in Red's instructions were for him to be "smart" about killing the policewoman. Richie had left from the apartment's fire escape, leading Guidry to the alleyway below. She was quaking in fear, but she obeyed.

Once in the alley, he pressed the knife against Guidry's back. Immediately, she started sobbing into her gag. Richie held her upright. "You're doing great. Just continue to play along a little more. When we're out of their view, I'll cut your bonds. Then we make a break for it."

The back alleys of the French Quarter were still deserted, most likely due to the strict curfew. But with Arsenault's SWAT team completely destroyed, there was no noticeable police presence. Richie hoped they'd run into a cop. He'd rather be arrested than ever have to deal with those hooded killers again. *Wait, isn't Bourbon Street nearby?* There had to be police on Bourbon Street.

As he crossed behind the apartments, he heard a lone engine, a motorcycle, stopping in front of the apartment building.

Shit, that's got to be Jacob, he thought. Guidry must have thought the same thing, because she started struggling, crying out into her gag.

Her thrashing made it hard for him to hold onto her. "Stop it! Look, he's as good as dead. I'm sorry. I can't save him. I can only save you."

She continued to struggle, and that made him nervous. *If she breaks free and tries to run back to save her boyfriend, she's dead and likely so am I. I need to get to a public place and fast.*

Looking around, Richie saw a doorway in the middle of the alley. He pulled Guidry along as she continued to struggle. "Come on! Stop it! Why are you so hysterical? Don't you realize I'm trying to save your life, you dumb-ass?"

He tried the doorway as soon as he got there. It was unlocked. With a sigh of relief, he went inside, pushing her along.

It was an abandoned art studio. There were a few easels in the room, and some covered paintings. A metal doorway led to what he figured was the front of the building. With a sigh of relief, he moved through the room to the metal door. "I think this building dumps out into Bourbon Street. Once we're out, we'll look for another officer."

He stopped and turned her around, looking her in the eyes. She looked positively terrified. He exhaled and tried to smile comfortingly. His mouth quaked. "Listen, you framed Sam. I want you to promise that you'll come clean. We'll tell the police the whole truth, about the Knight Priory, how they murdered everyone, including Jacob, and so on. We'll probably both do some time for this, but I swear to you, Emilie . . ."

Using her first name seemed to make Guidry lucid enough. She locked eyes with Richie, trembling.

". . . if you promise me right now that you'll tell the truth, I swear you'll get out of this alive."

Her eyes searched his for a long, silent moment. Then she nodded.

Relieved, he hugged her. She was still trembling. "I know you're scared. I'm scared, too. It's almost over. I promise. Let's go."

Turning back to the metal doorway, he opened it and stepped inside.

He was not expecting what he saw.

As soon as the door opened, a light turned on in the room. It looked heavily barricaded, with no other entrance or exit, and the windows riveted shut with sheet metal. In the center of the room was a large metal operating table fitted with leather straps and a drain board. Next to the head of the table was hospital monitoring equipment—heart rate monitor, breathing machine, and intravenous drip. Nearby was a side table, with trays of scalpels, forceps, knives, and other surgical equipment. Next to it was a side table with power tools—drills, jigsaws, circular saws, and a chain saw.

Beethoven's Ninth Symphony started playing from somewhere in the room.

As Richie stared, Guidry let out a blood-curdling scream. Struggling against his grip, she slammed her head back, right into his jaw. Everything seemed to be moving in slow motion as he fell backward while she stumbled into the room and collapsed at the base of the "killing table." As he reeled from the pain, she struggled to her feet, her eyes wide with terror. His head throbbed. He was aware of every sensation, every breath, every taste, and every sound—same as when the Knight Priory had saved him from Marcello's men. It was as surreal as it was distressing.

Guidry ran toward the open doorway. She was heading back outside. Still unable to move, he watched as someone entered the doorway and knocked her out with one punch.

Richie's eyes widened. It was a person in a black hooded coat, not like the motorcycle gang, but like the Knight Priory that worked for the Lady in Red.

Picking up Guidry, the hooded man carried her into the room. Richie struggled to get to his feet, but the pain was still making his vision blur. However, as the hooded man walked over to him, Richie glimpsed part of his face.

He was a Caucasian male, the same age as Sam or him, with a cocky sneer. At that moment, Richie realized that he was looking at the "traitor," the real copycat killer, the new Bourbon Street Ripper.

And like a dolt, he had delivered his next victim.

Once Guidry was laid out and strapped onto the table, the killer reached into his coat and took out a syringe filled with a clear liquid. He popped off the cap and advanced on Richie.

Richie tried to get to his feet, but it was no use. He couldn't move. His heart was pounding and his throat was tight. *It's like he's overpowering me with fear!*

"I'll let you live for now," the killer said. Richie swore he never saw the killer's mouth move when he spoke. The voice reminded Richie of how his own voice had sounded when he had showed up Olivier and Aucoin during the interview—arrogant and condescending.

"But tell that blond bitch I'm coming for her next." Again, Richie never saw the killer's mouth move. It was unnerving.

As the killer injected Richie with the syringe, his grin spread into a wide leer. Richie wasn't sure if he meant the Lady in Red or Sam, but the intent was clear—the nightmare wasn't over.

As Richie felt his consciousness fade, the killer said, "See you around, Richie . . ."

Chapter 23

The Blink of an Eye

Date: **Wednesday, August 12, 1992**
Time: **12:00 a.m.**
Location: **Tulane University Hospital**
               Downtown New Orleans

Tightening his tie, Michael looked at himself in the mirror in his hospital room. "Time to catch a killer."

First, he went upstairs to Dixie's room. The guard there let him in without a problem, letting him know that both she and Gino were asleep. As he entered, he saw Gino reclined in a chair near Dixie's bed. He was snoring softly.

Michael crept over to Dixie. The stump of her left arm, amputated above the elbow, was wrapped very tightly, tubes going in and out of the wrappings to keep the wound drained. She had a worried wrinkle to her brow, and her sleep looked labored. He took a moment to smooth back her hair. He had just tucked her hair behind her ears when she woke up.

"Hey there, Dixie," he said softly, offering her a small smile.

She smiled back. "Hey there, Michael. You look better." Her voice was weak, most likely from the sedatives.

He rested his hands on her abdomen and said, "Yeah. You look . . . like you've been better."

She laughed softly and coughed a few times. Gino stirred but didn't wake. She put her one hand over Michael's and said, "Sam . . . she's innocent."

Michael squeezed her hand. "I know, hun, I know. I've figured it all out. I'm going to go meet Rodger and put an end to it."

She furrowed her brow and nodded weakly, squeezing his hand. "Just be careful. Come back in one piece. Uh, I mean—"

Despite the somberness of the situation, he started to giggle, with her joining him. Both struggled not to wake Gino.

Dixie stopped giggling and looked up at Michael. Her expression was serious as she said, "Michael . . . if things had been different . . . if I had been . . . or if you had been . . . ?"

Michael felt himself flinch at the question. He cared for her very deeply, but while he had always known that she had feelings for him, he couldn't return them. All they could ever be was friends. Besides, there was Gino to consider. He knew that Gino could give her the life she deserved.

He said, "Dixie, about that." He cleared his throat and leaned down. His lips touched her forehead in a gentle kiss. "You're my best friend, and I will always love you. I couldn't have lived in this city without your friendship. Please understand how much that means to me. When this is over, we'll go shopping. I need a new suit. I'll even treat you to cheesecake. Won't that be fun?"

Dixie's eyes showed understanding. She nodded. "Yeah, that would be fun. You take care, OK, friend?"

Michael kissed her hand gently and said, "Of course. Get some rest." He left without another word.

Thirty minutes later, he was in the lobby of the Inn on Bourbon Street, waiting for Rodger to show up. In his hands, he held the key to Room 205, given to him by the front desk clerk, Viviane. She had confirmed that Irving Jennings was indeed in the room, alone, and had just received room service.

Irving Jennings. No. Kent Bourgeois. It's almost over.

Michael came out of his thoughts, noticing that Rodger was standing next to him.

"Hey there, partner," Rodger said. He was wearing one safety vest and holding another. He looked like hell.

"Hey yourself, buddy," Michael said, looking him over. "Wow, you got worked over something awful. Do I get to hear the gory details?"

Rodger just exhaled. "Yeah. Gory details. When this is over, I'll treat you to a pitcher of beer and tell you a story about a special house. One you will never believe."

Michael chuckled. That was the Rodger he knew. Smacking his partner on the arm, he said, "Yeah, I'm going to have to pass on the beer. Still recovering. But I'd love to hear the story."

Rodger motioned his head toward the elevator. "So, we gonna arrest Bourgeois or what?"

Michael nodded. "How long until Ouellette arrives?"

"Ten, maybe fifteen minutes," Rodger said as they got on the elevator.

Michael hit the button for the second floor and then put on the other safety vest. "So, the way I see it is this: if Nick is there, he's going to ambush us as we confront his father." It was a hunch given what he knew of the suspects.

"Yup, I agree," said Rodger, taking out his gun and making sure the clip was secured. He chambered a bullet, cocking the gun so that it could fire with just a pull of the trigger. Then he latched the safety on.

Michael had seen this look on Rodger's face before. Every time they went in to apprehend a dangerous suspect, he got very business-like. Michael was glad for it.

"So, here's my idea," he said, checking his own gun and preparing it as Rodger had. "I go in and confront Kent. I'll just knock and go in. Talk to him. Get him to confess if I can." *I may not be as good as Dixie at getting inside a suspect's head, but I've got to do this.*

Rodger rubbed his eyes. "You're sure you've thought this one out, right, buddy?"

"Yes, I have," Michael said. "Kent's a lawyer. He's going to lawyer up the moment it's obvious he's being arrested. If we can get a confession out of him before that, we can make it stick. "Besides, I told you before. We deserve to be the ones to get this guy."

"You're sure that Ouellette is OK with this plan?" Rodger asked.

"He's completely behind our plan," Michael replied. "He'll be here with backup soon, though. So we need to hurry if we're going to make the arrest."

Rodger eyed him for a moment, and then nodded. "All right. So what do I do?"

"You stay hidden, and if Nick shows, you apprehend him," said Michael.

"And if the whole gang is there?"

Michael grinned nervously. "Then we delay them until the backup arrives. But I think it'll just be Kent, with possibly Nick. No one else."

"Oh?" asked Rodger, arching an eyebrow. "Why do you think that?"

"Just a hunch," Michael said, winking at his partner. It was true. A week ago, he would have over-analyzed the situation with no regard to his gut instinct. Now, after all he'd been through, he was ready to believe in hunches.

Rodger must have picked up on this, as he winked back. "All right, partner. We'll follow your plan. Let's do this."

The doors to the elevator opened. Michael and Rodger, side by side and weapons drawn, headed down the hall toward Room 205.

Michael heard music coming from inside. It was the sweet symphony of "Serenade" by Schubert. He handed Rodger the key to the room and said, "Go ahead and hide."

Rodger took the key and moved to the alcove with the ice machine. Once Rodger was hidden from view, Michael went back to the door.

Taking a moment to enjoy the music, and hiding his gun in his coat holster, he took a deep breath and raised his hand to knock on the door. He stopped when he saw that his hand was shaking. Frowning, he closed his eyes and focused.

I can't think how there's a killer on the other side of this door. I have to focus on doing my job.

Taking a few more breaths to settle his nerves, he knocked on the door.

A minute later, a man in his mid-fifties with gray hair and reading glasses opened the door.

Michael politely flashed his badge. "Kent Bourgeois? Junior Detective Michael LeBlanc. May I come inside?"

Kent blinked in surprise. He then smiled a bit too cordially. Opening the door all the way, he said, "Come in. I was just about to have a very late dinner."

"Ah. Worked late tonight?" Michael looked for signs of trouble. None so far.

Kent led him into the room. "Sadly, yes. Work has been hell lately, Detective."

Stepping into Room 205, Michael saw that it was an executive suite. From the entrance foyer, the room spread back into a living area, complete with a sofa, a breakfast table, and a media center. A large set of glass windows, all curtained, faced Bourbon Street.

Kent sat at the breakfast table, where a covered dinner tray lay. He motioned toward the chair opposite him. "You're Rodger Bergeron's partner, aren't you? Will you have a seat?"

"I'd rather stand," replied Michael, looking around the room. So far, it was just him and Kent. *Nick has to show up at some point. If I'm lucky, it will be after the arrest.*

Shrugging, Kent lifted the cover of the tray, revealing a filet mignon steak covered with a sautéed mushroom and onion sauce and topped with caviar. Inhaling the dinner's aroma, he said, "I hope you don't mind me eating, then, Detective."

As Kent began to eat, Michael noticed the wedding band on his left ring finger. Remembering that Kent had married a woman in her eighties, he shook his head and leaned against the nearest wall.

"So you like to eat exquisite foods, Mr. Bourgeois?"

Kent placed a piece of the filet mignon into his mouth and chewed slowly, as if savoring the flavor in a spiritual way. After a few chews, he swallowed, patted his mouth and took a sip from a nearby glass of wine.

"Did you know, Detective, that there is a type of cow in Japan that is given a special diet of sake-soaked grain and is massaged to keep the meat soft? It is said to be the tastiest and most tender in the world."

"Kobe beef," Michael replied with a nod. "Sells for something like fifty dollars a pound. Pretty expensive."

Kent gestured toward his dinner. "With the wine, this dinner here is almost one hundred dollars. How often do you eat hundred-dollar meals, Detective?"

Michael could see where this was going. "Not often, why do you ask?"

"Well, you seem like a man of culture," Kent said, motioning again for him to have a seat. "If you sit, I'm sure we can work out a way to where you can have such lovely dinners every night."

In a way, Michael felt insulted, like his character was under attack. And this was after taking a bullet while chasing Blind Moses back in the bayou.

"Really, bribery is the best you can do?" he asked. "Honestly, Mr. Bourgeois, I am unpleasantly surprised."

Kent just shrugged, then resumed cutting his steak. "Why shouldn't we all benefit from Vincent Castille's generosity?"

Michael narrowed his eyes. He couldn't hide the disdain in his voice as he said, "Because innocent people have died for this fortune."

Kent sighed. "A lot more people have died for a lot less money, Detective. Now is not the time to get all self-righteous." He popped the food into his mouth.

"Perhaps, Mr. Bourgeois," replied Michael. He still didn't see any signs of trouble. "But I'd rather be known as self-righteous than as a serial killer."

Kent's cutting slowed down. "I'm not sure I have any idea what you're talking about, Detective."

Michael shook his head, not in the mood for games. "I just want to know why, Mr. Bourgeois. Why do this to Sam? She trusted you."

Kent chewed more slowly. "Sam is not the victim here." He drank some of his wine and finished the last of his meal.

Michael's brow furrowed. He needed Kent to open up more, to admit more. "I don't understand. Exactly what are you trying to say?"

Kent took his wine glass and headed toward the media center. Michael eyed him carefully, his hand inching up to his gun in case things went bad.

At the media center, Kent asked, "Do you like Schubert, Detective?"

"Yes," Michael replied, trying not to get bored. "Why do you ask? Did Schubert tell you to do it?"

Kent opened the media center and put the CD player on auto-repeat. "No, I just wanted to know if I needed to change CDs. That's all, Detective. No need to get insulting."

The sound of the Austrian composer's music started up again. Kent waved his finger in the air as if conducting. "You were too young to remember, but the Bourbon Street Ripper murders involved so much more than death. Take Vincent Castille, for instance. He sabotaged his own defense so that he'd get executed. He wanted to die. Now that is crazy."

"Maybe he felt remorse," Michael said. He knew that wasn't the case, though. Vincent Castille was a text-book sociopath. There was no remorse.

Kent, still waving his finger to the music, said, "You know that's not true. But there was more to Vincent than just remorseless killing. On the day of his execution, I had a personal meeting with him. He told me a few things that I have not told another living soul."

He stopped waving his finger in the air and looked into Michael's eyes. "Do you want to hear?" He gently sloshed his wine around.

"Sure," Michael replied, making sure his gun was close by. He wasn't sure how the conversation would go, but he didn't want to be caught unawares.

"He told me," said Kent as he finished his wine, "that he had loved only one person in his entire life. His first marriage was arranged, and they hardly spent time together. So, obviously, the person he loved the most was Sam. Oh, how he loved that girl! She was his princess, his reason for living. He loved Sam more than anything else in the world, and that's the most important thing anyone can know about Vincent."

Michael, who had heard this before, said, "I kind of sorted that part out for myself by now, Mr. Bourgeois. Why is that important?"

"Because Vincent confided in me that he committed all those murders for Sam," said Kent with a smirk.

Michael narrowed his eyes and looked at him. This was the first time he'd ever heard something like this. "He killed all those people for Sam?"

"Indeed," Kent said. "Every single one of them, including his own son. Vincent said that he killed them all just for Sam."

Shaking his head, Michael said, "I know that Vincent was crazy, but that doesn't make any sense. Why murder so many people for a little girl, even if you do love her?"

Kent shrugged. "Detective, I asked him the same thing. Do you know what he said?"

Michael shook his head again.

"He said that it was to protect Sam from harm. He said it was so she could live a life without fear. I've since given up trying to decipher Vincent's madness." Kent flicked the rim of his wine glass. A crystal clear tone rang out.

Michael sighed and wondered if he should give that up, too.

"You know what else he told me," Kent said, almost as an aside.

"What?" asked Michael. *I need to get him to trust me more, to open up so he'll confess.*

Pouring another glass of wine, Kent said, "Vincent told me that if I took good care of Sam, he'd make sure that I would be taken care of. He promised that I'd never want for material needs."

He raised his glass and observed the red color. "Like he'd be able to help from the grave. What a crock of shit."

Michael shook his head. The motivation was basic greed, and all the sad stories in the world wouldn't change the fact that Kent was facilitating murder to get at Sam's money. *That's pathetic.*

Shrugging, he said, "But you got screwed. You couldn't put yourself on a nice, fat retainer because Sam refused to run the household. She chopped up all the Castille family assets. You haven't been able to consolidate that fortune and do anything with that money. So for the past twenty years, you've floundered."

"I've more than floundered," Kent snapped so viciously that Michael jumped. "I've all but failed! Vincent Castille paid me more than I could ever dream. And as soon as he died? Nothing! Do you know how hard it is to get new clients when you're the family lawyer of the Bourbon Street Ripper? Even the Marcello family wouldn't touch me. I've been making do with Sam's minuscule retainer and the small pittance I get for managing her estate. Hell, I'd have had better luck moving out of Louisiana."

Michael felt a twinge of triumph. If he could keep Kent on this path, he could get him to confess. He just needed to play up the sympathy more.

Walking more toward Kent, he said, "But it's not right. What Vincent did was wrong. You deserved something—anything—after all you gave to that twisted family."

"All I gave, indeed," said Kent as he rubbed the lower part of his face. "I gave everything to keep that family and that little girl safe from the public. Sam wanted her grandfather's money to go away. Gladys and the others wanted it to be someplace safe until Sam 'came to her senses.' So I split that fortune up amongst hundreds of investments. In the past twenty years, the Castille fortune has grown far beyond what it once was. Sam doesn't even realize it, but she owns considerable percentages of some of the most successful companies in the world. Her wealth is immense."

Michael just stood there for a few moments, letting that sink in. *Sam isn't just rich, she's super rich?*

Exhaling, he asked, "OK, so, approximately how much is the Castille fortune now?"

Walking over to the nearby desk, Kent tapped a ledger. "Sam is worth, with her investments and holdings, close to five billion." He drained his glass of wine.

Michael whistled. While he was glad that his hunch was accurate, he was still surprised by the sheer amount of wealth. *However, here is my best chance to get Kent to confess.*

"So that's what this is about," he said, faking his surprise. "This is about getting a five-billion-dollar fortune? You framed Sam for murder so that you could get her money?"

"Are you so surprised?" asked Kent, his face starting to redden. "I gave everything to that family. Everything! I even hid my own bastard son so that I wouldn't bring shame to the good Castille name as their lawyer."

He sat down on the edge of the sofa, wringing his hands. "Then Vincent goes and messes it all up with that Bourbon Street Ripper nonsense. And then Sam goes and gets so screwed up in the head that everything just stalls. And here I am, cleaning up their mess for twenty years without so much as a Mercedes to say 'Thank you, Kent.' So you're damn right it's about the money."

He ran his fingers through his gray hair. "I admit that sometimes, I get sick to my stomach over how I've screwed over Sam. I have loved that girl since her birth, you have to believe that, but there's nothing more I can do to help her. She's far too damaged to ever live a normal life. Framing her for murder ensures she gets locked away. And when she is, she'll finally get the help she needs." He looked up. "And I'll finally get what's mine."

Michael smiled. "Checkmate."

Kent blinked and rose, his face getting red. "You little piece of sh—"

In a flash, Michael had his gun out. "I don't think so, Mr. Bourgeois."

At that moment, the door to the room burst open and in came a man in his thirties. He was wearing black leather pants, a fishnet T-shirt, and a leather jacket. His torso, visible through the shirt, was positively covered in tattoos. He had a wild, untamed, and angry look. His eyes were puffy, like he was strung out or had been crying or both.

Michael recognized him from the information on the *Times-Picayune* as one of its editors, even though he looked different when out of a suit. Michael turned and trained his gun on him. "Jacob Hueber," he said.

"Nick. Son. What the hell are you doing here?" exclaimed Kent.

Michael blinked as the connection fell into place. *Jacob Hueber is Nick Bourgeois.*

Nick looked at him, then looked at his gun, and then asked, "Dad, what the hell is going on?"

"Nick, you and your dad are in some serious trouble," Michael said. He knew that Rodger would be here any minute. He also noted that Nick was alone and looked pale and frightened.

"We're not the ones in trouble, Detective. You are," said Kent.

Michael heard the sound of a hammer cocking. His heart rate increased. Quickly, he re-trained his gun on Kent, who was aiming a 9 mm pistol at him.

"You had it in the sofa," he said, realizing his mistake.

"Of course," replied Kent, arching an eyebrow. "I just needed you to let me sit down. I didn't expect you to make me confess. Brilliant tactics, Detective. You pulled one over on me."

Michael looked for some signal or sign that Rodger was watching. Nothing. *OK, partner, let's not wait too long here.*

"It's true I feel bad about what I've done to Sam," Kent said. "But like I told you, she's damaged beyond what anyone can do to help. She needs to be locked away for the rest of her life. For her own good."

Another hammer cock resounded behind Michael. Looking, he saw that Nick had a .45 automatic, a very sizable handgun, aimed at him. "Father, we have some problems. My biker group is—"

"Shut up, Nick," interrupted Kent. "We have to deal with one thing at a time, like I always tell you." He narrowed his eyes. "Son, are you high?"

"I did a line before coming here," said Nick, sniffing. "If you had seen what I saw, you would—"

"Jesus Christ, Nick," Kent said with a shake of the head. "Do you know how to do anything right? Let's deal with this cop first, then we'll sit down and rationally talk about your prob–"

Michael heard Nick spit and say, "No, Father, you listen to me right fucking now! Someone murdered my entire posse. Snuck in from the fire escape and cut them into little pieces like they were in a Cuisinart. You hear me?"

He raised his voice. "Fucking spread everyone's guts around my pad! And whoever it was, they took Emilie. I did all this shit to Sam, years of pretending to be her friend, so you'd fucking approve of me. And now my real friends are fucking dead! So forgive me for doing a fucking line, but someone other than this cop is onto us and is killing us. So, yeah, we have to fucking deal with this, too, Dad!"

For a moment, Michael processed what Nick had just said. He felt a bit ill. Was it possible that there was someone else involved? Could he have gotten his accusation wrong?

"OK, OK. I apologize, son. But one step at a time," said Kent. "First, we take the detective to the bathroom and shoot him. Next, we get someone to remove the body and toss it in the river. Then, we call the police at your apartment. Finally, we go find your girlfriend before she gets herself hurt. She's probably doped up beyond belief right now, since she's a bigger cokehead than you."

Behind him, Michael could hear Nick muttering to himself. He figured that the mixture of trauma and drugs had likely made Nick less focused. Otherwise, Michael figured he'd be in serious trouble right now.

Still, he wondered what was keeping his partner. *Rodger, I know you love dramatic entrances and all, but I really need you right now.*

"All right, Dad," said Nick. He inhaled deeply. "Let's do it your way. But let's make sure we don't waste too much time here. I've put too much energy into pretending to be that psycho-bitch's friend, putting up with her screwed-up family and her faggot writer boyfriend, just so we can cash in her fortune, to get gutted like a fish."

Kent reached for Michael's gun. "Let's go, then, Detective. Time to write you out of this story."

The sound of a third cocking gun came from the entrance hall, followed by a gruff voice saying, "Don't edit Michael out just yet."

It was Rodger.

Michael breathed a sigh of relief. "Hey, partner, what took you so long?"

"I wanted to hear these two pieces of trash admit they've spent all these years lying to Sam so that they could screw her out of her money. Especially this little shit who was supposed to be her best friend." From the hallway, Rodger motioned toward Nick with his gun.

Backing away, Nick continued to aim his gun at Michael.

Michael held his gun on Kent.

Kent held his gun on Michael.

Rodger, his gun trained on Nick, came into the room. "It's over, Kent, Nick," he said calmly. "You've lost. Ouellette and the others will be here any minute. You're going to jail."

"Don't be so high and mighty, Detective Bergeron. It's because of you that Edward is dead. We all remember that lovely story," replied Kent, keeping his gun aimed at Michael. "And maybe you'll be the cause of your new partner's death, too, hmm?"

Michael kept his gun trained on Kent. It was a classic stand-off. All they had to do was wait for Ouellette to arrive and it would be over.

"If you shoot Michael," Rodger said matter-of-factly, "you're dead."

"I've lost more than you've ever lost, Bergeron." Kent's eyes were fierce.

Rodger shook his head. "That's the biggest load of bullshit I have ever heard. I've lost more than a narcissist like you can ever dream."

Kent winced and stomped his foot like a child would, yelling, "All I want is what's mine!"

Rodger sighed and again shook his head. "That doesn't excuse anything that you've done. In the end, you're just a pathetic con man."

"What do you know?" Kent spat out with growing rage. "So what if Sam goes down for murder? You know the whole damn family is evil. All those sick voodoo rituals and shit they used to do! What kind of a man tortures dozens of women to death and then laments that he didn't kill enough? The whole family deserves to burn in hell."

"You're babbling. And it's starting to bore me," said Michael. "We can be here like this all night, but as soon as the rest of the precinct arrives, life is going to get very uncomfortable for you two."

Just as he said that, the night sky lit up with dozens upon dozens of red and blue flashing lights.

Nick jerked his head toward the window. "What's that?"

"The entire eighth precinct," replied Rodger, keeping his gun on Nick. "Ouellette had to rouse everyone, I'm sure, and our numbers are reduced after the bullshit at the wharf, but we all have a way of pulling together when it counts."

"Crap!" exclaimed Nick. "So what do we do, Dad?"

Michael wasn't surprised that Nick was cracking under the pressure. He just hoped it wouldn't result in someone's gun going off by mistake. Whatever had happened at Jacob's apartment had thrown a monkey wrench into everything.

"Shut it, son," replied Kent, smirking. "This isn't how it's supposed to end. We'll get a few months, a year or two at the worst, for framing Sam. So what? You won't get us on those murders and you know it. There's no evidence. And this won't stop her from being committed. What will you gain, Detective Bergeron?"

"Closure. Something I need," Rodger replied. "Cuff him, Michael. Let's go back to the hospital. Sam started moving her eyes about half an hour ago. I want to see my niece."

Michael felt nothing but pride in both his partner and their department. Finally, after all that had happened, something had gone right. For the first time in weeks, it felt great to be part of the Eighth Precinct Homicide Division.

Moving toward Kent, he said, "Kent Bourgeois, you are under arrest for conspiracy to commit—"

Then a shot rang out.

Michael stood there, shocked. Looking down, he saw blood leak from a hole in his left pant leg. He could feel the pain spreading throughout his thigh.

Looking back up, he saw Kent with an expression of absolute horror on his face. His hand was shaking, and while he was holding the gun, his finger was nowhere near the trigger. In that instant, Michael knew what had happened. Somehow, the gun had gone off without Kent doing anything. It was a horrible, horrible mistake.

Rodger yelled, "No!" He aimed his gun at Kent, while Nick aimed his gun at Rodger.

Michael wanted to yell that it was an accident. But it was already too late. Nick and Rodger were seconds away from shooting—everything was unraveling in the blink of an eye.

If I don't act, Nick will shoot Rodger.

Michael felt any hope of a peaceful end to this standoff slip away. He could hardly remain standing with a bullet in his leg. All he could do now was save his partner's life. Biting his bottom lip, Michael aimed his gun and fired it point-blank at the side of Nick's head.

The gunshot rang out and Nick fell back, dead.

Michael heard Kent shout out his son's name, heard a bang, and then felt pain explode along the left side of his neck.

Kent had shot him again.

As Michael fell backward, he heard Rodger yell again. Then he heard three shots ring out. As he fell to the floor, he saw Kent fall back onto the sofa, holes in his chest, dead.

Then Michael landed in a heap.

As he lay there, he tried to breathe. It was very difficult. Blood was pouring from the side of his neck. Looking up, he saw several pieces of folded paper slip from Kent's pocket. His gut told him it was important.

That has to be it. The final piece of evidence. Please let it be that!

Rodger ran to Michael's side, pressing his hand to the wound. His voice was distant as he took out a walkie-talkie and cried out, "Officer down! Officer down!"

Michael pointed at the folded pieces of paper. His hand was shaky; his voice was raspy. "Evidence?" He hoped it was important.

Rodger looked toward the paper. "Don't worry about that, bud. We gotta keep pressure on the wound. Gotta keep—"

"Please," Michael said, feeling his body getting colder. "Gotta know . . . if we got the killers." He needed the paper to be important.

In the distance, he could hear the sound of someone digging.

Rodger gave him a despairing look before quickly heading to where Kent lay. He grabbed the pages and hurried back, dropping them on the floor where he could read them while compressing Michael's wound. His face showed no emotion.

"Was I right?" Michael asked, straining. He could hardly hear anything but that digging sound.

Rodger nodded. "It's a letter, partner. You were right. It was them. They were the killers."

Michael started to laugh, although it was more of a series of gasping chortles. Despite Rodger's best efforts, already Michael was losing his sight. "We did it . . . Thank God, we did it . . ."

"You did it," said Rodger, tossing the letter to the side and holding him close.

Michael smiled, even as he felt wetness on his face. *Is it raining?*

Looking up, he wondered why the lights were dimmed. He could hardly see his partner with the lights out. The sound of digging was all around him, enveloping him. "No, we did it, buddy. I'm glad we're partners . . . friends. I'm so . . . happy . . ."

With a smile on his face, Junior Detective Michael LeBlanc quietly passed away.

Chapter 24
A Neatly Folded Letter

Kent Bourgeois,

You don't know me, but I know everything about you. For the past twenty years, you have been scamming the Castille family for millions of dollars. Moving the money around investments and umbrella corporations, you have been skimming off the top and living high on the hog. Your pathetic story about starving on Vincent Castille's pickings is nothing more than lies. You lied to Vincent when you hid Nick, and you lied to Samantha when you said you'd take care of her.

In short, your entire life is a lie.

If you doubt my knowledge, see the attached records of your personal bank statements. Getting them was easy, and at the push of a button, I can send them to every newspaper and law enforcement agency in Louisiana.

But I am offering you a chance at salvation. I am offering you a chance to make this right. If you follow my instructions to the letter, I guarantee that you and your son will live well for the rest of your lives. But if you break a single rule, you will die as nothing more than a petty criminal.

In six months, I will arrive in New Orleans and begin a copycat killing spree modeled after Vincent Castille's twenty years ago. You will help me accomplish this killing spree.

I have vetted the original four accomplices to Vincent Castille and know which ones may be useful. I have also cased the townhome of Samantha Castille. She will be the one to take the fall for my killing spree.

Here is how we will do it:

Included are four drafts of four different letters. Three are to be typed on a typewriter. The one to Blind Moses is to be typed on a Braille machine. You are then to have all four letters anonymously delivered. Do not let it be traced back to you.

You are then to use some of the money you have swindled from the Castilles to purchase one Soviet Dragunov semi-automatic sniper rifle, one standard-issue Armed Forces .45-caliber pistol, and enough standard and explosive ammunition for both to have two full weeks of use. This should be simple—all of these weapons are available on the black market for those with enough cash to throw around. You are to stash these weapons and ammo in a cache at the address provided on the included dossier.

There are six addresses listed as "locations." These are where I will perform my executions. They are all abandoned, so purchase them under one of your many fraudulent accounts. I'll use the ones I see fit when I need them. I may or may not use them all.

Starting the second week of July, rent Room 205 at the Inn on Bourbon Street under a pseudonym.

Stay there every night. If I have additional instructions, I will have them delivered to your room via courier.

I will begin the murders within the first few days of August. Be ready.

After the first murder, have your son, Nick, meet with Samantha Castille and make sure she is publishing murder mysteries regularly with the Times-Picayune. It would be best if the stories were about the Bourbon Street Ripper, but any murder mysteries will do. I will do the rest.

While Nick is meeting with Samantha Castille, have him collect some of her skin cells. I don't care how you do this. Preserve the skin cells.

After the second murder, have Nick break into Samantha Castille's home and vandalize it, accusing her of being the murderer. It will also help if Nick attacks her or any of her friends. Make her think she is being targeted for vigilante justice.

After the third murder, have Nick find a way to plant her skin cells in the third victim's body. I suggest using a police officer for this task. Nick is good with the ladies, so perhaps he can seduce a policewoman.

Enclosed is a modem that will fit the type of copier Samantha Castille owns. Send me copies of the manuscripts of the story she is writing. I will use them to further discredit her.

Make no move to acquire control of the Castille family fortune until I say otherwise.

From your embezzling, you clearly want Sam's money. If you follow my instructions, this money will be yours after the final murder. If you attempt to oppose me, or in any way deviate from the instructions in this letter, you and your son will die.

I look forward to our mutually beneficial business relationship.

Sincerely,

The Bourbon Street Ripper

Chapter 25
Hot August Rain

Date: **Monday, August 17, 1992**
Time: **10:00 a.m.**
Location: **Oakland Cemetery**
               Shreveport, Louisiana

"Let us commend our brother, Michael Stephen LeBlanc, to the mercy of God."

The raindrops fell like gentle kisses from the heavens above, as if angels were weeping for the lost soul being laid to rest. The rows and rows of uniformed officers stood, saluting the casket as it was lowered into the earth to the minister's prayer, which mixed harmoniously with the rain and the sound of "Taps" being played.

"Give him, oh Lord, your peace. And let your eternal light shine upon him."

Rodger held a salute, watching the beautiful brown coffin lower slowly into the ground. To one side, Dixie, Gino, Aucoin, and Cathy stood, the detectives saluting as well. To his other side, Richie stood, holding the handles of Sam's wheelchair. Her body was still, but tears were streaming down her face. Ouellette stood near the minister. His face was pained, but as strong and resolute as ever.

"We therefore commit his body to the ground: earth to earth, ashes to ashes, dust to dust."

Across from Rodger was a plump middle-aged woman crying in an older gentleman's arms: Michael's mother and father. Next to the parents stood a girl in her mid-teens: Michael's sister, Alexia.

"In the sure and certain hope of the Resurrection of eternal life."

Rodger felt distant, as if he were barely standing there, even with the gunshots of a three-volley salute. Twenty years ago almost to the day, he had buried Edward Castille in a similar manner.

As the casket finished lowering into the earth, a procession of people approached the grave, throwing flowers on top of the coffin. Rodger looked around at the large turn-out to Michael's funeral. Most of the precinct was able to come, although Rivette and Landry offered to stay behind while Ouellette attended. Michael's family was extremely large, and every aunt, uncle, and cousin seemed to be there.

Rodger watched as Ouellette handed Michael's mother the folded American flag that had rested over his coffin. Ouellette looked exhausted. He had been attending funerals for the victims at the wharf all week. Michael's was the last one, right after Guidry's.

Michael's mother took the folded flag and started crying harder. Michael's father shook Ouellette's hand and then took his wife into his arms. A Baptist minister, he had given a solemn eulogy that dripped with remorse. Rodger knew that Michael's relationship with his father had been strained. However, it was obvious that the man had been fighting back tears all morning.

The only one who wasn't openly crying was Alexia. Rodger was amazed at how strong she seemed.

Even though it was the middle of summer, she was wearing a formal black dress, with a silver cross embroidered over the chest, and silver cross earrings. Her hair was as black as Michael's, but punky and unkempt. She had strength in her eyes that reminded Rodger of his partner. He could see why Michael had been so close to her.

He came out of his thoughts and realized he and Alexia were the last ones standing over the grave. Looking in her eyes, he could tell she wanted to be alone with her brother. Nodding, he knelt down and tossed the bouquet on top of the coffin.

"Goodbye, buddy. See you around," Rodger said. He got up, leaving Alexia to get on her knees in silence.

He figured he should offer his condolences to Michael's parents. He was just about to head over when he heard Richie say, "Hey, Rodger?"

He looked over. Richie was drying Sam's face. Rodger knelt down to look at her. She actually shifted her gaze over to him and grunted. But she didn't speak, nor did her head move. Although her progress the past couple of days had been remarkable, she was still a long way from a full recovery.

"We're gonna probably need to go soon," Richie said, wiping away the last of her tears. "This weather can't be good for Sam. And with both of our hearings coming up, we need to be healthy and rested."

Rodger kissed her forehead, and then patted her knee. "Good idea. I'll be ready to go in a bit."

He was glad he had come up with Richie and Sam the night before, as he got to spend time with her. Her commitment hearing for the various assaults committed as Sam of Spades was within a few days. Dr. Klein was doing all he could to get her committed to his care.

As Richie started to wheel Sam away, he stopped and turned back to Rodger. Despite having refilled his medication, he still looked extremely anxious. "Rodger, do you think things will end up OK for Sam and me?"

Rodger forced a smile. Richie's situation was not as bad. After having been found naked and badly beaten in an alleyway off Bourbon Street, he had led the police to the remains of Officer Guidry. He had then told the police everything: the group calling themselves the Knight Priory, their assassinations of Marcello's and Nick's gangs, and meeting the new Bourbon Street Ripper face to face.

Even though Richie's story seemed like the most convoluted jumble of facts, it conveniently filled in all the remaining holes of this sordid tale. It also seemed to satisfy the district attorney's office. Richie was scheduled to testify on Wednesday in front of a grand jury in return for not being charged with obstruction.

"Well, you sat on important information, but the DA is more concerned with wrapping up the case than with sending you to jail," Rodger said, shrugging. "As for Sam? Well, I think she'll be fine. A lot of people are on her side now."

Richie said nothing. He wheeled Sam back to her car.

Rodger shook his head slowly. There hadn't been any more murders, so most people were convinced that Nick was the killer and that

Guidry was the last victim. The timelines barely added up, but it was plausible. Rodger didn't buy it, though.

The killer is still out there.

He took out a cigarette. He needed a smoke.

As he puffed on his cigarette, he became aware that Gino and Dixie were standing by his side. Her ruined left arm was in a sling, where it would stay until the stump was healed enough for a prosthesis. She seemed to be taking it well, all things considered.

"She gonna be OK?" Dixie asked about Sam, heaviness in her voice. She had cried for almost two days when she found out Michael had died.

"Hope so," said Rodger with uncertainty in his voice. "That bastard Dr. Klein is doing everything to get her. And the way Sam reacts when he hears his name? She's terrified of him."

Dixie shook her head. "There's something wrong with Dr. Klein, Rodger. He visited me in the hospital, and he's called me twice since I got out. I feel like he's stalking me or something. It's really creepy."

"I told him if he came near Dixie again," said Gino, "that I would break him in two. The little prick laughed."

Rodger had never heard him swear before.

"Well, one thing at a time," Dixie said, turning back to Rodger. "I'm going to use my time off to see if I can find out what this guy is about. Like we agreed, Rodger. You just handle your end of things."

He nodded. The agreement between him, Dixie, and Ouellette was as under the table as it could get. "I'll keep my end up. Gonna go talk to Ouellette now. Take care, Dixie."

He approached Ouellette, saw that he was talking to Aucoin and Cathy, and waited nearby. He knew that Aucoin was on administrative leave for the next few months, and that his marriage with Cathy was on the edge of oblivion. Rodger found himself wondering if Aucoin would remain on the police force or not. Cheryl's death had caused irreparable harm to his life.

When Ouellette was done, Aucoin and Cathy walked off with distance between them. Then Ouellette came over. "It's late, Bergeron. Shouldn't you be getting Miss Castille home?"

"Heading out now, Commander," Rodger said, finishing off his cigarette.

Ouellette didn't look at him. Instead, he surveyed the dispersing groups of people. "Well, Bergeron, my precinct is under investigation for the next few days. Why don't you take some time to rest and recuperate? You know, put this ugliness behind you and focus on what's important?"

Nodding, Rodger replied, "That's a good idea. I might get bored, though, doing nothing at home." It was a simple verbal code Ouellette, Dixie, and Rodger had worked out.

Ouellette said, "I've already taken the liberty of lending you some reading material. You should enjoy it. I left it at your apartment this morning."

Rodger nodded and said, "Thank you for that, Commander. See you in a few days."

He was almost at Sam's car, where she and Richie were waiting, when Alexia stepped right out in front of him. She had the same intense look Michael had had right before he punched Rodger out.

Rodger flinched.

"Detective Bergeron," she said. "May I have a moment of your time?"

He blinked. "Sure. Just . . . don't surprise an old man like that."

"Sorry." Her eyes were puffy. It was obvious that she had been crying over her brother's grave. "I just want to say 'Thank you.'"

Blinking, as the rain started coming down more heavily, Rodger said, "Um, you're welcome? Thank you for what?"

Alexia sucked on her bottom lip. "My brother hated New Orleans. He was only there because he loved being a detective and wanted to make a difference. But he always felt out of place, like he never belonged."

Rodger nodded.

"But you made it worthwhile to him. He's told me so many times on the phone that the only reason he stayed in the eighth precinct was because of you."

Rodger felt a lump forming in his throat.

She bowed her head. "So, thank you. For all you did for my brother. For being his best friend. All's well." She left to join the rest of the LeBlanc family.

He was thankful for the rain. It hid any tears he might have had.

The drive home was long and quiet. Several times, Richie tried to strike up a conversation, but Rodger wasn't interested. He was mentally preparing himself for when he got home. The arrangement made between Ouellette, Dixie, and Rodger was simple: Ouellette would run interference for a few days, Dixie would find out what Dr. Klein was up to, and Rodger would figure out who the real killer was.

This was everyone's last chance to make it right. And they knew it.

It was six thirty when Richie dropped Rodger off at his apartment.

On his way through the courtyard, Rodger heard the familiar voice of Ms. Parkerson saying, "There you is, Rodger Bergeron. I needs to speak with you."

He turned to his landlady and smiled through heavy fatigue. "I am thoroughly exhausted, Ms. Parkerson. Can this wait?"

She shook her head and clanked her cane on the concrete. "I made some of my famous chicken and dumplings. I figured you could use a good cooked meal."

"That would be nice, Ms. Parkerson, just bring it over when you have a chance." He tried to sound congenial. He had already informed her of Michael's death, and while he appreciated her kindness, he really didn't want to be social right now.

As Rodger headed toward his front door, Ms. Parkerson, still clanking her cane, said, "Oh, and your mail arrived a little bit ago. Mail slot is busted, so I brought it inside so it wouldn't get soaked. I'll bring it over with your chicken and dumplings."

Despite himself, he chuckled. For years, she had brought his mail inside when it rained. He was OK with this. However, she always found it necessary to explain herself. It was a quirk that he found amusing. "Thanks, Ms. Parkerson. I'm going to shower off. Bring it over in half an hour."

As she muttered that she'd bring the food over when her soaps were done, he entered his apartment. The entire front room, from front to back, was stacked with boxes. Reports, profiles, notes, and more, ranging from 1972 to today—his home was filled with every file the police had on both Bourbon Street Ripper cases.

A note from Ouellette read: "You have three days. Get the bastard."

Rodger sighed as he crumpled up the note. He had already agreed to take the fall should the wrong people find out about this arrangement. He was risking his retirement, his pension, and his freedom—but he didn't care. Considering what both of his partners had lost, this was a small chance to take.

All right, Edward, Michael, first I take a nice, cool shower. Second, I get a glass of whiskey. Third, I solve this goddamn case.

Thirty minutes and one cool shower later, he was sitting in his favorite chair amongst the literally hundreds of files making up the entire Bourbon Street Ripper case. He was dressed in a change of clothes and nursing a glass of whiskey on the rocks. He was ready to begin the arduous task of solving the mystery.

"I know that Kent and Nick were being blackmailed by our killer, who has masterminded everything from start to finish."

Ice clinked in his glass as he sipped the liquor. *But who is this guy? He's so good at covering his tracks, it's like he's a ghost.*

He shivered. All talks of voodoo and loa aside, he was pretty sure he was chasing a living, breathing murderer—someone with the cunning and financial means to orchestrate a massively successful killing spree while simultaneously killing off all the accomplices and police involved in the original Bourbon Street Ripper case.

"A mastermind murderer who wants to erase everyone involved in the original case," Rodger said out loud, taking out Michael's notes on the case. Everything had started with Vincent Castille's accomplices: Topper Jack, Mad Monty, Fat Willie, and Blind Moses. And each one was now dead.

The killer used Blind Moses to kill Topper Jack and Mad Monty. Fat Willie died by accident. Sam killed Blind Moses. Did the killer know that Blind Moses would go after Sam? Was the killer banking on Sam killing Blind Moses?

His thoughts were interrupted by a knock on the front door. When he opened it, Ms. Parkerson came storming in like an alligator charging its prey. She was holding a covered cooking pot nearly half her size. Mail was resting on the top. "Gotta gets this on your stove and warms it up, Rodger Bergeron. Move aside."

It was all he could do to sidestep the elderly landlady, who managed to take the mail off the top of the cooking pot and put it in his hands and close the front door before an errant mosquito flew inside.

I swear to God, Rodger thought with an internal laugh, *this woman has four arms.*

As she barged her way into his kitchen, mumbling something about "too many boxes" and "fire codes" and "raising the rent to include someone's take-home work," he looked down at the mail.

On top was the *Times-Picayune,* the front page showing the images of Kent and Nick Bourgeois. The article was about their involvement in the new Bourbon Street Ripper murders. It was the usual unsubstantial sensationalism. He could tell that Caroline was doing all she could to separate her paper from Nick, which was an alias for Jacob, one of her editors. "Well, I can't say I blame her."

"Can't say you blame who-what, Rodger?" crackled Ms. Parkerson from the kitchen. The sound of clanking metal and the smell of chicken and dumplings floated into the main room.

Rodger, realizing he had spoken out loud, snorted playfully. "Nothing. Just talking to myself. Those chicken and dumplings smell good, by the way."

"Of course they good," came her reply. "I cooked them."

Still grinning at his landlady's antics, he returned to the mountain of notes, focusing on the paper trail that had led Michael to Kent and Nick Bourgeois.

Pretty good detective work there. From the trail of logic, it looked like Kent and Nick had been given just enough rope to hang themselves.

Rodger rubbed his chin as a realization came to mind. "We all cleaned up the killer's loose ends. He used Kent and Nick to facilitate these murders and then we killed them. Just like Blind Moses killing Vincent's accomplices, the killer used other people to remove his trail."

He shook his head at what that implied. "The killer has been planning this for years. There's no way there's not some underlying reason behind everything. The killer had a real agenda here."

"What you say?" asked Ms. Parkerson as she came into the room. She was carrying a large bowl of scrumptious-smelling chicken and dumplings.

"Oh, talking about the Bourbon Street Ripper case," he said as she set up the bowl on a tray table in front of him.

"I thought that hogwash was over with," she said as she emphatically replaced his glass of whiskey with a glass of iced tea. "Besides, never much liked the name anyway."

Rodger shrugged. "Well, it may be over, but . . . Who what now? The name? You mean 'Bourbon Street Ripper'?"

Nodding, she said, "Always bothered me, the papers using that name. Both times. Too much like Jack the Ripper."

His brow wrinkled as he gulped down some food. It was amazing, as always. "This is really tasty. But what did you mean by 'too much like Jack the Ripper?'"

"Oh, that's all ramblings from an old hen," said Ms. Parkerson as she walked back into the kitchen. "Just that some folks think that Jack the Ripper murdered a whole lot of women to cover up one real murder."

Rodger stopped mid-gulp at that. Michael had believed that Vincent's killings were like Jack the Ripper—many killings to disguise one killing. *What if that logic applied to this copycat?*

He ate very slowly as he spoke out loud. "Who could the killer have really been after? If he was just killing those associated with Vincent, the torture murders would be too much work. No, one of those victims he tortured and killed was a real target. But who?"

He counted off the victims in his head.

Virginia Babineaux was the daughter of the first original Bourbon Street Ripper victim, Henrietta Babineaux. *That was likely the real killer being poetic.*

Rebecca Clemens was the second victim. She was a tourist. *Nothing there. Just the wrong place at the wrong time.*

Cheryl Aucoin, the third victim, was the daughter of Detective Kyle Aucoin. *A possibility. But why target a child directly? Why not target Kyle?*

The fourth victim, Officer Emilie Guidry, was the one who had found the first three victims. *Almost like the killer was cleaning up his mess.*

As Rodger looked down at his empty bowl, the answer came to him. "Cheryl Aucoin was the actual victim here. The others were distractions."

It made sense. Using Blind Moses, the real killer would kill Vincent's accomplices, while the police who supposedly botched the original investigation, such as himself, wouldn't die until the last victim was killed. *So Cheryl was murdered to make Kyle suffer!*

He went over to the stacks of papers and looked for Aucoin's involvement in the original Bourbon Street Ripper case. "Kyle Aucoin discovered the bodies of Maple and Dallas Christofer. It was Kyle who found the body. The copycat killer wanted to punish Kyle, who found Maple and Dallas. Why?"

"Why what, Rodger?" Ms. Parkerson asked, picking up his dirty bowl. "Want some more chicken and dumplings?"

He nodded. "Sure thing." Truth was, he was focused on the report. Ms. Parkerson, with one comment, had set him on what felt like a path to solving this case.

After reading the report, it became clear why Aucoin was chosen to suffer. Originally, he had found the disturbed soil in the morning, but he hadn't actually come back with officers to dig it up until the late afternoon. *That means Dallas was lying in his mother's remains for over twelve hours.*

In the report, Aucoin had stated that an emergency call had sidetracked him from the investigation. He had received a reprimand for his lack of judgment, but nothing else. The top brass had decided that Aucoin's guilt over the situation was enough.

"But that wasn't enough to the murderer," Rodger said to himself. Taking a fresh bowl of chicken and dumplings from Ms. Parkerson and setting it to the side, he figured that for the killer, Aucoin's mistake demanded the loss of his only child.

"You gonna eat your food, Rodger? Or you gonna let it get cold?" asked Ms. Parkerson.

He smiled nervously and said, "Sorry. I'm just thinking about the killer still. I think you're onto something. I think he was killing all those women to hide the murder of a policeman's child."

She arched an eyebrow and asked, "That so? Whatever for?"

Rodger shrugged and picked up the bowl to take a bite. "That policeman was remiss on helping a victim in the original case. I think the two cases are linked."

"Is that so?" she asked. "If that be the case, then wouldn't the killer kill the children of the other policemen involved at the time?"

His eyes widened. Once again, Ms. Parkerson had, with just a comment, set off a chain reaction of thought within Rodger's mind. "Wait! What if Cheryl Aucoin wasn't the first child of a policeman this murderer killed? What if he killed someone else years before, but we didn't recognize it because it was a different kind of murder?"

She leaned against the stacks of boxes and asked, "Who you talking about, Rodger Bergeron?"

"Jason Ouellette." He stood up. He had something to check.

"Wait, Rodger, yo food!" she called out as he headed to the back of his apartment.

"I can't," Rodger called back. "I'm solving the case!"

In his bedroom, he kept a scrapbook of sorts—mostly newspaper clippings from every major event of his life, the lives of his friends, or the lives of his coworkers. Everything from his own graduation from the police academy to when he and Douglas had busted some of the Marcello family to when Vincent Castille was executed.

Flipping through the pages, he found what he was looking for— the article on Jason Ouellette's death. In it was a list of Jason's friends, the attendees at the party where he had died. It took Rodger only a few seconds to see a name he partially recognized.

"Julius Bernard."

Rodger looked at the name until something clicked. *That could be an alias for Julius Boucher. Oh, God, Michael's theory was right!*

At the front of his apartment, Ms. Parkerson was packing things up. "Sorry, Rodger. Gotta go deal with Earl Mastadon. Extra food's in the fridge, if you want some. Your bowl there gonna get cold soon."

He walked up to her and hugged her. She tensed up and said, "What's with you?"

"Thank you," he said. "You don't realize it, but you may very well have helped me solve this case."

Ms. Parkerson stared back up at him for a long moment before adjusting her glasses. "Ain't nothing. Don't forget the rest of your mail. Something from the city came, not that I looked or nothing."

Rodger said "thank you" to Ms. Parkerson again before showing her out.

As soon as she was gone, he called Sam's townhome. A few rings later, Richie picked up. "Hello?"

"It's Rodger. Is Sam OK?"

"Hey. Yeah, she's fine," Richie said. "What can I help you with?"

Rodger looked over the article on Jason. "Yeah, I need to know about your visit with Rosemary Boucher," he said, recalling Richie's affidavit about her murder. "Specifically, what did she say about Julius Boucher?"

There was another pause before Richie said, "Oh! It was crazy, Rodger. She was sure Julius was alive because she got this letter from him. I only got a glimpse of it before, you know, those people came. But it seemed like it was the real deal."

Rodger harrumphed. It was not the information he was hoping for. "Did you see anything else on the letter? Anything at all?"

There was one more pause, and then Richie said, "Yeah, I remember. The name 'Annie-Mae Bernard' was on the letter."

Rodger felt as if he had just come through the other side of a dark tunnel. "My God. Thank you so much, Richie!"

He was just about to hang up when Richie said, "Rodger, wait!"

"What?" he asked. "Is there something wrong with Sam?"

"No, no," replied Richie. "It's just that you asked me to inform you if anyone came over. Well, right before you called, Mason, the Castille family butler, called. He's coming to deliver a package for Sam. Something willed to her by, well, Vincent."

Rodger paled. "What?"

"Yeah, I know," said Richie. "I thought 'what the heck,' too. But, apparently, Vincent had specified that something was to be delivered to Sam on the twentieth anniversary of his arrest."

Rodger looked at his wall calendar. Sure enough, it was the exact date he had arrested Vincent on twenty years prior. His brow furrowed. "OK, don't do anything when Mason gets there. I will be there in a few minutes. I need to make just one more phone call. OK?"

"OK," Richie said. "Lemme go take care of Sam. Later."

Rodger hung up. *I can't let myself get sidetracked. Vincent Castille is dead. I will deal with whatever he's sent to Sam after I solve this case.*

Picking up the phone, he dialed the Acadia Vermilion Hospital.

Chapter 26
A Chance at Happiness

Date: **Monday, August 17, 1992**
Time: **6:00 p.m.**
Location: **Esplanade Apartments**
                New Orleans City Park

"Do you need anything else, Dixie?"

Dixie looked up at Gino as he finished feeding her some hot soup. She hadn't been very responsive since they had gotten back to New Orleans from Michael's funeral. She felt numb, like she had lost something more precious to her than she could ever know.

"No, thanks, Gino. I'm OK for now."

She knew it was a lie, and she knew that he knew. She was far from OK.

With a nod, he headed out of the bedroom, saying nothing else. They hadn't spoken much since Michael had died, and they hadn't talked at all about Michael's death. She hadn't felt the desire to open up to anyone, even Gino.

"If Dr. Lazarus or Ouellette calls, I'll take it," Dixie shouted down the hall after Gino. "Otherwise, I don't want to be disturbed."

"All right, Dixie," Gino called back.

She had been shutting herself away for the last few days, particularly avoiding Dr. Klein. Try as she might, the only record of him she could find was his practice on St. Charles Street. And despite Gino openly threatening him, which garnered nothing but a contemptuous laugh, Dr. Klein continued to try to get her to come work for him. She was considering filing for a restraining order.

The guy is a total creep, Dixie thought as the bitter memory returned. *I don't know why anyone trusts him.*

She leaned back and tried to think about something pleasant. She remembered hearing Gino mention another vacation, maybe an extended one to Greece to visit his family. She wasn't sure what she wanted.

Actually, she was sure. She wanted her best friend back.

Michael. God, I miss you so much. Why did you have to die? It's not right. It's not fair.

She struggled to keep her feelings in check. At times, she'd had a crush on her best friend; other times, she had loved him as a sister would a brother. It was strange to her, that a man other than Gino had impacted her life as Michael had. She had hidden her feelings for so long that even now they felt foreign.

"Dixie."

Dixie, who had started to absently nibble on her thumbnail, realized that Gino was standing in the doorway. He was holding the phone.

"It's that Dr. Lazarus," he said quietly.

She smiled back and said "thank you" before starting to reach for the phone with her left hand. She then stopped and remembered that she didn't have one. With a sigh, she reached out with her right hand.

Gino noticed the mistake. "The doctor said that this will happen for a while. Don't worry, we'll get you in physical therapy soon."

Dixie nodded to him without replying. Instead, she spoke into the receiver. "Hello, Dr. Lazarus?"

Gino left without a word.

"Yes, Detective Olivier," Dr. Lazarus said. In the background was a lot of commotion.

"What's going on over there?" she asked. "It, um, sounds like you're busy."

"Oh, no," he replied. "I'm just moving some things to another office. Nothing major."

Dixie heard a female voice and guessed it was Camellia. All she made out were the words "*tkeeus*," "Abel," and "reports." Dr. Lazarus was holding his hand over the phone, muffling the conversation.

"I can call back another time," she said, feeling considerably awkward.

"No, no," he said. "I've told everyone to rest a bit. Anyway, I apologize for taking so long to get back to you. But we've been very busy here. How can I help you?"

Dixie paused for a moment to consider everything. She wasn't one hundred percent sure Dr. Lazarus could help. *Well, I've got nothing to lose.*

"Do you know Dr. Lucius Klein?" she asked.

"Ah, yes," he said. "A very unpleasant fellow. I cannot say I am a fan of his methods at all."

"He seems to think even less of you."

He chuckled. "Is that so? Well, Detective, I am a big boy. I can handle critics."

"Yes, but that's not why I'm asking you about him." She sighed softly. "He's been pushing very hard to have Sam committed to his care. And . . . he's been bothering me to work for him and his colleagues."

The line was silent for a second too long before Dr. Lazarus said, "I see. That's very disconcerting. What can you tell me about his colleagues? Did he mention them?"

Dixie shook her head. "No. Not at all. He only mentioned that they were a group. I got the feeling it was some kind of secret. He made it sound very suspicious."

"I bet he did," he said. "Did he mention what he wanted you to do?"

"He wanted me to hunt down serial killers for him to study."

Again, the line was silent a second too long. "How very interesting. You were right in coming to me, Detective. While I don't think he's part of some clandestine group, Dr. Klein is a very dangerous man. He is well connected in local, state, and federal governments. He has very Spartan views on personality disorders and the treatment of psychosis. And he holds grudges remarkably well for someone who is supposed to be an adult."

She chortled nervously. "Yeah, well, he's been harassing me pretty regularly since I was in the hospital. And he did say that I'd never be allowed to walk away from him like nothing ever happened."

"He threatened you?"

She gritted her teeth as she relived the memory. "Yes, he did."

Dr. Lazarus's tone was grave. "Please listen, Detective, and listen carefully. I advise you to report this to your commander immediately. You may not think it, but Louis Ouellette has a lot of influence. He can protect you."

The commander?

Dixie thought that over, then decided that it made sense. After all, he was the police commander. "OK. Gino and I were considering a restraining order."

"Very bad idea," Dr. Lazarus replied. "Dr. Klein knows too many people. He'd get it denied and then flaunt it as a show of power over you and then make your life miserable. No, I highly recommend you going to your commander. If there is anyone who can keep you safe, it's him. And Louis likes you quite a bit. I'm sure he'll understand."

He calls the commander by first name? She was unsure what to make of that. "Thank you for that, Dr. Lazarus, I'll do this tonight."

"Just be careful," he said with more urgency in his voice. "There are things in this world, Detective, which are just plain dark and evil. You may not believe in them, but they exist. Sometimes, people like Dr. Klein invite those dark and evil things just by being themselves, much as a flame draws a moth."

Dixie had no idea what Dr. Lazarus was talking about. "Um, thank you? If there's anything I can do to repay this, just let me know."

"Not yet, but soon."

Now it was her turn to be silent for a bit too long. "Come again?"

"Well, I apologize if I am being too forward. But I wanted to say that if you are serious about repaying me, I will take you up on it. Soon. Very soon, I'll need your help in saving someone. It's going to be an ugly situation, and I'll need the help of an able-minded detective. You are my best hope."

She blinked. "Who would I be helping?"

"Sam."

She sat there in silence. *Sam? Dr. Lazarus needs me to help him save Sam. How? Why?*

"Before you say anything, listen closely," said Dr. Lazarus. "Sam is in a world of trouble. You wouldn't believe me if I told you, but even once the killer is caught, she still has some problems to deal with. I suspect that Dr. Klein is misinterpreting those problems as a psychosis. As you just confirmed, he is trying to get her into his custody. And I suspect that Sam's condition would only worsen in his care."

Dixie didn't say a word. She was riveted to the phone.

"When this happens," he continued, "whenever this happens, if you can fully commit yourself to helping me save Sam, I will be grateful beyond measure."

It didn't take her long to answer. "I'll do it. Count me in. I did Sam a great disservice when I accused her falsely. If I can ever correct that, I will."

"Then we have an accord," he said. "Just remember to keep your wits about you, watch your back, and don't forget to call your commander about Dr. Klein's threats."

"I will. I won't," she said. "Good night, Dr. Lazarus."

"Good night, Detective Olivier."

He hung up.

For several minutes, Dixie sat there in silence, her eyes closed.

If I hadn't convinced myself that Sam was the killer, I never would have arranged the confrontation at the wharf. If I hadn't done that, Blind Moses wouldn't have attacked us all. Then I wouldn't have lost my arm. Then Sam wouldn't have been so badly hurt. Then maybe, just maybe, with all of us healthy and working on the case, Michael wouldn't have—

She hung her head in shame.

Michael would still be alive. Oh, God, what did I do?

Covering her face with her only hand, she sobbed.

I'm so horrible! I killed my best friend. I killed Michael!

For several minutes, she wasn't even aware that Gino was holding her.

Leaning into his broad chest, Dixie sobbed. "Oh, Gino! If I hadn't been so quick to ruin Sam, so many people would still be OK. I'm sure a useless bitch."

"Never say that," he said, kissing the top of her head. "Never think you are useless. You are a good woman, Dixie. You have a good heart."

"But I killed Michael," she sobbed. The wellspring had opened, and everything was coming out at once. For nearly a quarter of an hour, she cried into his arms.

When she finally calmed down, Gino dried her tears. "No. Kent killed Michael. Do not ever think otherwise."

Nodding slowly, Dixie shuddered a few more times, then lay back on her pillow.

"I'll go get you some water," he said, getting up.

She barely heard her boyfriend. Nibbling on her thumb, she went deep into thought.

I cannot do enough for Sam to make up for how I treated her. She tried to reach out to anyone who would listen, but we all shunned and hated her. I effectively treated her like how my father treated my sister and mother.

Gino returned with her water.

If it takes me the rest of my life, I'll make it up to Sam. I'll make sure people forget the bad and only remember the good about her.

An hour later, Dixie had gotten cleaned up and was ready for bed. It was then that she remembered Dr. Lazarus's warning. *God, I've never forgotten something like that. These pain meds must really have me out of it.*

She went up to the front room. Gino was watching a stand-up comedian and drinking a glass of wine. The phone receiver was on the coffee table in front of him. She slid behind him and kissed the back of his head. "I need to call my boss, OK?"

He tousled her hair. "Of course, Dixie. Then you go to bed. I'll join you soon."

Dixie took the phone and went back to the bedroom. She dialed Ouellette's office at the precinct.

"You should be asleep, Olivier," he answered.

She blushed. She had forgotten that her commander's phone had Caller ID. "Hey, um, sorry," she said, taking a moment to recover. "I'm calling because Dr. Lazarus asked me to tell you something."

Dixie expected her commander to ask who the heck Dr. Lazarus was, or demand a complete and full explanation. Instead, Ouellette just said, "All right, tell me what's going on."

Odd. He must know Dr. Lazarus, she thought. "It's about Dr. Klein. I haven't said anything, but he's been trying to recruit me as a manhunter for him. And I'm not interested. And he's been threatening me because of it."

The line went silent.

His tone was cold when he finally said, "I see. Thank you so much for telling me, Olivier."

Dixie was expecting more of a response. "So that's it? Nothing else?"

"What else do you want?" His voice raised a little. "I've worked with Dr. Klein before, as distasteful a man as he is. We've built up a trust. He shattered that trust like goddamn glass by overstepping his bounds. I told him you weren't going to be interested, but he practically begged me to permit him to contact you. I knew he'd try some sort of bribery, but to threaten you? Hell, no!" His voice had gotten deeper and louder. The receiver of her phone was starting to vibrate, and she held it away from her ear.

He knew that Dr. Klein was going to ask me to work for him? She couldn't imagine that being the case. She couldn't imagine Ouellette knowing Dr. Klein or Dr. Lazarus, or any of those people, on a professional or personal level.

"Excuse me, sir," she asked. "What's going on here? How do you know all these people?"

His voice had started to reverberate unnaturally. "It's my damn job, and I'll thank you to stay out of my damn business, Olivier."

She gasped at the roughness of her commander's voice.

Ouellette immediately apologized, his voice returning to normal. "That was out of line for me. I'm sorry, Olivier. I'm waiting to hear back from Bergeron, and sitting here on my hands is more painful than any torture, let me assure you."

Despite the apology, Dixie felt a little freaked out. *Did that just happen?*

She didn't ask about Rodger's investigation. Before Michael's funeral, it was decided that Rodger would have to work this alone. Anything more and they risked the mayor's office coming down on everyone. But she was confident he could solve the mystery.

"You know, Olivier, I'm going to break protocol."

His words pulled her out of her thoughts. "What do you mean, Commander?"

"I was going to wait until you came back to the office, but you need some good news." He cleared his throat. "You're going to be promoted to lieutenant when you return to duty. Top brass have decided on it. You're going to help me run homicide. Congrats, Detective."

She sat there, stunned.

He harrumphed. "Your jaw is probably on the floor. Typical. Well, go celebrate with Gino, Lieutenant. Get plenty of rest. And don't worry about Dr. Klein. I have a few phone calls to make. See you soon."

Dixie was still in shock when she heard the dial tone. She hung up the phone as Gino came into the bedroom.

He looked at her with concern. "Is everything all right, Dixie?"

"I just made Lieutenant." The words felt surreal coming out.

With a laugh, he swept her up into his arms, swinging her around. That shook off the shock and she started to laugh as well. As the two of them settled into each other's arms, he kissed her lovingly. He then held her close and started a slow dance, humming to her.

She pressed herself against him. She couldn't help but smile. Despite all the ugliness and darkness in the world, despite everything vile that had happened recently, there was something to cherish.

Maybe, just maybe, we all have a chance at happiness.

Those happy thoughts carried Dixie into the night.

Chapter 27
The Knight Priory

Date: **Monday, August 17, 1992**
Time: **8:00 p.m.**
Location: **Sam Castille's townhome**
                 Uptown New Orleans

After he hung up the phone with Rodger, Richie looked over at Sam, who was lying on her bed making gentle whimpers. She smelled awful. *Man, you never know how much you love someone until you've changed their diaper.* Kneeling down by her head, he smoothed back her blond hair and looked into her eyes. Somewhere within those blue depths, he could see what she was feeling: shame, regret, anguish—but, most importantly, love.

He smiled softly as he gave her a gentle kiss.

"Come on, beautiful. Let's get you cleaned up."

The same night Michael was murdered, she had started to respond to the outside world again. At first, the doctors feared that she was brain damaged and that her eye movements and occasional grunts were just instinctual. However, after additional testing, they concluded that she was indeed mentally cognizant, even though she was locked in to her body.

Most of the doctors were amazed that she was even alive. The consensus was that the damage to her nervous system, the loss of blood, and the physical trauma sustained from fighting Violet Patterson were so severe that she should have died. Her survival was being called a medical miracle.

Despite Sam's condition, the state of Louisiana was still prosecuting her for the several dozen assaults committed by Sam of Spades. Everyone, including Dr. Klein, was treating it as a multiple personality disorder. As soon as she was declared mentally competent, she was arraigned in her hospital room, grunting once for yes and twice for no. Soon after that, Dr. Klein made a move to have her committed to his private facility somewhere in Louisiana.

She had responded to that news with something akin to a throat-trapped screech.

Fortunately, the parts of her fortune that could be easily accessed paid for her bail bond and her legal representation. So, despite facing either commitment or jail time, she was allowed to go home under Richie's care. To make sure she was cared for, protected, and certain to make her court date, a nurse and two police officers were stationed at her townhome.

The nurse helped in all things except for changing Sam's diaper and cleaning her. Richie said that as her lover, he'd do that.

"Rodger seems to think he's on the verge of solving this case," Richie said as he scrubbed her back. Seated in her bathtub in a mere two inches of water, she just grunted briefly, which he took as an affirmation.

He had become really good at reading her grunts the past week.

"So you know what that means, right?" he asked as he flipped Sam's hair over her shoulder and washed the back of her neck.

When she grunted in a higher pitch, which he took as a question, he said, "That means we'll finally be safe soon. No more worries about the Knight Priory or the new Bourbon Street Ripper coming for us. We can move on with our lives."

She didn't reply. He fought back against his anxiety. Even though he had gotten his prescription filled, the pills no longer worked. It was like something had bubbled up inside him during those days without the medication that wouldn't go away. He just dealt with it, no longer bothering to take the pills.

"When all this is over," Richie said, washing down just below the small of her back, "I'm going to move here to New Orleans—in with you, if you'll still have me."

Sam grunted a few short grunts. They sounded happy. Richie smiled and pushed his anxiety away. Even though Gordon Rockway, his publicist, had abandoned him when he had failed to go to the next round of interviews, and even though sales of *The Pale Lantern* were plummeting as he broke his commitments, Richie was happy. Despite it all, he had succeeded in the one thing he truly cared about—being with Sam. To him, this was his happy ending.

"At this point, I'm convinced that Julius Boucher is the killer. Everything adds up to it, ya know?" Richie chuckled to himself as he finished rinsing Sam. "At least, that's how I'd write the big reveal of this story."

The bath over, he drained the water and carefully dried her off. Then he picked her up and called for the nurse, an older African American woman who had been assigned by the state, to help him carry Sam to her bed. The nurse dressed her in a fresh diaper and then in her nightgown. Once Sam was in bed, Richie pulled the sheets up to the middle of her chest and kissed her softly.

"I'll be back in a little bit, hun," he said before leaving with the nurse.

"Do you need me to stay with her while you go downstairs?" she asked.

Richie shook his head and said, "I think she wants to be alone for a while. She's been a recluse most of her life. You can wait out here, though, in case she needs something."

When the nurse nodded, he headed downstairs. The two police officers who were on duty were sitting in the kitchen. He had invited them inside because he figured Sam would be that hospitable.

"Can I get you officers any more coffee?" he asked, going to pour himself a cup. Despite being from the North, he'd learned to love the taste of coffee and chicory. It had a taste that almost felt like home to him.

When the two policemen accepted, he poured the water, measured the grinds, and set a new pot to boil. He was just setting out the cream and sugar when there was a knock at the door.

Everyone in the kitchen jumped a little. Richie froze, and the two policeman got up, hands on their sidearms.

"Stay here," one of the policemen said before heading toward the front door. Richie nodded and waited in the kitchen, fighting back worry about who it might be. He feared the Lady in Red and the Knight Priory. Technically, to save Sam, he had betrayed them to the police.

"Mr. Fastellos, it's the Castille butler," said the policeman from the front door.

Richie breathed a sigh of relief. He had all but forgotten that Mason was coming over tonight. He went to the front door, wondering if Rodger would show up soon as well, like he had promised.

Mason stood at the doorway. In the driveway was a beautiful black Mercedes-Benz, parked right behind Sam's car.

"Master Fastellos," Mason said from the front porch. "Is Lady Samantha Castille awake?"

"Yes."

"I need to deliver this box to her," Mason said, his old voice somewhat hoarse. "As specified by the late Master Vincent Castille."

"Right," said Richie. "I don't want to be rude, Mason, but Sam is in something like a coma and cannot respond to anyone."

Mason sniffed and said, "My instructions gave no indication that a response was needed. Just that the box be laid before her and a message be read."

"You can refuse him entry," the policeman said.

Richie nodded and was about to do just that when a random thought appeared in his head. He felt that this could give Sam the closure she needed from the nightmare of her grandfather. The thought was overpowering. He needed to let Mason inside to see Sam.

It was weird to get a thought, a feeling, that powerful, but he didn't want to question it. For once, it felt less like the anxiety talking and more like a deeper, more aware part of him.

"Nah, let him in," Richie said, motioning for the old butler to come inside. "But after you give her the box and deliver the message, you're gone, OK?"

"As you wish, Mr. Fastellos," Mason said.

"Come this way, then," replied Richie as he led Mason upstairs.

As they approached Sam's bedroom, Richie saw the nurse still waiting patiently outside. *Crap, I forgot about her.*

"Hey, there's some fresh coffee downstairs if you want some," he said.

The nurse muttered her thanks as she headed downstairs.

Once inside the bedroom, Richie went quietly to Sam's side. Her eyes were still open. "Sam, honey," he said, putting his hands on hers. She looked at him.

He cleared his throat. "Your old butler, Mason, is here with a gift from Vincent."

She started to make whimpering noises.

He rubbed her hands and said, "I know. I know you hate him, honey. But he's dead, remember? Mason is just going to give the gift, relay a message, and then leave."

She made another whimpering noise and then moaned. Richie frowned and wished Rodger were here to offer her even more reassurance.

"Go ahead and get it over with," he said to Mason. "She obviously wants nothing to do with her grandfather."

"I understand," Mason said, approaching Sam. "Lady Castille, I apologize if this causes you any distress, but the late master was very specific about my performing this task on the twentieth anniversary of his arrest. And as you know, I have always served the Castille family without question."

The noise she made was as close to a mocking "nya, nya, nya" as someone in her condition could make. Richie didn't suppress his grin.

Mason appeared to ignore both and said, "Lady Castille, on this day, the twentieth anniversary of Vincent Castille's arrest, he bequeaths to you this box." He laid a black lacquered box on the bed at Sam's feet.

She followed the box with her gaze as best as she could. The box was about the size of a videocassette tape, only twice as thick.

"Master Castille also asked me to read you this message," Mason said, taking out a sheet of what looked like very old paper. Clearing his throat, he began to read.

> Dear Princess,
>
> If you are hearing this, then it is August 17, 1992, and I am dead. Twenty years ago tonight, Rodger Bergeron arrested me after I murdered my only son, Edward.
>
> I don't apologize for the actions I have taken, but I am sorry for the pain I have caused you. I want you to know that in the end, it was worth it.

Sam had made a whimpering sound a couple of times already. Now she rolled her eyes away from Mason and looked at Richie. A strained whine came from her throat.

"Can you wrap it up?" Richie asked, starting to get angry.

"I am reading as quickly as I can," said Mason.

> I don't know how events will reveal themselves to you, but if my calculations are correct, you and those closest to you will be in mortal danger soon.
>
> The person after you is a seed of incredible evil that I planted by my own actions. It's possible that others have already suffered his uncontrollable rage.
>
> I apologize, Princess, for being unable to directly protect you, but his acts of evil will be necessary for me to keep my promise.

Richie grabbed Sam's hand and squeezed. Had Vincent known that there was going to be a copycat murderer?

Mason read on.

> Therefore, Princess, I leave you with something to protect you. Should my experiment have been in vain, should all my calculations and work been for naught, the contents of this box may be the only thing that can save your life.

Forgive me, Sam. You are the only one I ever loved.
And I still love you, even in death.

Vincent Gilles Castille

Richie looked over at Sam. Although she was incapable of any facial expressions, her eyes were wide in terror. *God, what is going on here? What "evil" did Vincent create?*

"I should go, then," Mason said, backing up. He looked shaken.

"Hold on," Richie said, going to the foot of the bed. "Don't go anywhere just yet."

Opening the box, he saw that the interior was lined in satin with an embroidered "C" on the inside cover. On a satin cushion was a small envelope with the name "Samantha" on it in calligraphy. The envelope was sealed shut.

OK, now I'm even more confused. Holding up the envelope for Sam to see, he asked, "May I open this?"

Sam grunted. He took it as a yes.

As he opened the envelope, he felt his heart start to beat more rapidly. He honestly didn't know what to expect, and his anxiety was bubbling forth once more.

My heart hasn't beat like this since the Knight Priory attacked. I'm already starting to sweat. What's going on?

Feeling a chill in the air and a tingling sensation in his spine, Richie shivered. It was a wholly unpleasant sensation. Taking a deep breath, he quickly opened the envelope.

Inside were three capsules of pink powder. Just like the kind Sam and Blind Moses had used that fateful night at the wharf.

"What the hell?" Richie asked. Some of the excess powder had smudged onto his fingers. He sniffed it. It had the scent of fruit to it. He sniffed again, harder, trying to identify it. The powder flew right up his nose, bringing on a sudden and powerful headache.

Richie put the capsules and envelope back into the box and closed it. Carrying the box with him, he approached Mason, who looked upset.

"You know anything about this stuff?" he asked, pushing the box under Mason's nose.

Mason tried to keep his dignified composure but shuffled back. "No, sir, nothing! The master had a name for it that I never could pronounce. He got it from one of the Priory members who stayed in Africa during the—"

"Do you have any idea how much damage this stuff has caused Sam?" Richie asked, getting angrier. His heart palpitations were increasing, the anxiety constricting his throat. His head was already pounding. "This stuff nearly killed her, you twit!"

"I am sorry, sir," Mason said, his voice cracking with fear. "Please, I'm just a servant. I just—"

"Shut up," Richie said, glaring at him. "Just get out of here and never bother Sam again. She's through with her fucked-up family."

Mason hurried downstairs as quickly as he could.

Richie started to feel sick, like he was going to pass out. The pounding of his heart, combined with the sudden headache, made standing next to impossible. Leaning against the banister, he thought, *Fuck, I inhaled some of that shit. Am I going to start tripping or running up walls or something?*

He headed downstairs to the kitchen. *Water. I need water.*

In the kitchen, he put the box by the phone and the knife set and quickly got himself a glass of water. It felt good going down but did nothing to alleviate the pounding in his chest or the aching in his head. He was just about to go looking for aspirin when he slipped on some liquid and fell onto the kitchen floor.

He lay there for a moment until the nausea passed. Once it was gone, he got up and looked at the liquid he had slipped on.

Blood.

Richie turned pale. *What the fuck?*

Turning, almost against his will, he looked at the two policemen sitting in the kitchen. Both were slumped forward in their chairs, their heads resting on the breakfast table, their throats slit. The blood was still pouring out.

He screamed and backed up, struggling to get to his feet.

Not again! Not them again!

The door to the back porch opened, and in came the nurse with a cup of coffee. As soon as she saw the bloody mess, she let out a tremendous shriek. He squealed in unison with the nurse. She didn't appear to hear him as she backed away from the scene.

A moment later, a figure appeared behind her and, grabbing her tightly, slit her throat with a butcher knife. Her coffee cup fell to the floor and broke, the contents spilling. She struggled in the figure's arms, gurgling helplessly until she went limp. The figure let the nurse go. Her body fell to the floor in a heap.

Looking up, Richie saw the same hooded figure who had taken Officer Guidry—the one Richie believed to be the real killer.

He grinned at Richie. It was that same wide, condescending sneer as before.

Richie screamed and ran from the room.

Silently, the figure ran after Richie, staying close behind him.

Richie's heart was pounding, his head throbbing. Once again, he was covered in blood. All he could think about was getting to Sam. He had to get to Sam. Lock the door. Call Rodger. Call the cops. Call anyone.

Richie scrambled up the stairs so fast he was almost crawling, whimpering the entire time. Each time he looked back, he saw the killer just coming around the corner, that sadistic, murderous grin underneath the hood.

When Richie reached Sam's room, he quickly shut the door and locked it. He heard Sam grunt.

"It's the killer. The real killer," Richie cried out. Running to the nightstand, he picked up the phone.

No dial tone.

"The line's dead—oh, God, Sam, we're in trouble," Richie cried, slamming the receiver down.

Sam grunted again, her tone questioning.

The door to Sam's bedroom started to shake as someone pounded on it. Richie ran to it as Sam grunted questioningly again. "He's trying to break in!" Richie exclaimed, holding the door shut.

Richie felt another slam against the door. It was harder than the first one. "I can't hold it."

Sam let out a whine of concern.

Richie felt a third slam against the door. This time, the door shook in his hands. "Oh, shit! Sam! We need to get out of here."

Sam's whine started to rise in panic.

There was a final slam against the door, and this time, Richie flew back as it crashed open. He slid across the bedroom floor as Sam cried out in confusion, the sound trapped in her throat. Looking up, Richie saw the killer enter. His hands were covered in blood.

The killer looked over at Sam. His mouth opened, his teeth bared like fangs. "Samantha . . ."

"Sam!" Richie jumped to his feet. Both he and the killer got to Sam at the same time. Richie grappled with the killer, trying to force him away from Sam. "I won't let you have her. You won't hurt a hair on Sam's head!"

Sam continued the confused and terrified cries in her throat, eyeing Richie fearfully.

The killer just laughed. The sound dripped with venom.

With blurring speed, the killer kicked Richie in both shins. He wailed, and as he felt his knees buckle, the killer picked him up and threw him onto the bed. The impact pushed Sam right off, her throat-clenched yelp of confusion turning into a grunt of pain as she hit the ground. Richie tried to get up only to have the killer punch him right in the groin.

Richie felt his entire world reel, his vision blurring, and curled up into a ball. The pain was unbearable. As he doubled over on Sam's bed, he saw that the killer suddenly had a scalpel in his hand.

"Time to die," said the killer in a hushed voice. As before, his mouth didn't move from that awful sneer.

Oh, God, no. Richie was unable to move from the pain.

The killer grinned sadistically at him.

I'm gonna die. Oh, God help me, I'm gonna die.

Then Richie saw a figure behind the killer, stealthily moving toward them both.

It was the Lady in Red.

Oh, thank God.

As the Lady in Red crept forward behind the killer, she drew out a butterfly knife and flicked it open. Even as the killer moved toward him, Richie felt that salvation was in reach. *She's here to help. The Knight Priory is here to help.*

From below, Sam groaned in pain.

Just as the killer reached the foot of the bed, the Lady in Red grabbed him from behind, placing her knife at his neck. "Julius," she said to the killer.

Richie felt the relief of triumph. *I was right.*

"It's you," said the killer.

The two turned and embraced each other before pressing their lips together in a chaste but lingering kiss.

Richie cried out in despair. From the ground, Sam started sobbing.

"Thank you, little boy," said the Lady in Red to Richie, resting her head against the killer's chest. "We couldn't have pulled all this off without you."

What the fuck?! Richie mentally cried out, still reeling from the killer's blows. *They're on the same side?! That doesn't make any sense!*

"He doesn't understand," said the killer with a smirk, stroking the Lady in Red's hair.

"Of course he doesn't get it. He's stupid. He needs it spelled out to him," she said, running her finger up and down the killer's chest. She sneered cruelly at Richie. "We used you. We wanted to kill one person. It's always been about killing just one person."

Sam continued sobbing.

Richie was finally able to move. He wiggled, one inch at a time, to the edge of the bed. "What? Who the fuck do you—?"

He stopped as the revelation dawned on him. "It's Sam? This whole thing has been about killing Sam?!"

From below, Sam cried out in confusion, her throaty screams sounding choked and tight.

As the Lady in Red untangled herself from the killer, and as Richie tried to slip off the bed, she grabbed him and pushed him onto his back. He saw a flash of metal and then felt a hard pinch as she stuck a needle in his neck.

"Congratulations, little boy, you figured it out," she said as she drained a syringe into him. Instantly, he felt his muscles seize and lock up. "The ritual Vincent performed on her made her damn near invincible. You saw her at the wharf. Even with the *tkeeus*, we could never hope to match her strength."

Richie couldn't move. He could feel every sensation as the Lady in Red laid him on his back and secured him to the posts of the bed with leather straps.

"Julius came up with the brilliant idea of using Samantha to kill Blind Moses. Why not? Violet Patterson hated Sam. It was like a powder keg waiting to explode. They just needed a little spark to set them off."

They used Sam to kill Violet, Richie thought in a mixture of frustration and fear.

Now that he was strapped in, the Lady in Red leaned over him, face-to-face, saying, "We just needed someone to keep Samantha busy until we were done getting rid of everyone else. So we used you. And even though you have been a pain in the ass, you did exactly what we wanted, little boy." She leaned down and kissed his lips, passionless and without feeling. "Thank you."

Richie glared. *Fuck you, you bitch!*

"Did Mason escape?" asked the killer. Richie could see only the pale glint of his sadistic smile.

Looking up at the killer, the Lady in Red said, "My boys got him, Julius. We've already killed him."

"Good," said the killer. He pointed down at Richie. "I'm going to get rid of him now. He's baggage."

Richie's heart started to pound in his chest. He had never been so frightened. All he could think about was Sam. Holding her. Kissing her. Feeling her warmth against him.

"As you wish. But don't take too long," the Lady in Red said, looking at a pocket watch. "Rodger Bergeron will be here soon. We need to get Samantha out of here before then."

Richie felt sick to his stomach. He heard Sam weeping on the floor below. She sounded so confused and frightened. He felt utterly helpless. He couldn't move. He couldn't make a sound. All he could think was that he'd never get to hold her in his arms again.

"When you're done with Richie, bring Sam downstairs," the Lady in Red said, before leaning down with a sneer. "Goodbye, little boy."

As the Lady in Red left, Richie tried to distance his mind from what was happening. He couldn't move. He was stuck as the killer opened a case, producing a series of sharp, dangerous-looking tools— scalpels, pliers, miniature drills, a bone saw, and a pair of forceps.

"I won't lie," said the killer, as he checked a scalpel's blade. "This is going to be hard for you." Grinning evilly, he opened Richie's shirt.

The world started to become a haze as Richie felt like he was watching the killer prepare to cut into him. The sensation of detachment was overwhelming.

Struggling to keep his thoughts his own, he focused on the taste of Sam's kiss, the soft texture of her skin, the sweet smell of her hair, the gentle hum of her voice as she sleepily muttered his name, the si—

"Very hard indeed," said the killer as he cut into Richie's chest.

Inside his mind, Richie screamed in anguish, and gave in.

Chapter 28
Everything Made Sense

Date: **Monday, August 17, 1992**
Time: **10:00 p.m.**
Location: **Sam Castille's townhome**
              Uptown New Orleans

When the receptionist at the Acadia Vermillion Hospital picked up, Rodger said, "Hello. This is Detective Rodger Bergeron. I'm . . ." Rodger paused and sucked back a sigh. "I *was* Michael LeBlanc's partner. May I speak to Dr. Lazarus?" It was hard to think about Michael being gone.

"Of course, Detective," replied the receptionist. "One moment."

Rodger didn't have to wait long, as Dr. Lazarus soon picked up. "This is Dr. Lazarus. Is this Detective LeBlanc's partner?"

"Yes," said Rodger. "I was hoping to ask some follow-up questions from Michael's visit."

"Of course," replied Dr. Lazarus. He sounded tired. "Also, I heard about what happened a few days ago. My condolences for your loss. Detective LeBlanc was a truly remarkable person. His death is a terrible loss to many people."

Rodger, who felt that Dr. Lazarus was laying it on a little thick, said, "Well, that's all well and good there. You know his funeral was today, correct?"

"Yes, yes," said Dr. Lazarus. "Again, my deepest sympathies. I wasn't able to make it. I had to take care of something here in the hospital that is vital to my research. I did send flowers. Did the family get them?"

Rodger felt like he was getting side-tracked. He cleared his throat. "Dr. Lazarus, you spoke with Michael about Dallas Christofer. But what can you tell me about Julius Boucher?"

There was a pause before Dr. Lazarus said, "Funny you should ask that, Detective. I was cleaning up old files and happen to have Julius's with me right now."

Rodger blinked in surprise. Could luck be on his side? "Please tell me everything about him."

"Of course. Here we go," replied Dr. Lazarus. Rodger heard the sound of papers moving.

"Julius Boucher. A gifted but troubled boy. He was what I referred to as a cast-away child. His mother worked at the Jean-Lafitte Theater under the stage name Rose. His father was an oil dredger. He was born of their affair and given up for adoption at the age of five."

Rodger nodded. Everything Dr. Lazarus was saying fit with Michael's notes on Julius. "Continue, please."

"At age six, Julius was fostered out to a family in Donaldsonville. Julius's foster parents were very abusive. They kept him locked up in a storage shed and made him clean their house. They fed him scraps and physically abused him whenever the mood struck them. Monstrous people."

Rodger shook his head, feeling ill. Despite being on a roll with the investigation, he couldn't help but feel sympathy for an abused six-year-old boy. "So what happened? Obviously, someone rescued Julius and placed him in your care?"

"That would be the state of Louisiana," replied Dr. Lazarus, his tone unmistakably sympathetic. "At age ten, Julius broke free and murdered his foster parents. He was taken into custody by a state trooper. Given the nature and sheer brutality of the murders, he was committed very quickly and remanded to my care."

Murdered his foster parents! Rodger felt he was on the right track. This boy had already killed someone. "So, what kind of patient was Julius? Did his violent streak continue?"

"Very much so," replied Dr. Lazarus. "He was personable to other children—charismatic, even. But to adults, he was very violent.

Nothing worked. No type of therapy or treatment had any effect. As I told your partner, he was being considered for a lobotomy."

Rodger shook his head. That thought disturbed him greatly. "So did Julius get along with Dallas and Samantha?"

"They were close friends, as far as patients go," Dr. Lazarus replied. "Although Samantha and Dallas had an almost familial bond, Julius was adopted into their group. They used to play word games, especially Dallas and Julius. If you recall the term 'Nite Priory,' spelled N-I-T-E? That was the result of Samantha telling them about the Knight Priory of Saint Madonna. If I recall, Julius came up with 'Nite Priory' at Dallas's request."

Rodger hummed. "So, then, I take it that Dallas and Julius were particularly close?"

"Yes. All three were close, although I would say that Samantha was more removed than the two boys. They weren't with me terribly long, but they formed a very quick bond and then created a social pecking order. It was the topic of a paper of mine. Samantha was the leader, Julius was the charismatic one, and Dallas was the quiet, thoughtful one."

Rodger whistled to himself. Despite this being a bit of a side conversation, he was amazed to hear how these three troubled children had come together and formed a group so quickly. It must have been because all three had been so badly abused. *How awful!*

Rodger moved to get the conversation back on track. "Was Julius impressionable at all?"

"By adults, not so much. Definitely impressionable by other children," Dr. Lazarus said, "especially by Dallas. They were inseparable at times. Dallas would even visit Julius alone whenever they got the chance. It was refreshing to see the two boys becoming such good friends."

A light bulb went off in Rodger's head. "What was the positioning of the rooms? Who was next to who?"

He heard the sound of paper shuffling for a few seconds. Then Dr. Lazarus said, "Samantha, then Dallas, and then Julius."

Rodger grinned to himself in triumph. His hunch had been right. "Did Dallas and Sam tell Julius about what they had gone through?" Maybe Julius had taken on their anger as well.

"Dallas did, yes," Dr. Lazarus said. "Samantha did not. Samantha did not want to talk about her experiences with anyone. That's why I have always been worried about her."

Rodger ignored the comment about Sam. All he heard was that Dallas had told Julius about his experience with Vincent. *So then, Julius would hate Aucoin and Ouellette for not "fixing" Dallas's problems faster. Julius could have associated himself with Dallas and taken on Dallas's feelings of hate.*

Seeing a light burn through the darkness, he asked, "So then, Dr. Lazarus, did Julius actually die the night of the fire?"

"Of course," replied Dr. Lazarus. "Well, he was one of the boys who were burnt to ash. Dallas did go in and try to save Julius and . . ." He cleared his throat. "I get it. You think that Julius survived and ran away, don't you?"

Rodger gave himself a check mark. "I do. If Julius took on Dallas's experiences himself, he may have wanted to do something about it. It looks like this boy could very well be our killer."

Again, there was silence. Then Dr. Lazarus said, "It's entirely plausible. A lot of life was lost that night. Your theory is a stretch, though, since it would require Julius to have hidden amongst the general populace all these years. This is a person who has uncontrollable rage."

There was another long pause before he said, "However, my only way of confirming this is to question Dallas about the night of the fire. He gets very upset when I bring it up. However, if it's vitally important, I will try to talk to him about it again."

"Would you do that, Dr. Lazarus?" asked Rodger. "That may very well put an end to this case."

"All right," replied Dr. Lazarus. "I'll talk to Dallas in a little while. I'll call you back here when I do, OK?"

"That's fine. And thank you, Dr. Lazarus." Rodger hung up.

So this is it. Julius is the real killer, I'm sure of it. I just need confirmation from Dallas. Now to get to Sam's townhome and find out what Vincent willed to Sam.

Rodger headed out, grabbing the mail Ms. Parkerson had brought in. As he got into his car, throwing the mail onto the passenger seat, a large envelope addressed to him from "Orleans Parish Courthouse" fell to the floor. After putting the envelope on the top of the pile and struggling for a minute to get his seatbelt to click shut, Rodger headed toward Sam's townhouse.

The rain started to come down in heavy bands.

When he arrived at the townhouse some thirty minutes later, everything seemed quiet. Sam's car was still in the driveway. The porch lights were on, classical music was playing from inside, and the lights were on in the study and Sam's bedroom on the third floor.

When he reached the front door, however, he saw that the latch was off and the door was cracked open.

"What the fuck," he said, drawing his gun and delivering a swift kick to the door before heading inside.

The front hall was in a shambles, with obvious signs of a struggle. Near the broken grandfather clock lay Edward's service revolver, the bullets scattered about. In the study, books and papers lay everywhere. At the base of the stairs was some blood and Sam's overturned wheelchair.

He didn't see Sam or Richie.

"Sam!"

Rodger went into her study and then her office. Both rooms were ransacked.

"Sam! Richie!"

Moving into the kitchen, Rodger saw that everything from flour to coffee grinds had been scattered everywhere. The ground was soaked in blood and coffee. It looked like a war had taken place.

Going out to the back porch, he saw the two police officers and the nurse that the state had sent to watch over Sam. They were arranged on the large swing, holding cups of cooled coffee, leaned back with their throats slit and their mouths split open in wide, disturbing grins.

He was horrified. The brutality looked like the Knight Priory slayings Richie had mentioned.

Quickly, he moved upstairs.

"Sam! Richie! Goddammit, answer me!"

When he reached Sam's bedroom on the third floor, Rodger stopped and stared. His mind took a moment to process the horror. A scream built inside him like steam in a pressure cooker.

Lying on the bed, arms and legs bound, was a male body so brutally treated that it was utterly unrecognizable. The head had been skinned and scalped, and the eyes had been pulled out. However, the clothes were unmistakably that of a certain novelist from Pittsburg.

"Richie! Oh, my God, no!"

Rodger rushed to the corpse's side, not knowing where to begin. Richie had been secured by leather straps and obviously tortured to death. It wasn't clinical or methodical like the other murders. This one had been quick and brutal.

Shit, Julius got Richie!

Fuck!

But don't touch the body.

Leave it for the crime lab.

God, Richie, I am so sorry, man!

Dammit, I let this kid die, too.

Inside, Rodger felt his guts churning, tearing him apart. Another one dead because he wasn't fast or smart enough. The shock of seeing the mutilated body was almost too much for him. Leaning against a wall, he buried his face in his hand. For a minute or so, he rubbed his head. Then he looked up. Immediately, he saw something written in blood on the ceiling. It was obscured by the canopy of Sam's bed, so he moved to the side. There were two words.

"Nite Priory."

Wait, why is it spelled wrong? He furrowed his brow and again thought of the anagram. Iron pyrite. Fool's gold. A trick. A lie.

"Is Julius fucking with me?"

Rodger headed downstairs to the kitchen. Near the phone was a lacquered black box. Inside was a small open envelope with the name "Sam" in calligraphy on it. Inside the envelope were three pink capsules. He had seen similar ones before, on the night Sam had fought against Blind Moses.

"The *tkeeus*," he said, pocketing one of the pills and closing the box.

For a minute, he stood there, his face in his hands. "Julius killed Richie but took Sam. Why? Why take Sam?"

The answer came in a swift revelation.

"Of course," said Rodger. "Julius wants to hurt everyone associated with the original Bourbon Street Ripper case. I'm the last one. The only person Julius can kill to get at me, now that Michael is dead, is Sam!"

That thought made him feel sick to his stomach. Julius was now targeting him. "Once again, I have failed to see the writing on the wall until the very end."

Very end. That resonated in his mind. As he stood up, the part of the letter to Blind Moses that dealt with the final victim's identity made sense: "You will know who that is when the time arises."

Rodger felt weak in the knees as he said, "My God, the last victim has always been Sam. The bastard was going to kill Sam from the very beginning. All of these murders weren't leading up to Cheryl. They were leading up to Sam."

He knew he had to act. Picking up the phone, he quickly dialed the eighth precinct.

The voice answering sounded totally bored. "New Orleans Police Department, Eighth Precinct, Homicide Division, Detective Landry speaking."

"Landry, this is Rodger. Contact Ouellette and let him know that the real killer is Julius Boucher. He's killed Richie Fastellos and kidnapped Samantha Castille. I'm at her townhouse right now. Also, send a uniformed patrol to my apartment complex. The people there might be in danger."

Before Landry could say so much as "um," Rodger hung up.

OK, there has to be some kind of clue as to where they went. Where would Julius take Sam?

As he started looking around, he remembered his conversation with Dr. Lazarus. "Dr. Lazarus treated Julius," he said to himself. "He may know of a place that is important to Julius. He was going to call me back at my place, so he's probably waiting for me to call him."

Picking up Sam's phone, he quickly dialed Dr. Lazarus's number. His heart was pounding as he waited for the other side to pick up.

When it did, Dr. Lazarus's voice was trembling. "Detective Bergeron?"

Rodger was instantly concerned. "Dr. Lazarus, what's wrong with your voice?"

"I am positively terrified," replied Dr. Lazarus. Rodger heard a female and male in the background shouting instructions to other people. "After we get off the phone, I am calling the FBI. We need to start a massive manhunt."

Rodger's mouth started to dry. "What happened, Doctor?"

Dr. Lazarus sounded like he was sipping something. Rodger heard the distinctive clink of ice in a glass. Dr. Lazarus said, "Well, I went to speak with Dallas about Julius. I wasn't hoping for much, considering his injuries, but I thought maybe I could get something to give you."

"Yes? What did Dallas say?" asked Rodger. The tension was palpable. *What the fuck happened? Spit it out!*

"It's funny," Dr. Lazarus chortled nervously. "He's been so quiet. So calm. The moment I mentioned Julius, however, he completely lost it. He started crying and hitting his head and rubbing out the scribblings of the words 'Nite Priory' on his wall, like by writing them, he had been revealing a secret he could get in trouble for."

Rodger's heart was pounding in his chest. He was so choked with anxiety he could barely ask, "But what did he say about Julius? Is he alive?"

"Yes, Julius is alive," replied Dr. Lazarus. "I just confirmed it with his dental records. And I've been fooled. We've all been fooled. I should have figured it out. I can't believe I was this negligent. There's no way Dallas would be that obsessed with word games. All these years, the person I thought was Dallas has been trying to tell me that he's not Dallas."

Rodger felt the blood drain from his face. "What did you say?"

"I said, the person in Room Six is Julius Boucher. The night of the fire, he helped Dallas Christofer escape. They switched places!"

Rodger was stunned.

"Did you hear me, Detective?" asked Dr. Lazarus. "The implications are incredible. Julius is . . . he's positively terrified of being referred to as himself. Dallas must have threatened, harmed, maybe even burned Julius to keep him quiet. He must have been planning this all along. That would mean he's a psychopath and sociopath of the highest level, an insanely genius mind that orchestrated an escape at the age of ten. We are dealing with someone who is far beyond the normal definition of dangerous."

Rodger felt like he couldn't stand. Leaning against the cabinet, he asked, "So . . . why hasn't anyone seen him? Where could he have gone?"

Dr. Lazarus sighed heavily. "I don't know. Some place important to Dallas's memory. That's all I have. I . . . I can't talk. I need to report this . . . this is bad. Detective, we will talk in a few days." He hung up.

Slowly hanging up the phone, Rodger just stared blankly at the world. As he walked out into the hallway, he saw Edward's revolver and bullets still on the floor. Not knowing why, he gathered them up and pocketed them.

It was Dallas all along. My God. He manipulated Julius into taking his place. But, why . . . ? Why does Dallas want revenge on Sam?

He stumbled out of the townhouse, feeling utterly lost. He never would have guessed that Dallas Christofer was the killer, that Sam's story would end up being reality. *I just want to know where he is with Sam.*

The rain had stopped. Inside the squad car, he saw the large envelope from the parish courthouse. He shook his head.

"This is almost useless to me now, but I might as well open it."

Opening the envelope, Rodger was surprised when two certificates of marriage fell out, along with a letter from the clerk of court. He read the letter first.

> Detective Bergeron,
>
> Here are your marriage licenses for "Castille" in the sixties. However, since you did not specify which license you wanted, we are sending both.
>
> Sincerely,
>
> Derek Malone, Clerk of Orleans Parish Court

"The hell," Rodger said, and then looked at the marriage licenses. He gasped.

The first license was between Edward Pierce Castille and Maple Marigold Christofer.

The second license was between Vincent Gilles Castille and Mary Magnolia Christofer.

Immediately, things started falling into place.

"Oh, my God," he said, the shock forcing him to sit down inside the squad car. "Edward and Maple. Vincent and Mary. That means . . . Holy shit!"

Rodger closed his eyes, feeling completely overwhelmed.

Vincent was Sam's father. And Dallas was the child of Edward and Maple. That meant Dallas was a Castille. But he would never have been considered an heir because Sam was Vincent's child. That meant Maple would have felt angry and jealous at Magnolia.

Suddenly, everything from twenty years ago made sense: the secretive relationships between the M&M sisters and the Castilles, the reason Vincent ran to Mary's side when she collapsed, and the reason Magnolia was murdered. It made sense.

"Maple was jealous," he said, his brain assembling the entire sordid tale from two sheets of paper. "Because even though she married the next in line for the Castille fortune, Vincent's marriage to Mary ensured that Sam would be the heir. Not Maple and certainly not Dallas. So Maple killed her sister."

Suddenly, he stood up. "And Vincent did all those murders to hide the real one, to get revenge on Maple for killing Sam's mother. And Vincent cared about Mary because she gave him Sam—the only person he ever truly loved."

Pacing in the driveway of Sam's townhouse, he continued to talk out loud. "But then there's Dallas. His mother was murdered in front of him. He let his rage grow for years—his rage toward everyone he believed let his mother die. Ouellette loses Jason. Aucoin loses Cheryl. Kent is used and then killed. Topper Jack is killed. Mad Monty is killed. Fat Willie is killed—oh, I bet that was no accident after all. Blind Moses is set up to get killed. Everyone who helps him is killed. Until . . . until it's just him and . . . Sam . . ."

He realized that Dallas, the mastermind, had set up the final confrontation on his terms. "And me . . . He wants to confront me . . . he wants to punish me by having me arrive too late to save Sam, just like I was too late to save Edward."

Everything had snapped into place for Rodger. Only one question remained.

Where is Dallas now?

Looking back at the townhouse, his mind raced. He had to move quickly or Sam was dead. Closing his eyes, he went over every clue from inside the house. Richie's body. The black box. The writing on the ceiling. All of those things were out of place.

Moving to his car, he started to speak to himself again. "The box from Vincent was there, so Dallas attacked them after Mason left. Mason would have gone back to the Castille mansion. Dallas murders Richie and then kidnaps Sam. Dallas would want to take Sam someplace where they could be alone. Someplace significant to Dallas."

Once in his car, he closed his eyes again, concentrating on the last thing that was out of place, the reuse of the phrase "Nite Priory," an anagram for "iron pyrite."

Nite Priory. Iron pyrite. A misdirection. Is it possible that Dallas is leaving me a clue as to where he's gone by leaving that phrase above Richie's body?

Rodger's eyes flew open and he said, "What if 'Nite Priory' wasn't the only anagram? Why not use another? He wants me to find them, to arrive too late. Giving me a puzzle might accomplish that. This may work."

Taking out his notebook and pen, Rodger thought of all the words significant to the case.

"Let's try 'Knight Priory.'"

It took a few minutes for him to dismiss that one.

"How about 'Samantha Castille'?"

Again, a few minutes later, he realized it wasn't working.

"Maybe 'Bourbon Street Ripper.'"

By the time he was finished ruling that out as an anagram, he felt he was wasting precious time.

Then Rodger looked back at the names on the marriage licenses.

He tried "Mary Christofer," then "Maple Christofer," then "Magnolia and Marigold."

Nothing.

"I'm overthinking this again," he said, taking a deep breath.

Starting at the top of the page, he wrote down the name of his prime suspect.

"Dallas Christofer."

His pen scribbled and scratched, creating line after line, crossing out letters and rearranging them. Several side tangents were started upon and then discarded.

In the end, despite weeks of investigating a tortuous plot, it took Rodger only a few minutes of solving an anagram before he was looking at the name of the serial killer who had been terrorizing New Orleans.

"No goddamn way."

The answer had been in front of them, all of them, the entire time.

"Son of a bitch!"

Suddenly, a certain person's weird—at times, almost psychotic—behavior made sense. The inconsistency in that person's stories with what everyone else experienced made sense. The involvement of the Nite Priory, the Knight Priory, and the group of hooded assassins, made sense. Even Dixie's innate distrust of that one person—it all made sense.

The madness surrounding the recent string of serial murders, from start to finish, now made sense to Rodger. He was also pretty sure he knew who was dead up in Sam's bedroom. The entire sick scenario fell perfectly into place.

When you saw who Dallas Christofer really was . . . everything made sense.

His seatbelt clicked into place as he turned the key, the squad car roaring to life. Skidding out of the driveway, he sped toward Lake

Pontchartrain and the Castille mansion, where he had arrested Vincent—the place he was certain Sam was being held captive.

He wouldn't be too late this time.

"Don't worry, Sam," Rodger said between gritted teeth. "I'm going to save you."

Chapter 29
A Sheet of Notebook Paper

Dallas Christofer

~~Christal Salofer~~

~~Flash Dracoliters~~

~~Collared Starfish~~

~~Heraldo Falstris~~

Richard Fastellos

(maybe a joke?)
retard?

Salad?
drac?
card?

rist?
rish?

Rich? Falls?

Chapter 30
The Bourbon Street Ripper

Date: **Monday, August 17, 1992**
Time: **11:00 p.m.**
Location: **Castille family mansion**
               Lake Pontchartrain

The euphonious and harmonious tranquility that was the third movement of Johannes Brahms's Symphony No. 3 cascaded over the Castille dining room. The only light was from the faintly glowing gold and glass chandelier above, which barely illuminated the suits of armor and marble statues lining the walls alongside portraits, only their golden frames twinkling in the darkness.

The scent of wine graced the room like the scant light and gentle music. The black walnut dining table, large enough to fit more than a dozen, seated only two people, one at each end. Before each of the pair was a fine china plate with an exquisite cut of red meat, dripping with a deep crimson sauce, and garnished with a sprinkling of sumptuous herbs. Sitting at the foot of the table was an elderly woman in formal attire, her gray hair up in a bun. At the head of the table was a young man wearing a black tuxedo and tails, a butler's uniform.

The young man's dark hair was combed back, held in place with what must have been a sizable amount of grease or gel, as not a single strand stood up. His back straight, his mannerisms poised, the young man slowly cut the meat and, tasting it, made an approving sound, following it up immediately with a sip of the red wine from a nearby crystal goblet.

He uttered a sigh of contentment. "God, that's lovely."

Gladys Castille must have been staring intensely at the young man, as he stopped and offered her a nod of his head, waving his knife toward the meat on his plate.

"My compliments to the cook, Aunt Gladys," Dallas Christofer said with a smile. He had never expected something as delightful as this, not on such short notice.

However, Gladys still stared at him from across the table, her eyes fixed on him without emotion. In the dimly lit room, the shadows played off her face. She had a tight-lipped and tense look.

He mused to himself, sipping some more wine, before asking, "Do you know about Kobe beef, Aunt Gladys? There is a type of cow in Japan that is given a special diet of sake-soaked grain, as well as having its muscles massaged to keep the meat tender. It's said to be the most tender and tasty meat in the world."

Across the table, Gladys said nothing, her eyes fixed upon him like a hawk.

Dallas shrugged and cut another slice of the meat. He so dearly loved marinated tenderloin, especially when cooked rare. "Yes, Kobe beef. Your husband, Kent, was interested in trying it. Why don't we order some for tomorrow night, Auntie? We can have it flown in from Japan."

The stretch of silence as Gladys stared at him like a statue was uncomfortable.

Following the meat with a lingering sip of wine, he hummed to himself, only then understanding the immensity of what he was asking. "You're right, Auntie, that was a stupid idea. We'll need to give it at least a few days. My apologies for being so impulsive."

Looking up, he could see the old woman's eyes glinting in the light as if they were glass baubles. He could feel Gladys staring into him and could see that her expression was extremely stern.

"Right." Dallas sighed, then muttered to himself, "Such a charming dinner companion you are, you old bat."

Finishing his meat, sopping up the last of the sauce, and washing it down with the last of his wine, he put down his silverware and leaned back. "Truly marvelous."

Dabbing his mouth clean, he got up and bowed to his aunt. "Thank you for dinner, Aunt Gladys. I'll be sure to tell the cook it was her best creation yet."

Walking along the length of the table, Dallas stopped at Gladys, who was still staring icily ahead. He placed his hand on her shoulder and said, "Get some rest, will you, Auntie? Tomorrow is going to be very busy."

Giving her a gentle push, he watched as she fell forward, landing face first on her plate. Reaching behind her, he pulled out the stiletto knife which had been embedded in her spine for the past two hours.

"Thanks for holding onto this," Dallas said, smirking at the dead woman and heading out of the dining room.

Walking through the dimly lit hallways of the Castille mansion while twirling the stiletto knife between his fingers, he started to slide his feet in time to the Brahms symphony as it played over the house's sound system. He passed by the entrance to the kitchen, spun inside, and called out to Miss Cooper, the cook. "Fantastic meal, Miss Cooper. Such wonderful work this evening!"

Miss Cooper, who was standing up on a stool in front of the stove, leaned over a large pot where her intestines spilled out of her stomach. They were boiling quite nicely. Her assistant, kneeling before the oven, had his head inside. Smoke billowed out as the smell of burning flesh and hair wafted through the room. Neither had much to say.

"Carry on," Dallas said before waltzing down the hallway. A young maid leaned near the doorway leading to the study. In a moment of boldness, he swept the maid into his arms and danced around. The maid's head leaned back, the little flap of skin that was holding her head on snapping. Her head hit the floor and rolled out into the hallway.

"Oops," he said and placed the maid in the plush chair behind the desk. He tapped his fingers together and cleared his throat, bowing politely to the corpse. "Sorry."

Sliding to a bookcase in the back, he perused the volumes until his fingers rested on a certain book. "Ah, here we are. Hematology!"

Pulling on the large book, he heard a clicking sound. The book slid back into place, and a few moments later, the bookcase opened up. He headed down a stone staircase into the darkness below, sighing with contentment. "All right, time to get to work."

When Dallas reached the bottom, passing through a stone archway, he entered a square chamber made entirely of stones. Dust was thick on devices such as a rack, a Saint Andrew's cross, a spiked chair, and an iron maiden. At the far end of the torture chamber was a metal door that latched from the outside. To the side of the door was a large valve. Over the door was a dusty sign that said "Crematorium."

He was still waltzing to the music, which was no longer audible, when he stopped in the center of the torture chamber. In the middle of the room were the stained remains of a circle of blood. Dallas had heard that the circle had been used in a pair of rituals performed in 1967.

Amazing that after the Knight Priory stopped meeting at the Castille estate, Grandfather turned the gathering place into his torture chamber. I suppose if you're going to try to summon forth the powers of voodoo through human suffering, this is the place to do it. Go, Gramps.

His gaze flashed over to the crematorium. *I do wonder what the purpose of that room was. Grandpa never cremated any of his victims. Oh, well. I killed Aunt Gladys before I could ask. I guess it's not important.*

He stopped in front of an operating table. Next to the table was a metal pan filled with ethanol. Dallas tossed the bloody stiletto knife into the pan and then turned his attention to the centerpiece of the table and the centerpiece of the entire torture chamber—the nude, blond woman tightly secured there.

Sam Castille.

"Hey, Sam, sorry to keep you waiting," Dallas said, looking down at her. She just stared back up at him, her eyes wide and wild.

"Yes, I know, it was rude to make you wait." He shrugged innocently. "But you know how demanding Aunt Gladys is, right?"

From Sam's throat, a strained whine issued forth. Her chest started to rise and fall more quickly. Her eyes slowly moved away from him.

"I know, I know. How can Richie do this to you, right?" he said, patting her shoulder. "But believe me when I say this . . ." He grabbed her face so that she was looking at him. "This may be the face you know as Richie, but I can assure you, only Dallas is here. Earlier tonight, I made sure he experienced his own death. That should be the end of Mr. Fastellos."

Sam's eyes widened more. The whine took on a strained gurgle.

He looked her over, admiring her terrified expression. "Was it confusing to watch Richie struggling at the doorway to your room? Was it scary to watch him beat himself up and talk as three different people? Were you terrified when he advanced on you?"

Dallas leaned in and whispered, "God, I hope so."

He released her face and patted her cheek, then walked over to some hospital equipment. He counted to make sure everything was there, and then he nodded. *Well, at least Kent and Nick's money was good for something.*

Selecting a device, a large box with a screen on it, he pushed it toward the operating table.

She stared wordlessly at him.

"Still locked in, eh? I have to admit that at first, I was really disappointed." With the device next to the table, he started to attach the pads to Sam's chest, arms, and back. As he did so, he said, "I mean, part of the point is to savor all five of the senses. With you locked in there, it's going to be a lot of whimpering and gurgling instead of screaming in agony."

Dallas hit a few switches on the device, turning it on. The heart-rate monitor started to beep. Seeing that the machine was in working order, he stepped away and went to another device, one with two clear bags held up on poles.

He chuckled as he pushed the intravenous machine over. "But now that I think about it, this works out better for three beautiful reasons."

The IV machine in front of Sam, he took two small plastic tubes and attached a catheter needle to each, and then started tapping on one of her arms to make the vein bulge. Her eyes were focused on those needles. The beeping of the heart-rate monitor started to speed up.

"First, this part would be harder with you kicking and screaming. I would have to use anesthesia, and I really don't have time tonight to wait for anesthesia to wear off again," he said, gently sliding the first catheter into her vein.

Sam whined in her throat as the needle was pushed inside. Her eyes followed him as he walked around her.

"And second, there's all the whining and pleading and 'Please don't do this to me.'"

Dallas went to her other side and started tapping her other arm, getting the vein to stick out. "And the bribery. My God, the bribery! Did you know that Cheryl Aucoin said she'd be my love slave if I didn't harm her? Me?" He pointed at himself incredulously. "Have sex with a sixteen-year-old? Please, I am *not* a sicko. I have morals," the serial killer said.

Taking the second catheter and pushing it into Sam's other arm, he said, "The third reason is that I'll wager that this is infinitely more terrifying. There you are, all locked inside your little head."

The needle in and the IV machine hooked up, he leaned down and kissed her forehead. Her heart rate continued to increase. "You can see and hear and feel everything I do, and you can't say a word."

Lowering himself down to her ear, Dallas again whispered, "And I bet you are so scared right now. Oh, God . . . that is such a turn on." He gently licked her cheek. She tasted like fear.

Getting up, he went over to a small black bag and pulled out a set of syringes. "And to be honest, I'm not entirely sure I completely destroyed Richie earlier. I always figured he'd be weak, him being the subordinate personality. But near the end there, he turned out to be not so weak. I think it was his love for you. Anyway, we can't have him coming back if you start pathetically calling out his name, can we?"

Picking up a syringe, he took out a small vial labeled "Epinephrine" and drew some into the syringe. Sam's heart rate sped up again, causing him to say, "Oh, this won't hurt you, Sam. It's just adrenaline, to keep you from passing out. We can't have that."

The adrenaline measured out in the syringe, he headed to the IV machine and injected it into the plastic bags. "Speaking of Richie, wanna hear how he came about? Story time! The night you were released from Dr. Lazarus's facility . . . remember that power box you found in the utility closet? Yeah, I wired it to short out and explode. The fire nearly killed everyone, including our buddy Julius and dear Dr. Lazarus. After saving the doctor, I made sure Julius took my place while I ran off, and I made sure he was burnt beyond recognition."

Dallas checked the tubes going into and out of Sam's arms. "Anyway, after my escape, I wandered around for weeks, stealing from truck stops and doing things I'd rather forget, finally arriving in Houma. A nice old lady named Annie-Mae Bernard picked me up. Told her my name was Julius Boucher. She bought it and decided to just raise me on her own. That's what I love about bayou folk, they are so nice . . . so gullible . . . ya know, good people."

Her heart rate was more pronounced now, and she was whimpering more audibly. He noticed this and decided to get things moving along. "Side note! Julius Boucher, by the way, was totally my bitch. You may have run our little group, and Julius may have acted like he was the front man, but every time we'd get alone, I'd hurt him in ways that would trigger the most horrific flashbacks."

Laughing, he shook his head and made a mock trembling motion. "Julius was so scared of me that the night of the fire, he ran deep into the burning building to get away from me, even though I was going to save him. I needed him to pretend to be me. It was great fun, though, to hold Julius down while his head baked. Had to make sure his face was burnt beyond recognition."

He stood there recalling the memory fondly. Looking over at Sam, he blushed and said, "Sorry, I always get lost in the recollection of pinning him with his face near the flames, hearing him cry and blubber, and telling him that if he ever stopped pretending to be me, I'd finish the job. All the while, his hair and face were burning right off. Good times."

Sniffing, he cracked his neck to relieve some tension. *I'll need to get a massage soon, my neck is killing me.*

"I have to thank Grandfather, though. If he hadn't made me watch him murder Mom, I never would have learned about how pain can be a motivator. Not to mention, I never would have met you. Then I never would have learned about the real Knight Priory, the *tkeeus*, or any of that other stuff you told me about in the hospital."

Sam, who had been moaning in fear, sobbed in her throat. A few tears spilled down her cheeks.

Heading over to a large black duffle bag, Dallas took out a box and carried it to the operating table. He opened it and took out scalpels, forceps, scissors, switch blades, tourniquets, and hemostat clamps.

Sam started to whimper again.

"So, back to the story! I actually got to live a regular life until a high school friend invited me to a party for Ouellette's son. And on a boat ride, no less. Then I realized that I could get my revenge on Ouellette. I mean, how could I not take that opportunity? Luckily for me, Sam, the old bat who adopted me took Amobarbital like it was candy. Just ground up a few, popped them into Jason Ouellette's beer and, splash, one dead Marine."

The tray filled with operating equipment, he headed back to the duffle bag and started taking out tools—sanders, drills, a chainsaw—and placed them on the nearby rack. Sam's whimpers got louder and the beeps of the heart rate monitor got more rapid.

"After that, I slit Mama Bernard's throat and hitchhiked to Pittsburg. Why Pittsburg, you ask? No reason. Anyway, I needed to create a pseudonym, since Julius Bernard was now not safe, Julius Boucher was supposedly dead, and hell if I'd call myself Dallas Christofer."

Dallas went "hmm" and tapped his lips with a dentist drill. "Well, one day, I started noticing this other personality coming up inside of me. I think it was an icky desire to live a normal life. Ya know, like back in Houma. So I started to cultivate that personality. I started pushing it memories and thoughts of a life in California, of fleeing to Pittsburgh with a battered mother and growing up there. It took a lot of work, but in the end, I had a mask I could wear any time I chose."

He nibbled on the head of the dentist drill. "The hardest part was a name. Oh, I could have chosen any old name, but anagrams are more fun. Do you remember how we used to make anagrams at the hospital?

That's how we came up with 'Nite Priory' as an anagram for 'iron pyrite.' You were telling us about the Knight Priory, and Julius kept insisting they were fake, like fool's gold. So I pressed him into making an anagram that would make people think of the Knight Priory but actually mean a misdirection. I was already plotting. Years later, I was able to use what Julius came up with to fool the police.

"Think about it, Sam. They get all worked up over 'Nite Priory.' Then, when they finally figure out that it's a 'misspelling'"—Dallas made air quotes with his fingers—"of Knight Priory . . . they start chasing that tired old group like they're the culprit. But all of that, every bit of it, is just some silly game three mentally troubled children used to play. Poetic on so many levels. The ultimate 'fuck you' to every detective out there!"

He cleared his throat. "Sorry, I'm getting sidetracked." Winking at Sam, he said, "Anyway, I remembered the anagram game. And that is how I got my eventual alias, Richard Fastellos. All thanks to you, Sam!"

He turned back and saw tears rolling down her cheeks. He quickly rushed to her side. "No, no, no! Don't cry, Sam. Don't worry." He wiped the tears away and licked his fingers for the taste. "The love Richie has for you is real. But me, I love something else. I love the pain Grandfather taught me about. I mean . . ." He motioned around the torture chamber. "This is my world, Sam. I can no more help torturing and murdering than a spider can help spinning a web."

Leaning against the table near Sam's head, he gently tapped the blunt end of the dentist drill against her nose. "So that's how Richie came about. He popped up one day because a part of me wanted a normal life, and I cultivated him into the perfect disguise."

Using the dentist drill, Dallas turned her head to look at him. She whined through her throat in protest. "See, Sam," he said in a low voice, "Dallas Christofer is the real deal, while Richard Fastellos is the mask. He, like everyone else in my life, is my bitch."

He tapped her nose once more. "Just like you're about to be."

Tossing the dentist drill into the tray with the scalpels and surgical tools, he said, "Every now and then, parts of me would come out in Richie. He'd get paranoid if people jumped out at him, he'd get emotionally detached way too easily, and the anxiety attacks—my God, the anxiety attacks! Did you know that his pills actually made it harder at first for me to take back control to do the killings?"

With a wink, he headed back to the rack, where the heavier equipment lay, and started to carry the industrial devices to the operating table, placing them down one at a time. "Anyway, the whole point of Richie was to hide myself, so imagine my shock when he became a wildly successful author years later."

Dallas had a good chuckle over that, the irony too much for him. "But it gave me a ton of time to research the Bourbon Street Ripper murders and learn who all needed to be punished."

Holding a chainsaw in front of Sam, who moved her eyes away from it, her breathing getting heavier, he said, "And believe me, Sam, a lot of people needed to be punished."

Putting down the chainsaw, he went over to a nearby basin and started to wash his hands.

No reason to risk infection.

"See, the whole problem is that everyone was down on Maple because she had a temper. But my father, he saw the passion in Mom and just knew she was a good woman. Meanwhile, your mom, Mary, was Little Miss Perfect. So perfect that while Maple married Edward, my dad, Mary had to one-up her sister and marry Vincent, your dad."

From the operating table, Sam let out a confused and horrified shriek that stuck in her throat.

Dallas winced. "Oh, shit, that's right! You didn't know. Sorry, I didn't mean to break it to you so conversationally. Yeah, your father was actually Vincent and my father was actually Edward. Which made Edward your half-brother, not your father. Which technically makes you the sister of my father, which means . . . hello, Auntie!"

Turning off the water and patting his hands dry with a towel, he heard a strange sound coming from her. It was a rhythmic whining sound, like a puppy whimpering. Finally, it occurred to him that she was crying.

With a nod, he said, "Yeah, I know how you feel, Sam. I was grossed out, watching from the back seat while Richie did all those things with you."

He held out his hands.

"And believe me, I had no idea what freaks the two of you would be. Seriously, that's the most mentally deranged thing I have *ever* come across—an aunt and a nephew screwing like little rabbits."

He then shrugged and walked back over to her side. "But, hey, it got your trust, right?"

Ruffling her hair, he added, "And that's all that was important. Gaining your trust so that I could get you here. Which, by the way, is the point of everything I've done these past twenty years. To kill everyone around you and then kill you. Revenge. Oldest plot in the book."

Finally ready, he looked at the setup appraisingly. "Yes, this will do nicely."

Sam's heart rate sped up again as Dallas took off his jacket and started to undress. With his shirt off, the crescent-shaped scar was visible—the scar caused by Vincent as he buried Dallas alive with Maple.

"The hardest part was keeping Richie engaged in what was happening here, so we could stay in town and near all the right people, but without letting him realize he was a part of me. So I had to keep sending him these delusions of the Nite Priory, hooded figures, and a Lady in Red to keep him under control. When he found out that 'Nite Priory' was an anagram for 'iron pyrite,' I changed his delusions to have the Knight Priory spelled properly.

"Heck, I even sent a special delusion, a hooded figure Richie thought was Julius, at the very end. It was the kind of convoluted crap you'd write in your stories, Auntie, but it worked. Any time the hooded members of the Priory or the Lady in Red or any of that crazy crap appeared to Richie, it was in his head. It was me manipulating Richie. And by God, it worked like a charm. Fooled him completely."

He stretched a few times. *I need to start working out again. I'm getting too tight.*

"Good thing that when I murdered all of Marcello's men and when I killed off Nick's gang there were no witnesses around to see my particular brand of psycho. It would have looked very unusual to see Richie Fastellos going between arguing with himself to pissing himself to going batshit insane and murdering everyone around him."

With a snort, Dallas said, "It's a shame what I did to those dogs."

With a sigh, he recalled the mental effort needed to create that much delusion for his subordinate personality. "One thing I can't figure out. When I first started fighting Marcello's men, I thought I was going to die. Then time slowed down, I got stronger and faster, and . . . oh, you know the drill. You did it, too. All I know is that Grandpa injected me with that *tkeeus* before burying me with Mom. But the *tkeeus* only seems to work when my adrenaline starts pumping. So what is it?"

He looked over at Sam and arched both eyebrows. "Think maybe there might be some truth to that whole voodoo thing? I'm starting to wonder about that, too."

She stared back at him, gurgling out a whine.

He tapped the scar on his chest and slipped on a green scrubs top. "Just so you know, Sam, I hate Grandpa, too. We are totally simpatico there. He refused to acknowledge me, even though I am his grand-child, just because he didn't approve of my mother. Hell, he had my dad take your mother out to the Comus Ball, not mine, because he couldn't stand mine."

Dallas dropped the tuxedo pants and then, holding out his arms, exclaimed, "But Dad loved Mom. Maple was spicy and passionate. She had a temper, but she had such a love of life. She was the perfect match for Dad. Mary was just, I don't know . . . sweet. Nice. Bland. Kinda like Gramps."

Rubbing his head, he muttered, "Mom told me, the night before we were kidnapped by Grandpa, what she and Dad did to Mary. Of course, you realize it was an accident, right? You see, Grandpa was so controlling that even after Mom and Dad got married, they couldn't live together or even acknowledge each other. Edward had to raise you as his own child so you would appear to be part of the normal lineage."

Shaking his head, he looked at Sam with a frustrated frown. "Seriously, who doesn't let a husband and wife live together? Vincent Castille, that's who! The bastard wouldn't even live with his own wife—your mom. All to keep the Castille family image. Seriously? Break up a family for that? What a crock of shit!"

Sensing her staring wildly at him, he took a few deep breaths. "Sorry. I was out of line there, Auntie."

Once he was calmed down, he said, "So, Mom and Dad came up with a plan to distract Grandpa with your mother. They wanted her to be hospitalized. That way, Grandpa would be solely focused on her, and Mom and Dad could take me and move far away. But Mary's heart was really weak, and she died in the hospital. That's what drove Grandpa over the edge. That's why he made me watch as he killed Mama."

Pulling on the rest of the scrubs, Dallas shrugged. This was, after all, ancient history to him. He had only gotten upset because he couldn't understand Vincent's elitist logic. He didn't want to appear unhinged in front of his magnum opus.

"So, anyway, that's what drove me here. I spent years researching the Bourbon Street Ripper murders, learning about the accomplices and police who messed up, and everything. I started by getting that douche Kent and his greedy son to facilitate everything, then I got Blind Moses to think I was the Knight Priory of Saint Madonna. Lastly, I got my stuff set up, gave that escort Virginia a call—the daughter of the first original victim—and murdered the shit out of her. Pure poetry! And that's how I started setting up the bullshit murders to hide the first real one—Detective Aucoin's daughter."

Popping on some surgical gloves, he continued, "It was easy to pick my other victims. Miss Clemens seemed a good target, nice and drunk and a real 'Cock Teaser.' And Emilie Guidry made it so easy by being Nick's girlfriend . . . she was asking for it. The only sticky part was that Richie actually met every single victim after Virginia. He met Rebecca, Cheryl, and Emilie. I am so lucky no one ever picked up on that."

Gloves on, he headed over to the tray of surgical tools. "So you see, Auntie, the only one I was really worried about was Detective

LeBlanc. His death was a remarkable bit of good luck, although it seemed almost like, once again, some dark voodoo power was forcing the hand of fate that day."

Turning around, he perused the instruments.

Finally, he chose a scalpel.

"Really, hindsight being twenty-twenty and all, I should have just settled on killing you, Sam. I do tend to overcomplicate things. Kind of like your stories, you know? You see, all of this happened because Vincent, your father, loved you the most. My mother and father were murdered, and I, after being forced to watch my mother suffer for over five hours, was buried alive inside her guts. All because that evil bastard loved you the most."

He approached her. She was staring at him, the fear in her eyes like an aphrodisiac. He felt himself choking on the desire to cut into that beautiful flesh. The sight, the sound, the smell. It would be intoxicating.

"The only way I will ever lay my mother's soul to rest is to murder that one thing Grandpa loved the most, in the same way that he murdered my mother."

Winking, he lowered the scalpel to her left elbow joint, the tip piercing the skin just enough to make a droplet of blood appear. Sounds of terror gurgled in her throat. Her heart rate shot through the roof.

"Ya know," he said, pulling back and looking up at the ceiling, "the one thing I never figured out is how Fat Willie's death happened so conveniently. I mean, I suspected that Violet would attack you. But Fat Willie? An accident right after you visited him?"

Dallas waggled his eyebrows at Sam. "Again, it's like there's some truth to this 'Voodoo Hoodoo' thing after all, isn't it?"

He patted her left breast, lifting the mammary up and looking at where it connected to her chest. Nodding to himself, he placed the scalpel there. The heart rate monitor started beeping like crazy, her breath increased, and her whimpering got more labored.

"Honestly, though," he said, pulling back again and drumming his fingers on her stomach, "I'm really on the fence about that voodoo stuff. I mean, I've seen the *tkeeus* in action. Heck, one whiff of it back at your place and I was able to put Richie down for good. Usually, I had to make Richie think that something like Rosemary Boucher hitting him with her heel was the Lady in Red kicking him, or Officer Guidry's head-butt into his face was an accident instead of self-defense. You know, more delusions to explain away real-life injuries. But man, the *tkeeus* . . . wow . . . that stuff was potent. And what it did with you and Violet. That was beautiful!

"But the rest of the coincidences, the little things here and there that have happened . . . I really don't know. Were they flukes? Are we just crazy? Or is there something darker and more sinister at play? Sam, let me know when you're dying if there's any truth to this stuff, like hearing Baron Samedi dig your grave. I really want to know."

Shrugging, he looked down and saw her eyes wide and wild, her chest heaving rapidly, her cheeks wet with tears. The heart-rate monitor beeped uncontrollably.

"I guess you're pretty anxious. All these false starts aren't very fair. All right, let's get started. I promise not to make you wait anymore."

Dallas lowered his lips to Sam's ear and whispered, "I'm going to go as slowly as I can. I won't let you bleed to death, I won't let you choke on your own vomit, and I won't let you have a heart attack. I won't let you die until I'm satisfied."

He kissed her ear tenderly. "I won't lie, this is going to be a very hard night for you, Samantha Castille. Very hard indeed." He nipped her ear almost playfully. "Suffer for me."

Standing up, he moved down to her hips and placed his hand on her pubic bone. He then rested the scalpel to the side of her groin. Looking up into her eyes, which looked back with exquisite fear, he grinned and then pushed the scalpel into her flesh.

Her throat opened and a shriek gurgled out, her body immobile but her eyes as wide as could be. Blood welled up in copious amounts from the wound as he drew the blade down, stopping just to the side of her genitals. The blood pooled on the operating table.

"Whew," Dallas said with a nervous chuckle. "I came inches from the femoral artery. I could have killed you right then! Isn't that exciting?"

Sidling up along the side of Sam's body, he noticed that she had managed to turn her head away and shut her eyes. "Got a little motion back, eh? That's good. Maybe you can scream for me near the end. That would really be thrilling."

Pressing the scalpel into her left shoulder joint, he cut a sizable slit. Again, her cries only gurgled in her throat, but her head whipped to the side violently. "See? You have some fight in you, Sam. That's wonderful. Please, let me know how much you're suffering. I've waited my whole life for this."

He dropped the scalpel into the pan and took out a retractor, then pressed it into the shoulder wound and opened it up. Her chest heaved as her throat rattled with another scream that couldn't completely come out.

"Interesting bit of trivia," he said as he picked up the dentist drill. "Do you know what Vincent Castille's last words were before being executed?" Starting up the drill, he moved it toward the bundle of nerves in Sam's open wound. The sounds she would make as he ripped into them would be exhilarating.

From the entrance to the torture chamber, a voice said, "Yes. He said 'Pull the switch. I have no regrets. She was worth it.'"

Quickly, Dallas turned to see Rodger Bergeron standing at the doorway and pointing Edward's revolver at him.

"Checkmate," said Rodger, a look of focused resolution in his eyes.

Chapter 31
Just the Mask

Date: **Monday, August 17, 1992**
Time: **11:59 p.m.**
Location: **Castille family mansion**
                    Lake Pontchartrain

For several long seconds, Dallas stared at Rodger in disbelief. The old shit had actually figured it out in time.

Dallas blinked a few times before lifting up his hands. "OK, I'll admit it. I thought you'd never figure it out. Good game, Rodger. Good game, indeed."

"Yeah, tough luck for you, asshole," said Rodger as he slowly circled around the rack, heading toward Dallas. He only stopped when he saw the tuxedo on the floor. "You realize that even if I hadn't figured it out it was Mason you murdered in Sam's bed, the moment the body was taken before the medical examiner, they would have known?"

Dallas rubbed his nose. "Meh. I was in a hurry, I had to improvise with Richie, or else I would've been late for dinner with Aunt Gladys."

"You think this is funny?" asked Rodger, anger in his voice.

"No," replied Dallas with a slight shrug. "I think it's hilarious."

By now, Rodger was in front of him, the revolver level with his chest. "Turn around, Dallas. Put your hands behind your back."

"Really?" asked Dallas, his voice bored. He turned around, lowering his hands and putting them behind his back. "You're going to arrest me? Wouldn't it be easier to put a bullet in my head and call it justice?"

Dallas could hear the sound of jangling handcuffs, along with Rodger saying, "Don't tempt me. I am seriously considering it."

As Dallas felt the cold metal of a handcuff lock into place on his right wrist, he heard Rodger say, "What the hell is that thing in your hand?"

Dallas's grin widened, his adrenaline starting to pump. He could feel the *tkeeus* slowing down the world around him. "It's a dentist drill. It's great for drilling teeth, torturing wounds, and—" Quicker than the blink of an eye, he spun around, slapping Rodger's gun out of his hand, turning on the drill, and slamming it into the side of Rodger's neck, drawing blood. "—it's great for getting fat, old cops off your ass."

Spinning around again, this time in a full circle, he kicked Rodger in the gut, sending him sprawling back against the rack. Dallas looked at the handcuff around his wrist and said, "Not my kind of kink, you old fart." Reaching into the tray of surgical tools, he grabbed a pair of scalpels.

"Seriously, Rodger, you need to retire," he said, jamming one scalpel into Rodger's shoulder. "You're too old to be doing this shit." The second scalpel went for Rodger's chest, but the detective was able to block it, the blade sinking into his forearm.

Rodger cried out from being stabbed and, with a grunt, head-butted Dallas in the face. "You resisting arrest is all the excuse I need." He quickly removed the two scalpels from his body, making the smell of blood thicker.

Seeing stars explode from the head-butt, Dallas stumbled back, holding his bleeding nose. All desire to be charming and witty was swept away with a tidal wave of rage. "You're so fucking dead, old man!"

He grabbed a pair of switchblades and dashed at Rodger. The rush of adrenaline was complete, in full force as it had been at the Riverwalk. Time slowed down once more. He felt a tingle down his spine and a rush of cold air. Whenever he got this sensation, he became a whirling dervish of death. He took numerous swipes at Rodger, who jumped back and rolled behind the rack to avoid getting hit. Planting his foot on the rack's frame, Dallas jumped over it with a forward flip. Landing behind Rodger, Dallas stabbed at him several times, the blades lacerating his face and hands.

Fresh blood began to pour out as Rodger stumbled back, taking a wild shot at Dallas.

The killer ducked, his body moving with *tkeeus*-induced speed. The bullet flew overhead. "Ha!" He rushed forward. With two swift moves, he plunged his switchblades into Rodger, getting him in the shoulder and the side. When he pulled back, he saw that one of the knives had stayed in Rodger's torso.

Rodger spat up blood on him, his eyes wide with shock as he pulled out the blade. It clanked to the floor.

"Surprised?" asked Dallas with a cruel smirk, twirling the remaining knife. "You can thank Vincent for this. Looks like he's still haunting you, eh, Rodger?" Doing a back flip, he kicked Rodger in the face, knocking him against the spiked chair.

As Rodger fell on the chair, he let out a cry, the spikes piercing his flesh and the latches falling down to secure his arms in place.

As Dallas landed, he took his remaining switchblade and slammed it into the table near Sam's head. "Hold that for me, will you, Auntie?" He winked at Sam. She stared at him in both fear and rage as he grabbed the chainsaw. Revving it up, he turned to Rodger, who was struggling to get free of the spiked chair.

Rodger looked up as the chainsaw roared, his face horror-stricken, before struggling even more with the metal latches.

"You know, Rodger," said Dallas as he approached, waving the chainsaw side-to-side, "I am sorely tempted to make you sit there while I kill Sam. I think it would be a brutally ironic ending to all of this."

The chainsaw was close enough that he could easily start carving off Rodger's fingers like the old man was a Thanksgiving Day turkey.

Rodger's eyes were fixed on the rotating blade.

Dallas revved the machine a few more times. "But I want Sam to be the last one who dies. It's how it needs to be. And then, once she's dead, I'll burn this place to the ground and just disappear. Maybe I'll continue writing. Maybe I'll get married and have a family. Maybe

I'll go kill elsewhere. Who cares, so long as I never have to see New Orleans again. I hate this fucking city. This city is hell!" With a sneer, Dallas raised the chainsaw and brought the whirring blade down—

Sparks and smoke flew everywhere.

Standing between Rodger and Dallas, holding up the very IV stand she was attached to, was a very nude, very bloody, and very angry-looking Sam.

"This fucking city . . . " she yelled back, her blue eyes positively glowing with rage, ". . . is my home, you asshole!" Jumping up, she kicked Dallas in the chest.

He stumbled back. Shaking the blow off, he roared and lunged at her with the chainsaw.

Sam jumped in and blocked the blow. She then flipped back and, using the IV stand, broke Rodger's bonds while in mid-air.

Rodger hit the floor and scrambled for the revolver. "Sam! How are you doing this?"

Dallas ignored Rodger, leaping over the spiked chair and coming down on Sam with the chainsaw.

Sam swung the IV stand in a wide arc to parry Dallas's attack before sliding underneath him. "Whatever Vincent put inside me when I was a child, she calls herself Sam of Spades, but that's not her real name."

Dallas gritted his teeth. He faced the spiked chair and gave it a hard kick. That knocked it off its foundation and right at Sam.

As the spiked chair slammed into her, she cried out and stumbled back.

"So you think Vincent put something inside you instead of just injecting you with the *tkeeus*?" He roared his question. "Why do you once again get the better deal?" Seizing his chance, he rushed forward and thrust the chainsaw at Sam.

She must have seen the attack coming, for at the last moment, she slammed the IV stand into the side of the chainsaw. Sparks flew everywhere. "It's not the better deal, Dallas," she said before bashing his left arm. "I've had a few days to talk to Sam of Spades. As Dr. Klein's drugs wore off, she remembered more of what she really is. She's nothing good. She's something dark. Something that feeds off my hate. Something that wants to harm others!"

The pain was the first real thing Dallas had felt in days. With a cry, he lunged at her, starting a series of fast, high-powered slashes with the chainsaw. She was barely able to parry them, and the IV stand was getting more and more damaged.

He laughed madly as he attacked. "Sounds like you're not possessed, Sam. Sounds like you're just crazy. Crazy as me! Isn't that wonderful?"

Something about that last phrase seemed to strike a chord with her, for even as she parried his attacks, she roared, "Shut up! None of this is wonderful. It's all ugly!"

With a final grunt, she parried the last of his attacks, then rushed forward and flipped over him, swinging the IV stand at his head.

This time, he was ready and ducked the attack. As she landed, he heard the hammer of a gun click. He dodged toward the tray of medical instruments as the bullets Rodger fired from Edward's gun missed him.

"Mind your own business, old man," Dallas said, grabbing the same stiletto knife that had been buried in Gladys's back and throwing it with a deadeye's accuracy.

The knife embedded itself into Rodger's other shoulder. His arm went limp.

"Your time is long past, Detective," Dallas said. He turned back toward Sam, who was starting to rush at him. He snarled and kicked the tray of surgical tools up into the air. He glared at her. "Time to die, bitch!"

Jumping into the air, he spun around and kicked the tray of surgical tools at her, again exhibiting prefect precision. He crouched as he landed, revving up the chainsaw.

She cried out as she got hit by a dozen or so sharp instruments, her nude body getting cut in multiple places. Her skin was now almost completely crimson from the blood.

Dallas was amazed that any human being could survive that much blood loss. It was like she was damn near immortal. Closing the distance, he side-kicked her in the gut.

Dropping the IV stand, Sam flew back into the iron maiden. The IV ripped out of her arm, making even more blood flow. She let out a scream, which was wholly satisfying to Dallas, and tried to move forward, but she was apparently stuck on one of the spikes of the torture device.

Chainsaw still whirring, he moved to the iron maiden and grabbed the door. "This will make a good coffin," he said, his eyes narrowing. "Goodbye, Auntie."

Then he heard Rodger's voice. "Her name is Sam!"

Dallas sighed, turning to face him. "I guess I need to kill you first, eh, Rod—" He stopped in mid-sentence, staring.

Rodger held a small pink capsule—the *tkeeus*.

At that moment, Dallas remembered that he was the one who had said, out loud, that inhaling the *tkeeus* would increase a normal person's abilities.

"Fuck . . ." inhaled Dallas.

Rodger cracked open the capsule and inhaled the *tkeeus*.

". . . me . . ." exhaled Dallas.

Rodger's entire demeanor shifted. He drew his own gun to companion Edward's. "It's your time that's over." He fired both guns at Dallas.

Dallas couldn't move fast enough. The hail of bullets that flew at him was like lightning strikes. They penetrated his arms and legs with incredible precision. The pain was like fire. He was sure that when the *tkeeus* wore off, he'd be unable to walk.

Breaking through the pain, he starting rushing at Rodger until something jerked him back and turned him around. He was face-to-face with the glowing blue eyes of a very pissed-off-looking Sam.

"Go to hell, Dallas," she said. She vaulted over him, landed, and kicked him in the back of the head.

Everything went white as he stumbled, blindly swiping with the chainsaw. Barely able to see, he felt himself get kicked in the chest so hard he flew back. He kept his grip on the chainsaw like his life depended on it.

When he became aware of his surroundings, he saw he was in a dark room with pipes on the walls and ceiling and holes in the floor.

A single valve had a sign above it: "Emergency Controls."

He had been kicked into the crematorium.

He shook off the pain in time to see Sam rushing at him, Rodger just behind her, both guns aimed at him.

Dallas was so angry, all he could see was red. Nothing mattered, not even his own life, so long as he got to kill these two. As he charged, he roared, "I swear I'll kill you both!" Rushing forward, he swung a series of blows at Sam.

This time, she dodged every blow, finally hand-springing back and calling out, "Now, Rodger!"

Turning toward the entrance, Dallas saw Rodger had both guns aimed at him. As Rodger fired, Dallas swung the chainsaw, knocking the first two bullets out of the air with perfect accuracy. The rest of the projectiles hit him in the abdomen, making him stumble back. He looked up just in time to see Sam jump-kicking him square in the chest. Hitting the back wall where the gas pipes were, Dallas could only stand there, limp, body shaking. It was all he could do to not fall over.

"I've . . . lost . . ." The words came out in an incredulous tone, his eyes wide with disbelief. His entire body hurt, everything was getting fuzzy, and his teeth were starting to chatter. "Why? Why are you so much more powerful? It doesn't make any sense. Dammit, tell me why!"

"I have no idea," she replied as she walked forward, holding the switchblade that he had cast aside. "And I don't care. I just want this to be over. It's time for you to die." She put the knife to his throat.

The metal felt so good.

"Sam, no!" Rodger exclaimed. "Don't kill him. We've already won!"

Dallas looked into Sam's eyes as she held the knife against his throat. Her eyes held the same rage he'd had most of his life.

"Fuck that, Rodger," she said, her voice trembling with anger. "He . . . he tortured me! He was going to kill me. He doesn't deserve a trial. He deserves to die."

Dallas leered at Sam with his sadistic grin. He locked eyes with her. *Yes, exactly. I don't deserve a trial. You and I are just the same. You're as sick and twisted as I am. We are both Castilles.*

"When you were the prime suspect, you deserved due process," Rodger called out, his voice thick with concern. "Sam, there's no way he's getting acquitted. Not with the evidence we've gathered."

"He'll just get committed," she cried out, pushing the knife's blade against his neck.

The metal started to cut into the threads of his flesh. It was pure ecstasy. Dallas's leering grin broadened. His heart rate remained slow and steady. "And I'll escape. You know that, don't you, Auntie? You have to kill me. And when you do, you'll become me. The seed of evil that rots the hearts of all Castilles will blossom into something beautiful within you. Won't that be wonderful?"

Sam's eyes began to widen as she stared at him.

Rodger's voice was more urgent as he called out, "Sam, please! Don't let people like Michael die in vain. Don't become what he is!"

"You already are a killer like me, Sam," Dallas said. "It's just a matter of time. In the end, you'll always be happiest when you're making others suffer. That's what it means to have Vincent's blood in your veins."

The sharpness of the metal grew more painful as she pressed the knife further into his neck, the threads of skin popping more quickly. Hot blood was flowing. She bared her teeth in a grimace. "You are a cruel, remorseless bastard. You are more like Father than I could ever be. I really want to kill you, Dallas Christofer. And I know I'd enjoy every second of it."

He looked up, his cold eyes staring into her simmering ones. "I know you do. So do it. Prove that you're Vincent Castille's daughter."

For a long time, they locked eyes. He never felt his pulse quicken or his breath deepen. He just waited, waited for that final moment. She would narrow her eyes and swipe the blade. He would felt a sharp pain at his throat, then a gasping sensation. Taking in breath would be impossible. Then his knees would weaken as he bled out. He'd be dead in a matter of seconds. It would be euphoric beyond words.

"Kill me," he said.

Sam's eyes narrowed, her wrist flicked . . .

. . . and she threw the knife into the adjacent wall. "No. I may be Vincent's daughter, but I'm not him. And I sure as hell am not you. I am Sam Castille. And Sam Castille is not a killer."

Dallas watched in growing indignation as she turned and walked away. Seeing Rodger advancing with a second pair of handcuffs, Dallas felt molten-hot rage course through every nerve.

The hell with you, bitch!

He squeezed the trigger of the chainsaw. The machine roared to life as he raised his weapon and aimed it at Sam's head. "*Then die, Sam Castille!*"

Click.

The chainsaw fell out of his hand, hit the ground, and shut off.

Sam turned quickly, ready to fight, and then stared in shock. Rodger stared as well.

Dallas's right hand was raised. But the handcuff around his right wrist, the one Rodger had put on him before the fight, was now secured to the pipe above him. And Dallas's own left hand had closed the cuff, trapping him.

"What the hell?" said Rodger, confused.

Dallas stared at his left hand in horror, feeling his body twitch as a part of him he thought he had murdered and buried away pushed forward. "No way! No fucking way," he said. "You can't still be there."

Another voice strained through Dallas's throat. "Don't . . . you . . . dare . . . hurt her . . ."

It was Richie.

Sam began to pale. Her voice sounded shocked. "Oh, my beloved . . ." Covering her mouth, she peered at him in growing horror. "Richie, can you hear me?"

Dallas glared at her, his eyes fierce. "I told you, I'm the one in charge. He's just a cover. A mask! I'm the real thing. And I got rid of him! I—"

But as those words left his mouth, his left arm moved once again on its own to a valve on the pipes. With a quick turn of the handle, the room began to fill with the hissing sound of building pressure and the smell of natural gas.

"What the hell are you doing?" Dallas yelled at his left hand. Even as he shouted, his left hand broke the valve's handle. There was no shutting it off now.

"Holy shit," Rodger said, starting to back out. "The nutcase is going to light the fire. Sam, we have to get out of here now."

"Richie," Sam repeated, her chest heaving. She turned to Rodger. "For God's sake, Rodger, shut it off from the outside!"

"Yes, shut it off!" cried Dallas in a panic, his heart rate spiking. He couldn't die like this, not being beaten by his own mask. He'd go to jail or to the sanitarium. He'd take years, if he had to, to reestablish control. He had to have control. "For the love of God, Rodger, shut it—" Even as he said that, his left hand covered his mouth.

Rodger ran outside the room. A moment later, he ducked his head back inside. "Sam, it's busted! Must have been broken in the fight."

She seemed to ignore him, instead calling out, "Richie, if you are in there, answer me."

Dallas was sweating, from both the rising heat and from the fear welling up inside him. But even as he uncovered his own mouth, he felt his subordinate personality push forward and speak through him. "It's OK, Sam."

Gritting his teeth, Dallas closed his eyes and cried out, "No! It's not OK. Get me out of here, Rodger! I swear I'll surrender. I'll confess. Just don't leave me to die like this! Not on his terms!"

He looked up in time to see Sam before him. She touched his face in a way so gentle it reminded him of his mother. "I love you, Richie," she said, her voice choking. "Please. Please don't do this . . ."

"I'm not!" He felt the urge to bite into her neck, to tear out her throat. Instead, despite his best efforts, Richie spoke through him again. "Sam, I know I'm screwed up. I'll never live a normal life. Even if I get help, Dallas is who I really am. And I can't live with the pain I've inflicted. On other people. On you. I love you too much."

The heat in the room had become intense and Dallas saw Sam's face start to redden. His own skin was painfully hot.

Rodger, now at the door, called out, "Sam! I can't turn it off. You've got to get out of there!"

Sam looked into Dallas's eyes.

Dallas tried to whisper, "Sam, I beg you. Please. Let me live."

That was what he wanted to say. But instead of his desperate plea, Richie again spoke. "Sam, I beg you. Please. Let me die."

Her lips trembled as she leaned in and pressed them to Dallas's. He felt utter repulsion. To his horror, his own body returned the kiss. It was the most tender thing he had ever experienced. He didn't know how to respond to that kind of genuine affection.

When the kiss parted, Richie spoke once more. "I love you. I'll see you on the other side, Sam."

She stepped back, tears in her eyes. "You better, you doofus, or I'll be pissed."

"What the hell, bitch," Dallas cried out, again in control. "No, no waiting on the other side! Save me now! You can break the handcuffs with your super-whatever strength. Come on! Save me!"

The air was so hot now that their hair was starting to smolder. She rushed toward the exit, stopping only to look back and say, "Dallas . . ."

He looked up at Sam, spat, and said, "The hell you want?"

Her eyes looked sad. They were filled with something he couldn't place. It was the kind of look you gave someone when they managed to screw up everything about themselves, but you couldn't bring yourself to feel contempt. *What is that? Hate? Disgust? Or is it . . .*

Suddenly, he knew what he was seeing. It made him even angrier. *That's . . . pity . . . in her eyes.*

"Dallas, you're wrong," she repeated, shaking her head. "You aren't the dominant one. You're just the mask. Richie was the real you. Good. Kind. Loving. The person you didn't have the courage to be."

He roared with rage as she exited the crematorium and closed the door.

"Sam! Come back, Sam!" he cried out, tears in his eyes. "You goddamn sadistic bitch! You are as evil as your goddamn father. *Bitch!*" He lowered his head and sobbed in anger and fear.

Then he heard a familiar sound. Even as the bottom of the room started to glow with fire, even as the gas pressure built, even as he smelled his hair sizzling—he heard it. The clicking of heels.

Looking up, he saw the Lady in Red approach him.

"What do you want?" he asked, spite in his voice.

Sighing, she shook her head and patted the side of his face.

He tried to shrug her away. "And why are you here, anyway? I created you to manipulate Richie, you shouldn't—"

"Because Sam was right, you are the mask. And Richie's using me to do this."

The Lady in Red's fingernails sank into the flesh of Dallas's face. As she ripped, he felt his consciousness getting torn away, replaced by the person he thought he had destroyed. He screamed.

When Richie's eyes focused, the Lady in Red was gone. The side of his face had a gashing, bleeding wound. And the fingernails of his left hand were soaked in his own blood. *I did it. I beat him.*

It had been a hard-won battle. Dallas had created the delusion of the pale-faced killer, the one believed to be Julius, to give Richie the hallucination of being brutally murdered. Though it had kept him dormant while Dallas kidnapped Sam, it did not destroy him. All of his experiences in New Orleans had made him too strong. So he started meticulously chipping away at Dallas, hoping he'd not be discovered.

Dallas's arrogance proved to be his undoing, and bit by bit Richie gained a silent foothold. When the fight with Sam began, and Dallas became completely distracted, Richie used every ounce of his will to gain dominance. In the end, he used the very same delusion that had been used on him—the Lady in Red— to destroy Dallas and become the sole remaining personality.

"So that's it," Richie said, as the heat made his lips crack, his skin peel off. He felt like he was being baked alive. "I created a delusion of the one person I'd listen to . . . to manipulate . . . myself."

"The Lady in Red was made in the image of my mother," he said, tears welling up in his eyes, sizzling on his blistering skin. "My real mother. Maple Christofer. Man, I am a very special kind of crazy."

He looked at the door where Sam and Rodger had left minutes ago. "At least Sam will get to live," he said to himself. "That means everything to me. I hope her story has a happy ending."

The sound of pressure building stopped, and he heard a series of clicks—the safety valves releasing. His throat tightened and tears rolled down his cheeks, boiling halfway.

"Goodbye, Sam. I love you."

As the flames shot up, filling the room with such a blaze that the air itself caught on fire, Richard Fastellos, author of *The Pale Lantern*, closed his eyes. In the distance, he heard the sounds of someone digging. He knew what that sound meant. Baron Samedi was digging his grave.

I'm dying . . . Ya know, it's funny. In the end, I'm not all that scared. I didn't piss myse—

Death came before Richie could finish the thought.

Chapter 32
A Tale of Two Sisters

Date: **Tuesday, August 25, 1992**
Time: **5:00 p.m.**
Location: **Sam Castille's townhome**
                   Uptown New Orleans

"You sure you'll be OK?" Rodger asked Sam.

She had been thinking about Richie, and Rodger's words pulled her out of her thoughts. With a small smile, she leaned over in the squad car and kissed him gently on the cheek. It felt like she was ten years old and kissing "Uncle Rodger" again.

"Honestly? I don't know anymore. But I'm going to try," she said.

It had been one week since the final confrontation with the new Bourbon Street Ripper, Dallas Christofer, alias Julius Boucher, alias Richard Fastellos. It had been just one week since she, nude and covered in blood, had left the Castille mansion with Rodger after sealing Dallas in the crematorium. It had been only one week since the gas pipes in the crematorium had burst after killing Dallas, engulfing the Castille mansion and all its secrets in purifying flames.

It had been only one week, but to her, it felt like it had been a lifetime ago.

As she started to get out of the squad car, she felt Rodger's hand on hers. In a gentle, paternal tone, he asked, "Would you like some company for a while? I don't have anywhere to be."

Sam looked at the man who was an uncle, a friend, and a savior to her. "You know what? I think that would be nice. A little coffee? Like old times?"

Rodger smiled back. His face showed the stress of their ordeal, the lacerations from Dallas's attacks still healing. She knew that the stab wounds to his sides and shoulders would take longer to heal. He grumbled as he got out of the car, his voice strained. He was definitely showing his age.

The stress of the battle with Dallas had also taken a toll on her. The doctors concluded that she had only recovered from the locked-in syndrome due to what they called a shock to her system caused by the torture she suffered. And she had sustained major injuries in the fight as well.

Both Sam and Rodger had ended up in the hospital again, where they had stayed for the better part of a week. Her quick recovery from her injuries was being considered another modern miracle. The only explanation anyone could give was "mind over matter."

That had all ended up working in her favor. After Rodger had presented the district attorney with all the evidence he had uncovered, she was formally cleared of all charges. Dr. Klein, who was still pushing for a committal hearing, was delayed while the Bourbon Street Ripper case was formally closed. For now, Sam was free of being Dr. Klein's patient.

Sam of Spades was still being treated like a multiple personality disorder, much like Richie and Dallas. Sam was also diagnosed with acute schizophrenia and was placed under the care of a state-appointed doctor. She received new anti-psychotics specific to her condition while the district attorney decided what to do with her. While she was still adamant that Sam of Spades was something else, she agreed to try the medication out anyway. Anything to keep Dr. Klein out of her life.

But Dr. Klein was the last thing on her mind as she and Rodger, sitting in the kitchen of her townhome, waited for the coffee to brew. The only thing she could focus on was how much she missed Richie. Despite everything, he had been the first and only person she had ever truly fallen in love with.

And she had killed him.

"I'll give it to that maid service Dixie got in here. They cleaned this place up better than I could have imagined," Rodger said, chuckling morbidly. Both of them had become a bit more morose since the confrontation with Dallas.

Looking around, Sam said, "I agree. I'll have to give my thanks to Dixie and Gino when I see them again."

Rodger shook his head. "It's not just about cleaning your house, Sam. Dixie's trying to reach out to you. You should meet her halfway."

Sam tried to smile again, but she didn't much feel like smiling lately. "Well, it's nice that someone wants to be friends with me, but I'm not ready to come out and live again. Not after all that."

He nodded and, reaching up, patted her hand gently.

Now she smiled softly. His touch was the only thing that felt real right now. Her uncle Rodger.

"Don't be too hard on yourself, and don't take what this old man says seriously," he said. "Take time to grieve. I know you loved him. And the real Richie? Well, he was a good man."

She nodded back. She thought maybe tears would come to her eyes, but they didn't. She had long since cried them all out.

"Anyway, it'll be a while before Dixie'll want to be social again," Rodger said, leaning back in his chair. "And then, once she finishes her physical rehabilitation, she'll be a lot busier. You heard that she was made a lieutenant, correct?"

"I heard," Sam said in a low voice. While she was happy for Dixie, she felt that Rodger should have also been rewarded. "It should have been you, though. You caught the Bourbon Street Ripper. You caught him both times."

He shook his head. "No, no. I just put the pieces together. Every-one caught him. You, me, Michael, Richie, Dixie . . . and Aucoin and Douglas and Ouellette . . . heck, even Rivette, Landry, and the others. We all did it."

With a slight nod, she said, "Yeah. We all did it."

The coffee machine beeped. She got up. "Well, you should have at least been promoted to something. You are a hero, after all. You have a medal of valor presented by the mayor himself, right?"

His cheeks flushed. He cleared his throat before casually lifting the lapel of his new overcoat to show the medal. "You mean this little thing?"

She smirked gently as she poured them both some coffee. "Show-off."

Rodger gave the kind of helpless grin a man gives when he's OK with showing a little bravado. Covering up the medal, he said, "Well, the real reward is that my pension is intact, my record is clean, and I'm being given my gold watch at the end of the month."

"Retirement, eh?" Sam asked as she finished doctoring the coffee. She carried his cup to him. "Why, Detective Bergeron, whatever will you do with all that free time?"

Taking the cup, he chuckled again. "Honestly? I think I'll travel. I didn't realize until Michael's funeral that Shreveport is the furthest I've ever been from New Orleans. I'd like to see the rest of this country."

As he sipped his coffee, she chuckled as well. "Well, if you want some company, and don't mind your niece hanging out with you, I'd love to come."

He locked eyes with her, looking genuinely touched. "Thank you, Sam. I'd like that."

Her smile, as she sipped her coffee, was small but sincere.

"So what will you do?" Rodger asked. "Other than go gallivanting around the United States with your fat old uncle?"

Sam's smile grew as she snickered into her coffee cup. When she was a child, he had always had a way of making her life better. Now, twenty years and one serial murder investigation later, she felt like that old connection was back.

"Honestly, Rodger? I don't know," she said. "I want to write. I have a lot to get out. A lot of darkness that is bursting forth. I'll finish this copycat story just to do it, but then I'm done with mysteries. I think I'll write something else. Maybe supernatural horror?" She sounded as unsure as she felt.

"Well, whatever you decide," he said, "you'll do fine. You're a good woman, Sam. Edward would be proud."

She looked down at her coffee and felt life return to her heart by degrees. "Thank you, Rodger." Still looking down at her coffee, she finally asked, "So Rodger, can you tell me, you know, the whole story? About my mother, my father, my . . . real father . . . everything?"

He sloshed his coffee around in his cup. "It took me days to sort through everything and get the full tale. It's a sordid story, Sam. You sure you're up for it?"

She nodded. She wanted to know everything.

Rodger leaned forward, again resting his elbows on the table. He began the story. "Back in the early sixties, Vincent Castille and his childhood friend, Carlos Marcello, founded a cabaret nightclub called the Jean-Lafitte Theater. It was created as a throwback to the Prohibition era.

"At the time, there were two nurses—twin sisters—who worked at the St. Jude hospital alongside Vincent. The sisters were from a lower-middle-class family and needed the extra income. They found out about the club from Vincent and ended up getting jobs as singers. The twin sisters were Mary and Maple Christofer."

Sam nodded. "Mine and Dallas's mothers."

"Right, exactly," said Rodger. "The Jean-Lafitte Theater became a place where anyone who was anyone in New Orleans would go. The mayor. The top businessmen. Pretty much anyone who was a part of the social elite—"

"You mean the Knight Priory of Saint Madonna?" asked Sam.

"Exactly. People like Jonathon Russell and Vincent Castille. Now you wouldn't catch the Castille women like Gladys or Marguerite there." Rodger took a long sip.

Sam shook her head. "Of course not. It was a different era. Women of high society probably didn't even go to cabarets."

Rodger chuckled. "And neither did poor-ass bum detectives like me. But Edward Castille went, as did Giorgio 'Blue-Eyed' Marcello. Anyway, over the months that he attended the theater, Edward fell in love with Maple, who sang under the stage name Marigold. Giorgio started moving in on Mary, who sang under the stage name Magnolia."

Sam finished her coffee and got up. "Please continue."

Rodger said, "However, at that time, Giorgio came under investigation by Ouellette for a string of serial rapes. So, even though Edward was actually interested in Maple, he publicly pursued a relationship with both sisters. To further protect Mary from Giorgio, Edward took Mary, not Maple, to the Comus Krewe Ball. That's where your mother got the charm you squeeze."

Sam looked at the red plastic shoe charm, which was dangling from a belt loop, and patted it gently. "So Edward started to date both sisters to protect Mary from Giorgio," she said, pouring herself another cup. "More coffee, Rodger?"

"Yes, please," said Rodger, holding out his cup. "And so began Edward's fall from grace in the Castille family's eyes. Not only was he a police officer, which they considered a gross profession, but he was dating two sisters, both of whom were the equivalent then of a stripper today."

Sam poured him a second cup. "So Edward was publically involved with both Christofer sisters, but only had eyes for Maple. How does Grandpa . . . I mean, Father . . . I mean, Vincent fit into this?"

Rodger sipped his coffee. "She was the only person at the theater who Vincent actually liked. Vincent's first wife, Edward's mother, had been dead for many years. They say that Mary was similar to her. Quiet. Kind. Gentle-hearted. Maybe it stirred a memory deep inside Vincent. Either way, only Mary was allowed to sit with him. I suspect that at the time, only Edward and Maple knew. I imagine they were OK with it. And why not? If Vincent and Mary were together, that left time for the two of them."

Sipping his coffee again, he added, "The end result is that Vincent married Mary about the same time that Edward married Maple."

The sequence of events was falling into place for Sam. Sipping her own coffee, she asked, "And soon after the weddings, Dallas and I were born. Also roughly at the same time?"

"Exactly," said Rodger. "The sources I've dug up said that the sisters were sequestered in a beach house on the North Shore during their pregnancies. That was Vincent's doing. Since both women were basically no more than harlots in the eyes of the social elite of New Orleans, Vincent had his and Edward's marriages hidden from the world. The sisters were not allowed to live with their husbands. Mary, Maple, and Dallas lived in a private townhome in the French Quarter. You, as Vincent's daughter and his heir, were allowed to live in the Castille mansion. However, to keep up the appearance that you were Edward's daughter, you also lived with him."

Sam looked down at the coffee in her mug, noticing that it was so dark, it could pass for blood. Shaking that thought away, she said, "So I was told that my mother had died soon after I was born. But that was a lie. Mary was still alive. To keep up the ruse, I spent half my time with Edward, the other half with Vincent. Meanwhile, Mary and Maple were forced to live as if they had never married into the Castille family. Is that correct?"

Rodger looked away for a moment, sighing in obvious disgust, then looked back. "I told you it was a sordid tale. I'm sure there were threats made to Edward and Maple, and even to Mary. You see, as the patriarch of the Castille family, Vincent wielded considerable power in New Orleans. Even after the older generation of the Knight Priory retired, he was still one of the most powerful men in southern Louisiana.

"And of course, the Knight Priory went through all those changes because of the ritual they did on you and Violet. It scared people so badly that most of them just stopped gathering. Nowadays, the Knight Priory consists mostly of their grandchildren and other politically connected people. I don't really know who belongs to the current Knight Priory, and I don't think they'd ever reveal themselves to me. And I don't care."

Sam didn't say anything at that. While locked into her body, she had had many conversations with Sam of Spades. She had become thoroughly convinced that Vincent, after finding out she had a weak heart like her mother, had put something inside her at the age of five. That something had forgotten what it was and reformed its psyche as Sam of Spades. After the drugs had worn off and Sam of Spades had had a chance to sort things out, it had started referring to itself by a new name.

Marinette.

The thing inside her had the same name as one of the loa hag sisters. What more proof did she need of what Vincent had done to her?

"Anyway, Sam," Rodger said, breaking her out of her train of thought, "over the years, the tension between Edward and Vincent grew. When Giorgio was actively investigated and Edward, suspected of being an accomplice, fell under the scrutiny of Internal Affairs, it must have driven Edward over the edge. All Edward wanted was to live with his family, but his own father wouldn't allow it. The sad truth, Sam, is that I can assure you that Edward wanted you with him. However, Edward knew that if he took you, the Castille princess, away, Vincent would spare no expense or manpower to hunt him down. So he concocted a plan to run away with his wife and their child, Dallas."

Sam lifted her coffee cup to her lips. She felt the steam rise over her face. It felt real. Finally, she said, "So that's when Edward and Maple poisoned my mother?"

"Not poisoned," Rodger said cautiously. "They just wanted her to collapse and be hospitalized. Edward would then take Maple and Dallas and flee the state, maybe even the country, knowing Vincent wouldn't leave Mary's side to pursue them. The problem, however, was that Mary had a weak heart. Back then, that wasn't something they knew how to treat. So those nicotine pills did make your mother collapse, but instead of putting her in the hospital, they killed her."

"And that broke Vincent," Sam said, feeling the story was done.

"No," Rodger replied, his tone getting serious. "You don't just wake up one day and decided to torture people to death. Vincent had the makings of a sociopath years before he became the Bourbon Street Ripper. I mean, why did he keep Edward away from Maple and Dallas? What kind of man does that? No, Vincent was already a bad egg. He just needed a reason to start acting like one."

Although she nodded in agreement, she somehow felt like that wasn't the full story. She recalled how, soon after Mary's death, she had come across Vincent crying. On that day, Vincent had seemed genuinely frightened. Frightened that she, Sam, his princess, would die. So, being ten years old, she had promised not to die. Ever.

It was one of many memories she wouldn't share with anyone.

"So that's where we end our tale," Rodger concluded. "Vincent became the Bourbon Street Ripper, and involved Topper Jack, Mad Monty, Fat Willie, and Blind Moses. All of this was to capture and torture dozens of women, all to cover up his real intended victims: Edward, Maple, and Dallas."

"Whom he blamed for Mary's death," Sam said, draining her coffee cup. "And while he was at it, Vincent decided to inject Dallas with the *tkeeus* to further test it. So he punished Dallas just for being born, used him as a guinea pig, and ended up sowing the seeds of a future serial killer."

"Correct," he replied, draining his cup as well. "And I honestly don't know what to make of the *tkeeus*. It does seem like voodoo magic to me, and after using it myself, I can believe anything. Magic. Spirits. Wonderdrug. The stuff is dangerous. Ouellette has personally overseen the efforts to make sure all of it is destroyed. And we're waiting to hear back from Dr. Lazarus on his findings."

Sam was silent for a few moments. Like everyone else, she wanted to know the truth behind that mysterious pink substance. Among other things, it would confirm whether she was possessed or simply insane.

Finally, she said, "That's all the questions I have. Thanks, Rodger."

Nodding and getting up, he said, "Then I should get going, Sam. I have to start cleaning up my desk at the precinct before tackling those reports. Plus, Michael's family is sending someone to get the personal stuff out of his desk."

Sam was distracted, remembering that she needed to call Dr. Lazarus. But as Rodger stood, she focused on him and followed him to the door. Hugging him once more, she leaned up and gave him a final peck on the cheek. "Take care, Uncle Rodger."

He hugged her back, patting her shoulder. "You, too, little Samantha." He winked and went out to the squad car.

She watched him fiddle with the front seat belt, his frustration plain on his face. She couldn't help but smile at his efforts. She was glad he wouldn't have to drive that car for much longer.

Finally getting the seat belt in place and giving her a helpless shrug, Rodger drove off.

Sam watched as he left, fondness in her eyes. She loved that old guy.

Later that evening, after ordering pizza for dinner, she was in her study listening to the radio.

She had spoken briefly with Dr. Lazarus. He had reassured her that the new medication given by the state-appointed doctor would help with any symptoms of schizophrenia. He had also reassured her that he was both analyzing samples of the *tkeeus* and doing all he could to stop Dr. Klein from interfering with her new treatment. Dr. Lazarus ended the phone call by promising her that eventually he would have answers about the *tkeeus* and her special abilities.

When she had pointedly asked him if he thought she was possessed, he had just said, "I can't tell you anything now. But soon, I will tell you everything."

As satisfied as she could be, she sat down to write. Another cup of hot coffee sat on her desk, and her typewriter had a fresh sheet of paper in it.

However, Sam's attention was on the notebook directly in front of her, where she was tapping a fresh page with her silver pen. Rodger had given them back after her discharge. It felt good to touch that pen once more.

"And in other news," said a voice on the radio, "the mysterious fire that burnt down the historic Castille mansion has been ruled an accident. It has been confirmed that Gladys Castille, the matriarch of the Castille family, along with the mansion staff, were killed when several gas pipes combusted. The property, which has been donated to the city, will be converted into a public park."

She shook her head, trying not to snort. It was obviously false information, but she knew why. The public would demand to know every single detail, and there was too much that couldn't be explained. The fight at the wharf, the *tkeeus*, the Knight Priory, and more. She hated lies, but this time it was better to withhold the truth.

The radio continued, crackling with a little static. "There is still no word from the heir to the Castille fortune, Samantha Castille, who was recently cleared on all charges relating to the new Bourbon Street Ripper."

Sam wasn't rushing into matters regarding her inheritance. While the thought of having nearly five billion dollars was amazing, she wasn't sure what she would do with that much money.

"The murderer, Dallas Christofer, a long-term resident of Acadia Vermillion Hospital, who committed suicide during a police standoff, was cremated in a private ceremony earlier this week."

A small sigh escaped her lips, and she closed her eyes. She was just glad that the police, the district attorney, and the mayor had all decided not to include that Richie was actually Dallas. Richie's obituary was two paragraphs, simply stating that he had drowned in the Mississippi after drinking too much. She hadn't saved that clipping. She preferred to keep her signed copy of *Darkness Rising* as her way of remembering him.

"And lastly," crackled the radio, "Mayor Sidney Barthelemy announced today that he will not be calling for the resignation of Commander Louis Ouellette of the New Orleans eighth precinct. In a press conference, Mayor Barthelemy stated that he believed that the eighth precinct had suffered enough these past few weeks, and that without Commander Ouellette, who has had a flawless track record up to this point, the French Quarter and wharf would be the only ones to suffer. And now for some music."

As the radio started playing a catchy dance tune, she thought about the other survivors. So many had suffered, and she didn't want to hold a grudge anymore. Dr. Klein, Aucoin, even Ouellette. She would try to stop hating and move on.

"Enough. I need to write. Let me finish this stupid copycat story and move on with my life," Sam said, looking back at her notebook.

She hadn't touched her notes since before her fight with Blind Moses and still needed to come up with an ending. She did have a lot of notes, however.

She had sketched out a final fight between the lead detective and the killer. In that fight, she had listed over four different ways for the killer to die, including falling, fire, shooting, and impaling. She decided to stick with fire and have the entire building burn down, just like the Castille mansion did. That would be poetic.

Other notes, such as one of the accomplices dying in prison and another murdering a police officer with a shredding machine, were too close to what had actually happened. So she deleted those scenes. She also removed the part where one of the detectives died in an arrest gone wrong, as she felt it was too close to what had happened with Michael.

But Sam kept in the sequence where the heroine and an assassin have a fight to death—despite the similarity to her fight with Blind Moses—because she liked the idea of two strong female characters fighting. She also kept the bit about an escape from a house full of traps, because she found that to be deviously wonderful.

Now with the words "building burns down" written on the page, she moved to a fresh line to start on the ending.

She didn't want to have a happy ending. And she didn't want to continue this story. It was best if she killed off her remaining two characters.

She examined them: Horatio Benoit and Julia Castille. Horatio had caught the villain, but the stress had destroyed him, so he had turned to Jack Daniels to numb the pain. Julia was horribly depressed from her own loss during the case and was slowly going insane.

"Heh, this is sinfully easy," Sam said, uncapping the silver pen and writing: "Horatio Benoit gets drunk and is killed in a car crash. Julia Castille commits suicide by jumping out of a window."

Capping the pen, she said, "There. Now, once I write this ending, I'll start something new. New story. New characters. New genre. I'll need to read up on voodoo some more if I want to switch to supernatural horror. Maybe I'll even go straight to an agent with this. I wonder if Gordon Rockway was serious about representing me?"

She looked at the Rolodex where she had scribbled Gordon's number. He had contacted her soon after her discharge from the hospital and had let her know that, because of Richie's praise, he wanted to give her a chance.

Sam sat there for what felt like a very long time, her eyes closed as she listened to the sound of distant thunder. Sipping her coffee occasionally, she felt truly and genuinely at peace. *Thanks, Richie. You looked out for me until the very end.*

Suddenly, the air conditioning kicked on and the temperature started to drop.

"Shit, it's getting cold. Why the hell is the heat gone?"

The radio stopped playing music. The DJ's voice could again be heard. "Ladies and gentlemen, we have a breaking news report."

She headed out to the hallway, then stopped at the thermostat and jiggled its controls. The needle was dipping below seventy degrees.

Ugh, my thermostat is broken. She held the cup of coffee near her chest. The steam felt good.

The voice on the radio continued. "We have just received word of a fatal car accident at the corner of Saint Peter and Bourbon Street."

Sam shivered as a tingle ran down the base of her spine.

Chapter 33
Exiting the Stage

Date: **Tuesday, August 25, 1992**
Time: **7:00 p.m.**
Location: **New Orleans Police Department**
             Precinct Eight, French Quarter

"A toast to Rodger Bergeron," said Detective Rivette.

He, Landry, Breaux, Gravois, Dixie, and about half a dozen other detectives lifted their champagne glasses to Rodger, who lifted his as well. He had been surprised by most of the homicide division waiting for him with a champagne basket and cards of congratulations—for both his success in closing the case and his impending retirement.

Rodger took it all in stride. He was pretty sure that Dixie had set up the party, because she was the only one who had known he'd be in the office that evening. The somewhat cheeky smile she had didn't do much to convince him otherwise.

After the toast, the detectives chatted around Rodger for a little while longer, giving him more congratulations and asking him particulars about solving the case. He kept up his smile and good cheer, but the attention was making him feel a bit uncomfortable. Just like twenty years ago, with the party after arresting Vincent, he felt like he didn't deserve it.

Finally, Ouellette came to the rescue, coming out of his office. "All right, everyone, in case you hadn't known, the Bourbon Street Ripper is dead and New Orleans is back to being a normal cesspool once again."

As the detectives all dispersed, giving Rodger final congratulations and claps on the back, Ouellette said, "Bergeron, my office, please."

Rodger was slightly taken aback. Ouellette hardly ever said "please."

In his office, Ouellette once again sat down and poured a glass of whiskey for them both. "Here, better than that crap they gave you outside."

While Rodger didn't much feel like drinking, he took the whiskey anyway, swishing the cup gently in his hands.

"I want you to know that I'm sorry," Ouellette said, also swishing his whiskey around.

"Commander?" Rodger asked, unsure what he meant.

Ouellette snorted and sipped his whiskey. "It's the same goddamn thing as when Douglas retired. You gave your all to this city. You gave your blood, you even gave your partner's life, and how do they repay you? They make you retire."

Rodger blinked and looked away from Ouellette. He hadn't really thought of it that way. He had figured that retirement was a reward for all the sacrifices he'd made. Not once did he ever think he was being swept under the rug like Douglas had been.

"It really is a goddamn shame, Bergeron," Ouellette said. "You turned out to be one hell of a cop."

Rodger chuckled and said, "I really didn't solve all that much, Commander. You know Michael—"

"That's not what I meant, Bergeron," interrupted Ouellette. "I don't mean a detective, I mean a cop." He paused for a moment to sip his whiskey. "Let me tell you a story."

Rodger sat back and looked at his commander questioningly.

"Before I joined the police, I served in the Armed Forces during the Vietnam War. You know that, right?" asked Ouellette.

Rodger nodded.

Ouellette continued. "My platoon and I were stationed in the A Shau valley during March of 1966. We had seen a lot of violence, a lot of killing, a lot of bloodshed. To say that my men and I were desensitized to violence would be an understatement."

Again, Rodger nodded. He knew of his commander's military past but had never heard him tell a story about it.

"So there was this girl from the village right next to our camp," Ouellette said, sliding his glass back and forth between his hands. "Twelve, maybe thirteen years old. Absolutely adorable. Rode her bike past where my platoon was stationed every day. The men would cat-call her, because for some reason soldiers stationed abroad lose their shit the moment a girl goes by, even if she's more illegal than going AWOL."

Rodger, despite himself, snickered at Ouellette's remark.

Ouellette seemed to ignore him and continued the story. "So they'd cat-call her, and try to get her to come over, and all the demented crap horny soldiers do. But she'd always just smile at them, wave, and say '*Cam on ban*.' Do you know what that means, Bergeron?"

Rodger shook his head. "No, Commander, I'm afraid I don't."

"It means 'thank you,' Bergeron," Ouellette said. "Some of my men were pretty dumb and thought she was thanking them for the compliments, because obviously a pre-pubescent girl loves being told she has a fine ass."

Rodger held back a second snicker by sipping his whiskey. "Obviously."

"So, anyway, every day this girl comes by, says thank you, and heads off. But then, March 9, 1966, comes around."

Rodger blinked. The date was significant, but he couldn't recall why. Vietnam War history wasn't his strong point.

"The battle of A Shau."

"Ah. I remember reading about it. It was one of the biggest battles in the war next to the Tet Offensive, right?"

Ouellette nodded, his countenance darkening. "Those VC bastards came in and turned our camp into a bloody graveyard. Worst fight I'd ever been in. Read about it, Bergeron, cause I sure as hell am not going to relive the details for you." He took a deep drink of his whiskey.

Shaking his head, Rodger said, "No, I remember enough about the Vietnam War to remember how awful that battle was."

"When the smoke finally cleared, when the VC finally withdrew, three of us were all that was left of my platoon. The camp was lost and the village next to it was a goddamn massacre."

Rodger shook his head again. He had been lucky enough not to have been drafted. Without dismissing the horrors he had experienced with both Bourbon Street Ripper murders, he couldn't begin to imagine what Ouellette had experienced.

Drinking more of his whiskey, Ouellette continued. "So I'm walking around these killing fields and helping identify bodies. Soldiers in my platoon. Soldiers I knew since arriving at the camp. Doctors. Teachers. Journalists. I'm walking around as if in a daze, figuring that this is how the soldiers who opened up the Nazi concentration camps must have felt." Leaning forward, he said, "So I'm at the end of this one field, and guess who I see?"

Rodger felt he knew where this story was going. Frowning, he said, "The little girl, right? Dead in a grave?"

Ouellette shook his head. "Nope. The little girl, alive and kneeling in front of a dozen or so bodies. Her whole family. All dead."

Rodger just stared at him. He didn't know what to say.

Ouellette wiped sweat off his temples. His voice lowered to almost a whisper. "There she was, this little girl, barely old enough to be considered a woman. She's kneeling on the side of the road and just praying. Praying over her mother. Her father. Just praying. And when she saw me, when I walked up to her, do you know what she said?"

Rodger felt a lump in his throat. He shook his head.

"She said *'Cam on ban,'* Rodger."

Rodger swallowed the lump in his throat.

A few tears rolled down Ouellette's face. It was like he wasn't even aware of them. "I never saw her during the fighting. I didn't even look for her. I didn't save a single person she knew. Hell, I didn't even try. And here she was, with nothing, nothing at all. And she was thanking me."

Rodger took a deep, silent inhale and finished his whiskey. It burned going down.

"I asked her why. Why she would thank me, when I hadn't done shit for her. She looked at me and said, 'You're a soldier. Your job is to die so I can be safe. If I'm alive, it's because you did your job. So, thank you.' And with that, she got on her bike and rode off. I was re-stationed in Guinea shortly afterward, so I never saw her again."

He sat back, drank the last of his whiskey, and said, "So when I say you're a good cop, Bergeron, that's what I mean. It's not about the case. It's not about the suspects or the deductions. It's not about the arrests, and it sure as hell isn't about the convictions. It's about you going out there and maybe dying, so that little girls like that can live."

Rodger felt a few tears run down his cheeks.

Ouellette appeared to notice this, since he wiped his own tears away and said, "Enough of that crying crap. You're a good cop, and it's a shame that the city's shitting on you like you committed the Rape of Belgium. Now that was some screwed-up shit."

Rodger dried his eyes and chuckled. "Sounds like a bad memory. What was it?"

Ouellette blinked and quickly chortled, shaking his head. "Just an old saying from an old soldier who's buried too many comrades. What I mean to say is that you're being made to be a patsy, and you don't deserve it. Anyway, it's getting late. You better head home. If you ever need anything, you let me know."

Rodger slid his empty glass back to Ouellette. "Thanks for the drink, Commander. I'll keep in touch once I'm gone."

Rodger left Ouellette's office. He needed some fresh air.

An hour later, he was outside enjoying a cigarette when Dixie joined him. Sitting next to him, she said, "Hey. Douglas is on the phone."

Rodger had been lost in his own thoughts, and her sudden arrival jerked him out of them. When what she had said registered, he put out his cigarette. "Thanks, Dixie."

As he headed inside, she called out after him. "You know, Rodger, I'm going to be a lieutenant soon. And while Kyle just got off of administrative leave, he's going to be on probation for a while. Point is, I could use someone like you underneath me."

Rodger stopped at the doorway as she continued. "If you want, I can try to get your retirement postponed. Someone like you could really do a lot of good."

He smiled and shook his head. "I have done a lot of good, Dixie. It's time for this old player to exit the stage." He headed inside, adding, "You be the one to play the lead now, Dixie. It's your time, anyway."

Back at his desk, Rodger paused a moment to look at Michael's. His personal belongings were stacked up on one side of it. At the center of the desk was a photograph of Michael from when he had graduated from the police academy, along with several bouquets of flowers. Rodger took a moment to touch his partner's desk. "Yeah. We did it, buddy."

Picking up the phone, he said, "Hey, Douglas!"

Douglas sounded overjoyed. "Hey, hey, you old bastard. I hear you're getting the gold watch soon."

Rodger laughed. It felt good. "Yeah, yeah, I'm getting shuffled out for a newer model. You know how that goes, right?"

Douglas chuckled and said, "Yeah, I sure do, bud. I sure as hell do."

"So what's up?" asked Rodger, settling comfortably into his chair.

Douglas said, "Well, Mabel and I were going to have a potluck tomorrow and she wanted to know if you could come over. I think even Boudreaux wants to see you."

Rodger liked the idea. "Sure thing. What time, and do I need to bring anything?"

"Come at six. And if you're offering, bring the beer," Douglas said. "But make it a light beer, bud. Mabel wants me to watch my weight."

"Watch it grow, right?" asked Rodger with a good-natured snort.

The two shared a good, friendly laugh over the pun.

"Ah, Rodger," said Douglas. "Don't sweat the retirement thing. You'll never stop being a cop, but you'll learn to love not working as one."

"Good to know," muttered Rodger. That advice was the best he'd heard all day.

Douglas continued. "Anyway, I need to get going. Mabel wants some help in the kitchen. You be careful, see you tomorrow night."

"Thanks, Douglas. Good night," Rodger said, hanging up.

He spent another thirty minutes cleaning up his desk. When he was done, all he had remaining were the reports on the new Bourbon Street Ripper case. It was shaping up to be a good start to the weekend.

As Rodger was getting ready to leave but still sitting at his desk, he heard a female clear her throat. Expecting it to be Dixie, he was surprised when he turned in his chair and came face-to-chest with Michael's little sister—Alexia LeBlanc.

She was wearing a black polo shirt with an embroidered white cross, a pair of blue jeans, and a pair of black boots. She was still wearing the silver cross earrings and silver cross necklace from the funeral. With her punky, unkempt hair, she looked like a younger, sloppier Michael.

Except Michael never had a chest quite that size. It was very noticeable now that she was out of a formal dress.

"Are you going to say hello, Rodger, or are you going to gawk at me?" she asked, arching an eyebrow.

He averted his eyes, remembering that she was not only Michael's sister, but a teenager. *What do they feed that girl? I swear, kids are becoming adults faster and faster.*

"How can I help, Alexia?" he asked, looking her in the eyes.

She smiled softly and said, "I'm here to get my brother's things. His personal stuff? Remember?"

"Oh, right," Rodger said, going to Michael's desk. There were two boxes of Michael's personal belongings—books on logic and reasoning, puzzle books, IQ test booklets, notebooks, and binders of newspaper clippings. "These are both his, and they're heavy. Need any help?"

Alexia went over to one of the boxes and, with a sharp inhale, effortlessly picked it up.

He whistled. "Stronger than you look."

"I work out a lot," she replied. "If you want to help me, please carry that one to the car. It'll save me two trips."

"Car?" he asked, grabbing the box. It was heavy with books and papers. He felt both its weight and his age as he followed her. "Did you drive here?"

"I'm sixteen, Rodger," she said. "I'm old enough for a license. Besides, Papa is too busy with the church to come and Mama hasn't been able to drive since Reagan was in office."

Rodger followed Alexia in amazement. He could completely see how this was Michael's little sister. The personalities were very similar.

Outside, she headed to a black sedan and popped the trunk. They both loaded the boxes in the back. When they were done, she closed the trunk and waved goodbye. "All right. Thanks again, Rodger. Take care."

She was halfway to the front when he called, "Hey, wait a second!"

She stopped and looked at him, blinking.

He rubbed the back of his neck. "Can we talk for a few minutes?"

When she again arched an eyebrow at him, he waved his hands in front of himself and said, "I mean, you're one of the few people who knew Michael well. I just want to know a bit more about him."

Alexia shrugged and got up on the trunk of her car. She placed her hands on her knees. "What do you want to know about him?"

Rodger stuffed his hands in his pockets. It wasn't like he had a list of questions. "Really, I just want to know what kind of guy he was before he became a detective. He never talked about himself. Heck, I don't even know why he became a detective. So, just . . ." He shrugged again. "Just talk about him."

She furrowed her brow some and exhaled. "All right. Fine."

He could instantly tell that she was just like Michael. She liked to get straight to the point. In fact, in some ways, she was even more direct than Michael.

She started talking. "Michael was a good older brother. A lot of times, the boys in the neighborhood would mess with me, because I've pretty much always been a tomboy. It didn't help that as soon as I hit puberty, my cup size shot up to a C. So, yeah, boys would mess with me, and Michael would stand up to them. He kicked their butts and made them leave me alone until I learned to fight for myself."

God, is she a master of Muay Thai Kickboxing as well? Is the whole family like that? Remembering how slovenly the rest of the LeBlanc family had looked at Michael's funeral, though, he doubted it.

Alexia continued. "Anyway, Michael always wanted to work in law enforcement, especially in forensics. He loved Agatha Christie and Sir Arthur Conan Doyle. Loved mysteries. He really wanted to join the FBI as a profiler."

Remembering hearing Michael say something about that once, Rodger asked, "So why did Michael become a police detective instead of joining the FBI?"

She sighed and looked away. "Our papa sabotaged him. Michael graduated top of the class. He passed his tests with flying colors. He was all set to be accepted into the FBI when Papa made a few phone calls to people he knew in the Louisiana branch and had Michael rejected at the last minute."

Rodger was stunned. He had never heard of anyone doing something so cruel to their own child before. It was utterly incomprehensible. "Why?" he asked. "Why would he do that?"

"You do know that my brother was gay, right?"

Rodger cleared his throat and nodded. Much like the sun rising and the moon setting, it was something he had always known but never talked about. It wasn't polite.

"Yeah," she said. "Papa and Michael never got along because of it. Michael always knew. Mama knew. I knew. Papa didn't. When Papa found out, he lost it. Every time he'd push Michael, Michael would push back. The FBI thing was just the result of many years of fighting."

Rodger shook his head. "To think that someone would do that to their own son."

She frowned. "Well, Papa is a Baptist minister. To him, Michael was sinning, plain and simple. To Michael, Papa was being a bigot. It was never meant to work out."

Alexia kicked her feet a bit, doing the first real teenage thing so far. She shrugged. "After that incident, Michael left for the New Orleans Police Academy. I'm sure in a few years he'd have tried again for the FBI. Maybe not. He didn't like talking about it. Very sore subject."

Nodding, Rodger asked, "So why did he choose New Orleans? Because it's far away from Shreveport? Because of the open culture here?"

"Nah," she said as she jumped off the trunk. "He wanted to work with the guy who solved the original Bourbon Street Ripper case. So all's well, ya know?" She winked at Rodger.

He felt himself suddenly choke up. It was becoming a regular thing. "Well, Alexia, it was nice chatting with you. Are you heading back up to Shreveport tonight?"

Alexia shook her head and walked back to the front of the car. "Nah. Brother's apartment still needs to be emptied. I'll be here a few more days. We can do lunch this weekend if you want. I'd love to hear about Michael as a detective. Call his apartment and leave me a way to get in touch with you."

Rodger nodded again. He liked this directness. And swapping stories with Michael's sister sounded like fun.

"All right then, Alexia," he said. "Have a good night."

"Good night, Rodger. God bless." She waved and then got into the sedan. In a minute, she was gone.

Watching her drive off, he chuckled to himself. "Already an adult, eh? Sixteen going on sixty. Man, do I feel sorry for the guy who falls in love with that girl."

Taking out a cigarette, he started to light it and then stopped. He looked at the unlit cigarette for a moment, then put it back in the pack. *I should probably cut down if I want to make it past my sixties.*

When Rodger finally finished up at his desk, it was late and he was looking forward to his nice, warm bed. The only one still working was Dixie, wrapping up her reports. He stopped by her desk and said, "Good night, Dixie. Get some sleep soon."

Dixie smiled sweetly, got up, and hugged him. "You have a good night, Rodger. And don't worry about me. That which does not kill me, makes me stronger."

He winked and said, "Well, make sure nothing kills you. The world needs more people like you."

Rodger walked to his squad car and got inside. The safety belt clicked in on the first try. "Stupid thing finally works and I'm on the way out."

Putting the car in gear, he headed toward home.

He stopped at a street light at the corner of Bourbon Street and Saint Peter. He saw people walking around Bourbon Street, laughing, drinking, and partying—having a good time. The French Quarter, and all of New Orleans, was already starting to heal.

He smiled as he saw the street-side vendors dispensing liquor by the boatload. He smiled as he saw the topless and bottomless bars advertising their cheap sexual thrills. He smiled as he saw people on the balconies of the hotels goading the passersby to flash for a handful of glass baubles. Everything about the city was beautiful. Every speck of dirt, every puddle of vomit, and every drop of human decadence. He loved it all.

It was New Orleans. It was the Big Easy. It was hell. It was his home.

"Time to go home," Rodger said as the light turned green. He hit the accelerator and drove across Saint Peter.

Just as a delivery truck swerved and hit his car head on.

He didn't even see the truck coming. One second, he was driving into the intersection; the next second, the truck was hitting him. The force was so strong that he was thrown forward. As soon as he hit the safety belt, the latch gave way, and he crashed through the front window and out into the street.

The pain was excruciating as he tumbled along Bourbon Street, coming to rest in a heap. He couldn't move anything. Out of the corner of his eye, he saw the wrecked remains of his squad car. He heard people screaming in his direction. He smelled blood. Lots of blood.

He saw his own blood pooling around him. As he blinked a few times, he realized that there was hardly any more pain. Instead, he felt a coldness that seemed to come from within.

I don't think I'm getting up from this one, Rodger thought, amazed at how calm he felt. *I'm sorry, Sam. I guess Uncle Rodger won't be there after all. Forgive me.*

In the distance, he heard sirens.

Something caught his eye. His cigarettes were scattered on the pavement.

He mentally chuckled. *I always thought those things would kill me.*

In the distance, he heard the sound of someone digging. The sound was getting louder.

Despite his vision darkening, Rodger thought he recognized someone in the crowd. A cloudy figure came into focus, leaning against a lamppost with folded arms, watching him. This figure had a small, sad smile. Rodger recognized him as the digging sound grew louder still.

Michael.

The figure walked toward him, reaching out his hand. As everything else went out of focus, Rodger saw that it was indeed Michael, but translucent. His deceased partner's lips mouthed the words "Time to go."

The digging sound was all around him.

Rodger's vision went dark. *All right, buddy. Let's go home.*

Rodger Bergeron died at 9:52 p.m. on Tuesday, August 25, 1992.

Chapter 34
Isn't It Wonderful?

Date: Tuesday, August 25, 1992
Time: 10:00 p.m.
Location: Sam Castille's townhome
Uptown New Orleans

With a loud crash, Sam's mug of coffee hit the ground, shattering across the wooden floor. She fell back against her staircase, her face frozen in horror. Her blue eyes were wide, her pupils were dilated, and her breath was shallow.

Her heart and head started to pound.

Rodger . . . Rodger is dead? How?!

Outside, rain began to pour. Thunder crashed in the distance.

The radio crackled. "Commander Ouellette, at the scene, stated that Detective Bergeron was just heading home after completing his reports on the new Bourbon Street Ripper case. It is reported that the driver of the delivery truck which collided with Detective Bergeron's vehicle had been drinking at the Jean Lafitte Blacksmith Bar. Police have . . . already started . . . pieces of . . ."

The radio started to crackle with static.

Sam felt like she was about to throw up. Quickly, she rushed into the half bath underneath the stairs. She barely made it to the toilet in time. The vomit burned as it came up, only making her head pound more.

I can't believe he's dead. Rodger's dead! How did this happen? How?

Once Sam had finished puking, she flushed and went over to the sink. She splashed water on her face, rinsed out her mouth, and fought against hyperventilating.

Shutting the water off, she stared down into the sink for a long time.

The radio's static continued to worsen as the rain poured down harder and the thunder crashed closer. "The coroner has been . . . police are sectioning . . . keeping crowds back . . ."

OK. Get a hold of yourself, Sam. Call Dixie. Get the facts.

Sam exhaled, the pain in her head lessened enough to where she could think clearly. She looked up into the bathroom mirror at her reflection, ready to move.

Her reflection's eyes were gone, just blank flesh covering up the sockets.

With a blood-curdling shriek, she fell back, landing in the open toilet bowl. As the cold water hit her ass, she threw herself forward and scrambled out into the hallway. Her head pounded with incredible pain.

Stopping in the hallway, Sam could barely hear the radio, which was thick with static. The sound of the heavy rainfall and the thunder outside was so much louder. "So much blood . . . a beautiful crimson . . . such a lovely treat . . ." The words from the radio sounded garbled and twisted.

Getting up slowly, she braced herself on the grandfather clock. Her heart was still pounding hard enough to thump in her ears.

What the hell was happening? Had she finally lost her mind?

The grandfather clock began chiming very loudly. The sound made her stumble back against the rise of the staircase, her head bouncing off the railing. Pain exploded in her head.

Chime!

The new pills, Sam thought, holding the back of her throbbing head. *I have to get those pills!*

Tripping forward, dizzy and off-balance, she fell to the side, landing in the entrance hall of her townhome.

Chime!

The radio was almost all static now, the voice distant and crackling with every word. "Most beautiful thing . . . shown in the history . . . we are blessed . . ." The radio was giving off nonsensical static-riddled phrases.

Grabbing onto the console table, Sam pulled herself up. In doing so, she came face-to-face with her reflection in the entrance hall mirror. She flinched back in instinctive fear, the memory of her fleshed-over eyes still fresh in her mind.

Chime!

Her reflection was not monstrous at all. Sam breathed a sigh of relief. "At least you're normal," she muttered.

Chime!

At that, the reflection's eyes grew wide and black, the face gray and pale. Its jaw unhinged and its mouth opened into a wide black maw with razor-sharp teeth. It let out a high-pitched caterwaul.

Chime!

With a terrified squeal, Sam jumped back, hitting her coat rack and falling on the floor in a heap. From there, she could see right into her office.

Chime!

The copier was running, but instead of paper coming out, it was squirts of blood. The fax machine was on, constantly making that grating connection sound. The keyboard of the personal computer was rapidly typing by itself.

Chime!

I'm having a full-on schizophrenic episode. I need those pills.

Only able to crawl, Sam pulled herself to the study. The radio was just pure static now. Outside, the rain was pouring down in sheets, thunder crashing loudly. Sam's head pounded so hard she thought it would crack open.

Chime!

Reaching her desk, Sam grabbed her bottle of new medication, opened it, flipped her head back, and slammed back its contents.

Only a single object fell into her mouth. It wasn't a pill.

Chime!

With a retch, Sam threw the bottle to the side and spit. A rolled-up piece of paper fell to the floor. She looked at it in confusion. The pounding in her head was like hammer strikes to her skull.

Chime!

Outside, the thunder crashed with frightening intensity and lightning flashed so often it seemed like daylight. The rain was so heavy it was like hail.

Chime!

Hands trembling, Sam unfurled the paper and looked at it. It had only three words on it.

Chime!

"Isn't it wonderful?"

Sam looked up slowly. She hadn't just read those words, the radio had said them in a voice she hadn't heard in twenty years.

Chime!

Vincent Castille.

Sam whispered, "Father?"

Outside, the rain had stopped. There was no thunder. There was no lightning. There was no wind. The air conditioning wasn't blowing, but the house was very cold.

Sam's headache and dizziness were completely gone. But every single fiber of her being felt like something was wrong.

"Isn't it wonderful? Isn't it wonderful, Sam?"

Sam punched the side of her head several times. "This. Is. Not. Happening."

"You shouldn't hit yourself like that, Sam. You'll get hurt."

Sam broke into laughter, pulling herself to her feet. "That's it, then. I've gone completely crazy. I've gone over the edge."

"Far from it, Sam. You have never been saner."

Leaning against the fireplace mantle, Sam covered her mouth as she continued to laugh morbidly. Then she noticed the photo of her and her father at City Park. Edward was a decomposed corpse. Little Samantha had sunken-in eyes that were bleeding, and a sharp, toothy grin, making the child look positively demonic.

"Yeah. I'm in crazy land," she said, turning away from the picture. She rubbed her eyes.

"On the contrary," replied Vincent. "This is not your world. This is the world between life and death. Isn't it grand, Sam? Isn't it wonderful?"

"Stop saying that!" Sam shouted at the radio.

Rushing forward, she grabbed the radio from the table and pulled it out of the wall. "Because of you, I've lost my goddamn mind." She threw it onto the floor. It cracked open. She stomped on the coils and tubes until they were pulverized.

"Just shut up! Shut up! Shut up!"

She struggled to catch her breath, wrapping her arms around herself. She was shivering violently, from both the cold and fear. Then she heard a scratching sound coming from the record player as the needle moved into position and started playing.

"Your confusion is understandable, Sam," Vincent's voice said through the record player. "But believe me. Your mind has opened to a new plane, to a place far beyond the mundane reality of the tired and trite world of the living."

Sam felt her knees get weak.

The fireplace lit up in a pale green fire. The typewriter at her desk clanked, typing on its own.

Sam, still holding onto herself, slowly walked toward the record player. Her lips trembled as she shook her head violently. "Shut up! All that bullshit about neuroscience and drugs that increase your brain power—I don't care! You're dead! And the dead stay dead. That's reality!"

"Is that so? And this is coming from someone who's been convinced for over a week that she's possessed?" Vincent sounded amused. "Then you need to read something, Sam. I think you'll find it enlightening."

Sam's advance toward the record player was halted by a large book falling down and opening up at her feet. She knew that book. She had taken it out when she, Richie, Michael, and Rodger had met in her house weeks ago.

Modern Voodoo.

Picking up the book, she saw a passage circled in red ink.

> Loa can influence minor aspects of the world when a priest or priestess commands them through a focus. The direct influence of a loa is always preceded by a tingling sensation down the host's spine, signifying that the loa has attached itself to the host. These attachments are useful for brief tasks, giving the host physical power and enhanced perception. The strongest attachment, however, is a full possession. Possession requires a complex ritual that binds the loa to the host, creating a symbiotic relationship for an extended period of time. Possessions are much more powerful than standard attachments.

Sam fell back, dropping the book. It landed with a thud as she struggled to catch her breath. "No way! No goddamn way!"

It was one thing to suspect that she was possessed. It was one thing to place stock in voodoo, witchcraft, or even magic. However, it was an entirely different thing to suddenly be told that was the truth.

"No way?" replied Vincent. "Think about it, Sam. How else would a blind woman be able to fight so well? How else would an aging detective like Rodger be able to save himself time and time again? How else would a normal man like Michael be able to run along a wall?"

Sam fell to her knees by a curtained window, digging her fingernails into her flesh and trembling. She wasn't getting a chance to process what she was hearing.

"And do I even need to bring up the power you've possessed?" asked Vincent.

A tapping sound caught Sam's attention. It was coming from behind the curtain in front of her. Moving the curtain aside, she saw what looked like dozens of bony fingers tapping on the glass. A skeleton with many arms came into view, grinning lifelessly, its glowing eyes focusing on her.

She closed the curtain and sank to her knees again. "That night . . . when I was five years old? Was that when . . . ?"

Vincent cleared his throat. "My first great success, Sam, and my first great failure. After watching you collapse one day and fearing that you had inherited your mother's heart condition, I called down a loa and bound it to your body. Possessing you, if you will. It gave your body a strength I never knew possible, but at a terrible cost."

"Marinette. You put Marinette inside of me."

"I did."

Sam needed to sit. Pulling herself along the desk to her chair, she asked, "What was the cost? What the hell did you do to me, you sick bastard?"

"Mind your tongue, young lady," Vincent said crossly. "The cost was that the loa Marinette lost awareness of who she was. She became a second you. Sam of Spades, I believe she called herself. The problem was the *tkeeus*, you see. We used too much and Marinette entered you too quickly. There were horrible side effects, like nightmares and delusions. I am sorry for that."

Sam reached her chair and sat down. "And Violet? What about Violet Patterson?"

"Ah, yes, my favorite dog," said Vincent. "When we called down Bwa-Chech to possess her, we used the correct amount of *tkeeus*. Therefore, Bwa-Chech was conscious of herself and was able to form a more complete bond. Sadly, Bwa-Chech's awareness made her act as a parasite. Violet's health was always frail after that."

Vincent chuckled. "Still, though, it made her a perfect assassin, don't you think? Imagine that! Being blind, but having a loa physically guide you. Isn't it wonderful, Sam?"

"God sakes, shut up, you old snake," Sam said, clawing again at her face. "Will you stop saying 'Isn't it wonderful?' already!" Her head didn't hurt, but her stomach was in knots.

It made sense, though. Marinette and Bwa-Chech, the hag sisters, despised each other. They each sought to kill the other as much as they sought to cause others pain.

No wonder Violet and I were destined to fight . . .

Sam looked down at the typewriter. It was typing "Isn't it wonderful" over and over again. Covering her face, she sobbed, the feelings of confusion, anger, and frustration overwhelming her. "Why are you doing this to me?"

"Why am I doing this to you?" asked Vincent. "Sam, I did all of this for you. Every torture. Every murder. I did it to grant your wish. I did it so that you could be free."

Sam looked up from behind her hands, her eyes narrowing. She felt confused. "What I wanted? You sick bastard! I never wanted you to torture or murder or kill anyone. How can this be what I wanted?"

The needle on the record player hit the end. Quickly, the needle lifted and returned to the beginning.

"Do you remember what I told you about how a person is most alive when they're in pain?" Vincent asked.

Sam nodded.

"Life creates energy, Sam," explained Vincent. "You cannot see it. You cannot touch it, but it's there. Energy that can be manipulated. Energy that can be used. The agony I put my victims through created the energy I needed to perform an even greater ritual. This ritual was so complex it could not be completed while I was still alive. It required me to die and finish it here in the spirit world. But I needed someone alive to finish it for me."

Sam felt dizzy. It was almost too much for her to deal with. But as she sat there, a horrible thought came to her. Covering her face once more, Sam said, "Oh, my God . . . Dallas . . . his murders . . . everything that has happened . . ."

"Exactly!" exclaimed Vincent's voice. "Good, Sam. I am very proud of you. You see, even once I was dead, I needed more energy, more victims. So I chose Dallas to unwittingly carry on my work for me. It was easy. By murdering his mother before him, injecting him with heavy amounts of *tkeeus*, and burying him alive, I created the perfect future copycat killer."

Sam uncovered her face and stared blankly ahead. "But that was twenty years ago."

"Sam," replied Vincent, "time has no meaning here. Even in your current location, which is between the living and spirit worlds, time has slowed to a crawl."

Sam looked up at the clock on the wall. Vincent was right. Since the world had gone crazy, the second hand had barely moved.

"Of course," said Vincent, "since Dallas was alive and had free will, I couldn't force him to act. Yet I couldn't have him deviating too far from my plan. I couldn't even be sure he'd end up as a murderer. So that is where my loa came into the picture, to make sure Dallas did those things."

"Your loa?" asked Sam.

"Yes," replied Vincent. "My loa. I say 'my loa' because they work for me now. Just sending Dallas the occasional vision of a certain type of loa that resembled the old Knight Priory was enough. Soon, the poor boy had created his own intense fantasy involving his mother's supposed ghost, an entire group of Knight Priory members, and . . . Ah, but he told you that little tale already. Point is, it was very convenient."

Sam felt sick.

Vincent's voice grew louder, more triumphant. "In the end, I just needed to nudge him to complete the ritual. He did the rest on his own. And when he killed the Aucoin girl, the ritual was complete."

Sam looked back down at her desk. She felt so tired, like all the will to move was bleeding out of her. Hearing how Vincent had managed to manipulate everything from beyond the grave was utterly disheartening.

And for what? What was the point?

Vincent continued. "And to keep events on track, I needed my loa to make sure certain things happened. Things that would give me all the energy I needed. But loa cannot influence the world of the living without a ritual, without someone using a focus. So I devised a way for a ritual to be performed without the person realizing it. Instead of the focus being something like a wand, it was something far more mundane."

Sam's eyes widened.

"Someone with a heart darkened by watching torture and murder. Someone who would unconsciously direct the loa to influence both events and people. Good little events, like helping someone run across a roof or aiding someone in escaping a deadly machine, and bad little events, like making a gun go off by accident or making a loose seatbelt come undone. Little things that would happen at the worst possible times and would cause great calamity. All I needed was someone macabre enough to give the loa those little, awful suggestions."

Sam's eyes, puffy and red, continued to widen. She looked at where her notebook lay. She already knew the answer.

"You, Sam," said Vincent. "I bequeathed my focus unto you, the same focus I recorded the suffering of my victims with. And you used my focus well. You far exceeded my expectations."

Sam trembled, pieces of her mind starting to fall away like shards of broken glass. She looked over at an object. The object she had used to add little details to her story, such as escapes from death traps, adrenaline-fueled fights, and death-defying chases. The same object she had used to suggest how a fat accomplice, a junior detective, and her own uncle might die.

The silver pen.

Inhaling, she screamed as loud as she could. It was like she was exhaling her sanity.

"*Nooooo!*"

Grabbing her typewriter, Sam threw it across the study. With a loud crash, it smashed the record player into hundreds of pieces. Still screaming, she slammed her fists down on the desk over and over again.

"It was me. I killed them all. I did this!" Her voice tore at her throat.

Tears poured down her face. All those people: Fat Willie, Michael, Rodger. And who knows who else. Killed by her suggestions to the loa. If she had not used that pen, the situations where they had died might never have happened. Without realizing it, she had helped turn an already bad situation into something far worse.

Vincent's voice moved all around her. "Don't be so hard on yourself, Sam. After all, you are my precious princess, my darling daughter. You're a Castille. We have always lived in darkness and worked in shadows. This pen is more than a focus. It is your legacy."

Sam lifted her leather chair, her increased strength making it easy, and slammed it against the back wall. With a roar of rage, she started breaking furniture, throwing loose items, flipping over her desk, and trashing her study.

"Legacy! You call this a legacy? You possessed me with a loa when I was a child. You forced me to watch you torture my father to death. You gave me a pen that helps me kill people. And then you dropped me into this madness! You do all this, and you call it a legacy?"

She looked at the mirror on the mantle. Her own reflection, which appeared as the hag Marinette, grinned sadistically at her. Sam grabbed a nearby paperweight and threw it. The mirror shattered, shards tumbling through the air before slowing down. She watched as those shards reassembled into a construct—the face of the late Vincent Castille.

She glared at Vincent. "You used to tell me how much you loved me. How can you love me and do all this to me?"

Vincent looked away, then back. "Why, to grant your wish, of course."

"What wish?!"

"To live a life without fear. A life without the fear of dying."

Sam stared as the glass shards fell to the ground. Shadows moved in on her. In her gut, she felt that Vincent had done something truly terrible.

"Father. God help me. What did you do?" Sam asked.

"It was the purpose of the ritual," replied Vincent, his voice all around her. "I have bound Baron Samedi, King of the Loa, to me. The result is that Baron Samedi cannot dig your grave. No matter what injuries you sustain, no matter how ill you become, Sam, you can never die."

Sam fell to her knees and dry-heaved. Her stomach was empty. Her throat burned. Her body shook. "Are you serious? I can't die? How is that granting my wish? No matter how much I suffer, I'll never know peace? And won't I grow old? What will you do when I'm a hundred? Two hundred?"

Vincent shouted, "You've been given the gift of immortality, Sam. Who are you to question it? You can go out and live your life as you see fit without the fear of death. Isn't it wonderful?"

"Stop saying that! You're crazy," Sam said, wiping her mouth and trying to focus. The world was cold and terrifying. Nothing seemed real anymore. "You're fucking crazy."

Vincent's voice took on an indignant quality. "Crazy, am I? How did you survive the injuries from fighting Violet? How did you recover so quickly from your fight with Dallas? Think about it, Sam. You had a weak heart and I strengthened it. You had a limited life and I expanded it. You, my dear daughter, the only one I love, will live forever."

Sam felt her guts churn in agony. "No! I don't want this. You have no idea how much pain I've suffered through. And to have that pain last forever? To be unable to die? Vincent! Please take this back. Undo this thing you've done. Let me die now if that's what it takes, but please do not do this to me!"

"No," replied Vincent. "I cannot undo this ritual. The Baron and I are bound together so long as I exist. And I will exist for a very long time." His voice deepened. "And you, my princess, my daughter, are being very ungrateful."

Sam had stopped trembling. *It was because of me that Vincent did all of these horrible things. All of this blood. All of this suffering. For me.*

Slowly, she got up. All of her dread, fear, sickness, and nausea were slowly being replaced with stern resolution. *I'm done. No more deaths. No more suffering.*

"Good girl. No more whining and fighting. We will embark on this adventure together. This part of the spirit world is ruled by the voodoo loa, but the rest of the world . . . oh, Sam, the spirits are so different everywhere you go. It's a beautiful world of so many dark wonders. And something is happening. Something big. You think I'm the only one? No, my daughter, this is only the beginning. With you directing my loa, we can accomplish so much—father and daughter."

"No." Sam had a fierce look in her eyes.

There was a very notable pause before Vincent replied, "What did you say?"

"I said 'no.' I will not be party to this." Sam's voice choked with anger.

Vincent's voice turned cold as ice. "Oh, but you will, Sam. Don't make me have Marinette overpower you. She has her memory back, and she wants to be in control again. She wants to feast on the suffering of others. And if you try my patience, I'll let her play for as long as she wants. Maybe I'll have her start with that new friend of yours, Dixie Olivier. Wouldn't that be fun?"

Sam's eyes narrowed. *Big mistake. You will never threaten someone I care for again.* Grabbing the silver pen, she headed down the hallway.

"Just where do you think you're going, daughter?" Vincent sounded increasingly agitated.

"If you think you can take me that easily, go for it. I fought down Marinette once and I'll do it again."

Sam rushed into the kitchen. It was a bit . . . different. The refrigerator was open and white smoke rolled out of it. Two skeletons sat at the breakfast table, playing cards. The cabinets were open, with glowing eyes peering from within. The coffee machine was percolating a dark red substance, and around it were odd little creatures that looked like black clothespins with large white eyes at the tips.

Both skeletons looked quizzically at her as she entered. Some of the cabinets slammed shut. The clothespin creatures spoke in high-pitched gibberish, many of them stopping to look at Sam curiously.

Sam ignored everything and went to the stove. It was lit, with a pot of boiling water on it, containing a head with hands for a neck, relaxing in it as if it were a hot tub. The head looked up at Sam and said, "Wait your turn, Princess."

Sam slid the pot off the stove, making the head complain. The burner was lit with a pale green flame, which she held the silver pen over.

"Sam, have you gone mad?" snapped Vincent, rising panic in his voice. "If the pen is destroyed, I will lose my ability to influence the living world. Do you hear me?"

Sam inwardly grinned. She lowered the pen toward the flame. "That's the plan. I don't care what happens to me, but I refuse to let you harm one more innocent person."

"No!" cried Vincent. "I cannot allow this. Seize her!"

Movement to the side caught Sam's attention. The two skeletons at the table were advancing on her. She felt the energy from Marinette course through her as she delivered two quick kicks, knocking off one's head and snapping the other in half. "After I defeated Violet and Bwa-Chech, you think two little skeletons are a threat?"

As she turned back to the stove, she felt something pulled from her, like a weight taken off her back. She felt her strength lessen. Had Marinette just left her?

"Sam, don't do this," replied Vincent. "Don't make me hurt you."

"Go to hell," Sam said, lowering the pen to the flame, letting it burn her fingers. "And this time . . . stay there."

Before the pen even started to smolder, she was struck hard in the chest and fell back. Shaking off the impact, she looked up at her attacker. It was the same hag that was once her reflection, but now with hot coals for eyes. She wore a dirty dress made of moss and rags. The hag opened her mouth, her maw filled with pointy yellow teeth, and let out a deafening screech.

Sam recognized the hag. The anger, the desire to hurt, the hatred for life. "Marinette," she said, stepping back. "But how? I thought she was inside me."

"My loa, my world, my rules," Vincent said in a stern voice. "I took her out so you'd lose your power. Now she will tear into you and weaken you further. And when she re-possesses you, she'll be in total control."

Marinette sank her claws into Sam's shoulders.

Sam winced in pain. Her great strength had vanished.

Vincent's voice was icy. "I warned you to obey, Sam. But you have been very bad. Now you must be punished. I think I will give your body to Marinette for a year. Enjoy watching yourself murder everyone you know. Marinette, take her!"

Marinette let out another screech, this one much louder. The sound slammed Sam back against the wall again, indenting the plaster with her body.

Falling to her knees, Sam raised her arms to defend herself.

Marinette slashed at her with razor-like fingernails. Blood poured down Sam's ripped-open arms as Marinette stepped back, inhaled, and screeched at Sam once more.

The silver pen fell from Sam's hand as she hit the wall again. This time, she hit the back of her head so hard she went limp. Unable to move, she felt Marinette ripping into her, as if literally trying to dig into Sam's body. The pain was excruciating and unyielding.

Oh, God! Someone help me! Please!

Sam was answered a moment later. She felt time come to a stop. The world around her darkened and went out of focus. Then she heard footsteps. Looking up, she saw someone before her. It was a woman, a dark-skinned beauty with jet-black hair and fiery red eyes, walking toward her.

The woman wore a purple shoulder wrap that barely covered her large chest. She also wore a purple skirt, one that was split along the right side, which showed off her ample hips. Her waist was ornamented with a sash made of gold. She exuded both a fire of intense sexuality and a deep maternal glow.

Sam felt groggy. In her mind, she summoned up the strength to think, *Do I know you?*

The woman stopped and placed her hands on her hips. As if she could hear Sam's thoughts, she nodded.

Sam strained to focus on the woman. Blood trickled from her nose as she steadied her thoughts and searched her memory. Then she remembered the woman from the Patterson voodoo tour.

Wait, I do know you. You're a high loa, right? You're the Queen of the Loa, Madame Brigitte.

Brigitte nodded.

Please, thought Sam weakly, *please help me.*

Brigitte tilted up her head and pointed off in the distance.

As Sam looked where the other woman was pointing, her vision suddenly moved, rapidly traveling outside her home and over a dark and gray landscape—the spirit world. When her vision finally stopped, she knew she was looking at a place that was very far away.

Her sight was obscured, as if looking through a clouded pane of glass. She could make out only one thing, a crossroad. And there, she saw a tall skeletal figure wearing dark purple formal clothing and a top hat. The figure was holding a shovel and was completely bound, ankles and wrists, by what looked like a chain made of snake coils.

Baron Samedi. King of the Loa.

Sam's vision returned to Brigitte. *I get it. We share the same goal. I want to be free of this curse, and you want Baron Samedi back. So, we can help each other. Correct?*

Brigitte nodded again. She then slowly caressed her fingers down the length of her body. Her expression was sensual.

Sam felt words form in her mind.

Integration.

Fusion.

Symbiosis.

Immediately, Sam knew what was being asked of her. *You want to merge your spirit with mine. We'll be as one. Is that it?*

Brigitte nodded once more. She then ran her forefinger over her throat. Her expression was grim.

Sam felt the weight of the request. The image of her own lifeless body floated before her. It was all she needed to confirm her suspicions. *I have to find a way to get to Vincent. I have to destroy him. But then, for us to separate, for you to be set free, I'll have to die.*

As before, Brigitte nodded.

Sam appreciated the honesty. *So long as we can take that bastard Vincent down, I don't care. Everything I've ever loved is gone. I have nothing left to live for.*

Brigitte looked solemnly at Sam. It was clear she was waiting for explicit permission.

All right, then, Sam thought. *I permit you to become one with me. Tell me what I must do.*

Brigitte said nothing. She crouched before Sam and leaned in close.

Sam tried to pull back, but Brigitte grabbed her head.

Staring into Sam's eyes for only a moment, Brigitte covered her mouth in an all-consuming kiss.

Sam was not expecting that. She didn't kiss back. She didn't have to. Within seconds, she felt the integration begin.

She felt a tingle go down her spine. It attached itself at her tailbone, then ran back up into her skull. Then the tingle spread throughout her entire skeleton, then her nerves, then her muscles, and then her very skin. It felt like she was being consumed by the sensation.

Sam's consciousness faded. The last thought that was solely her own was . . .

Vincent, if I cannot die, then I will dedicate my immortal life to stopping you!

Chapter 35

A Life Without Fear

Date: **Tuesday, August 25, 1992**
Time: **10:30 p.m.**
Location: **Sam Castille's townhome**
                  Uptown New Orleans

When Sam regained awareness, she could feel it. She was no longer just Samantha Castille. Brigitte was within her, a part of her very being. Every thought and every action felt like it was of two minds, two souls, intertwined as one. She even felt more like Brigitte. She felt focused, majestic, confident, and extremely powerful—filled with both arrogance and sexual assertiveness.

Although she was still consciously Sam, she had Sam's memories and thoughts combined with things Brigitte intrinsically knew. Not only did she now have the ability to fight unlike ever before, but she also knew exactly how to reduce loa to their base energy, effectively killing them.

As powerful as she had felt when Marinette had possessed her, this was in a class all its own. Sam felt like nothing less than a god.

She felt a shock wave of energy fly out from her. *Hell, yeah.* With a smirk, she opened her eyes. The world was speeding back up. Marinette, who had been blown back, was rushing at her with a slashing claw.

"I don't think so," Sam said, moving so fast that Marinette seemed to be standing still. In a flash, Sam was behind her. As she pulled back for a punch, she focused her will through her arm, creating what looked like an arc of white and purple energy flowing down to her fist. Her arm felt hot. With a single strike, she sent Marinette crashing into the wall, creating a hag-shaped hole. Marinette shrieked in pain. Energy poured from the hole, then black dust flew out and drifted away. Marinette was dead.

Sam felt Vincent's presence. It was far away, deep within the spirit world, but it was focused here through one object—the silver pen.

"What the hell is going on, Sam?" Vincent asked, his voice stern.

Picking up the silver pen, she said, "Don't you know how to address royalty? Call me Princess . . . no . . . call me Queen!"

Several of the lower cabinets exploded as three dog-like beasts burst forth. Their mouths were filled with razor-sharp teeth, and their drool hissed and sizzled like acid as it dripped on the floor.

Sam knew that her power was in its infancy, since she had just merged with Brigitte. It would take time for her to reach her full potential and be able to go after Vincent. Her only hope now was to run before she depleted her energy and was unable to escape the spirit world.

Right, first things first. I need to get out of here and destroy this pen.

The three dog-beasts charged at her. She rushed forward, her movements faster than theirs. She ducked under the first two and hit the third with a shoulder blow, energy flowing through her. The impact was so strong that the beast flew into the counter. The little clothespin creatures bounced in shock and then scattered as the beast slammed into the stove.

The stove exploded, fire going everywhere. The two remaining dog-beasts jumped up at her, and she destroyed them with a few powerful kicks before flipping over the flames. As the flames consumed the kitchen, she grabbed her mother's charm and rushed into the hallway.

Once in the hallway, she bolted toward the front door. Before she could get to it, however, dozens of skeletal arms peeled away the door as if it were a decal. Within a few seconds, only wall was there. She was trapped.

Of course! The only place I can escape is the attic, because I wrote it that way. Fine, then, the attic it is.

Sam was confident that she could survive a three-and-a-half-story fall now that Brigitte was inside her.

As she neared the stairs, the mirror in the front hallway exploded. Out came a gray-skinned hag in a shroud running at Sam. The hag's face elongated. Her eyes were black except for fist-sized fires, and her tooth-lined mouth opened wide enough to engulf Sam in one bite.

Sam recognized her. "Bwa-Chech. How many of you have betrayed your queen and gone to Vincent's side?"

Bwa-Chech did not respond.

Reaching out, Sam grabbed the banister of the stairs and swung around, but her feet narrowly missed that gaping maw. Letting go, she threw herself into her office, where she skidded to a stop. As Bwa-Chech came at Sam, shrieking once again, Sam grabbed her copier.

As Sam lifted the copier over her head, white and purple energy charging from her into the machine, Bwa-Chech stopped with a horrified look on her face. If the hag sister hadn't been so ugly, it would have been comical.

Sam grinned menacingly. "Bye-bye!" She threw the copier at Bwa-Chech.

As the copier fell on the hag, black dust scattered everywhere. Bwa-Chech was dead.

Sam didn't have a moment to rest, as a crackle behind her got her attention. A skeletal figure made of lightning was emerging from the computer monitor. She figured the spirit world must adapt to human innovation, developing loa for electricity and technology.

She jump-kicked the monitor, destroying the electric loa. She then rushed toward the stairs. The piercing cold of the spirit world was rapidly being replaced by heat as the kitchen fire spread. As she reached the stairs, she heard the sound of glass breaking from within her study.

The large, multiple-armed skeleton had crashed through the window and was charging at her. Without stopping, she kicked the copier that had killed Bwa-Chech right at the skeleton, sending a charge of white and purple energy along with it.

She didn't wait for the impact. She headed up the stairs. But when she heard the sound of hundreds of bones crunching, she smirked once more. *Serves you right, traitor.*

On the second-floor landing, Sam saw the entire hallway heading to the stairs covered in hundreds of pitch-black, ghostly arms. They were of various shapes and sizes and grasped at her with clawed hands.

She sighed. *Why can't this be easy?*

Hearing a sound behind her, she turned to see four large creatures with alligator heads and bodies and crawfish tails and claws, walking on dozens of human hands. She curled her upper lip at them, saying "Ew," and rushed toward the gauntlet of arms.

Sam stopped short of jumping through the morass. *Do I have an idea!*

Turning away from the arms, she waited until the first alligator creature was almost upon her. She then jumped over them with a triple flip and landed on the fourth creature, destroying it. As black dust went everywhere, she rushed forward, kicking all three of the creatures, one after another, over the grabbing arms.

Once all three alligator creatures were flying over the hands, she took a breath, rushed forward, and jumped. She vaulted from creature to creature, using them as flying platforms to get to the other side of the gauntlet of arms. She then flip-kicked one of the creatures back into the other two, destroying all three of them.

She felt some approval coming from the part of her that was Brigitte. *You're impressed and you know it.*

Seeing the hot glow of fire from downstairs, Sam didn't hesitate. She rushed up to the third floor.

Once there, she saw about a dozen figures coming from stairs leading to the attic. Black hooded figures. Loa that looked like the Knight Priory. *These are the ones Vincent used to mess with Richie and Dallas.*

Sam charged the black hooded figures, bellowing, "This is for Richie!"

Rushing in, she dodged two of them, kicking one and punching the other. As they exploded into black dust, three more jumped down on her, so she jumped to the side and landed on the wall. She ran along the wall, leaving those three behind, until she reached a wall sconce. Tearing the sconce loose, she jumped into a group of four different figures and, spinning the sconce in a wide circle, destroyed all of them.

When she landed, every figure she had hit had turned to dust. About half were gone. The three that she had initially dodged were running along the ceiling at her, and the three behind her were running along the ground. A lone figure was standing off to the side with a look of extreme disbelief.

Grinning cockily, Sam flipped up to the ceiling and engaged the three there. Catching the punch of one of the figures, she twisted its wrist and threw it to the ground. She then bashed one of them with the sconce and punched the other figure several times, destroying them both. Finally, she leapt down and landed on the one she had just thrown, destroying it as well.

The three running along the ground were almost upon her. Sam threw the sconce to the lone figure, yelling "Catch!" Then she spun around onto her hands, her legs out like the blades of a helicopter, and pushed herself toward the three. They were destroyed by the spinning kick.

When she flipped back to her feet, she was right in front of one lone, very scared-looking hooded figure, still holding the sconce. The third-floor landing was covered in black dust.

The lone hooded figure looked for an escape route and then offered her the sconce. She waggled her finger at it and said, "Unh, unh, unh!" With a full backflip, she kicked the figure in the face. It flew back and broke apart into black dust. As she landed from the attack, the sconce fell to the ground with a loud *clank*.

She felt the heat rise again and saw the fire coming up from the second floor. *Time to get out of here.*

Sam rushed up to the attic. Much of it was packed densely with boxes, chests, and furniture, stuff that hadn't been dealt with since before Edward had died.

So much for ever cleaning this out. Anyway, there should a window facing the street on the other side of this mess.

Checking her pants pocket to make sure the silver pen was still there—it was—she jumped up to the ceiling and ran along its vaulted surface on all fours. As she landed on the other side of the clutter, she heard Vincent say, "Sam, you have been a very, very bad girl. I will not tolerate this kind of behavior from my princess."

"I am not your princess," Sam yelled. "I am the loa queen. And I am no longer yours."

Vincent snorted and said, "You get no choice, little girl, loa queen or not. I will have my way. I am the loa king now, and you will submit."

She had started toward the window when a glowing circle of runes appeared on the floor before her. She heard Vincent say, "You give me no alternative, Sam. I will use a servant, a very special one, to stop you. Destroy him if you can. You brought this on yourself."

She got into a fighting stance. From the circle of runes, beams of light flew upward until they obscured her vision. When they dimmed, a single figure stood there. A ghost. His skin was pale, and he was dressed almost like Dick Tracy. His eyes were lifeless and dull.

Sam recognized him at once. "Dad!"

Edward Castille reached into his coat. "Sorry, little magnolia. I have no choice. I must do what the king says." Taking out two machetes, he rushed forward. "Forgive me!"

She jumped back just in time to avoid getting cut. For the first time since she had united with Brigitte, she felt internal discord. She couldn't do this. She couldn't destroy him. He might not have been her birth father, but he was her daddy. She loved him.

Her jaw was tightly clenched. Her stomach was in knots from growing frustration. She dodged a blow by handspringing back, but he relentlessly pressed the attack. As she dodged yet another strike, this time by flipping over him, he cut one of her legs.

Sam felt the approaching heat from the fire. The attic would be burning soon.

I have to escape!

Edward jumped and kicked at her, then swiped at her several times. She barely dodged.

Think! There has to be a way to stop him without destroying him. Think!

The answer came from deep within. *Fight a ghost with other ghosts.* With that came Brigitte's knowledge of how to summon the spirits of the dead.

Pressing her hands to the ground, she felt energy flow from her body and into the floor. The feeling was ecstatic, like she was controlling the world. Soon, she saw three similar circles of runes appear on the floor in a triangular pattern.

I hope this works.

Sam rushed in to fight Edward, to delay him until her own help arrived.

He slashed at her. She spun to the side like a top to avoid it. Then she punched at him. He slapped her fist aside with one machete and cut her arm with the other. She jumped back defensively, then flipped forward, bringing her legs crashing down on his shoulders.

"Useless failure of a son," chided Vincent. "Can't you even defeat one woman?"

"Leave him alone, you damn coward!" yelled Sam.

Edward, recovering from the kick, threw the two machetes at her. Sliding underneath the weapons, she pushed up and wrapped her feet around his neck. Then, with a twist, she threw him down to the hard floor.

She yelled to Vincent, "Edward was not a failure. Hell, he was the best parent that ever lived. Yes, he made a lot of mistakes, like with Mom. But any man who was able to love his wife and son whom he almost never saw, as well as the girl whose birth tore his family apart, was a hell of a parent. And you know what . . . 'Father'?"

As Edward got up, the attic began to fill with thick, black smoke. Sam's lungs began to burn and her vision became obscured. Taking advantage of those distractions, Edward rushed forward, this time with knives for fingers. He swiped at her again and again, pushing her back to a wall.

As she dodged, Sam yelled, "Edward is ten times the father you ever were. In fact, you don't deserve to be called 'Grandfather' or 'Father' anymore. For the rest of my life, you're just 'Vincent.'"

Vincent snarled angrily as Edward rushed in, jabbing with his knife-tipped fingers. Both sets of claws easily sank into her midsection. She cried out, blood gushing in alarming amounts.

"Samantha, I am so sorry," Edward cried out in anguish.

Sam coughed up some blood. All around, the fire grew until Sam's flesh was starting to redden. If she didn't get out of there soon, she was going be burned alive. She didn't know how long it would take to recover from that kind of damage, if it was even possible, and she didn't want to find out. She needed to end this fight now.

"Sorry, Dad!" Sam cried out and thrust both palms at him, stepping forward and focusing all of her will into the blow. She wanted to push him back toward the three circles of runes and then make her escape.

Edward flipped back, avoiding the strike. When he landed, he stopped and stared at Sam's hands.

They were glowing. Wisps of white and purple energy, like the corona of a star, were coalescing into a sphere in front of her hands. She could feel her power focusing from every fiber of her being into that sphere. Her stance was making it happen. *What is this?*

As the sphere of energy reached the size of a baseball, she instinctively knew to circle her hands around it and then again thrust them forward.

She did so. The result was spectacular.

The blast of white energy that flew out of the sphere spiraled with raw power, purple lightning crackling around it. The blast crashed into Edward. He flew back and landed between the three circles of runes. He was flickering and looked extremely weak.

My God!

If she had used any more power, she would have destroyed him.

As Edward got up, the three circles of runes exploded in energy, sending beams of light upward. Sam shielded her eyes. When the light dimmed, standing there were three people she was truly glad to see: Rodger, Michael, and Richie.

"Impossible! I command the dead in this region," said Vincent.

She knew that they were ghosts. But for the moment, she was no longer fighting alone. She felt connected to them all one last time.

"I get the feeling ghosts have much more free will than loa, Vincent. I don't think you're as powerful as you pretend to be."

Vincent roared with rage.

The three other ghosts rushed at Edward. He swiped at them each in turn, but it didn't help. He was soon overcome. They held him back and started pulling him through the floor.

"Go now and live," whispered Rodger's ghost to Sam.

Michael's ghost looked at her. "Sever Vincent's connection to this world."

"Set your heart free," Richie's ghost whispered, smiling at her.

Sam felt a tear in her eye. She smiled. "I will, guys, I will. And one day, I'll set you free. I swear it!" Seeing those she loved trapped in this world and unable to move on just strengthened her resolve against Vincent.

The three dragged Edward back into the ground. Just before vanishing, he cried out, "Live for me, my little magnolia. Live for me!"

Turning, Sam rushed toward the glass window. The outside didn't look nightmarish. It looked like New Orleans. It looked real.

The attic was completely covered in flames. As she took a few steps back, preparing to jump through the window, she heard Vincent make one final plea.

"Please, Sam! Please! I just want you to live a life without fear."

"Then you succeeded, Vincent, because I'm no longer afraid. Of you or anything else!" Gritting her teeth, Sam covered her face and then jumped toward the window.

She crashed out into the warm August night as if in slow motion. The particles of glass moved past her like twinkling stars. Turning in midair, she saw the sudden intake of air feed the fire as if it were a hungry beast. *The fire's going to flash over. I have to hurry.* Cocking her right arm back, she prepared to throw the silver pen into the inferno.

And then the attic exploded.

Sam lost track of the silver pen as she flew back. The flesh on the left side of her body, closest to the explosion, burst into flames. Her hair and clothes caught fire as well. The concussive force was so great that she felt some of her bones shatter. She landed in a heap outside her townhome as it burnt to the ground.

As she lay there, she felt the cool rain extinguish the fires on her body. She couldn't move. Her left arm was blackened, and she could feel similar burns on the entire left side of her body. It felt like most of her bones were broken. Each breath felt like she was taking in water. Her eyes watered from the immense pain.

Only her headache seemed to be gone.

The pen! Did she destroy it? Did she sever Vincent's connection to the world?

She didn't know. She couldn't see the silver pen from where she lay.

Sam searched within for any signs of Brigitte. However, she couldn't find any traces of the loa queen. It was as if the damage Sam had suffered had made Brigitte vanish. For a moment, Sam wondered if the experience had been real.

Her adrenaline wore off. Her consciousness was slipping. If she died now, that would mean the whole thing was in her head. She would just be a crazy chick who went psycho and killed herself, just like she wrote it. *Wouldn't that be a fitting end?*

She was aware of flashing red and blue lights and of sirens getting closer. She was also aware of something in her blackened hand. Opening those burnt fingers hurt. Nestled in her palm was a partially melted red shoe. The only memento of her mother. The word "Comus" was illegible.

Mother's charm was ruined.

She closed her scorched fingers back around it. She wanted to keep it. She wanted to remember her.

As Sam heard car doors open and Dixie's voice calling her name, she felt her body start to get cold. She knew she was moments away from dying. But she still didn't hear the sound of anyone digging. If what she had just experienced was real, then no one would be digging her grave—she couldn't die.

This is it, then. Time to find out if I'm crazy and fucking dead . . . or immortal and just plain fucked.

Sam felt her breath start to still. She felt her body start to go numb. She felt her vision start to dim. She felt her world go silent.

The one thing she didn't feel, however, was fear.

She wasn't afraid. Not anymore. Wherever this took her, she was ready.

"Let's do this . . ." she whispered to the world.

Sam closed her eyes.

Epilogue

Date: **Wednesday, August 26, 1992**
Time: **12:00 a.m.**
Location: **Ruins of Sam Castille's townhome**
                    Uptown New Orleans

"They say Hurricane Andrew will be making landfall soon. No one knows why it got so strong all of a sudden," said the police officer to Detective Aucoin. "Did Cathy go shopping for the essentials yet?"

"Cathy's upstate with her mother," Aucoin said, shrugging. "As for the hurricane? Hell, at this point nothing will surprise me."

Truth was, Aucoin had the night off and did not want to go out. He was trying to put an unpleasant chapter of his life behind him. He had lost his daughter, was about to lose his wife, and was losing any chance of advancement in his career. Most of it was due to how he had acted, how he had allowed himself to become an ugly, hateful person. He was past trying to make excuses for his behavior. He was ready to accept the costs of his actions.

But he could live with every consequence for just one chance to apologize to Sam. He knew he had done her a great wrong, casting her in a villain's light when she was just another victim.

So when he heard that there was a fire at Sam's townhome, he rushed there as fast as he could. Ouellette didn't object. He was too preoccupied with Rodger's death from earlier in the evening. Aucoin tried not to think about it. Rodger was a good man and hadn't deserved to die in such a violent way.

When Aucoin arrived at the scene, he saw the remains of Sam's townhome, still smoldering. The New Orleans Fire Department was keeping it contained. After briefly chatting with an officer, he spotted his former partner, Dixie, surveying the scene. He quickly approached her. "Hey, Dixie."

She looked over. "It's 'Lieutenant' now. But hi, Kyle." She glanced back at the ruins of Sam's house, clearly preoccupied.

Aucoin nodded and then looked over the wreckage. "What happened?"

Dixie shook her head. "Honestly, I have no idea what happened. Witnesses report they heard her screaming up a storm. Next, there was a massive racket, like she was destroying the townhome from the inside. Then the whole place was on fire. Everyone's just extremely lucky that the flames blew out into the street, or half of Uptown would be burning right now." Her expression was dark.

He nodded. "Just like the Castille mansion. Totally destroyed." He looked back at Dixie. "Is Sam still alive?"

Dixie lowered her head. Her voice strained. "If you can call it that. Reports say she jumped out of the attic to escape the flames. But she's still been horribly burnt, and most of her bones are broken. Kyle, it's just like before. She shouldn't be alive. I'm told it'll be a miracle if she makes it to the hospital."

Aucoin clenched his jaw and watched as Dixie's hair fell over her face. It was obvious that she had grown to like Sam. And once again, Sam was critically injured. Both times before, she had somehow recovered, but he wasn't sure that she could escape death once more.

If she does survive, she must have the devil himself looking after her.

He could see tears traveling down Dixie's cheeks. He wanted to comfort her, but he felt he could no longer comfort anyone. Instead, he said, "Anyway, with your permission, Lieutenant . . . Dixie, I'm going to go see if I can help out."

Dixie rubbed her forehead and nodded again. "Go for it, Kyle. I need to take a moment and collect my thoughts. This is really too much. I really thought we all had a chance at happiness. Now, Rodger . . . and Sam . . ." She turned toward her squad car.

Aucoin watched her leave. Something was changing in Dixie. She wouldn't be the person she once was anymore. Not after all this.

As he headed toward the remains of the townhome, his thoughts returned to Sam. It was best that he had missed her being taken away. It wouldn't have been right for him to apologize to a comatose woman. She deserved the chance to tell him to fuck off.

Aucoin felt it would be fitting to hold onto his guilt for the rest of his life.

He reached the smoldering ruins. It looked even worse up close, like a bomb had leveled the place.

A few firefighters were rummaging through the rubble. Aucoin joined them, looking for anything that could shed light on what had happened.

Sam, what kind of demon possessed you to destroy yourself like this?

Aucoin had never felt so bad for someone who wasn't family. He didn't know why he cared so much. It might have been guilt, or maybe shame. Or maybe even compassion.

Who was he kidding? *I'm just a washed-up old shit with nothing left.*

A glint on the driveway caught his eye. He headed over and knelt down, clearing away some ash.

The light glinted off a single item, still very much intact.

A silver pen.

Huh. I wonder what this pen is doing here?

Aucoin reached for the pen, and thunder rumbled in the distance.

Afterword

Two down and one to go.

As you figured out, what started as a normal mystery/suspense thriller has evolved into a supernatural thriller. I hope you've enjoyed the journey as much as I've enjoyed writing it.

As I mentioned in the afterword of *The Bourbon Street Ripper*, I was able to put back in a lot of content that was originally cut when these two books were just one. Most of that content is in *A Life Without Fear*.

So what exactly was restored? Let's see, the outings with Jacob, the motorcycle gang side story, most of Dixie's chapters, and the entirety of Jonathon Russell's storyline. While the main story of the copycat killer, the influence of the loa, and the rituals performed on Sam didn't need that content, I feel their addition really rounded out the overall experience.

And now you know for absolute certain that *Sins of the Father* is really about Sam. To quote the Lady in Red, "It's always been about Sam."

So that leads us to the ending of this book. Where do we go from here with most of the major characters killed off or in a coma? The third book, *Face Behind The Mask*, resolves everyone's stories and gives a few characters that haven't had a chance to shine their moment in the spotlight.

No, Boudreaux is not one of those characters. I already told you, he's truly innocent!

See you in Book Three, when we bring this sordid tale full circle and give Sam's story a full and definitive resolution.

—Leo King

About the Author

Leo King was born in New Orleans, Louisiana, and moved to Houston, Texas, in 2005 after Hurricane Katrina. He works during the day and writes at night, usually juggling several projects at once.

He lives with his wife, his Playstation 3s, and more stuffed lions than an adult should probably own. His education is in game development, and he often uses the structured approach of game design in developing his stories.

Connect with Leo

Email
leoking@foreverwhere.com

Twitter
@leokingauthor

Website
www.foreverwhere.com

Facebook
facebook.com/leokingauthor

Grey Gecko Press

Thank you for purchasing this book from Grey Gecko Press, an independent publishing company that focuses on new and emerging authors, bringing readers the best in fiction and non-fiction at reasonable prices in all formats.

With books in nearly every genre of fiction and non-fiction, there's something for everyone, and you can be sure that buying books from us leads directly to the support of independent authors. Grey Gecko pays our authors some of the highest royalty rates in the business and strives to produce only high-quality books.

Visit our website to purchase our titles, pre-order upcoming books at a discount, sign up for our free monthly newsletter, and find out about two great ways to get free books, the Slushpile Reader Program and the Advance Reader Program.

And don't forget: all our print editions come with the ebook free!

Authors First!

www.greygeckopress.com

store.greygeckopress.com